THE STICKLEPATH STRANGLER

THE
STICKLEPATH
STRANGLER

Michael Jecks

HEADLINE

First published in 2001
by HEADLINE BOOK PUBLISHING

10 9 8 7 6 5 4 3 2

British Library Cataloguing in Publication Data

Jecks, Michael
The sticklepath strangler
1. Furnshill, Baldwin, Sir (Fictitious character) 2. Puttock, Simon
(Fictitious character) 3. West Country (England) – Fiction
4. England – Social conditions – 1066–1485 – Fiction 5. Detective
and mystery stories
I. Title
823.9'14[F]

ISBN 0 7472 6919 X

Typeset by Avon Dataset Ltd, Bidford-on-Avon, Warks

Printed and bound in Great Britain by
Clays Ltd, St Ives plc

HEADLINE BOOK PUBLISHING
A division of Hodder Headline
338 Euston Road
London NW1 3BH

www.headline.co.uk
www.hodderheadline.com

This book is for
Shirley and Dartmoor Dave Denford,
the blacksmith who 'don't do 'orses'.

Cast of Characters

Sir Baldwin de Furnshill The Keeper of the King's Peace in Crediton, Baldwin has been marked by the injustice of the destruction of the Knights Templar. As a result he seeks justice for common folk.

Lady Jeanne Baldwin's wife, who was once widowed and now fears losing her second husband.

Edgar Baldwin saved Edgar's life in Acre, and since then Edgar swore loyalty to him for life. He is Baldwin's most trusted servant.

Simon Puttock Long a friend of Baldwin's, and an official of the Stannaries, the tin miners of Dartmoor. Simon and Baldwin have often worked together on investigations.

Roger de Gidleigh Coroner Roger is one of only two Coroners who must investigate all sudden deaths and wrecks in Devonshire.

Nicole Garde The French wife of Thomas Garde; mother of Joan.

Thomas Garde Thomas is a freeman, who works his own little plots, but he is an incomer to the vill of Sticklepath and has never been fully accepted.

Joan Daughter of Nicole and Thomas, Joan has found a corpse.

Ivo Bel Brother of Thomas, and Manciple to the nuns of Canonsleigh. He lusts after Nicole, his sister-in-law.

Serlo Warrener	A gruff, hardy man, crippled years ago, who tends to the warren up on the moor.
Athelhard	Athelhard was killed by the vill when they thought him guilty of murder.
'Mad' Meg	Sister to Athelhard, and simple from birth, Meg avoids the vill since the death of her brother.
Ansel de Hocsenham	A Purveyor to the King, Ansel last visited the vill during the 1315–16 famine.
Emma	Close friend of Joan who found the corpse with her.
Swetricus	A peasant of Sticklepath who lost Aline, his daughter, several years ago. Three daughters survive.
Samson atte Mill	The miller, known for brawling and drunkenness.
Gunilda	Samson's wife, a downtrodden woman.
Felicia	Samson and Gunilda's daughter.
Alexander de Belston	The cautious Reeve of Sticklepath who is determined to preserve the reputation of the vill and its people.
William Taverner	William is the master of the only inn.
Ham	Taverner's son, who was killed in the recent floods.
Mary	Daughter to Taverner, who often serves visitors to the inn.
Gervase Colbrook	Parson to the little chantry chapel of Sticklepath.
Drogo le Criur	Leader of the Foresters, charged with the duty of guarding the Forest of Dartmoor and travellers over it.
Peter atte Moor	A Forester under Drogo, Peter lost his daughter Denise to the murderer some years ago.
Adam Thorne	Also a Forester, Adam has a bad limp, but is known for his strength and integrity.

Vincent Yunghe   The youngest of the Foresters, Vin is still learning his duties.

Miles Houndestail   A traveller who was first to see the corpse with the two girls.

Author's Note

There is a natural series of stages in the creation of a new book. For me, a central scene comes first, something which drives the whole of the rest of the story. In *The Leper's Return*, for instance, I wanted to look at leprosy in the Middle Ages, while in *The Crediton Killings*, I examined the role of mercenaries. Often, though, I find myself chewing over a curious beginning and wondering how I could develop it into a story. *The Sticklepath Strangler* belongs to this category, and I have to thank Deryn Lake, author of the excellent John Rawlings stories, for the initial idea.

It was while we were walking over Dartmoor – not, I have to add, the sort of thing that Deryn's friends would expect of her – some few years ago that she and I swapped ideas for new novels.

My idea for her was for a deserted ship suddenly arriving at a Devon port, a concept she used in her novel *Death in the Port of Exeter*, while hers gave me the initial scene of this book, with Joan and Emma's hideous discovery. I must add that her suggestion that I should write about a skull falling from a wall came only from an appreciation of a two-thousand-year-old wall – not from any wishful thinking about what she would like to do with the struggling author who had promised to show her an attractive walk to a not-too-far distant pub.

And if Michael, who later gave us a lift back from the Northmore Arms in his Audi, should ever read this, I would like to thank him too.

Sticklepath is a fairly typical and relatively unspoilt village, but it has had a confusing past.

Take the Church: Sticklepath has been split among the parishes of Sampford Courtenay, South Tawton and Belstone. Then again the roads have all changed their routes; the main road used to suffer gridlock for the whole of the summer until the dual carriageway was built, which avoids Whiddon Down, South Zeal, Sticklepath, and Okehampton itself, so that now, instead of stationary vehicles belching fumes on the old A30, locals have no passing traffic whatever. Good for the children walking to and from school, but less so for the many pubs and cafes which were built on the old road. Most have been forced to close.

Sticklepath itself has had a great history. There is the Finch Foundry, until the 1960s a working tool-manufacturer which exported its billhooks and spades all over the world. Nowadays the foundry is a National Trust museum dedicated to water power, and I would recommend anyone who has an interest in metalwork and smithing to visit it, especially since 'Dartmoor Dave Denford', to whom this book is dedicated, can often be found there giving demonstrations of blacksmithing. Just remember not to ask if he makes horseshoes. He is keen to point out that 'I don't do 'orses', since he is not a farrier. Yes, there *is* a difference.

A short way further up the river from the foundry's water-wheels is the old mill of Tom Pearce, made famous in the song 'Widecombe Fair'. Now the main buildings have gone, to be replaced by houses. The mill too has been converted, but not so long ago, a thick serge-type of cloth was still being manufactured here from wool shorn from the sheep on Dartmoor; it was then worn all over the British Empire by soldiers and sailors alike. All this from a tiny little village hiding in a valley in the middle of Devonshire.

The success of the place came from two factors: its abundant water power, and its location on the main road to Cornwall. The village supplied the needs of visitors and travellers, because during the age of horse travel, everyone going to Cornwall passed through Sticklepath and made use of its inns, cooks and grooms. While other villages lost their trade, like South Zeal, which was bypassed centuries ago so that the mail coach horses didn't have to cope with the two hills at either side of the town, Sticklepath somehow survived.

There was no bypass for the hilly part of the road which gave the 'Stickle' or 'Steep' path its name until fairly recently. In fact, there are many local families who can still remember grandparents talking about the time when the road went up the hill.

In reality, it seems that the road has changed direction twice. If you walk along Sticklepath's High Street heading westwards, you will come to a left-hand turn towards Higher Sticklepath and Belstone. Follow this, and only a matter of a couple of yards down from the road junction you will notice a narrow track on the right which has been partly metalled over. This is the start of the old Sticklepath, now replaced by the modern roadway itself which follows the countours of the hills towards Okehampton. Walk on up this old track a short way, and soon you'll find that there is a flagpole on your left. Between this track and the 'White Rock' pole is a sunken pathway, now largely obliterated by bushes and straggling brambles, gorse and ferns, but clearly visible early in the year. This is the old Exeter to Cornwall road. And if you try to walk up it, you will see why it was necessary to build the new road, because, by God, it's steep!

At the other end of the village is a relatively modern bridge. This would not have been here in the Middle Ages. However, before the bridge was built, the River Taw would have been easily fordable at that particular point. Often when bridges were thrown up over rivers, the builders then charged money for people to use them in order to recoup the cost of construction. And equally often, the more wily travellers would bypass the bridge and find a new ford. I think that this is what happened at the Taw. While there were charges for the use of the bridge, people went a little upriver along Skaigh Lane to where there was a ford, and when the charges were dropped, they returned to the new bridge and used it.

Like so many small settlements, there is little written down for Sticklepath during the Middle Ages. We know that there was a chantry chapel, which seems to have been established in the reign of Henry I, but there are no maps and few documents.

Apparently in 1147 Robert Fitzroy (illegitimate son of Henry I) and his wife Matilda d'Avranches gave lands to Bricius, Empress Matilda's Chaplain, so that he could build a small chapel. It was to be called the church of 'St Mary of Stikilpeth' in the manor of 'Saunforde Curtenay' or 'Sandy Ford' over the Taw. Later, in 1282, Robert de Esse was installed as priest to the church by Hugh Courtenay. The latter's son, Hugh II, provided 'a messuage and one carucate of land' to the two chaplains of the church. The messuage is thought to be where the present Chantry Cottage now stands, while I am told that there is still a field off the back lane called Chantry's Meadow.

Sadly, though, there's little proof of the precise location of the land, and nobody knows where the priest would have lived, nor how the vill would have been set out in those far-off days. All we can do is extrapolate what we know about other vills and use some logic to see what the place might have looked like, seven hundred years ago.

For those who are interested, the Sticklepath Women's Institute has produced an excellent history which is available in the West Country Studies Library in Exeter.

There is one facet which will no doubt concern the casual reader, and that is my use of vampires. I know that I will be told off for bringing foreign bloodsuckers into my stories, so here is my defence.

Vampires were brought to the public's mind by the marvellous story of Dracula, written by Bram Stoker. It is known that vampire stories were once quite common on the continent, especially in Transylvania and Slovenia, but it is less well known that such stories existed in England too.

The earliest examples I have found were written by Canon William of Newburgh (1136–98). He details four cases of *sanguisugae* or vampires in his account of English history: one in Buckinghamshire, and three others in the north of the country. Of course, the stories of vampirism covered a wide range of offences; it is only since the invention of Dracula that it came to mean drinking blood and nothing else. Before that, vampires were thought of as especially evil people, probably infested by demons, who would torment an area. Some accusations were undoubtedly malignant, made by neighbours who coveted a patch of land or a pig, perhaps; others derived from genuine fear and superstition.

The worst period, as one can imagine, came after a famine. We know that there was talk of cannibalism in the British Isles during the terrible famine of 1315–17, and to an ill-educated and starving population of peasants, it is no surprise that in order to explain away such a hideous and inconceivable crime, some might have suggested that a supernatural agency was responsible.

In this tale, I have taken only the details which Canon William wrote down. I have not invented these elements of the story, although I have of course elaborated on them. Some readers may be surprised by the exhumation scene. I can only say that the villagers', Gervase's and Baldwin's views are borne out by research in several countries.

For those who are keen to find out more about the subject, look at Jean-Claude Schmitt's excellent *Ghosts in the Middle Ages*.

There is one final point I must make. As always, this book states that all characters are fictitious and any resemblance to the living or the dead is entirely coincidental, and I should like to say here that I have been as careful as I possibly could be to avoid using the names, characteristics or features of any of my friends from Belstone, South Zeal or Sticklepath.

This is particularly important because, as with any work of crime fiction, so many of the folks in this book are unpleasant, motivated by questionable urges, with deceit, dishonesty, racism, adultery, greed and corruption forming a large part of their make-up. All I can say is, I have encountered *none of these traits* in any of the people of the area – and I hope that all my friends will understand that a crime book which features only pleasant, laughing and above all honest men and women like themselves, would make for a less than riveting read.

I cannot complete this note without expressing my immense gratitude to the people of the three villages who have made my family and me so welcome since we moved to Devon some years ago.

Our thanks to you all.

Michael Jecks
North Dartmoor
March 2001

Preface

Sticklepath, 1315

They were out there.

In the darkness about his cottage, as he sat inside, panting like a wounded dog, he knew they were silently gathering, like rats about carrion, and Athelhard shivered not only from the pain of his wounds, but from the knowledge that he was soon to be slaughtered and burned until nothing remained, nothing but the lie that he had killed the girl; that he had drunk her blood and eaten her flesh; that he was a *sanguisuga* – a vampire. It was that thought, more even than the pain, that made him snarl in defiance like a bear at bay in the pit.

His leg felt as if it had been savaged. The hole through his flesh was more painful than he could have imagined, a pulsing agony that produced a sort of deadening cramp in his groin. Not that it compared with the injury to his back. That was sharper, like a knife thrust. That was the one which would kill him, he knew. The arrowhead was lodged deeply, and he could feel his strength seeping away with his blood.

Why? he wondered again. Why attack him? Why think *he* could have done that to the girl?

The arrow in his leg heralded the attack.

He'd had no premonition all that long day he'd been at his holding, far on the western outskirts of the vill, peaceably chopping and storing logs in preparation for the winter. At the beech tree that marked the eastern edge of his plot, he set down his axe while he ducked his head in his old bucket and rubbed his hair. It had been hard work, and tiny chips and flakes of wood were lodged in his scalp, making the flea bites itch.

Puffing and blowing, he shook his head, relishing the coolness, feeling the water trickling down his back. As he did so, he thought he heard something, an odd whirring noise which came from his left and disappeared to the right, but his ears were filled with water and he didn't recognise it. Probably a bird, he told himself.

Then the missile slammed into his thigh.

The jolt itself was vicious, yet even through his shock he was conscious of every moment of the impact: he could feel the barbs pierce his flesh, slicing through muscle, tearing onwards until they jerked to a halt against his thigh-bone. Even as he collapsed, he was aware of the arrow quivering in his thigh.

And then he was on his arse, while water scattered from his upturned bucket, staring at his leg, scarcely able to believe his eyes. It was tempting to think it must be an accident, that someone had been aiming at a bird or a rabbit, and the arrow had missed or skittered up from the ground, like a spinning stone on water, only to find him, a fresh target, but as the idea occurred to him, he realised it was impossible. There were no rabbits here, and an arrow wouldn't bounce upwards when it struck the ground; it would bury its entire length. Yet he had no enemies. Who could have deliberately aimed at him?

As the stinging grew more painful, he studied the arrow, seeking clues as to who might have fired at him. The fletchings were bright blue peacock feathers, moving lazily with the beating of his heart. Like most longbow arrows it was at least a yard long, a good missile over long range, he told himself, an ideal weapon for an assassin.

As the pain increased, he realised he must move. His attacker must still be there, perhaps drawing back the bowstring a third time. Athelhard stumbled to his feet and scurried around the tree's trunk like a vole looking for a hedge, leaning back against it while the nausea washed over him.

His axe was around the other side of the tree, right in the line of another arrow and he daren't reach for it, but somehow he must get away, and first he had to remove the arrow. Looking down at the slender stem protruding from his hose, the thought of what he must do made him retch. While a soldier he had seen others do the same often enough, but that didn't make it any easier. Swallowing the bile that rose in his throat, he touched it gingerly. He couldn't pull it out backwards, as the barbs would rend his flesh and do more damage. No, he must drive it forwards, so that the arrowhead cut through the thickness of his thigh and came out the other side.

It was firmly lodged at his bone, however, and he wept freely as he twisted and turned it, trying to move it away without harming himself more than he must. When he finally succeeded, he fainted as a gush of hot blood fountained from the wound, flooding his hands, but he came to only a moment or two later, shivering and nauseous deep in the pit of his stomach. At first he was fearful to see the bright crimson puddle, but he felt all right. No arteries had been broached.

It was done. He snapped off the remaining length with the fletchings, then tugged the splinter of wood which was left attached to the point through his leg, his face pulled into a mask of revulsion. Tearing off his hose, he fashioned a makeshift tourniquet which he bound as close to his groin as he could. He couldn't touch the arrowhead again. Slick with his blood, he was repelled by it. Instead he took up the piece with the fletchings and shoved it into the cloth, twisting it until the ligature was tight and the blood ceased flowing. Then and only then did he turn his attention to the man who had ambushed him, who must still be there, waiting for him.

A good bowman could hit a butt at four or five hundred yards. Trying to get a moving man was more difficult, especially if he could dodge and sprint, but Athelhard wouldn't be doing that, not with his leg in this state. He would only be able to hobble, presenting an easy target to the most incompetent archer.

There was the crack of a breaking twig and he knew that his attacker was edging forward. If he remained here, he would be killed. He climbed to his feet as quietly as he could, gritting his teeth as his ruined leg refused to support his weight.

With infinite caution he peered around the tree. That was when he felt his heart plunge. There was more than one man: he could count at least three at the edge of the nearest line of bushes. One held something in his hands – it must be a bow. Athelhard gripped his knife, frozen with indecision. Should he throw it now, kill one of his attackers, and then cry for help? The vill wasn't far from here. Someone would be bound to hear his screams, and it was possible that the remaining two would bolt if they saw their companion fall.

He was calculating the likelihood of the men in the fields hearing him when he saw one of the figures move.

It was a shambling gait, as though he was dragging his left leg, and in that moment, Athelhard knew he would soon die. The man was from his own vill: Adam. That limp was caused by a badly mended leg after he was run over by a cart. It was as distinctive as a coat of arms. Then he recognised another man by his voice, and felt the blood freeze in his veins. These three stalkers were his neighbours, men with whom he had drunk, eaten, fasted, toiled and prayed. They were men he had called his friends. He glanced down at the fletchings on the arrow and now he recognised it, knew who had made it, who had fired it.

That decided him. He couldn't get to his axe, so he must somehow make his way back inside his cottage and find another weapon. He had his own bow and arrows in there; with them he might yet be able to turn the tables on his attackers. If he could hit two of them, that might persuade the others to go, but even with God's help, it would be hard: he'd be lucky to get to his house before being shot again.

From here he could just see his cottage through the trees. There was a cleared space between the edge of the trees and his door, and the thought of covering it in his current condition made his flesh creep. No, ballocks to that: he'd have to work his way round to the back of the cottage and hoist himself in through the rear window.

He retied the shreds of hose about his leg and twisted the shard of arrow until the pain almost made him cry out, before beginning to crawl forwards.

Fear of making a noise forced him to move with exceptional care. The wound in his leg was smarting now, and he shivered in shock. He made it to a bush and slumped down, loosening the tourniquet. Immediately, or so it seemed, his leg was afire with stabs of agony flashing up and down, from his toes to his cods. It felt as if someone had wrapped his entire leg in a blanket of tiny needles, and was progressively shoving them in deeper and deeper.

There was a shout behind him, and he felt his heart lurch.

'Are you *sure* you hit the bugger, Drogo?'

''Course I am! I saw the arrow strike.'

'Where is he then, eh?'

There came another cry from further up, a thrilled call like a huntsman's. 'Blood! Gouts of it! You bled him well enough, like a stuck pig!'

'How do you kill them?' the man called Adam asked. '*Sanguisugae* are dead already, aren't they? How'd you kill someone who's dead?'

'You cut out his heart and burn it. That's what I've heard. If not, he'll keep coming back, keep attacking our little ones.'

'Cut out his heart? Ugh!' The voice came from dangerously close to Athelhard. He recognised it as the youthful tones of Vincent Yunghe, a hanger-on of Drogo's. Instinctively he tensed, but the lad was walking away, going to join the other three. 'I'm not doing that!'

'I'll do it, Vin. I'm not scared, and I want revenge after what he did to my little Denise, the devil!' The angry, bitter voice of Peter atte Moor choked off and there was silence for a while.

Athelhard gritted his jaw and set off again, his leg dragging. The tingling meant he couldn't stand on it for any time, nor could he bolt; all he could do was make for the uncertain sanctuary of his cottage. On he went, sticking to the line of low bushes he had planted to keep dogs from his hens, until he came to a gap.

The blundering of many feet was nearer now. Hell's fires, there must be half the vill up here, he thought to himself. They sounded as though they were congregating at the point where he'd pulled out the arrow, and he bit his lip when he heard someone shout. They were on his trail.

Ahead of him the window was a rough, square hole in the wall of his cottage. A matter of four feet from the ground, and ten yards from him, it looked almost impossible to reach without being seen and hit, but he had to try: inside was safety. He could string his bow, nock an arrow to it, and hold them off, at least until he learned why his neighbours had decided to kill him.

When he heard the command to follow the marks in the mud, he knew he must move fast or be killed like a beast at bay. Summoning up all his courage, he stood. There was a bellow, then a roared instruction, and he could have sworn he heard an arrow, but by then he was hurtling inelegantly forward, hobbling weakly on one leg, forcefully shoving himself on with the other.

One pace, two, and he was waiting for the arrow to pierce his unprotected back. Three paces, four, and his breath was wheezing in terror at being in the open. Five paces, six, and the window was so close he could almost reach it. Seven, and his hand caught the rough cob wall.

He crouched on his good leg, both hands on the ledge, then roared with pain and anger as he tried to leap upwards, wrenching with both arms, using all the muscles of his powerful shoulders. He was already halfway through when the second arrow struck him with a terrible, hollow, wet sound, like a stick striking a damped woollen cloak.

Not a sound broke from him as he thudded heavily to the ground, although the shaft struck the floor and wrenched the broad barbs of the arrowhead deeper into his back. It had found its mark. As he reached around tentatively and felt it, he knew that it would kill him: it had lodged in his liver. The pain was excruciating. Outside, the cries of glee showed that the success of the shot had been seen.

But he wasn't dead yet. He could sting back, he promised himself. Climbing slowly up the wall, he pulled the shutter over the window and tied it in place. Then he could hop along the wall to his stool. Once he was sitting on that, he could snap the arrow-shaft in his back with both hands. It was less painful than the one in his leg, perhaps because he was already growing weak and he simply couldn't cope with more pain; his frame had registered all it could. He didn't care. Now all that mattered to him was killing as many of them as he could. His *neighbours*, his *friends*, he sneered to himself.

The bow hung from a beam, away from the damp. He could just touch it with his fingers at full reach, and that was enough to knock it down, falling across his head and then down his back, where it snagged on the broken arrow. A scream broke from his lips. Standing, he grabbed the bow and with slow determination he rested one end on the ground and leaned forward, pushing the bow and bending it, shoving the gut string up and over the curve until it could fit into the two slots at either side.

It was done. His back was soaked, and he knew he was losing a lot of blood, but he carried on. The small quiver with his arrows was near the door, and he plucked one and nocked it on the string before dropping back with a grunt to his stool to wait.

But now the rats were closer. He had husbanded all the energy he could, and he rose, shuffled to the doorway and peeped out from behind the leather curtain. He hoped that the men would not notice him there but if they did, the leather might serve as some protection.

Outside, the light was swiftly fading, and he could scarcely make out anything, save the great trees which towered all around. He could see none of his attackers in the gloom, but he could hear them moving about. He couldn't be sure of hitting them, not aiming by sound alone.

When the man called to him, the sound of his voice was so unexpected that Athelhard caught his breath.

'Athelhard, surrender to us.'

He made no answer. The voice was coming from the right of the beech tree, and he squinted, but he couldn't be sure of a target in the gloom.

'Come out and we'll send you to Exeter to be tried by the justice of Gaol Delivery. Otherwise we will kill you. We have to.' It almost sounded as though the man was pleading. 'We've found her. We know what you did to her. We've heard of your . . . your *meal*!'

A shot of pain lanced his back, and the breath hissed through his teeth. He had no idea what the Reeve was talking about, didn't care especially. A moment later he caught sight of the man, a tall, powerfully built figure standing a little distance from the beech tree, roughly where Athelhard had pulled the arrow from his thigh.

He could feel his strength ebbing, but he was determined, and lifted his bow. Every week he had practised with his bow since his youth, and now he had a clear picture of his enemy. Raising the bow until the point of his arrow was on the man's face, Athelhard drew back the string.

Normally he could pull it back smoothly, the arrow resting on his knuckle while his hooked fingers drew the string back to reach his face, softly touching his nose, lips and chin, while he stared along the arrow itself, waiting for the moment to release it. Not today. He couldn't hold it steady, even when the string was only halfway drawn. Hauling back on it, he kept his eye on the man, gasping with the effort, but before the arrow's nock was six inches from his chin, his arm began vibrating madly. The bow wavered impossibly; his hands couldn't control it. The pull was too strong for him in his weakened state. Blood flooded from his wound, slick on his skin, glueing his shirt to his back. He couldn't aim, couldn't even be sure he'd get the thing to fire through the doorway – it would be more likely to strike the wall at this rate. Slowly, he permitted the string to inch forward without firing, then sagged, silently weeping, his chin falling to his breast after the expenditure of so much effort. There was nothing left. He was done.

That was when he noticed the light playing about the doorway, saw the torches. Instinctively he glanced up at the thatching of his roof.

There was an odd noise, like a pheasant in flight, and he wondered for a moment what it might be. He realised when he heard it thud against his roof that it was a torch. After so much rain, it had little immediate effect, producing a loud spitting and fizzing, but then he heard another thump above him, and a third. Soon he could hear a loud hissing and crackling as the thatch began to ignite.

It was enough. As the flames took hold, the fight left him. He had no more energy. The vital force which had directed him was fading as his blood dripped steadily to pool on the floor. With it, his urgent need for revenge was dwindling and in its place an overwhelming lassitude settled upon him. He fell back onto his stool even as the first whiff of burning thatch reached his nostrils, as the first glowing strands fell at his feet.

Resigned to death, he preferred to be consumed in the flames that devoured his cottage. Rather that than give his enemies the satisfaction of seeing him bolt from his door like a rabbit chased by a ferret, only to be shot and killed. He would have been pleased to die fighting, but it was too late. As the smoke began to fill his room with a greenish, yellow vapour, he inhaled deeply, welcoming the light-headedness that proclaimed the onset of oblivion.

The scream stirred him: *Margaret*, his responsibility, his sister. Her despair made him sit up, coughing painfully. In her voice he could hear her terror. She was too simple to comprehend what was happening, probably didn't know her only brother was inside, but seeing her cottage in flames made her give shriek after shriek.

'Go on! Throw her in with him!' he heard someone shout, and that was enough to galvanise him.

'NO!' he roared, stumbling to his feet. She cried out again, and he felt the fury take him over. Gripping his useless bow in both hands and leaning heavily on it like a staff, he limped to the door, then lurched on outside shouting for his Meg. It was there, before his threshold, that the three arrows found their marks.

One smashed straight into his shoulder, the heavy arrowhead spinning him around, making him drop his bow and stumble to the ground. He had just propped himself up on his good arm to face his tormentors when the second arrow flashed into his neck and flew through it, thudding on into the cottage wall. He coughed once, and even as he drew breath to cough again, the last arrow slammed into the left side of his breast, straight into his heart.

Just before he died, Athelhard used his remaining strength to scream one last defiant curse. All the men heard him; all would remember it for the rest of their lives.

'*Damn you! Damn you all! I'll see the whole vill roast in hell! You are all accursed!*'

Later, much later, Serlo the Warrener walked down into the clearing. He took in the smoking shell of the house and eyed the smouldering corpse which lay just inside the doorway where the departing men had thrown it, to be consumed by the flames.

A dead body was nothing to Serlo; he had handled enough of them in his time, although he had never burned one. That looked wrong. It was one thing to bury a man after listening to his confession, letting him answer the questions of the *viaticum* and giving him absolution, but to slaughter a man like this was repellent.

He shrugged and turned away; a man of few words has little need of contemplation, and for the present he had one pressing consideration.

The girl knelt not far from the wreck of her house, her eyes wild, her mouth dribbling. Her round face was enough to show that her mind was addled, and it was that which saved her, of course. Serlo knew that the superstitious folk of the vill wouldn't harm a girl like her. She was touched.

He gently crouched before her, blocking her view of her brother's corpse, and clasped her hands in his. It took a long time, much talking, a lot of reassuring and comforting, but at last, as the dawn lighted the eastern horizon, she complied with his gentle urging and went with him up to his house.

Chapter One

Seven years later

Joan bolted up the track as though the hounds of hell were snapping at her heels. Splashing through the ruts and puddles, she could feel the mud spattering her calves and thighs underneath her skirts, the brambles catching at her sleeves.

Gasping, she paused at the top of the steepest part of the hill, gripping her sides and facing back the way she had come. There, far below her, she could see her red-faced friend Emma panting and waving up at her. Soon Emma had recovered and set off again, pressing her palms on her thighs with each step as though it could ease her progress.

Emma was too chubby, that was why she struggled to keep up with Joan, not that either minded. Joan was fond of her friend, and Emma was devoted to Joan. There were few other girls in the area and although with Joan's fertile imagination she could populate the surrounding ten miles with different inhabitants, it was nice not to have to bother, and Emma had a similar sense of fun to her own. She was a good companion.

It was terribly steep here – Joan could recall her father telling her that 'stickle' meant steep – but now that they had climbed the sharper incline at the bottom of Greenhill, the slope rose less cruelly, taking them through the trees to the scrubby land above the vill.

From here she could see right over the clump of small cottages and the Reeve's own larger house, to the river and then the hill which stood between Sticklepath and South Zeal.

She loved this view. Below her she could just glimpse her own family's home, a large cottage at the edge of the vill under the hill that led up to the moors, a good-sized house for her and her parents. Behind was the mill, whose crunching and rumbling could be heard even over the steady rushing of the river. A short distance away was the chapel, sitting in the broad loop where the river curled around the bottom of the hill's slope with, beside it, the small cemetery with its twin defences: the hurdles enclosing it to protect the dead from scavenging dogs and wild animals, while their souls were protected from demons by the single large wooden cross planted like a tree in the middle.

After that stood the inn, always filled with travellers. Sticklepath lay on the main road between Exeter and Cornwall, and pilgrims, merchants, fish-sellers and tranters of all kinds passed by here. Even now Joan could see a man leading a packhorse down the slope from South Zeal. He followed the muddy trail to the ford and stood there contemplating it, then ran across quickly, feet splashing the water in all directions. At the far side he turned, but his horse hadn't followed him, and it stood for a moment, watching him with a kind of bemused surprise before wandering to the verge and nibbling at the grass. The man's angry voice couldn't reach Joan over the rumble and clatter of the mill, but she smiled to see him raise his fists in impotent fury before recrossing the river to fetch the beast.

The men and most of the women were outside, working, their legs stained brown from the mud in the narrow strips in the communal fields. Each little half-acre strip was separated by an unploughed, grassy path called a *landsherd*, and the women were bending to pull out the straggling fingers of couch grass before they could invade and establish themselves in the strips and threaten the new crop of oats.

It was a peaceful, comforting scene. Joan knew enough about poverty. It was hard not to, when everyone was struggling to make a living, when neighbours could scarcely find the money for grain to make bread and had to depend on the largesse of their lord, Hugh de Courtenay, whose serfs they were. Still, none of that could detract from the warmth she felt, surveying this serene little vill. It was her home.

As she gazed down she could feel her heart swell. The picture before her represented safety and comradeship; it contained all she knew of life and love. She had no idea of the trials which would soon afflict her and her family – those troubles were in her future, so today she smiled happily at the sight. The sun was shining down, the rains all but forgotten, and the fields glowed with green health and promise, shot through with blue and silver silken threads to show where streams and rivulets fed the soil.

All looked clean and pure, not like other places. Inevitably her attention moved beyond the fields, past the larger pastures and water meadows, all bounded by the river as it wound its way northwards.

She gazed in that direction, feeling faintly troubled. From here she couldn't see the hills. If she walked up to the warrens on the moorland nearer to Belstone, the long, low blue line on the horizon was plainly visible, but not from here. Her father had told her that it was far-distant Exmoor, and that beyond it was the sea, but she found it hard to believe. It was so far away, it was incomprehensible that it should in truth exist. She had seen far-off towns – she had been to Oakhampton many times, and had even joined her father when he went to market in Tavistock once, miles to the south and west – but to think that somewhere like Exmoor lay there, so distant that even massive hills were an indistinct smudge, was quite difficult to accept. It was scary.

Sighing, she glanced down at Emma. 'Come on! We'll have to set off back home before we even get there, at this rate,' she called imperiously.

Emma grinned up at her. Her breast was heaving and she was plainly feeling the warmth. To Joan's eye she panted like a dog. The sun was beaming down, almost directly overhead, and Emma's face shone like a cherry. 'There's no hurry. Everyone's out working. They won't notice we've gone for ages.'

It was rare that there was anything up here of interest. They both visited the moors often enough, sometimes to see the spoor left by the fox which lived up at the wall before the moor, or to steal eggs from the larks and other ground-nesting birds, but they were natural sights. Unusual sights, like the rotting corpse of the wolf which Emma had discovered last year, were unique; not that it stayed there long. The heavy springtime rains had dismembered the remains, washing them away as though they had never existed and the two girls couldn't even find the skull, no matter how long they searched.

What a spring it had been! Two houses down in the vill had been flooded and collapsed when their walls were washed away. Poor Ham, the son of William the Taverner, had died when a beam fell on him as he tried to help rescue the animals and belongings from the home of Henry Batyn. It was fortunate that the other buildings survived, and the houses built to replace the fallen ones were almost completed, but Joan still missed Ham. He had been a natural enemy, cat-calling and sneering at her, but sometimes even the loss of an enemy can be sad. His death had left a hole in her life.

The rains had been terrible. Not so bad as the famine years, all the adults said, but Joan and Emma wouldn't know that. This was the year of 1322, so the priest told them, when Father Gervase deigned to speak.

Samson atte Mill said that Emma and Joan were only two and three when the great downpours started. Not that they spoke to Samson much. He was a huge, fearsome man with red, slobbering lips and a brutal expression. Joan had heard horrible stories about him, and she tended to avoid him, but he seemed to like to get close to her. Once he tried to persuade her to kiss him. Not when her parents were around, though, and Joan felt sure it was because he knew it was wrong.

This year the weather had been worryingly similar to the famine

would starve ag̲___
persuaded the villagers to ou̲___
his own house, designed to slowly dry the̲___
using it to cook, hadn't worked well. In Devon, many ha̲___
during the famine. All feared another, and their trepidation as
they watched their crops being tortured by the torrential downpours was communicated to the children.

But the rains had stopped, mercifully, in the early summer.
Joan felt as though she would always remember that first delicious
day when the clouds parted and the sun could at last break through,
sending shafts of light to the ground. Before long the soil was
heated, so quickly that there was a thin mist of steam. She could
see it rising from the earth, as though there was a great fire
beneath the land, a health-giving, invigorating fire that soothed
and reassured, drying out the sodden fields and transforming
people's pinched grey faces into ones with fresh pink complexions
and cheerful expressions.

It certainly worked wonders on the poor serfs slaving in Lord
Hugh's fields. Joan's mother, Nicole, declared that it was the first
time in weeks that her own clothes had not been soggy. She
looked happy, revelling in the sun's heat, standing at the door of
their tiny cottage with her face to the skies, moaning in pleasure,
lifting her arms slowly as though in reverence, eyes closed, as
though she was drinking in the warmth. She looked almost like a
child again; it was odd to see her like that.

That wasn't the only great thing that day. The other was that
Joan wasn't told off or smacked once. It felt as though the whole
vill was starting a new life together.

If that had been a marvellous day, she thought happily, this was

[torn flap — inverted bleed-through text, partially legible]

weren't strong enough again. Even the little ovens which the Reeve had
the grain, spindly plants with feeble, non-nutritious grains which
weak, spindly plants with feeble, non-nutritious grains which
years, everyone said. Farmers took to watching the skies anxiously, for if
weeks, everyone said. The rains began in March and continued for
... the sodden grain before had died
... child in the communal bakery next to
... bake into bread or brew into ale, they
... were planted were to drown, or grew to produce only

...illside,

...y were passing

...king the road's surface

...s shimmer in the haze, while

t... ...g in among the banks were dappled
wi... ...shadow, as the breeze ruffled their leaves.

'...further is it?' Joan asked. Glancing back towards
the t..n, she saw that the man with the packhorse now stood at
the base of the sticklepath itself, looking up the narrow track
towards them. 'We'll have to set off home soon.'

Emma didn't see her glance. She didn't care about some silly
man traipsing about the place with a packhorse. Tranters were two
a penny during the summer when travel was less arduous.
However, she was always easily offended and now, upset by Joan's
tone, she answered sulkily, 'It's just a little further on.'

'Sorry,' Joan said quickly, not wanting to spoil the mood. Yet
for some reason she was feeling apprehensive.

'There it is!' Emma pointed a few moments later.

Following her finger, Joan saw that a small section of the bank
had been washed away. Loosened, perhaps, by the rains earlier in

the year, it had yielded to the weight of a fox or a dog, and the
wall of the lane had collapsed. An untidy mess of grey moorstone
rubble had slithered into the lane, borne along by the tide of damp
soil behind, although the trees and bushes on either side appeared
to bulwark the rest of the bank from further disintegration.

The two girls hurried to the rent in the wall. 'There, see?'
Emma said, excitedly.

They crouched side by side and peered. In among the roots
Joan thought she could see some cloth, filthy from long immersion
in the soil, but still recognisably material of some kind. How
peculiar! Someone must have buried it here. Emma had been
right when she'd begged Joan to come and see this, saying that it
was even more weird than the dead wolf.

'Do you think there's something wrapped in it?' Joan said at
last.

'Could be, but what would someone wrap in cloth and bury?
And why would they have buried it here?'

'It could be gold, stolen by a felon, and hidden here for
safekeeping,' Joan said, reaching out and touching it.

'Careful! You don't want the wall to fall on you,' Emma cried,
pulling her friend away.

'It's strong enough.'

'Remember how the houses fell in? I'll never forget seeing
Ham when they pulled him loose. Ugh! Blood everywhere, and
his arm dangling like that.'

Joan sniffed unsympathetically. 'If you don't dare stay, leave
me to it.'

Emma bridled. 'It was me found it! All I'm saying is, you
ought to poke it with a stick first, just in case the lot tumbles
down. It could trap you.'

For all her boldness, Joan could see the force of the argument.
The rocks which had landed in the road were some of them very
large. One was over a foot deep; easily massive enough to crush
her like a snail. Casting about for a stick, she found a thin branch

about a yard long. Methodically stripping the twigs from it, Joan fashioned it into a pole, using her knife to sharpen the tip, cutting a barb into it. Then, while Emma waited below, watching with some anxiety in case her friend should be overwhelmed by a fresh fall, Joan stabbed at the cloth. The stick caught, the barb snagging in the cloth, but when she pulled, although there was a light scattering of soil, the stick pulled free. Poking again, she managed to pull a shred of the material away, and crouched to gaze closer.

'What is it?' Emma called.

'There's nothing,' she returned. 'It won't come away, though. There's another rock behind it. Maybe it's trapping the cloth in there?'

She squinted in, beckoning to Emma, who sighed with relief, and began the slow ascent to rejoin her. Behind her, the man with the packhorse was climbing stolidly up the slope. And then something odd happened.

Joan had pushed her stick back into the cloth, trying to pull it away, and the stone behind had moved. It rocked, once, twice, and then the material tore. At the back of her mind Joan had been thinking that she might be able to rescue it to bind her hair or something, and now it was ruined. She screwed her face up with bitter disappointment. As she did so, the stone toppled out.

It wasn't the way that the stone fell from the hole, so much, although it bounced somehow more slowly than she would have expected, as though it was lighter than it should be; no, it was the hollow sound it gave as it rolled haphazardly towards Emma.

At first Joan thought nothing of it, but then Emma's horrified scream made her head snap around. 'What?'

To her astonishment, she saw that her friend had already turned tail, and was fleeing from the rock, screaming her way down the slope towards the vill. As Joan watched, her mouth gaping, Emma hurtled past the traveller and his horse, alarming the beast and making it rear and snort. The man swore loudly, yanking at the leading rein and smacking the horse on the nose to calm him.

As he approached Joan, he glanced down and enquired, 'Are you all right?'

'Yes, I think so.' Joan was still staring after her friend, wondering what could have so scared her. She glanced down, at the rock which had rolled so oddly from the wall.

But it was no rock. It was a skull, and it seemed to be gazing up at her as though in sardonic amusement.

Nicole Garde felt a stab of fear when the figure appeared in her doorway.

She hadn't been expecting anybody. At that time of day, before noon, in the last hour before the sun rose to the highest point in the sky, visitors were the last thing on her mind. She had been preparing her family's meal, squatting before the fire, teasing the embers into life with small quantities of wood chips and a lot of careful, steady blowing. Once she had the fire burning brightly, she would throw her large flat stone into the midst of the flames, getting it good and hot, while above it the pottage in her prized iron bowl began to bubble. When it was almost ready, she would drag out the stone, wipe it, and cook her bread.

But today the process was taking time; the fire was reluctant. She had already used up much of her store of tinder, and was worrying that she would never tempt the fire into roaring life. The room was smoky, so she had opened the door wide to release the fumes, and the sunlight streamed in, making everywhere look bright and cheerful when for so long the room had been dull and gloomy. That was how she knew someone had arrived, because the place was suddenly thrown into darkness again. Without even looking round, she felt the hairs on her neck rise, the breath catch in her throat, knowing it was *him*.

Only one man merited such contempt, mingled with fear: her brother-in-law Ivo Bel, Manciple to the nuns of Canonsleigh. He lusted after her, had done so for years. Thank God he was not often here at Sticklepath, and his nasty little eyes could not fix upon her with that unpleasing gleam, as though he had already undressed her in his mind and was mentally entering her. He wouldn't dare offer her an insult in front of her husband, of course. Thomas would avenge her honour without fear of the consequences. Ivo was here too often and if he attempted to rape her, she would be hard put to defend herself. He was wiry and powerful and a dangerous man. She had not forgotten his offer to have her marriage declared illegal, because he had some power over the Reeve, so he said. He had witnessd the Reeve killing a man.

Sitting up, she rallied her thoughts. Her knife was resting beside the dough, where she had been tearing up leaves of orach and good henry and chopping garlic. She grabbed it and whirled to face him. If she had to kill him, she would; if she couldn't, she would at least mark him. Only when she had risen into a crouch, the knife held out in front of her, did she see who stood in the doorway: Swetricus.

He was a hulking great man, one of Lord Hugh's serfs who worked the lands under Reeve Alexander, but he was no enemy of Nicole's. *His* enemy, since his wife had died and his daughter Aline had vanished, was the ale barrel.

'Oh, Swet. I am so sorry!' she gasped as she set the knife down again.

'You thought I was the miller?' He shrugged. Broad and heavily built, although not tall, he was bent with work and worry. At thirty-eight he was one of the older men in the vill and his dark hair was already shot through with silver. Grey eyes, which in the right light could look blue, were turned watery since the death of his wife. Now he must look after their remaining three daughters on his own, with a little help from the woman next door. It didn't leave poor Swet much time to relax, but he tried to with his ale. Often he had to be asked to be quiet, when his drunken shouting and weeping threatened the vill's peace.

'Yes,' she said. Everyone knew that he suspected the miller of having had something to do with Aline's disappearance.

'He wouldn't trouble you,' Swetricus said.

She suddenly saw something in his eyes, something almost like sympathy. A cold hand gripped her throat and she blurted, 'It's not Thomas, is it?'

'No. Your daughter. Found a body up the sticklepath. She's not well. Needs you.'

Nicole gaped, then rushed past him. Outside, she could see across the puddled soil of the roadway that there was a gathering crowd up on the sticklepath itself. Men and women were leaving the fields to go and gawp. There was a second, smaller group at the door to the tavern, and she guessed that her daughter must be there. Lifting her skirts, she ran, unheeding of the muddy water that splashed about her bare feet and ankles.

'Joan? Joan, where are you?'

Emma sat on the tavern's only bench, sobbing and incapable of speech, a large pot of strong ale at her side, but Nicole could see no sign of her own daughter. She was about to go to Emma's side and shake her, demanding where Joan was, when she felt a hand touching her arm. It was as if Swetricus understood her terror – as he would, she reminded herself.

'It's all right,' he said gently. 'She's with others – showing them where it was. Here she comes now.'

Seeing Joan walking down the lane towards them, Nicole was tempted to run to her and gather her up in a hug. She should be as petrified as poor Emma, she was only young, only ten years old . . . but something held the woman back. It was the tall, rangy traveller walking at her daughter's side. He had his hand on the girl's shoulder in a way that made Nicole's hackles rise.

The stranger was of a heavier build than Thomas, with long, unkempt hair of a pale brown, and eyes that might have belonged to a cat; they were a peculiar shade of green, wide-set and intelligent. His mouth had full lips, and although he wore a solemn and respectful look, he was quick to smile at Nicole as he approached the tavern.

In that smile there was something wrong. Nicole always judged people quickly, and this man, she felt sure, was false. There was a veneer of sympathy there, but no more than that. His sole interest was himself.

Joan rushed to her mother, burying her face in Nicole's skirt.

'It's all right,' Nicole said, gently tousling her daughter's hair.

Joan looked up, and in her face there was a mature, fearless expression. 'I wasn't scared, Mother. Emma was, but I wasn't.'

'She's telling the truth there, *madame*,' said the stranger, hearing her accent. 'She was more intrigued than fearful.'

'Who are you?' Swetricus demanded from behind her.

'Miles Houndestail, master,' the stranger said, bowing graciously. He was clad in simple hose, with a short tunic over a shirt, and a leather jack to keep out the wind. In his hand was a felt cap with several pilgrim badges pinned to it, and he wore a long-bladed knife in his belt, next to his horn. 'I'm a simple Pardoner, here to assist those who seek God's forgiveness.'

'What was so scary?' Nicole asked her daughter.

'The skull. It rolled down past me and finished up with Emma. She became hysterical.'

'Skull?' Nicole repeated dully.

'Yes. Drogo said he thinks it must be poor Aline.'

Nicole gasped and turned to see whether Swetricus had heard. He must have, but he merely stood and watched the men huddled about the body up on the sticklepath with an unreadable expression, saying nothing.

His daughter Aline had disappeared many years ago, but surely he would still show some reaction on hearing that at last her corpse had been found? Any father would – wouldn't he?

Chapter Two

Only a matter of days after Joan and Emma's discovery, Sir Baldwin Furnshill lay on a bench in his garden before his house, enjoying the warmth of the sun on his face as he dozed, listening idly to the peasants in the fields. Overhead, larks sang in the sunshine and a pair of doves called to each other in his oak. They sounded delightful, and he decided that he would have a pair or two killed. His wife loved the taste of them roasted with honey.

The sounds of laughter and birdsong were wonderfully soporific. Gradually he found himself slipping into sleep, but not into a happy daydream; this was a nightmare, the same he had endured many times before.

He was in some woods – he did not know where or why. All he knew was that he was pursued by a nameless dread, and as he rushed forward, raising his arms to protect his face against brambles and twigs, he scarcely knew which to fear most – the pursuit or the horror which awaited him.

Soon he could see it: a broad swathe of grass. The sun pierced the high canopy of leaves here, and he could detect an odour – of roasting meat – *of human flesh*. The smell was noisome, sickly sweet, and then he reached the clearing and could see the man bound to the tree, his body slumped forward, his legs consumed in the fire that raged about his feet. It was a Knight Templar, from the cross at his breast, and then Baldwin recognised him. He was one of Baldwin's friends, a knight who had died in the mass burnings in Paris after the death of Jacques de Molay, the Templar Grand Master. Even in his dream, Baldwin knew that this man had died many years before, and yet as he stared in horror, the scene was horribly real.

The knight was dead. No man could live with the flames licking upwards as they were now about his breast, but as Baldwin stopped and stared, he saw the head rise, saw the blackened skin about the eyes crack as the lids opened, and saw the mouth fall wide as though to call him . . .

He came to with a start, a cold sweat all over his face and back, a shivering like the ague, his breath coming in short gasps. Aylmer rose and padded softly to his side. The glossy rache, Baldwin's hunting dog, stood near him with his head set to one side, his tan eyebrows frowning and his forehead wrinkled with concern. Baldwin stroked the animal to reassure him.

Above him the swallows called, whirling and spinning in the warm summer air. A pair of buzzards circled lazily high over the fields towards Cadbury, and when he gazed southwards, he could see a hundred rooks slowly rising into the air as one of his villeins' sons threw stones or shouted at them. Looking about him, he could feel his heartbeat returning to normal, his breathing growing calmer. Feeling the sun on his face, he was aware of a curious sense of anti-climax. The world was unchanged. People strained and worked without fear, he could hear a woman singing, and cattle moaned gently as they chewed the cud.

The dream regularly impinged upon his sleeping mind, not every night, but often enough to unsettle him. Its roots lay in the violence which had begun long ago when his comrades in the *Poor Fellow Soldiers of Christ and the Temple of Solomon*, the Knights Templar, were burned at the stake. Baldwin felt a residual guilt for having survived the persecution, and the dreams were a reflection of that guilt.

Resolutely non-superstitious he might be, but he was still prey to the prickings of conscience, he told himself as he wiped away the sweat that filmed his forehead.

With that reflection, he broke wind and grinned to himself, glancing around to make sure that no one had heard him. It would not do for the Master of Furnshill, the Keeper of the King's Peace in Crediton, to be overheard indulging in such shameful behaviour.

Shaking off any lingering anxiety, he yawned, then stretched voluptuously. At once he had to stifle a curse. A pain shot from under his shoulderblade, a reminder of his recent joust at Oakhampton's tournament. His wounds no longer healed as quickly as they had when he was a young man, not that he would admit as much to his wife. She was already ruining him with her solicitous nursing. Much more of it and he would be as round as a football. Detestable sport that it was, he thought grumpily. Always led to violence and death.

Still, it was a glorious day. He could, in sunshine such as this, forget the horrors of his past and the annoyance of football. The reflection made him grin to himself, but when he cast a look over his shoulder, there was another stab in his neck, and the breath hissed softly between his teeth.

Baldwin was a grey-haired man in his late forties with the strong shoulders and thick neck of a trained sword-fighter. Only one scar testified to his past as a warrior: it stretched from temple to jaw, a souvenir from the battles about Acre. The sole incongruity about him was the neatly trimmed and still dark beard, which followed the line of his jaw. Not many men wore beards these days, especially among the knightly class.

Only two years ago his features had reflected the anguish which he had endured after the destruction of his Order and the slaughter of his companions, but recently his face had lost much of the torment, although there were still deep tracks scored at either side of his mouth, creases at his forehead, and a lowering wariness in his dark eyes that sometimes alarmed people when he stared intently at them. It had been said that he could see beyond a man's lies, through to a man's soul. He only wished that were true.

Since marrying he had found a new delight in life and had gladly thrown off the melancholy which had cloaked him for so long. As he must soon throw away this tunic, he told himself as he gazed down at his growing paunch. His wife had seen to it that his diet had subtly altered, and his frame was filling out. The proof of this was the way that his tunics fitted: tightly. It was partly due, too, to lack of exercise. Whenever he took his ease he found his weight increased alarmingly and he felt lethargic.

That was certainly the case after last year's Christmas celebrations in Exeter, and now, since recuperating for a week or two after the tournament at Oakhampton, he could feel his belly becoming uncomfortable once more. He needed a ride, a series of fast gallops and hunts to work off some of this weight. That would make him feel better. Not that there was much chance of that. Lady Jeanne would never let him take exercise until she was convinced that he was entirely cured.

He glanced at his dog, Aylmer, who stood, his tail sweeping slowly from side to side.

'So you want to go out too,' Baldwin muttered. He put out a hand to stroke Aylmer's head again, but the dog ducked away, springing back, ready to head for the stables, staring at Baldwin enquiringly.

'It is tempting,' Baldwin said, just as Jeanne, his wife, came through the doorway. Not hearing her, he had sat up and was about to throw off the thick woollen cloak that lay over his legs, when he caught a glimpse of her from the corner of his eye.

'Bugger! Too late,' he muttered ungraciously.

Aylmer saw her too, and slunk away.

'Coward!' Baldwin hissed, and then turned to meet Jeanne's steely gaze with an innocent smile.

'Baldwin, where were you going?'

He felt unaccountably like a mischievous urchin caught scrumping apples, and the sensation put him in a bad humour. 'I was only going to fetch some wine,' he grunted.

'There is no need – I have brought drinks.'

Baldwin looked up into the impassive features of his servant, Edgar. The steward gazed back without allowing his face to reflect his true feelings. 'What are you staring at?' Baldwin snapped.

'Don't be troublesome, my love,' Jeanne said soothingly. 'You know it is for your own good. Please sit back and rest.'

He obeyed, but with a bad grace, scowling at the view. 'A fine day like this, hounds bursting to be out, a destrier that needs exercise, and you have me hobbled like an old man. I can't sleep properly . . .'

'Have you had that dream again?'

'I need exercise to be able to rest,' he said quickly, recalling that Jeanne took dreams seriously, thinking them to be omens. 'I just woke up with a start, that's all.'

'Have you had another nightmare?'

'Superstitious maundering!'

'Don't mumble,' Jeanne said imperturbably. 'If you hadn't submitted to trial by combat, you wouldn't have hurt yourself so badly and I wouldn't have to nurse you, so lie back like a good wounded knight and drink this.'

'This' was a warming strong wine sweetened with honey and flavoured with spices. She motioned to Edgar. He held the cup to Baldwin, who irritably took it and sipped.

'There must be some magic in this,' he growled reluctantly after a few moments.

Jeanne sent Edgar away and smiled at her husband, her features pleasantly shaded and softened by the trees above. The gentle light emphasised the softness of her skin, making her blue eyes seem more sparkling and alive with humour. 'Magic?'

'What else can it be, my Lady? I was prepared to be angry, chafing at the silken fetters with which you have me bound here, yet one sip and I feel as though it is better to lie here for ever than get on with the thousands of little tasks which ought to occupy me.'

Jeanne laughed aloud. She was a tall, slender woman of some thirty years, but her red-gold hair was as soft and bright as that of a young woman, and her mischievous expression gave her an impish charm. Her face was regular, if a little round; her nose short, perhaps too small; her mouth over-wide with a full upper lip that gave her a stubborn appearance; her forehead was maybe too broad – but to Baldwin she was perfection.

'Well, my Lord, I am glad if my wine is so effective,' she joked, then grew serious. 'But I would rather you had not been so battered and had not needed my medicine.'

'I have my duties, my Lady,' he said sharply.

'And right now your duty is to yourself, Baldwin. God's blood! Will it help anyone if you work yourself into the grave? You must give yourself time to heal.'

'Very well, and I will try to avoid battles in future,' he said, only half mockingly. He had no intention of getting into any more fights, not at his age – although he was concerned about the current political situation, which could lead to an armed struggle.

'Are you troubled, my love?'

He smiled. 'You recognise my moods too well.'

'It is easy when you sigh like that. You are thinking of the King?'

'Not him particularly, but his advisers: the Despensers.'

News had filtered down to them gradually after the disaster of Boroughbridge. Earl Thomas of Lancaster had been caught there and executed by his nephew the King, and almost instantly King Edward II had reneged on the agreements won after so much strife. He had called a parliament in May and revoked the exile imposed on his friends the Despensers, but that was not all. Edward was still bitter about the way his powers had been curtailed. He had repealed the Ordinances which had been created to protect his realm from incompetent or corrupt advisers, and now, for the first time in his reign, he held supreme power.

This absolute control meant that he could reward those whom he considered his friends, and he lavished lands, wealth and titles on the Despensers. Hugh the Elder was created Earl of Winchester, while his son received many of the estates of the Marcher Lords, the nobles from the Welsh borders who had dared to stand against Edward II and his friends in the brief Despenser Wars.

'It will lead to disaster,' Baldwin said grimly.

'Perhaps we can look forward to a period of stability,' Jeanne said. 'The King's enemies are dead or imprisoned, and he will surely wish for peace himself.'

'I expect he will,' Baldwin said, but added heavily, 'It is not *him* whom I fear, though. The Despensers are dangerous, avaricious men. With the consent of the King they have acquired almost the whole of Wales over the claims of those who have remained loyal to Edward. And then there is the Queen. How must she feel, now that the King has his closest friend back with him?' Baldwin did not need to spell it out. The whole kingdom knew about the allegations that Hugh Despenser the Younger was the King's lover.

Jeanne was aware of her husband's tolerance for homosexuals. When he fought in the hell-hole of Acre, the last of the Crusader cities, until it fell, he had seen men who preferred other men to women. That he felt no disgust for such behaviour seemed peculiar in the extreme to her. Sodomy was sinful, and she agreed privately with Baldwin's friend Simon Puttock, who had made his own opposition to such practices perfectly clear. Simon never minced his words.

But she was sure that Baldwin was right to be thinking of the poor Queen. Isabella had recently given birth to another child, a daughter, while locked up in the Tower for her own protection during the King's successful campaign against Lancaster. Rumours said that the poor woman had been forced to give birth in a room with a leaking roof, and the rain spattered her even as the child was born. Jeanne shivered at the thought. It was an awful idea, as though the Queen was imprisoned so that the King might be free to enjoy his lover. 'How will she react to the return of Despenser?'

'I am sure she will tolerate her husband's . . . um . . .' Baldwin's voice trailed off.

Jeanne noticed he was staring at Aylmer, who frowned at a rider cantering along the road. As she watched, the rider reined in at the end of the track which led to Furnshill, then pulled his horse's head around and aimed for them. Aylmer stood, a growl rumbling deep in his throat.

Keeping an eye on him, Jeanne answered, 'I can guess at her reaction. She is French, Husband, and herself the daughter of a King. I have lived among the French, as you know, and I think I know how a Frenchwoman would react to learning that her husband had little interest in her. She would not be patient for . . . Baldwin? Perhaps you would prefer me to demonstrate how a French wife would behave when she was being ignored?'

Hearing the caustic edge to her voice, he tore his gaze from the approaching rider. 'Sorry, my Lady?'

'Nothing, Husband,' Jeanne said with poisonous sweetness. 'I am sure I was only talking nonsense. What interest could it be to you? Who is it on that horse?'

Baldwin was squinting in his effort to recognise the rider. 'I can't quite see.'

Jeanne cast a quick look over her shoulder, but she need not have worried. Edgar, who had been sergeant to Baldwin in the Order of the Templars, and who took seriously his duty to protect his master, was already approaching, a long staff in his hands. He stopped a short distance from Sir Baldwin, resting the staff on the ground, gripping it loosely in his right hand, ready to deflect an attack.

The rider was a young man, probably not yet twenty, with sandy hair and the thin, pinched features of hunger. He reined in before the door, near to where Baldwin, Jeanne and Edgar waited, and ducked his head like a man used to being polite to officials. 'My Lady, God's blessing on you. I seek Sir Baldwin Furnshill – is he here?'

Jeanne put out a hand to restrain her husband on his bench, but she was already too late.

'I am,' Baldwin said, sweeping the cloak away and standing. He studied the rider with a calm gravity. 'Who sent you?'

'Sir Baldwin, I am glad to have found you so soon. My master, Sir Roger de Gidleigh, asked me to request your help.'

'A murder?' Baldwin said. Sir Roger was one of the Devonshire Coroners. From the look on the messenger's face Baldwin realised that his eagerness must have sounded strange, but he had conducted two enquiries with Sir Roger, the most recent during the Oakhampton tournament in which Baldwin had received his wounds, and he respected his judgement. If Sir Roger was asking for help, it should prove to be a matter of interest.

'Of a sort, sir, yes.'

'What do you mean, "of a sort"?' Jeanne demanded.

The lad looked at her with a sort of weary acceptance that there was no way to ease the impact of his news.

'Madam, I fear Sir Roger is investigating a matter of cannibalism.'

Felicia could hear the row as she approached the mill, even over the harsh rumbling of the great stones grating over each other as they ground the corn. Her parents were at it again.

There was no surprise in it. The whole vill knew about them. Other families were normal, they lived easily with each other, with only the occasional flarings of anger, but not in her home. Her parents detested each other. The only surprise was that Samson had not yet killed her mother.

At the mere thought of her father, she shivered. Felicia was a strongly built girl of twenty-one, with thick dark hair swept back under her wimple. Her eyes were large and almost blue; her face had high cheekbones that could make her look beautiful when she was excited and flushed, but her mouth was thin and severe. When she smiled her features lit up as though with angelic calmness, but she never smiled when thinking of her father. He aroused too many conflicting feelings in her, ones she couldn't altogether understand. His large hands were as coarse and rough as moorstone, far better suited to clenching in anger than to soothing and stroking in love, although some women liked that. Felicia shivered again. That was the trouble. He enjoyed so many females, and Felicia's mother Gunilda raged with jealousy. Never, even in their bed, would he turn to her to fulfil their marriage duties, but always sought younger flesh.

Felicia stood at the door while their voices rose inside, his a hoarse bellow over the constant noise of the stones, hers a petulant whine. She wanted him, although Felicia couldn't understand why. The bastard hated her, just as he hated everyone.

She couldn't go in. The thought of coping with the pair of them fighting, him striking Gunilda then his rage overwhelming him so that he turned on Felicia too, made her panic. She scurried around the house and slipped away over the far wall, past the dogs' kennels, and into the church ground. She felt safe in the shadow of the great cross. It was far enough for her parents' voices to be overwhelmed by the grumbling of the mill's machinery and the noise of the river rushing past. For a while she could be at peace as she walked around the chapel.

It had been a dream of hers for as long as she could remember, the idea of escaping from Sticklepath. There was nothing to keep her here. Odd, to think that her father would find that idea shocking. He must think that she loved him in her own way, but she didn't. She obeyed purely from a fear of punishment. If it weren't for that, she'd never submit to him.

Yet as she walked she saw the one thing that could tempt her to stay: Vin. There he stood, guarding the place where the body of Aline had been found, up the hill. Several years ago they had kissed and cuddled out on the riverbank, a clumsy fumbling together in a clearing among the bushes, and although it wasn't very satisfying for Felicia, especially when he groaned and fell across her when she had only begun to play with him, she had been oddly gratified, and expected that he would want to marry her. Except they had heard Samson bellowing, and Vin had run off, terrified.

That was the last time she saw Vin with any intimacy. Afterwards he seemed to avoid her, as though ashamed of his behaviour with her, or perhaps it was simple fear of Samson. Or, more likely, he was put off her by what she did with Samson.

Whatever the reason, Vin never made love to her again.

Once the messenger had gone to the buttery to refresh himself, Jeanne followed Baldwin into the house. Her mood was not improved by his twisted grin. 'I know what you are going to say, my love: you are unhappy that I should consider going. That is fine, but—'

'But *nothing*, my Lord. You are a man and feel you must ignore your injuries and return to take part in an investigation many miles from here in the miserable waste of Dartmoor.'

'I have not yet agreed to any such thing,' he protested, smiling. 'And anyway, your own manor is as near to Dartmoor. You never complained about it before.'

'I am aware that Liddinstone is near to the moors,' she said, with dignity. And it was. Her comfortable, pretty little manor was out near Brentor. Although she had lived there during her first miserable marriage, the fact of her husband's cruelty had not changed Lady Jeanne's love of the place. But that was not her only memory of the moors. 'You haven't forgotten the hideous murder at Throwleigh, and that sad woman Katherine, losing first her husband and then her son?'

'Just because there was one murder there—' Baldwin began, but she cut through his emollient speech.

'Not just one murder. You haven't forgotten Belstone?'

'Ah, that was different,' he said, and gazed at her with suspicion. 'I never told you about that.'

'You didn't have to, Husband. A hundred little clues can tell a wife what she needs to know. Besides, I bribed Bishop Stapledon's messenger with several pots of ale when he came to thank you for your help. The simple fact is that the moors are dangerous – and for you particularly. Why, when you were at Belstone you were almost killed.'

'I survived,' he murmured.

'Yes. To go to Oakhampton and be all but ruined there instead,' she said acidly. She went to his side and crouched, holding his hand. 'I fear losing you, my love. And I feel you treat the dangers of the moors with scant regard.'

'I will wear thick clothing when I go, I swear.'

'See? You make light of my anxiety even now!' she said bitterly.

He saw that she was growing angry, and in an attempt to mollify her, took both her hands in his, looking attentively into her eyes. 'Come, now. What need I fear on the moors? There are bogs and pools in which a man may drown, but I can make sure that a guide shows me the safest roads.'

'Baldwin, it's not that. It's the spirits and ghosts I fear. If they have taken against you and choose to make you their plaything, there is nothing you can do to protect yourself.'

He smiled. 'Ghosts are things to petrify peasants. There is nothing in them for me to fear.'

She saw she had lost him. Her concerns had overwhelmed her to the extent that she had lost her powers of persuasion. He would listen to no more. She knew him too well, and the slight smile that played about his eyes told her that this particular conversation was at an end.

Yet for her the dangers were very real. The Church taught that souls could return to haunt the living, and sometimes, walking into a new house, or passing by a gibbet, or merely riding along a quiet road, she had the oddest sensations, as if someone else was nearby, although nobody ever was. Baldwin laughed at what he called her 'superstition', but the thrill of fear which shivered up her spine on these occasions felt very real.

He continued, 'No, do not fear for me, my love. There may be ghosts which the eyes can see, perhaps, but just because the eyes can accept them does not mean that they are real. They are illusions, no more. We need not fear them.'

'The priests tell us of ghosts which can take on violent forms! Ghosts which can kill, which can give birth to children and—'

'You have been listening to too many wandering friars. Once the body dies, the spirit flees to Heaven or to Purgatory. And now I must plan my journey to Sticklepath.'

She turned away, staring out over the many miles to the south, to where, dark and sullen on the far horizon, she could see the cloud-covered hills of the moor.

'I shall come with you and bring Richalda.'

'There is no need. I made the same journey returning here from Oakhampton Castle without your nursing,' he pointed out. 'And my wounds were fresher then. Surely now it will be much easier.'

'Baldwin, you know I fear that you may be injured and die and that I should be widowed again – this time with our baby daughter to bring up on my own. Can you not understand my concern? Can you not remain here a while longer, just until you have fully recovered?'

'You need not worry. I shall be perfectly safe. It is a journey of a little over a day and a half from here if the weather holds, no more. And by the time I arrive there, I am sure that the good Coroner will have arrested the culprit. After all,' he added with a chuckle, 'the vill of Sticklepath is only very small. Not above about ten households all told. There can't be too many suspects if Coroner Roger is correct and the crime is that of one man eating another!'

Father Gervase walked to the door of his tiny cottage and leaned against the post a while, waiting till he could force his feet over the threshold. He was physically exhausted, his rounded features grey after a day spent labouring in his little field. It was the same feeling that people had so often early in the year, when there were fewer vegetables and the meat was heavily salted, sometimes even rotten in the barrels. It was an all-but-unbearable lassitude, as though he was suffering from a malaise, one from which there could be no recovery.

Another death. Somehow, through all the intervening years, Gervase had hoped that she lived, poor little Aline; that her disappearance was caused by her running away, or perhaps drowning and being swept away. He had hoped that this was not merely further proof of his guilt. Yet she had been found.

They had thought years ago that this horror was ended, that when they slaughtered Athelhard in front of his hut, this evil would end. Instead it had enveloped the whole vill in a miasma so foul it infected everyone. Gervase could do nothing about it. It had been he who had caused the murder of Athelhard. His guilt was worse than all the others'; his crime had led to the curse which now lay on the vill.

This cottage was no sanctuary. It was here, in the room where he ate and slept that the memories flooded back, where the horror attacked him each night. His only comforts were the crucifix resting on his table and the wineskin. He knew he was drinking too much now; he was rarely sober even when conducting the Chantry for the chapel's patrons. That was no way to carry on, but he couldn't help it. Without the wine his every moment was bound up with thoughts of the murder and the innocent victims.

He was so tired. His muscles ached from his work in the fields, but that wasn't it, he could cope with that. No, it was the lack of sleep. He daren't sleep. Every time he closed his eyes, he saw the hideous vision again – that poor idiot girl's screaming face, her terror and pain as she watched her brother die, saw the men pick up his broken body, swing it once, twice, thrice and then let it fly back into the smouldering remains of their cottage.

Athelhard, the man accused of murder. Athelhard the innocent.

'God forgive me,' the priest whispered, grabbing his wineskin. 'Please, God, forgive me!'

Chapter Three

Simon Puttock didn't need a messenger to ask him to join Sir Roger. He was still at Oakhampton's great castle, recently renovated and modernised by Hugh Courtenay, because he had helped Lord Hugh to stage the tournament at which Baldwin himself had been wounded.

Tall, dark-haired, with the ruddy complexion of a man who spent hours each week on the moors, Simon was shattered, worn down by the grinding efforts of the last few weeks. First it had been the trial of creating the field, setting up the grandstands, laying out the positions of the markets and agreeing where the tents and pavilions for the knights and their men should be erected, but then he'd been forced into the hectic post of field's marshal, keeping the peace and ensuring the smooth running of the whole event.

If he'd succeeded, he might feel less emotionally drained, but he hadn't. There had been a series of murders, now resolved to the satisfaction of all, but that didn't hide the fact that people had died while he was there running the thing. The pageantry and festivities went off well enough, but Simon hadn't been in a position to enjoy them. Instead he'd spent his time working doggedly at uncovering the murderer with his friend Baldwin and the local Coroner.

All about him the roadway was filled with puddles. The detritus from the market and tented area had already been gathered up and burned or thieved by the poorer elements of the town, and all that was left was the inevitable mud after the rains. Sometimes Simon wondered whether he would ever see the predictable, seasonal weather he had known as a lad. It was all very well his wife laughing that he always hankered after better times from his youth when all was golden and wonderful, but things *had* been better. The winters had been cold and snowy, the summers drier and warmer.

He stopped and gazed about him, taking in the sodden grass, the dark, soaked soil rutted with cart-tracks and hoofprints, booted and bare feet, the marks of dogs and cats and children, and his lip curled. This was one of the worst summers he'd ever known. The famine years of 1315 and 1316 had been terrible, but this year of Our Lord 1322 was a continuation. It was as though there was some sort of blight on the country.

At least his wife and daughter were back home in Lydford. They would have hated being locked up in the castle during the rains. He missed them terribly. Margaret, his Meg, tall and slender as a willow, with her long fair hair and full breasts; his daughter Edith, the coltish young woman of fourteen or fifteen – it was hard to remember now – who at Oakhampton had proved that she was no longer merely his daughter, but was grown into an attractive woman.

He missed them, yes, but he was glad that they were gone. Edith was in so gloomy a temper since the end of the tournament . . . Simon pushed away the unpleasant memory, hoping that back in the happy, bustling town of Lydford, she would soon forget her misery. Her many admirers would see to that.

It was better than having them moping here. A castle filled with the retinue of a lord was a loud, exciting place, full of roaring, singing men, and wayward-looking women – not only whores: Simon had been surprised at the behaviour of some of the well-born married women. However, as the people faded away, Lord Hugh himself departing to visit Tavistock and then distant manors, taking his stewards, cooks, almoner, ostlers, ushers and bottlers and all the other men of his household with him, the place grew silent. All the local serfs commanded to serve Lord

Hugh had cleared out, and only the small garrison remained. It
was as though a burgh had been one day filled with people going
about their business, and the next the place was dead: all the
inhabitants struck down by God's hand.

A shiver passed up his spine. It was scary to think such things,
but he couldn't help it. He was of a cheerful disposition generally,
but he was also a Devonshire man, and that meant he was cursed
with a powerful imagination. His friend Baldwin treated his wilder
flights as the ravings of an irrational fool, although he usually
mitigated the harshness of his words with an affectionate grin.
Usually, anyway. Sometimes his irritation got the better of him.

No matter. Simon had been raised in Devon, meeting few
strangers, only the occasional traveller, and was accustomed to
hearing local stories about the strange things people had seen, the
odd things they had heard. Baldwin could dismiss all this if he
liked, but even the priests at Crediton's canonical church knew of
ghosts. When Simon had been a student there, he had heard them
tell tales around the fire of an evening which had frozen the blood
in his veins. Terrible stories of phantasms and ghouls, of ghosts
which haunted the living, or even *killed* them. Simon had never
seen one himself, but that didn't mean he couldn't believe in such
things. He'd never seen an angel, but he didn't need to in order to
believe in them.

The end of the tournament had been a relief, but only now,
with the stands pulled down, the castle all but closed, the lands
cleared and all the guests gone, could Simon begin to relax. And
it was a marvellous feeling, knowing that at last he could think
about packing up his belongings and setting off for home.

He had reached this conclusion when he saw Sir Roger de
Gidleigh cantering towards him. When the knight had drawn to a
halt at his side, Simon put out a hand to pat the mount's neck and
looked up at him. 'You only left two days ago. Did your wife
chuck you out again?'

'Her? She's probably glad to see the back of me. Doesn't like

me mucking up the place,' Sir Roger joked. He was a thickset
man, strong in the arm and shoulder, but with a paunch that
demonstrated his skill lay more with a knife and spoon than with
a sword and spear. For all that, he rode his mount like a man bred
to the saddle from an early age. His face was square and kindly,
with warm brown eyes and a tightly cropped thatch of hair which
was frosted about the temples – the only proof of his increasing
years.

'You mean you've come back here without even seeing her?'
Coroner Roger often derided his wife, but in reality Simon knew
he was devoted to her. 'What's going on, man? Out with it. This is
going to cost me money or time, I can feel it in my bones.'

'Oh no, Bailiff, this won't cost you. You and your friend have
been requested to visit a delightful inn not far from here, that's all.'

'That sounds painless,' Simon said suspiciously. 'When you
say "my friend", do you mean yourself?'

'I'll be with you, Bailiff, but I meant Sir Baldwin.'

Simon eyed the grinning knight sourly. 'Look here, I can't just
drop everything to come and view one of your corpses, Coroner.'

'It's already been discussed with Lord Hugh. He said, since the
work here is finished, you're free.'

Simon saw a loophole. 'I don't work for Lord Hugh. I'm a
Stannary Bailiff and I report to the Warden, Abbot Champeaux of
Tavistock.'

'Who has given his permission. Lord Hugh's staying with him
and has said all's well. Come on, Bailiff! Wipe that grim
expression from your face and join me in a jug of wine. I don't
have to see my wife for another week, and that's enough excuse
for a drink!'

Simon grimaced. In truth he was usually happy investigating
crimes, but he had hoped to return home and take his rest. 'Wine?
Yes, a pint or two would be good.'

'After all,' Coroner Roger said conspiratorially, leaning down
and winking at him, 'this one's better than most. I am informed

that it's the remains of a cannibal's feast – and well ripened, too! Surely you wouldn't want to miss a rarity like that, would you?'

Simon grunted, trying to instil an element of enthusiasm in the sound. He failed.

Approaching Sticklepath from the town of South Zeal, passing up the incline to the crossroads at the top, where he rested the horses and Aylmer, who sat and scratched with an intent expression on his face, Baldwin reflected that the view was attractive, with the vast rounded mass of Cosdon on his left and the rolling country-side of middle Devonshire ahead and to the right.

'Is it much farther now?'

Baldwin glanced across at his wife. She rode at his side on her white Arab, the gift he had given her on their wedding day. 'I am sorry. If I could, I would have placed you in the wagon, because it would be more comfortable.'

'The wagon would not have made it,' she said. 'The tracks are too steep, slippery and badly rutted. I'm more comfortable on horseback. Look at that hill. No wagon could climb that.'

He had to agree. The hill west of Sticklepath was a terrible climb. It was only a few weeks ago that Baldwin had travelled this route to the tournament at Oakhampton, but then he had not been considering the view, he had been contemplating the immediate future and the risk of being included in a joust. Now he looked at the trail, he could remember having heard that this must be one of the steepest sections of the road to Cornwall, and he could easily believe it was true.

The road curved away down the hill from Baldwin to become lost among trees and bushes. It reappeared on the far hill, but there it didn't twist from side to side, but set off almost as straight as an arrow's path upwards, defined by the moorstone walls at either side, which stood out clearly compared with the green tree-lined slopes.

'It is not far,' he said. 'The vill is down in the valley.'

'What is the vill like?' she asked as they began the descent.

'I cannot say that I noticed much. An inn, a mill . . . the normal things. When we got here, we rode through as quickly as we could, in our hurry to get to Oakhampton Castle. Do you recall anything, Edgar?'

'Good pasture, plenty of wood for timber, and well-maintained field strips. And oh yes, it had been flooded. Apart from that, no, I didn't see anything.'

Baldwin grinned. Edgar was a professional observer.

Their journey had not been as swift as he had hoped. They had set off the day before, but the clouds had opened and their journey from Crediton was hampered by thick mud on the roads. Twice Baldwin had been tempted to turn back, but each time the rains had seemed to lessen, and Petronilla, Edgar's wife and Richalda's nurse, was careful to keep the baby warm and dry beneath a thick woollen rug.

Although they now rode in bright sunshine, it was good to see that there were several fires roaring in the vill. That much was obvious from the smoke rising above the roofs. Baldwin felt clammy. His clothes needed drying and he knew that his wife and servants were just as damp.

Where the road met the river there was a shallow ford, and the horses splashed their way through it, leaving a dirty, streaming stain on the water as the soil was washed from their hooves. As soon as they left the pebbles that bounded the river, they were riding over an unmetalled roadway again, covered in glutinous, dark mud. The entire village was in this condition, and Baldwin wondered how anyone could remain clean for a moment.

As they rode towards the inn, a building on their left with a scrap of furze bush tied above the door to show that ale was on sale, Baldwin noticed some peasants watching him and his entourage. To his surprise, none looked at all welcoming: all were grim and suspicious, especially the four scruffily dressed men and one woman standing at the inn's door. Baldwin was reminded of the stories he had heard of travellers becoming lost on a journey and finding themselves in strange surroundings. All too often the inhabitants of such vills would be wary, fearful of 'foreigners' from far distant places – which could mean someone from two villages away – and might hurl stones or worse at newcomers. There was a merchant recently who had complained to him about being pelted with dogshit, and another who was on the receiving end of sticks and clods of earth.

It was fortunate that this vill was on the Cornwall road, he told himself, because the people here should be well used to seeing strangers riding through. Otherwise, from the looks on their faces, he might have been tempted to bend low over his mount's neck, rake his spurs along the beast's flanks and ride hell for leather out of this place.

Perhaps the people here were just put out at the thought of the Coroner's arrival. That would mean fines for breaking the King's Peace which would affect everybody in the vill, so it was no great surprise that they should eye strangers glumly.

At the inn he remained seated upon his horse while Edgar swung down from his saddle and strolled forward. There was a small group at the entrance, and Edgar stood a moment, waiting for them to part. Aylmer wandered along behind him and stood staring, head tilted.

Snatches of conversation wafted up to Baldwin even as the folk stared at him and his wife.

First he heard the woman. 'She was pregnant. She told me so in confidence.'

'Terrible if it's true. Poor Aline!'

'Would he kill her to silence her?' the woman asked.

'Who can tell?' a man sighed.

To Baldwin's surprise, the group did not give way to Edgar. Two men stood at the doorway, blocking it. A younger-looking man with startlingly fair hair planted himself next to them, while another, older man eyed Baldwin and curled his lip.

A broad fellow, with a rugged face and a badly broken nose, he looked the sort to have been involved in lots of fights, possibly the instigator of many of them. His gaze was unblinking, rather like a snake's, and Baldwin half expected to see a forked tongue flicker from between the pale lips.

Not that he was entirely reptilian. Aged forty years old or so, he had the ruddy complexion of a moorman, and Baldwin would have put him down for a miner if his hands had been dirtier or more calloused, but although he had the appearance of a man who has laboured, his hands were not ingrained with dirt. Dressed in a good linen shirt under a crimson tunic, he was clearly no peasant. From his shoulder dangled a horn, while the dagger which hung from his belt looked well made, with a leather grip wired into place and an enamelled pommel; the sort of craftsmanship that a peasant could not afford. His clothes and knife spoke of money, and his manner showed he was of some rank, and probably power, since he dared show such studied insolence.

It was the first time Baldwin had seen Edgar's swagger fail. Normally the controlled threat in his posture persuaded people to hurry from his path. Apparently folk here were less easily intimidated. Edgar stopped before the man, and Baldwin saw him rise on the balls of his feet, preparing for violence. Baldwin reached over his belly and felt for his sword, easing it in the sheath so that he could pull it free in a moment, but even as he shifted in his saddle, ready to kick his mount forward, the woman spoke up.

'Drogo, you should not stop travellers from eating and drinking. They need sustenance.' She had a pleasant, low voice, and Baldwin recognised her accent as French.

The man she called Drogo gently pushed her out of his way. 'Quite so, Nicky, but I have a duty to keep an eye on people around here.'

'Why is that your duty?' Baldwin asked quietly. 'Are you the Reeve of this vill?'

That earned him a short laugh. 'Do I look as stupid as
Alexander? De Belston, he's called, but only because his gut's as
great as a bell, the slug. No, I'm an official of the King, so you
can begin by answering my questions and not by answering me
back!'

'Drogo, you shouldn't.'

The fair, younger man, who wore faded brown hose and a
much patched green tunic, stepped forward as though to persuade
his companion not to intimidate Baldwin. He looked fit, maybe
twenty-two years of age, and had a pleasant face, with weather-
beaten brown skin and calm grey eyes under thick, carelessly
cropped hair that hadn't seen a barber for some weeks. His
eyebrows were delicately shaped arcs that sat high on his features,
giving him an expression of perpetual astonishment, which
Baldwin was sure would make him attractive to women.

Drogo shook his hand from his forearm. 'Want to take my post,
Vin?' he sneered. 'Is that it? You pathetic, poxed little turd. *I* lead
this group, not you. That means *I* make the decisions about who I
question and why.'

He stepped forward, carelessly allowing his shoulder to jostle
Edgar as he passed. Edgar said nothing; he merely altered his
stance a little, placing his feet further apart, while Aylmer sat,
gazing over his shoulder at Baldwin.

Baldwin was not concerned about his servant. Edgar had
survived many fights, probably more than Baldwin himself, and
yet bore no scars. He would be able to hold off the three men
ranged before him on his own.

'First of all, who are you, eh?' The man was near Baldwin's
horse now, moving to the beast's left side, where he would be
safer from Baldwin's sword arm. His eyes assessed the good
leatherwork at saddle and bridle, the enamelled badges declaring
Baldwin's heredity. 'Where are you from?'

'By what authority do you ask?'

'Just answer the question,' Drogo snapped.

'I am a traveller here, a stranger. Why should I answer your questions if you do not tell me the authority by which you ask?'

'I told you I am a King's man. Answer me!'

'I, too, am a King's official,' Baldwin said mildly. 'So what rank are you?'

'I have the rank of the man who demanded first, friend. I call you "friend" now, but soon I shall lose patience.'

He thrust his head forward, jaw jutting aggressively, but then he stopped. There was a low grumbling noise, and when he looked down, he met Aylmer's face snarling up at him, right near his cods. He sprang back, his hand going to his knife. 'Keep that brute away from me!'

Baldwin smiled, but there was no humour in his face. He was annoyed that this self-important bully should dare to delay him in his business. Edgar, he could see, was as ready as a cocked crossbow, waiting for the signal to attack.

Then his irritation left him. Drogo was a foolish man overcome with his authority in this, his own little sphere. It was ridiculous that he and Sir Baldwin should be standing up to each other like a pair of game cocks while men prepared to do battle on their behalf. If Baldwin pushed the matter, he might be forced to put the other to the sword, and Edgar would risk his life in battle against three. There was no point.

'I should hate to see you lose your patience, friend. So let me say, I am Sir Baldwin of Furnshill, Keeper of the King's Peace in Crediton, and friend to Coroner Roger de Gidleigh, who should be visiting you here shortly to investigate a body. Now, who are you?'

The man didn't answer him, but merely spat. 'A Keeper to help a Coroner! What a blessing. We are fortunate to have so many officials here to help us sort out a four-year-old murder. Maybe there's some mystery everyone forgot to tell us about, eh?'

'And you are?'

He stared up at Baldwin with unconcealed disgust. 'Nothing to do with you!' and strode from the place with every appearance of bitter fury. After a few moments the other men trailed after him, one of them with a pronounced limp. The last, whom Drogo had called Vin, stood as if working up the courage to speak, but then he too walked away, giving Baldwin an apologetic grimace before making off after his leader.

Only the woman remained. She was attractive, of middle height, and her hair was a mouse-brown. She looked as though her inclination tended more to laughter and singing than melancholy, but it was obvious that sadness had affected her, and as Baldwin gave her a politely welcoming smile, she looked away hurriedly.

Baldwin was intrigued by Drogo's assertion that there was a four-year-old murder to be investigated. He had expected something much more recent. Aware of Jeanne moving her Arab nearer to him as Edgar entered the inn, he thought she was nervous of Drogo and his men.

He was wrong. Jeanne knew he was capable of protecting himself, even with his bruises. No, it was the atmosphere. It felt as though there was a miasma of violence and fear about the place, almost as though it was infected by a malignant disease, and it reminded her of stories she had heard in France many years ago, stories in which evil spirits could invade a vill.

The fear which she had known as a young woman in France was with her again here. There was a curious deadness of sound. None of the usual squealing of children, none of the barking or yapping or whining of dogs, no whinnying – nothing. There was not even the hum of people talking, or the dull thud of axe hitting wood, only a low grumbling from the earth as though the soil itself was complaining. Seeing the mill she realised that it came from there.

Baldwin did not notice his wife's distress. He chewed at his moustache while they waited for Edgar to return, which he did a few minutes later with a large man who wore a long leather apron. He wiped his hands on it as he bowed to Baldwin.

'Master, I'm William Taverner. Your man said you want beds.'

He jerked his thumb over his shoulder towards Edgar, who now leaned nonchalantly against the doorpost, his hands in his belt, apparently staring into the middle distance and unaware of the conversation.

'Yes, master Taverner. I need a room for my wife and child and their servant, and somewhere for me and my servant. In the meantime, I want a jug of wine for each of us in front of your fire.'

The taverner was a short, fat man with straggling brown hair scraped over a bald pate. He rasped a hand over his poorly shaven chin as he considered. 'I have a small chamber at the back, but I'd have to throw out some others, and they've already paid for the use of it. It's not reasonable for me to evict them.' As if to aid his resolve, he fiddled with coins in the pocket of his apron.

'I am sure you will find a way,' Baldwin said with suave confidence. 'Has the Coroner arrived yet?'

There was a faint but noticeable stiffening of the man's manner. 'You're friends of his?'

Baldwin never liked being answered with a question, especially after the rudeness of Drogo and his men. His tone sharpened. 'Has he arrived?'

His answer was a surly grunt which persuaded Baldwin that Sir Roger had already made his presence felt. It gave him some little amusement, and he was pleased to have had the behaviour of the locals explained. If the Coroner was in the vill and throwing his weight around, it was no surprise that folk here were resentful.

'You will help my man empty the room for my wife and bring in all my belongings,' Baldwin said coldly. 'And I am sure your wife will be pleased to serve me in your hall.'

Will Taverner shook his head. Another bleeding knight. It wasn't enough that there was Drogo biting the head off everyone and the Reeve was like a feral cat being stoned, running all over and scratching at everyone, no, now there was a Coroner and a Keeper.

And he was expected to chuck out Ivo and Miles, both of whom had paid well, to accommodate this idle bugger's wife. Sod him!

It wasn't only the King's officials that were upsetting everyone, though. Since Swet's daughter had turned up – and no one doubted that it was Aline's bones up there – everyone had grown tetchy. People avoided each other's eye. They all knew why. Aline was only the latest of the Strangler's victims to be found.

Will made one last attempt. 'My wife, she—'

Suddenly the knight was off his horse. With one bound he landed immediately in front of Will, and the innkeeper gave a startled squeak and jumped back, only to find himself pressed against Edgar, who caught his upper arms.

Baldwin was flushed, and he looked enraged. Staring at the innkeeper with glittering eyes, he said quietly, 'Master Taverner, I have much to be getting on with to help the Coroner and I do not wish for delay. If your wife is busy, send your son or daughter.'

Taverner looked away. 'My son's dead. The flooding.'

'I am sorry. So many have died,' Baldwin said more gently, although not solely in compassion. His leap from the horse had jolted his flank and his injuries were aching dully. For a moment he thought he might topple over.

'God's will,' the taverner muttered, turning away. 'I'll fetch my daughter. She can serve you.'

'I am grateful,' Baldwin called after him. The French-sounding 'Nicky' had already gone, and when he glanced around, he saw that she was striding towards a small cottage at the western edge of the vill. 'Edgar, see to the wagons. I shall be back shortly,' he said.

'Where are you going, Husband?' Jeanne asked.

'To take a look about the place,' he said. 'Would you care to join me?'

She let her gaze sweep around the view, from the stained walls of the tavern to the sodden roadway, on past the chapel with its small, desolate graveyard to the grim, dark moors above.

'I think perhaps I shall wait here with a warming drink,' she said.

Chapter Four

Drogo le Criur turned and stared as Jeanne entered the inn. He saw Baldwin wander off westwards and frowned after him, chewing his lip.

'What's the matter, Drogo?' the fair young man asked him timidly.

'Shut up, will you, Vin,' he said sharply. It was difficult to concentrate. Drogo knew nothing at all about this Keeper. Fleetingly he wondered whether Baldwin was as corrupt as other men in official positions, but he knew he couldn't count on it. Bribing a King's Officer was a risky business.

The Coroner was the same. Drogo had met him briefly when he came to the vill earlier, a big, powerful man with the glowering mien that showed he was used to finding liars wherever he looked. With him was another fellow, tall and rangy, with an open expression that hinted at integrity. He, Drogo heard, was one of the Tavistock Abbot's men, a Stannary Bailiff charged with maintaining the law among the tin miners on the moors.

Three officials, all important men, none of them known to Drogo for corruption. He was convinced that he would be found out, and the thought made his belly turn to liquid. If the identity of his son's mother was discovered, he knew his life would be in danger; if the truth of his involvement seven years ago in the death of Royal Purveyor Ansel de Hocsenham became known, he would be executed. No doubt about that. The King couldn't allow someone who had offended his authority to live. Drogo would be hanged, his chattels forfeit to the Crown, his body left hanging to be picked at by crows and ravens. Not alone:

he'd take Reeve Alexander with him.

The Purveyor would never have died if the King hadn't decided to send him here. A Purveyor was only a spy, a thief, a bent, niggardly whoreson dog's shit who would take the food from a starving family's mouth without caring, and Ansel de Hocsenham was one of the worst. Always looking to see how he could enrich himself, and to hell with anyone else. He would have seen the whole population die. Bastard! Drogo knew the importance of power to control people, for without that power, people would run amok. Any King's Officer knew how vital it was to keep the King's Peace. Still, if Ansel hadn't died, Sticklepath would be a shadow now, a place filled with ghosts and nothing more. Drogo had been to Hound Tor, and had seen how a vill could be destroyed.

Hound Tor was a ghost-town all right. The famine had ruined the place; gradually families had given up, leaving their dwellings and taking their few remaining animals with them as they made their way down into the valleys seeking better soil in which to grow their crops, and better pastures for their cattle and the few sheep which had survived the successive murrains.

The place was desolate now. Only two years before he visited it, seven families had lived there, and their noise and chatter, the contented sounds of their animals, created a healthy row. The stream, dammed further up the hill, provided all their water, and the hillside was enough for their meagre crops of rye and oats.

That was then. When Drogo went that last time, just after the floods had washed away the crops for the second year, the place was empty. Two dogs scavenged among the weeds that grew in the Reeve's old house, searching for scraps, but the people were gone. As Drogo walked between the houses, looking in at the little ovens used to try to dry the sodden grain, he had encountered only bats and the odd rat. The roofs were sagging, the hurdles and fencing on the point of collapse. It was a depressing experience.

If that evil bastard had succeeded, Sticklepath would have ended the same way. It was one thing to take from a community in a time of plenty, but to try to steal from people when they had insufficient to tide them over to the next harvest was unforgivable.

At least the Purveyor's body had never been found. They had hidden it well enough up on the hill. Not like those little bitches killed over the last few years. Drogo had heard the complaints of the parents, their grief as the bodies were discovered, but he had no sympathy for them. His own little lass Isabelle had died during the famine, and he didn't remember anyone giving *him* much support. After his wife's death, he had not married again – it would have been an insult to his dead woman – so he had never sired another daughter. At least the fathers who mourned their children hadn't been forced to watch them starve to death.

'Drogo? You all right?'

It was Adam Thorne who spoke, a short, wiry man with the dark hair and features of a moorman. He was one of Drogo's oldest serving men. He had been a Forester for nine years now, and knew the moor like the back of his own hairy hands. His shambling limp tired him quickly, the pain from the badly mended leg a constant reminder of the cart which had run over it. Drogo had only seen him lose his temper once. Adam had picked up a farmer who was twice his weight and punched him twice in the face while the man was in the air, before hurling him through a door into the street. Drogo had made a mental note on the spot never to upset Adam.

At Adam's side was Peter atte Moor, who stood eyeing his leader anxiously. Slim, with ferret-like features, the man had never got over the death of Denise, his young daughter. Pale, with bright eyes, he always looked feverish. The only time he looked contented was when he saw felons paying for their crimes. There had been a hanging last year, and Drogo saw him lose his haunted look. Instead he became calm, serene, almost like a man in a sleep. As the condemned man's body twitched and jerked, Peter relaxed, as though the sight was soothing.

'I'm fine. Fine. I just don't like having strangers in my vill,' Drogo said.

'Do you think they'll be here for long?' asked Vincent. 'I'd have thought they'd soon go.'

Vincent Yunghe had the expression of a dog desperately eager to please, Drogo thought contemptuously. The youngest of the Foresters, Vin was only in the group because Jack Yunghe had asked Drogo to look after him when he was dying. Vin's mother was long dead by then, and Jack had been desperate to see his son under the protection of his old friend Drogo, but although Jack died pleased to know that his son was under the wing of a powerful Forester, he had not realised how much Drogo loathed the lad.

Vin was weakly and insipid, a pathetic fool. Drogo detested him – and yet was bound to him. It was a bloody nuisance.

Drogo hawked and spat. 'There isn't the Keeper born who can scare me. Nor Coroner, neither.'

'What, even if they find out about the Pur—'

He got no further. Drogo thrust him back against a wall, his fists gripping handfuls of the young man's tunic. 'So you think they might find something out, eh? I reckon they'd only do that if someone told them. Now who'd do a stupid thing like that, Vin?'

As he released Vin with a snort, Drogo noticed the faint twitch at Peter's cheek, and knew that if he gave the order, Peter would punch, kick, stab or batter puny Vincent to death.

'Now you listen to me, lad,' Drogo hissed. 'You forget everything you've heard about deaths in this vill. If I learn that someone has been blabbing to the Coroner or his friends, I'll come and find you, and when I do, I'll tear out your entrails with my bare hands and feed them to the dogs! Got that?'

'Y-yes.'

'That goes for you others as well. If anyone opens their trap, I'll make sure they suffer.'

'I wouldn't tell, Drogo,' Vin whispered. 'I'm your man, you know that.'

'You?' Drogo sneered. 'You serve me from fear, and that's good. Don't lose that fear, boy, because if you do, I'll ruin you.'

Adam Thorne watched without interest. As Drogo turned away, Vin stood with his head hanging. 'Better get a move on, boy,' he said, not unkindly. 'You don't want to upset the man.'

There was spirit in Vin's retort. 'Don't call me boy!'

Even with his misshapen leg, Adam was taller than Vin and now he pulled the lad up until Vincent's resentful face was on a level with his own. Adam wore a faint smile, as though he was amused by some joke that only he could understand.

'Boy, I'll call you anything I like. Anything at all.'

'Let go of me!'

Adam's face held only an expression of mild regret, almost sadness as he gazed at Vin. 'Don't ever raise your voice to me again, boy. Show respect for those who know more than you.'

'Enough!' Drogo said. He was staring back at Baldwin. The knight was at the far end of the vill now, walking towards the steep hill, and Drogo tried to put him and the Coroner from his mind. 'We have work to do. There's no point in fighting among ourselves when there are plenty of thugs out on the moors to keep us busy. Come on, back to work! And afterwards I'll buy you all ale in the tavern.'

After the long journey, Baldwin was relieved to be able to wander about the vill and stretch his muscles, Aylmer trailing behind, sniffing at every bush, corner and post.

Baldwin was aware of eyes watching him at every step, but now he knew that the Coroner was here, he was less bothered. Roger must have been throwing his weight about.

The road was a swathe of mud, and he took a straight line past the chapel and cemetery, which had a row of pollarded trees and a fence of hurdles to keep dogs from digging up the bones of the dead. At the far side, where the mill lay, there was a low stone wall. Baldwin circled around the cemetery and headed towards the mill. It had a great overshot wheel, and he stood watching it turn slowly as the water poured into the wooden compartments, some splashing over the sides, and listening to the dull rumbling of the massive stones grinding against each other inside. It was always good to see how mechanisation made life easier for people, he thought. The mill would help feed the place, saving men and women from the drudgery of grinding grain themselves, and earning Lord Hugh a little revenue from the miller's profit.

Baldwin passed the mill and found himself at the foot of the hill. This, he knew, was the road out to the west, towards Cornwall. He started up it, thinking that it might be interesting to see the vill from a different angle, and soon he found it rising steeply, but after a short way it levelled off and he could breathe more easily. Quite a way ahead, he saw two men standing close to a broken wall. One was a tallish fellow, clad in a faded blue tunic of some coarse-looking material, and gripping a polearm in his hand. However, it was the guard's companion who caught Baldwin's attention.

He was a thickset little man, not a dwarf, but only marginally taller than one. If he had been a child, Baldwin would have said he was some ten or eleven years old, but he was plainly much older than that. His face sprouted a thick dark beard, and there was only a small area between his wide-brimmed hat and moustache for his eyes to peer through, like a suspicious peasant watching a stranger approach his house through a crack in a wall. Although he was short, Baldwin had the impression of great power in his frame. His shoulders were broad, his hands the size of an adult man's, and his legs were planted widely apart like a fighter's.

While Baldwin watched, the guard let his weapon slip into the crook of his arm and lifted the front of his tunic to direct a stream of urine at the roots of a nearby tree. His companion nodded down the lane, pointing at Baldwin with his chin, and both eyed Baldwin with what looked like suspicion. Baldwin, who was growing heartily bored with being the object of so much silent observation, met the guard's stare with one that showed his authority. He would not knuckle under to some peasant.

Aylmer noticed the men too, and Baldwin heard him rumbling deep in his throat. The dog padded past Baldwin, his head dropping as his pace slowed to a more menacing stalk. Hackles up, it seemed as though he had a stripe of darker fur running from his nose to his tail, but then he looked sheepish when Baldwin called him back.

There was nothing strange about finding a man watching over the body; the law demanded that when a body was found, it was the duty of the local vill to protect it from predators, and Baldwin was pleased that the locals here took their responsibilities seriously. Not all did. There were many stories told by Coroner Roger of vills which, when they discovered a suspicious death, kept the fact secret, later arranging for the body to be carried away to another hamlet so as to avoid incurring fines at an inquest. There were other people who sought to avoid taxes by simply burying a newly discovered body without calling in the Coroner. They were always fined heavily for their attempt at evasion.

Not that it was always villagers who were guilty. Coroner Roger had once mentioned a corrupt Coroner who sought to line his pocket by charging to attend inquests. One village was shocked to learn that he demanded a whole shilling just to view the corpse, and the villagers were forced to argue with him, desperate to avoid yet another fine on top of all the legitimate costs they could scarcely afford. While they negotiated, they set bushes about the body to protect it from the dogs and wild animals. By the time the argument was concluded and the Coroner visited, the hedge had taken root and had to be hacked back to allow him to view the now putrefied corpse.

It was tempting to continue up the road, but Baldwin decided against it. His flank was still aching badly after his long ride, and he had no wish to be involved in another argument like the one at the tavern, so he began his descent to the vill. A short way down the hill, there was a track to his left and Aylmer stood at it hopefully.

'I should have thought you would be tired,' Baldwin chuckled, but he set off down the path, driven by no more than an idle whim. New paths always intrigued him.

He found himself being taken downhill through a dark section of woodland, away from the main part of the vill. On his right he could see the vill's buildings every so often, but for the most part the lane was deeply sunken and the only view was ahead, while the path continued ever gloomier and murkier in among the trees.

At gaps he caught glimpses of the system of strip fields running perpendicular to the main road itself. Men, women and their children were working there, bent double as they pulled at the weeds, the long lines of crops stretching away, each strip owned by a different person. It was a natural, peaceful picture, and Baldwin smiled as he took it all in, watching one man stand and walk many yards to another strip, presumably another of his own, for each man would hold chunks of each field so that if any field were to fail the vill, no single family would starve, but all would suffer a diminution of their crop. God's plenty was to be shared fairly, as the priests said.

Gradually, as he carried on, Baldwin became aware of the silence growing about him. It was as though the farther he went from the Cornwall road and the vill itself, the farther too he travelled from civilisation and security. The low growths at either side, which were obviously regularly harvested for firewood and building materials, began to look stunted and unhealthful. At their feet the grasses were yellowed, strangled by the vigorous brambles all about, and although the nearer bushes were short and scrubby-looking, there were enough taller trees beyond to send out great boughs overhead which effectively cut off the light, so that he felt as though he was walking along a dimly lit tunnel.

It was the lack of noise which he found most unsettling. The only thing he could hear was the padding of Aylmer's paws and the mud sucking at his boots. It made a liquid belching noise, almost as though it were alive – an oddly disturbing reflection. He found himself stepping more carefully in order to prevent that unpleasant sound.

Baldwin was used to peacefulness in the country, but this lack of noise was different. As he reminded himself, he was not superstitious, yet the very air seemed to hold something which was utterly antagonistic to mankind; something *evil*. His steps faltered. High overhead there was a dry rustle as a breeze caught the leaves, a quiet creaking as one branch moved against another, but apart from that there was nothing, or not at first.

From somewhere on his left he heard a sharp crackle, a sound so fleeting that he could almost have thought he had imagined it, but his senses were too well honed. After the destruction of the Templars he had often been forced to evade capture, and a man who has once been hunted learns to trust his eyes and ears. At this moment Baldwin's ears told him that there was a man in the woods: not close, but not far either. Baldwin was sure that the man was listening for him even as he himself waited, listening intently.

Aylmer cocked his head as if suspecting that his master had addled his brains, then padded onwards unconcernedly.

Baldwin followed after him, occasionally glancing back towards the source of that sound, but could see nothing. Then, as he turned his attention to the road ahead, he thought he glimpsed movement. Peering around a tree trunk, he caught sight of a clearing through the trees. Then, as he took in the scene, he felt the hairs on his back, on his arms, on his neck and head beginning to rise and his heart pounded with a fierce energy that left him breathless.

There, at a tree, was a figure, standing with head bowed. The face was concealed in the shadow of a hood which dropped down over the head almost as far as the chest. Slim, short, and clad in grey tatters and shreds, it was eerily similar to the figure he had so often seen in his dreams. He couldn't see the apparition's feet, for they were concealed by brambles, but even as he stared in horror, the hooded head began to lift, as though to meet Baldwin's gaze.

Later, he was not proud of his instant reaction. As the head rose and he could see the outline of a round, pale chin, his courage left him and he bolted. When he saw Aylmer disappearing around a bend in the lane ahead, unconcernedly trotting on, Baldwin felt a sudden panic at the thought that he should be left here alone, and bellowed to his dog. Aylmer faced him, his head on one side, an expression of mild enquiry on his face, and when Baldwin summoned his courage and looked back into the clearing, there was nothing there.

Only the certainty that he was being watched.

Chapter Five

Edgar helped the tavernkeeper carry his master's belongings to the room at the back of the inn, then removed the previous occupants' things.

'They won't be happy,' Taverner said morosely.

Edgar made no comment. His master required the room, so whoever had been there first must move. Lady Jeanne and Edgar's own wife Petronilla needed protection from the gaze of strangers. Here in the room there was a bed for them both with its own mattress. Petronilla went to it and sniffed at the bedclothes, pulling a face. It was normal enough to have to share a bed, to sleep between sheets which had not been washed for weeks and which had been used by all the travellers who had stayed at the inn, but that didn't mean Petronilla had to accept it. She was not content to sleep among the odours of another's sweat or worse.

They had anticipated rank bedding. Petronilla opened a sack filled with clean linen and good herbs to keep fleas and lice at bay. Edgar left her pulling the old bedding from the palliasse as a prelude to remaking the bed, while Jeanne saw to her child.

On the threshold he stood enjoying the sunshine. Edgar had never been here before, but he knew that his master had visited this inn during the previous year on his way to Belstone with Simon Puttock, and he guessed that this river came from high up on Dartmoor. From the sound of it, it was swollen by the rain. Usually any river would have its own background noise, a soothing sound as it wandered over smooth pebbles and rippled past grassy banks, but when it grew, it developed a new, angrier rushing as though furious to be constrained in so narrow a path.

He studied the inn dispassionately. It was a large, cruck-built place, but dilapidated. Moss was thick on the thinning thatch, and the walls were green where the mud hadn't spattered them, and Edgar didn't fail to notice the rubble at one end where an extension had collapsed. Now the inn's rafters projected some distance into thin air, and it reminded Edgar unpleasantly of a skeleton exposing itself as the corpse rotted.

Entering the main room, he found his nostrils assaulted by an eyewatering stench of sour ale and wine, rotted straw, damp, mouldy wood in the fire, and urine – probably from the dog which scratched by the fireside. Edgar kicked at the scruffy, emaciated creature, which slunk away, then took a seat on a bench.

The interior was dingy and smoke-filled. It was darker than Edgar would have expected at this time of day, but the window to the south opened onto a dim and gloomy tree-clad hillside. Already the sun had passed westwards, but in the western wall there was no window because the tavernkeeper had built himself a chamber up in the eaves. No doubt his room would be bright with the evening sun, Edgar thought to himself, at the expense of his guests.

There were men sitting at another table, but apart from them the place looked deserted. Edgar could not make out their faces in the gloom, but he was amused to see that the rough peasants said nothing after he walked in, merely supped their drinks from large pots and eyed him suspiciously.

Many years ago he had set off from a vill little larger than this one. His father was similar to those fellows over there. Burly, resilient, wary of strangers, capable of intense loyalty, but also acquisitive, vindictive and aggressive. Such men were the backbone of the King's Host, but they were also among the most troublesome and quarrelsome of his subjects.

When the tavernkeeper's daughter entered and ungraciously offered to serve Edgar, he ordered a jug of wine. He indicated the sullen drinkers at their own table. 'And drinks for them, too.'

It was always a good policy, he found, to keep an ear open in a new area. If he could pick up rumblings of discontent early on, it could mean the difference between Baldwin's safety, and danger for him and Jeanne. Edgar was happy to invest for security. One drink, he calculated, should buy the companionship of any of these villeins.

To a man they rejected his offer, stood and strode out, all ignoring him bar one: the slim fellow called Vin. Yet the others were not the friends this Vin had been with earlier. And it was curious that they should willingly turn down free ale.

He sipped his drink and made himself comfortable on his stool, his back to the wall facing the doorway leading in, for it was hard to give up the habits of a lifetime's wariness. Soon a new fellow entered, a tall, long-legged man with a face burned as dark as a nut. His features were open and cheery, and he looked the sort who would be good company on a long winter's night before a fire. Grey eyes twinkled when he pulled off his hat to expose a thinning scalp.

'Godspeed! Would you care for wine after your journey?' Edgar enquired politely.

'I am staying here, not journeying. Not until after the inquest, anyway,' said the man. He cast a long glance about the room. 'Has everyone died? Bleeding hell! I've never seen the place so quiet.'

'All's well, though the people are unfriendly,' Edgar said, and called for the serving girl. When she arrived, she took his order, but with every indication that she was unhappy. She stood near them, practically hopping from one foot to another, and Edgar had to ask her sharply to fetch the wine he had ordered.

'I am grateful to you, sir,' the man said. 'It is not common to be served so speedily here.'

'My master expects better treatment.'

'Your master?'

'Sir Baldwin Furnshill, Keeper of the King's Peace in Crediton. We are here to help the Coroner at the inquest.'

'Oh! The inquest into the body up the lane? I was with the two girls who found the corpse. Poor things. One didn't stop running till she got back here. The skull rolled from the grave, you understand, down towards her.' He reflected. 'The skull was only small. I'd imagine the body was that of a child.'

'It is always terrible to find a child who has been murdered,' Edgar said. He nodded and introduced himself. 'I am Edgar, servant to Sir Baldwin Furnshill.'

'I am Miles Houndestail,' his companion said. 'Pardoner.'

'Ah,' Edgar said, more coldly. Pardoners were disreputable characters in his mind.

'I shan't sell you anything,' Houndestail said with a chortle. The girl had returned with his drink, but she remained hovering at his shoulder. 'What is it?' he asked.

'Sir, your stuff – it's all been moved.'

'I should apologise,' said Edgar immediately. 'My master's wife wanted privacy so she has taken the room at the back.'

'I hope she will be comfortable,' Houndestail said easily. 'I shall look forward to a new bed which does not involve sharing with Ivo Bel. Odious man!'

With that, he finished his wine, thanked Edgar, and left to seek his clothing and goods.

It was some little while later that another man walked in, and Edgar was convinced that this must be Houndestail's bedfellow. His petulant expression would have curdled milk.

'You travelling through here? I'm sick to death of the drunken rioters in this bar. They keep me awake every damned night!'

'I am here for the Coroner's inquest,' Edgar volunteered mildly.

'Oh, Christ's bones! You're one of his entourage, are you? You don't look like a clerk.'

Edgar ignored his words. They were not spoken with intentional malice, but with a kind of unthinking rudeness.

'You should tell the Coroner to be careful of Thomas Garde.'

'Why?' asked Edgar. The man was sitting near him on the same bench, and he was leaning forward, whispering as though the two were spies.

'He's dangerous. Violent. And I have heard that he might have killed the girl. She died just after he came here.'

'You know whose body it is?'

The man leaned away, sipping his wine. 'We can guess,' he shrugged. 'One girl disappeared just as Garde appeared here. Her name was Aline, the daughter of Swetricus, a local peasant. She was never found.'

'Who are you?' Edgar asked.

'Ivo Bel, Manciple to the nuns at Canonsleigh.'

'I see.' Edgar wasn't surprised. The man had the look of an ascetic. If he was honest, Edgar would say Ivo had the look of a eunuch who would prefer holding parchments in preference to a young, fragrant girl. Edgar, a hot-blooded man, found that difficult to understand.

Bel was shorter than Houndestail. Slim of build, with narrow shoulders under his light cloak, his long nose gave him a singularly lugubrious expression. The first impression he gave was of painful thinness. In fact, with the miserable light thrown by a pair of candles and a few rushlights, the stranger's features appeared so drawn and cadaverous, Edgar thought they looked almost like a skull.

The girl reappeared in the doorway, then approached. 'Sir,' she said falteringly, 'I have to say sorry, but your things are all in the pantry.' She shot a look at Edgar and said spitefully, 'They were thrown from the room.'

Ivo's face was unmoving, but his voice became chilly. 'And who did that?'

'My apologies, friend,' Edgar said immediately and explained again. 'My master's wife wanted somewhere quiet for herself and her child. When we enquired, the innkeeper admitted that he possessed a room. We took it.'

However, the damage was done. Ivo Bel studied the wine in his pot. 'If your lady is comfortable, that is enough for me,' he said eventually. 'I am only glad to have been of service. Pray do not trouble yourself about me.'

His tone was calm, but Edgar could see the cold fury gleaming in his eyes. It made him smile, but at the same time he resolved to keep an eye on this fellow.

It had been a ghost.

Baldwin forced himself to stand and wait until the pounding in his breast was a little calmer, until the rushing in his ears had slowed.

There had been someone there, a figure he remembered from his dream. No, he amended, that was not true. It was not from his dream, but from his past: the body of the fat Prior, the man found in the clearing in the woods near to Crediton, whose death he and Simon had investigated six years ago. Yet the figure today was not so fat, nor was he clad in rich, embroidered things, but in miserable grey, like the poorest churl. Like a leper.

No matter. Baldwin, a proud knight, had wanted to flee, to bolt up the hill to the roadway and human company. He had been petrified by the mere sight of someone standing against a tree. It was pathetic.

Snapping his fingers to Aylmer, he turned his back on the scene and set off to the road, but he had only walked three paces when he glanced down at his dog with a puzzled expression. If the figure *had* been a ghost, surely his dog should have been scared as well? He had heard that dogs would always hurry away from ghosts, yet Aylmer had apparently noticed nothing.

The hound was frowning up at him as though concerned for his sanity, and Baldwin gave a dry laugh. His breathing was easier now, and his overriding feeling was of shame rather than fear. 'So there was no ghost, eh? And yet I do not think I shall share this escapade with Jeanne. She would not appreciate the irony.'

Before going to the vill itself, he noticed a freshwater spring and drank from cupped hands. It was refreshingly cool, if slightly brackish, and he drank thirstily before washing his face. Shaking his hands dry, he felt the anxiety drip from him as the sun's warmth seeped into his frame.

It was ludicrous. Although he could consider the affair logically and rationally, he would not feel completely easy until he was back among the cottages of the vill. There was nothing for him to be afraid of, and yet he was. With an effort, he put the dark shaw from his mind and took in his surroundings.

There was a series of buildings some little distance from the road and he let his feet take him along the puddled track towards them. Most were simple barns and sheds filled with farming tools and equipment, but the furthest was devoted to animals. This was where travellers left their mounts. Even as Baldwin approached, he could see Jeanne's magnificent Arab being groomed. His own mount stood patiently nearby, reins tied to a metal ring in the door, while the cart horse and Edgar's animal were tied to a post.

He made sure that they were all being looked after and glanced at the stalls inside. At once a smile spread over his features as he saw the unmistakable brown rounsey with the white star on his forehead.

'Simon's here, then,' he murmured to himself as he sauntered back to the inn. On his way, he noticed the entrance to the little chapel. He was about to pass, but the unsettled feeling was still lying heavily on his spirit, and he craved a moment's peace and reflection. Calling to Aylmer, he stepped through the gate and up to the chapel's entrance.

It was a poor little property, built of stone and thatch, but the thatch itself was old and leaked, and streaks of dirt had run down the walls and stained the paintings. The decoration of the ceiling itself was all but wrecked, with the paint falling from it. As Baldwin pushed the door wide, bending in a quick genuflexion as he noticed the altar, he saw that there was a damp mess of leaves and rubbish stuck to the flagstones. All in all, there was a feeling of melancholy and neglect about the building, as though no one cared for it. Even Aylmer was bemused. He stood in the doorway and gazed about him, as though he had no wish to soil his paws.

'You need sweeping out,' Baldwin muttered, and then felt stupid for talking to a building. It was all of a part with his trepidation in the woods, he thought irritably.

The altar was a plain table of roughly smoothed wood; a large pewter cross stood roughly in the middle of it, but when Baldwin studied it, he saw it was carelessly positioned, the arms facing away from the door, and just far enough from the centre of the table for the failing to be noticeable.

'May I help you?'

The words made Baldwin spin. Behind him stood a fat cleric, who nervously licked his lips when he saw how Baldwin's hand had flashed to his sword. His eyes were bloodshot, as though he had been weeping, and his tonsure looked ill upon him. The pate that showed was covered with a light stubble, like a man's chin after a week's growth, and there was a thick lump of clotted blood on the left of his skull as though he had stumbled. He had pale hair which, together with his tonsure, made it difficult to guess his age, although Baldwin thought he had already seen his thirtieth summer. The wrinkles at forehead and eye tended to support that. Overall, Baldwin had the unpleasant impression of a dissipated man.

'I fear I may have alarmed you, my Lord. My apologies. I am Gervase, Parson of this little chapel. I live opposite, and when I saw you enter, I thought I should come and ask whether you wanted . . . um . . .'

His voice trailed off, but long before the end of his speech Baldwin had realised that the priest was drunk. If his slow and careful pronunciation had not convinced him, the man's too-stiff stance, his red face, twitching eye and trembling hand would have sufficed.

'I am well, I thank you,' Baldwin said, keen to be gone. 'I only wanted to see what the chapel was like.'

'It was once a flourishing little church,' the priest said, almost to himself. He looked about him as though seeing it for the first time. 'People used to visit often. All the travellers on the way to Cornwall or back, they came and worshipped. Not now, though. Since the famine, people stay at home.'

'The famine was years ago,' Baldwin protested.

'People still don't come. Not in the same numbers,' the priest said, and there was a shiftiness in his manner as he lowered his head and avoided Baldwin's gaze. 'Please excuse me, I have . . . duties to see to.'

He carefully stepped around Baldwin, who watched as he walked unsteadily towards the altar, then dropped to his knees, hunched, hands clasped. Rather than a penitent making his appeals to God, uncharitably Baldwin thought he looked like a clenched fist making a threat, all knuckles and anger.

It was when he quietly left the chapel, pulling the door closed behind him, that he heard the gleeful shout. 'Baldwin! About time, too!'

Peter atte Moor stood watching the roadway, leaning against a tree. At his side, Adam picked his nose and studied the crust before flicking it away.

'This inquest on Aline,' Peter said. 'You think it'll be a problem?'

'No reason why it should be,' Adam said. 'It's high time we caught this bastard. What do you reckon to Drogo as a suspect?'

'Him? Nobody would dare tell the Coroner if they thought Drogo was guilty. Not when they knew they'd get us lot, all the Foresters on their backs.'

'He's not been the same since his wife and girl died, has he?' Adam said. Drogo had apparently thrown away any hope of ever finding another woman, and lived behind his own armour of cold dispassion, putting his all into his job. Perhaps it was because there was no one to blame, no one to attack over his daughter's death. So many starved during the famine, but no one could fight it or try to kill it.

'My Denise was an angel,' Peter said quietly, and Adam glanced at him. Peter, too, had changed greatly since his daughter's death.

Six, seven years ago now, everyone in Sticklepath had been starving, the women trying to eke out their meagre stores, some few helping their neighbours, but mostly the whole vill subsisting and jealously protecting their own. During the hardship, Denise was found – and for that crime Athelhard had been horribly punished. But the murders never stopped, and now they, too, were killers themselves. Adam shuddered at the memories of a burning cottage, a bloody corpse and the weeping idiot girl. The regret would never leave him. Nor would the speculation. Every time he observed his friends in the vill, he wondered which one was the killer, the real *sanguisuga*?

Peter lived only to find the killer of his girl. That was why he spent so much time up on the moors, he always said. He was looking for the murderer in case he ever returned. Aline and Mary had been killed up there, but Peter had apparently seen nothing.

Adam stared back towards Sticklepath. The girls' murderer could be someone local, who lived in the vill itself, or perhaps it was that miserable sod Serlo, the warrener up on the flank of the hill towards Belstone. The girls all appeared to like him, often visited him. Yes, Serlo was one possibility – but what about that weird bastard, Samson? There were enough rumours about *him*.

Peter was glowering at him, his shoulders hunched, his face dark with anger, and suddenly Adam realised that the killer could well be Peter himself. 'Something wrong?' he asked.

'There's no point being up here,' Peter said. 'Might as well get back.'

'All right,' Adam said, and he stood to one side, thoughtfully watching the other man before they set off back to the vill. Denise had been the first of the girls to die, and since then Peter had been very jealous of any man who had a living daughter.

Suddenly Adam wasn't happy to expose his back to Peter. Not until the killer had been identified and hanged.

Chapter Six

Simon wore a broad grin as he bore down on Baldwin, and the knight was glad to see that his old friend the Bailiff showed no sign of the strain of the last few weeks. Organising the tournament had been both an honour, because in former days it had been Simon's father to whom Lord Hugh had always turned, and an ordeal, since when Simon arrived at Oakhampton Castle, he had almost immediately become embroiled in arguments with the builders, and then there was a murder, which rather spoiled the whole affair.

Now, though, his eyes twinkled and he gripped Baldwin's arm enthusiastically. 'How are you? When did you get here? We arrived yesterday, but Christ's balls – the place is deserted. No one is about at all.'

Baldwin managed to pull away long enough to give his greetings to the Coroner, Sir Roger de Gidleigh, who stood at Simon's shoulder. 'I hope I am not too late for the inquest?'

The Coroner gave a crooked smile. 'Oh no, Sir Baldwin. You haven't missed anything yet.'

Gunilda heard the door open and she shivered against the wall as her husband stormed in.

'Where's my food, bitch?'

Samson atte Mill was a heavy, barrel-chested man in his mid-thirties; hefting sacks of grain all day had given him muscles like a cart horse. He had broad hands with stubby, dirt-stained fingers, thighs as thick as a young man's waist, and a neck so short it was almost non-existent. When Gunilda had married him, he was fabulously desirable, and she was slim and girl-like. He had loved her then.

Not now she was thirty-five. Gradually she had become aware that his love for her was fading, as her slim body filled and she became a woman. He had given her one daughter, Felicia, but now she wondered whether that was just so that he had another young girl to feel, to stroke, to slobber over in his bed, while his wife lay beside him weeping silently.

'I have it ready, Husband,' she blurted, and ran to the hearth. There was the loaf she had cooked that morning and the pot of hot soup thickened with peas and grains. She quickly brought them to him at his seat at the table, his small eyes watching her without expression. He kept his eyes on her all the time, as though measuring his complete control of her. Certainly not to protect himself against her; he knew she wouldn't dream of striking him. Too many years of obedience made that unthinkable.

When he glanced down, his lip curled, and then he swept both the bowl and the loaf to the floor. Instantly the dogs were on the bread, snarling at each other as they tore at it.

'It's ruined, woman. You useless bitch, you can't even cook a loaf of bread, can you?'

She was already crying; she knew what would happen.

'Is this the best you can do? A whore from the Plymouth stews could do better than this. How dare you serve me up with that pile of ox dung! All you have to do is feed me, woman, and you can't even do that, can you?'

As he spoke, he grasped the thick length of rope which he kept on the rafter overhead. He swung it through the air, and it whistled viciously, a serpent woken.

'Please, Samson, don't.'

He ignored her. He always did. The anger was a part of him, not a mood he brought on, but a permanent piece of his soul. In his eyes as he grabbed her wrist, there was a faraway look, almost of lust. His face was flushed, his lips parted slightly, his eyes

wider than usual, his breath coming in grunts, and as he lifted the
rope, she felt him shudder as though in extreme sexual excitement.

Later, she crawled to her palliasse on the floor. She was still
lying there when her daughter returned from her work in their
field.

'Mother! Oh, God in Heaven!'

Gunilda wanted to speak, wanted to offer her daughter words
which could make things better for her. Felicia was too young to
have to suffer this life. It wasn't fair! It wasn't *fair*! But the words
couldn't come. Gunilda knew that if she was to open her mouth,
she would scream.

'Mother, your back!'

Gunilda didn't need to be told. He had stripped the tunic from
her, yanking it from her neck and leaving her upper body naked.
Then he had beaten her with the rope, each blow slashing at her
like a sword, all over her upper body. Felicia could only see her
back, but her breasts and belly were scored with the same long,
raw wounds. Even breathing was hideously painful.

Felicia left, returning a moment later with a bucket filled from
the leat. Saying nothing, she used a scrap of cloth to wipe slowly
and gently at the weeping stripes.

Gunilda cried silently. All her pain, all her fear, all her futile
anger were bottled up. If she let them out, she must explode. The
heat and intensity of her uselessness would sear Felicia as well as
Samson, and Gunilda couldn't bear to think of the girl being hurt
even more.

Her silence didn't surprise her daughter, but Felicia's quiet
acceptance of her own suffering was a constant barb in Gunilda's
soul. Felicia was beaten as well, whenever Samson was displeased.
Not that she refused him often. She knew that when Samson was
in the mood for rutting, he preferred Felicia to his wife. He
always preferred younger girls.

Poor Felicia, she thought again, while the tears streamed down
both cheeks.

'Has he gone to the tavern?' Felicia asked in a still, quiet voice. Gunilda couldn't nod. Yes, her father was gone to the inn to drink again, washing away the sweet taste of his victory over his wife. He would stand there and brag, tell stories to impress his friends, and then he would return, filled with dark, amorous longings. Gunilda had no idea what went on in his head, maybe she never had, but she knew his routines. He would return drunk, ignore her, move over her to lie behind her.

And while Gunilda cried, he would rape their daughter.

Simon was pleased to meet Jeanne again. She hadn't been to the tournament, and it was six months since they had last met, thanks to her pregnancy and the safe delivery of Baldwin's first child, baby Richalda.

So far, Simon had avoided seeing the corpse. On hearing that the body was probably that of a young girl, he had grown still more unwilling to see the remains. He knew it amused Baldwin, and sometimes exasperated him, that he displayed such squeamishness, but he couldn't help it. Although Baldwin himself often expressed the wish that the victims of violence could have lived to a contented old age, Simon felt that he declared it a little too regularly for it to be entirely frank. And the way that Baldwin would leap into action at the sight and smell of a corpse was, frankly, repellent to his friend.

If there was one crime the Bailiff hated more than any other, it was the murder of children. To him, child-killing was the foulest crime imaginable. When his own son Peterkin had died some years before, it had felt as though a candle providing warmth and light to his family had suddenly been snuffed out, and the thought that someone could willingly destroy a child was horrific.

Baldwin didn't notice his quietness; he was more interested in the Coroner's thoughtful mien. 'What is it, Sir Roger? I do not remember you being so quiet before.'

Roger glanced at Simon before answering him. 'There's something wrong here, Sir Baldwin. Something very odd. The people . . . well, I'm used to being shunned in public, it's all a part of my job, because I can hand out more fines than anyone apart from the Sheriff, but this goes deeper.'

'I had noticed people avoiding me, too,' Baldwin mused. 'I thought my rank, and yours, explained their attitude well enough.'

'No. I have never seen a vill react in this way. There's something behind it, you mark my words.'

Simon wondered if he was right. 'They're only peasants, and you know how gormless they can be. Some children in Lydford tried to stone a traveller three weeks ago because they thought he looked dangerous. Scared the poor devil half to death. I had to put him up for the night just so he was safe.'

'Why did they do that?' the Coroner asked.

'Who knows? He might have kicked a cat, or stepped on a dog's tail, or muttered something under his breath about someone's cottage. They're all uneducated fools.'

'I don't think Baldwin's villeins are that foolish,' Jeanne said defensively.

Baldwin grinned at her protective tone. 'What of this suggestion of cannibalism?'

'I've heard of such cases,' Roger admitted. 'The poor, the dimwitted and the drunk have all been known to eat men when they couldn't afford food.'

'I heard of cases during the famine,' Baldwin agreed, 'but I have heard of others too, quite unconnected with starvation. Witches are rumoured to eat young flesh or use it to achieve their aims by black magic.'

'Absolute rubbish!' the Coroner scoffed.

'I know, but simpleminded peasants can get hold of these ideas and take them seriously.'

While Baldwin and the Coroner fell to discussing the inquest, Simon drained his pot. William the Taverner was working hard, and it was some time before he noticed Simon and nodded, going to fetch a refill.

Baldwin took a long draught of his wine and leaned towards the Coroner again. 'So you will hold the inquest tomorrow, Sir Roger?'

'Yes. Whether the Reeve will be able to organise it is a different matter; he seems a complete fool. The child's corpse has been left where it was found, apart from the skull, which was taken to the Reeve's house.'

Baldwin nodded. 'The jury has been called?'

'I told him to ensure that all the men over twelve years would be there, and to bring shovels.'

'The body is buried?'

'Up by the road, yes. That's why I was in a hurry to get here,' the Coroner said, 'before the vill's dogs could pull it apart. A man has been guarding the place, apparently, so it's safe from wild animals.'

'You have little faith that the Reeve will have arranged all this?'

The Coroner grunted. 'Like I say, he's either useless or deliberately unhelpful. Still, it can wait till morning. If it's not done, I'll give him a ballocking.'

One word the Coroner had used sprang in upon Simon's thoughts. 'You said "skull", not "head".'

Sir Roger shot him a keen look. 'The locals here told me that she died years ago.'

'Thank God,' Simon breathed, and gulped at his wine in relief.

'I heard four years,' Baldwin said, recalling Drogo's taunt. 'I am surprised that they have decided that the victim was cannibalised, since there can be no meat left on her bones. Perhaps there is more to this than we realised.'

Simon shuddered. He had no wish to hear these details about the body. To him it seemed almost sacrilegious: the poor girl would have to be exposed to the sight of the whole vill tomorrow, an appalling thought. He wondered how he would feel, if it were his own daughter, Edith. If this girl had lived, she might be the same age as Edith, not that her family would know. Peasants often forgot the year of a birthday. It was difficult enough to keep track, because years were measured by the King's reign, and trying to recall how long the present King had held power made one's brain ache. Edith was born in the first year of King Edward II's reign, which made her age easy to work out, but as many peasants spent their whole life in ignorance even of the King's name there was little likelihood that they would be able to make use of such information.

He turned, thinking to engage Jeanne in conversation, but as he did so he caught the eye of a man standing in the doorway.

Simon had not seen Drogo before, but he could tell that Jeanne had, from the way that she sat a little straighter on her bench. Baldwin and Jeanne had not told Simon of their brush with Drogo and his men, but he could tell that something was making Jeanne unhappy. He watched as Drogo sauntered across the room to take a table at the far end, his companions joining him as he loudly dragged a chair out and bellowed for ale. The men already sitting there gave up their table to the four.

There was nothing to distinguish the newcomers from other men. Apart from Drogo himself in his crimson tunic, they were all clad in worn and faded clothes like any of the locals. Ochres and greens made up their colours; they carried small horns at their sides, and all had daggers and heavy staffs – just like any other franklin.

There was an aura about them, though: an intimidating presence. They clearly knew that they were all-powerful in this area. In fact, they looked as though they were not truly a part of the vill, but were superior to it, like men who were above the law. Or who were themselves the law.

That impression was reinforced when the taverner's daughter appeared in the doorway. She carried a tray, filled with pots and jugs of ale, and was walking slowly and carefully towards a table at the far side of the room. A man stood there, smiling. 'Over here, Martha, love,' he called.

Simon had to smile at the sight of her. Young, probably not more than fifteen years old, she had wavy, raven hair pulled back and bound with a piece of coloured cloth. Strands had strayed and now dangled at either side of her face, and she concentrated hard, the tip of her tongue protruding as she crossed the floor. She was pretty, in a sulky sort of way.

And then the man in the red tunic stood, snatched the tray from her, and set it down at his table.

There was a moment's stunned silence, and Simon edged his stool slightly away from the table in case a fight should begin, but before he could warn Baldwin, Drogo had reseated himself, staring at the deprived drinkers, who scowled but turned away, waiting while the girl hurried back to the buttery to fetch more.

'They feel themselves superior to other inhabitants,' Baldwin observed.

Simon nodded. While he watched them, the man in red glanced up and caught his eye. He stared at Simon for several moments, meeting his gaze unblinkingly, as though it was a test, a trial of strength. Simon held the man's stare until someone else walked between the two tables and broke their locked concentration.

There were several men in the room now, and the ones between Simon and the Foresters consisted of a powerful-looking man with the curious cough and pallor which Simon associated with millers the world over, and another, taller man, who stood listening quietly.

Edgar leaned over to Baldwin. 'That is Ivo Bel.'

Simon hadn't heard of him, but thought he was worth watching. Although Bel looked educated and well-travelled, Simon could see that he was uneasy, his attention flying to the doorway whenever anyone entered. He was talking loudly, complaining about a man called Tom Garde.

William was soon with Simon, pouring from a great jug, and when Simon nodded towards the miller, the tavernkeeper said gruffly, 'That's Samson atte Mill.'

Simon soon saw why the tavernkeeper seemed upset: Samson appeared uninterested in listening to this Ivo Bel. His gaze was fixed on the innkeeper's daughter, a wolfish smile on his face. His attention was distracted only when William stood in front of him, deliberately blocking his view. Suddenly the place went silent, as though a blanket had smothered all noise.

'Do you want a drink, Samson?'

'I've got plenty here, Bill.'

'I think you ought to finish up and go.'

Samson smiled, but in his face there was no humour. Simon nudged Baldwin, and made ready to stand should Samson attack the tavernkeeper, but before he could put his hand to his sword, Drogo had stood.

'Time you were off home, Samson.'

'I want more ale.'

'No, you don't,' Drogo contradicted with conviction. He had his legs a short way apart, his hands hanging loosely at his side, in the stance of a fighter at his ease, but there was no mistaking the threat.

Samson stood as though fixed, and then he slowly emptied his bowl of ale onto the ground. Suddenly he laughed, tossed the empty bowl to William's daughter and walked out, still chuckling to himself.

Baldwin motioned to William, who approached their table still visibly shaking.

'What was that about?'

The innkeeper glanced about him. No one was paying any heed, and he felt secure enough to whisper quickly, 'That man, Samson the miller, there's talk that he's raped young girls. Orphans. They say he got his own daughter in foal. He's dangerous. If anyone killed the girl up the road, he did, God rot his guts!'

'Then why is he still alive?' Simon asked. In his experience a vill would quickly dispose of a child-murderer.

'No proof. Just suspicion, but if you saw how he looked at my daughter just now, you wouldn't doubt my words,' William said, and in a flash he was gone.

'There, I think, you have one suspect,' Baldwin murmured to Coroner Roger.

The room was quieter a few moments later when the smiling face of Miles Houndestail appeared in the doorway. He remained there a short while, his gaze passing over the people in the tavern, and then he walked towards Baldwin.

'Are you the Coroner, sir?'

'*I* am,' Coroner Roger rumbled, displeased that Baldwin could have been mistaken for him. 'What do you want?'

'My name is Miles Houndestail, the First Finder of the body. Well, the skull, anyway.'

'Ah! Would a pot of ale suit you?'

'Greatly, I thank you.'

When his drink had arrived, Coroner Roger watched him gulp at it, and when Miles set it down, the Coroner began, 'You don't live here?'

'Oh, no. I am a Pardoner. I was on my way to Tavistock and then to Plymouth.'

'Where are you from?'

'I hale from Bristol, but I have been down this way two other times. Once before the famine, once during it. In fact it was then, in 1315, that I met the Royal Purveyor here on his rounds. We stayed together at this inn.' He frowned at the memory. 'It was odd. He was going to meet me at Oakhampton a couple of days later, but he never arrived.'

'Probably got diverted.'

'I don't think so. He told me his plans, and we had a wager on the weather, which he won – and he didn't seem to me the sort of man to leave money behind.'

'Interesting, but what has this to do with me?'

Houndestail smiled mildly. 'There is something very strange going on here, Coroner. This Purveyor disappeared, and I believe he hasn't been seen since.'

'One traveller disappearing is hardly news.'

'Yet Ansel de Hocsenham was a man of stature and importance. He was huge – brawny and muscular. Most robbers would have steered well clear of *him*. His disappearance is a mystery that has never been solved, and I for one feel it has a connection with this ill-begotten place.'

'Is that your only objection to Sticklepath, sir?' the Coroner asked rather sarcastically, but his expression changed when the Pardoner answered him.

'No, it isn't. When I reported the appearance of the skull, the vill went quiet and I heard someone mutter, "Oh God! Not another one sucked dry and eaten." And then someone else said: "It's Athelhard. Dear God, it's Athelhard! Another child eaten!" '

'Who is Athelhard?' Baldwin asked, bemused.

'I don't know.'

'So you can tell us nothing conclusive,' Baldwin said. He eyed Houndestail keenly. The man was like an old gossip relating a tasty morsel of vill history, and Baldwin was sure he was withholding something.

'There was a feeling about the place even then,' the Pardoner persisted. 'Haven't you felt it? There's something wrong here. Something unwholesome.'

'You're dreaming, man!' the Coroner rasped. 'If you mean there's been murder or somesuch, say so, but if that was true, the Reeve would have stopped you from spreading rumours.'

'He tried, and he was most persuasive. Almost scared, I would have said. But I sent a man for you because I heard talk in the vill that this body was another one "eaten", as they said. I hadn't heard of cannibals in this area before.'

'So you sent for me,' Coroner Roger said heavily.

'I met a fellow who was travelling through and gave him a coin to find you.'

'Very public-spirited of you,' the Coroner said suspiciously.

Houndestail's face hardened. 'I have a daughter.'

'There is more, isn't there?' Baldwin said quietly.

'Yes,' Houndestail said, meeting his gaze. 'It was the other thing I heard the Reeve say. I heard him mutter, "It's Athelhard's curse again!" '

Chapter Seven

Vin stared over at the strangers in the tavern with a premonition of disaster. Every so often their eyes would move towards him and the other Foresters, and each time Vin flinched, wishing he had never joined Drogo's men.

At the time it had seemed the best thing to do. Vin had been lonely and terrified after his father's death, and Drogo, his father's only real friend, had been the one person he could go to, even though he found the man fearsome. Living alone as he did, after the death of his wife and daughter, he seemed still more daunting to the teenaged boy, but there was no one else to turn to.

That was years ago now. Since then, Vin had come to know Drogo's real nature. The Forester, quite simply, hated everyone. When he saw someone being happy, Drogo wanted to spoil their pleasure. It wasn't only the travellers passing by; Drogo wanted to hurt and offend the very people he had grown up with. He hated them all. And most of all Vin was sure Drogo hated *him*.

It was the sullen, measuring looks he gave him. There was contempt in those looks, and hatred, and although Adam had tried to explain to Vin that they were emotions directed at Drogo himself, the young man was unconvinced. Drogo despised him. He had done nothing which could have led to such loathing. Still, at least Drogo did not treat him particularly harshly, compared with the other Foresters. If anything he treated Vin with scrupulous fairness, as though he recognised his hatred.

Vin watched Miles Houndestail, and wished the Pardoner would clear off. He was a *foreigner*, a stranger to the vill, and he had found that grave. Vin glanced at Drogo, remembering that time when he had seen Drogo and the Reeve up there at that field, the Reeve carrying a shovel.

It had been a strange night, that; the night Vin's life was to change. Only a short while before, his father had died during the famine, and Vin was already starving. They all were. Desperate for food, everyone, and then that bastard Purveyor arrived and demanded their stores. It was no surprise that he'd 'disappeared'.

Felicia had met Vin the previous evening as he walked home, and she had teased him, flirting. They had kissed and cuddled a few times before, as friends do who have grown up together in the same vill, but this was more serious. Perhaps it was because both feared they might soon die. They knew that without food they wouldn't survive long. She had taken his hand and led him along the river towards Belstone, then, at a clearing, she threw her arms about him and kissed him again, before standing back and untying her belt, then her tunic, tempting him with her woman's eyes. They were both young, but suddenly both were adult.

Later he would remember the keen thrusting of her hips, the sweet melting explosion that stilled both, and the calmness, the overwhelming lassitude. They lay there for what seemed like hours, cradled in each other's arms, until they heard a hoarse bellow, her father Samson roaring with fury, then calling for Felicia. Hurriedly Vin had risen, pulling up his hose while Felicia watched, her face sad as she smoothed her tatty skirts.

'Will you come here again tomorrow?' she asked, but he hadn't answered. He was too scared of Samson. Everyone was. He had hurried away, darting into the bushes before Samson could see him, and hurrying back towards the ford behind the inn. There he floundered through the water before making his way to the roadway again.

And it was there that he saw them the next night, on his way to see her again: Drogo and Reeve Alexander pulling the heavy weight of a body from near the mill, Drogo shouldering it and making his slow way up the sticklepath while Alexander followed, carrying a shovel. The two made their way silently into the field beside the road, then stumbled cursing up the hill. There, Alexander began digging.

Vin hid and watched them from the road, tiptoeing near to where the rocks had fallen and had only recently been replaced, and there he saw the two men take turns to dig a hasty grave and roll in the body of the Purveyor.

That was why Houndestail was an embarrassment. The place where the Pardoner had found Aline's skull was dangerously near the spot where Drogo had buried the body of the Purveyor all those years ago – and Drogo wasn't one whit happy about it.

It was late when all the other drinkers had left and Simon and Baldwin could unroll their cloaks and blankets, taking up places to sleep on benches and tables away from the floor and the scurrying creatures that moved in among the noisome rushes.

Houndestail went to the stable, he said in order to protect his horse and his goods, but Simon thought he preferred to sleep in peace away from the Coroner and Keeper. Not many people would want to sleep in the same room as two senior officials. Even Ivo Bel declared himself too warm in the tavern and said that he would seek the cool of the hayloft.

Simon dragged a bench to the fireside while the Coroner was draining his last jug of wine. Stripping naked, he bundled up his clothes into a thick pillow, then spread his cloak over the bench, lay down and draped a pair of heavy blankets over himself.

'What did you think?' he asked the Coroner.

Coroner Roger was pulling his hose off and he grunted, pausing while he considered. 'Houndestail seems a reliable enough man. I wonder how many others he thinks might have been killed?'

'An excellent question. And why should they immediately think of cannibals?' Baldwin wondered from the other side of the fire.

'Or a curse,' Simon added.

'Ridiculous! Only a foreigner would think of such a thing,' the

Coroner said with disdain. He recalled the innkeeper's words. 'And if Samson *is* a rapist, that isn't the same as a cannibal.'

Stroking Aylmer's head, Baldwin recalled his horror in the lane. 'Perhaps there is a popular superstition here.'

The Coroner was pulling rugs and a thick sheepskin over him. He yawned and cast a sour eye at the knight. 'Oh yes? What are you speculating about now, Baldwin?'

The knight smiled weakly. 'It is that time of night, is it not, when men should tell tall tales to freeze the blood of others.'

'Not me!' Simon declared firmly. 'All I want is sleep.'

'What story were you thinking of, Baldwin?' asked the Coroner, ignoring him.

'Have you ever heard of William of Newburgh?'

'No,' said the Coroner. 'Who is he?'

'I don't want to hear this,' Simon said determinedly. 'Shut up and go to sleep.'

'*Was* would be more accurate,' Baldwin said, putting his arms behind his head and staring up at the blackened thatch that comprised the ceiling, 'for he is long dead now. He wrote a history of England, in which there were stories of ghosts in Buckinghamshire and the north . . . I think in Yorkshire near the Scottish March.'

'Do we have to hear this?' Simon growled.

'Oh, I merely thought there could be some bearing on the case,' Baldwin said innocently.

'I believe you,' Simon said with heavy irony. 'After all, it would never occur to you to try to ruin my night's sleep by telling me of hideous things that I could not possibly imagine on my own, would it?'

'Oh well, if you don't wish to know,' Baldwin said with a certain petulance. 'I should hate to bore you with a tedious story.'

'Good. Now will you just go to sleep?'

'What was this story, Baldwin?' the Coroner chuckled.

Baldwin sat up and swung his legs down, frowning at the fire.

The flames lighted his face with a yellow glow and left his eyes in shadow. Simon thought it made him look solemn – and alarming. His eyes gleamed, and Simon shivered in anticipation. He knew he would regret hearing this, whatever it was.

'William told of many fantastic things,' Baldwin said as Aylmer walked to sit at his feet. He stroked the dog's head as he spoke. 'There were miracles and wonderful omens. I read his book many years ago, in the last century, and most of the tales have slipped from my mind, but some were so intriguing that they have remained with me.

'Those which caught my attention most of all were the tales of the men who had died and been buried, but continued to live. There have been many accounts of such things. I remember one story of a man who returned from burying his wife, only to see her dancing with other women at his vill. He caught hold of her, and took her to his bed, and fathered three sons by her. The boys remained, so this story must be held to be true.

'But there are others, men and women who died, but who were apparently still alive when their graves were opened. These beings would walk about the world at night, victimising an area, killing people and eating them, drinking their blood. William called them by a special name: he called them *sanguisuga* – vampire.'

Simon growled, 'I suppose there is a reason for this tale, other than to give me nightmares?'

Baldwin continued, 'The people who found these strange beings asked the parson what they should do, and in almost all the cases he referred the matter to higher ecclesiastical authorities. They told the people to break open the tomb or grave and place a piece of paper on the breast of the dead man, with instructions to the soul explaining how to find absolution and free their spirits.'

'Did it work?' asked Coroner Roger.

'It was not attempted,' Baldwin chuckled. 'Do you really think a vill which suffered from pestilential creatures like that would be so merciful? No. The graves were opened, the poor fellows inside were removed, their hearts were cut out, and they were flung onto pyres.'

'Why cut out the heart?' Simon asked, horrified.

'Otherwise the body would not burn, apparently. William said little about it. In fact, he made practically no comment of any sort; I gained the impression that he thought it not unnatural. Certainly he mentioned that all unpleasantness stopped. The air was cleaner, the noises which had been heard in the night ceased, and dogs which were wont to howl at night suddenly were calm. The burnings were successful, by all accounts.'

Simon stared at him across the fire. 'You made that up, didn't you?'

'No, Simon. I assure you, I got it all from William's book.'

Simon's face was bleak. Then he sighed, 'You miserable poxed bastard. I'll never bloody sleep now.'

He was right. Simon tossed and turned all night, and it was only in the early morning that he finally dropped off, dreaming of funeral pyres with bloody bodies tied to stakes, and although all had hideous wounds in their chests where their hearts had once beaten, they were all alive and stared at Simon with bitter hatred.

Eventually he was woken by the taverner, whistling cheerfully while he walked about, and crouching at Simon's side to stir the fire into life. The Bailiff was forced to rasp, 'Get out, you heathen bugger, or I'll have the Coroner amerce you for violence to my ears and breaking the King's Peace!'

The man left with amused unconcern, but by then Simon's rest was ruined; especially because his hoarse voice and the innkeeper's whistling had been sufficient to wake the other two.

Edgar had slept at the door to Jeanne and Petronilla's room to protect them from intruders, but by the time Simon sat up, blearily gazing about him, his mind muzzy from lack of sleep, his belly rumbling and acrid from the mixture of rough wine and thin ale, Edgar was already at Baldwin's side with a jug of water.

Christ's bones, the place stank! Simon thought. The odours of vomit and urine made him feel queasy. It was always the trouble with cheaper inns; few tavernkeepers would bother to keep the place clean. At least there were no other people staying here. A big city inn might have real beds to sleep in, but the casual visitor had no choice of bedmate. A man could climb naked between his sheets to find that on one side his companion for the night was a grubby merchant who reeked of fish and whose breath wasn't cleansed by chewing spices, while on the other was a tanner who stank of ammonia, or worse. Perhaps that was why Houndestail was not unhappy to have lost his bed with Ivo Bel.

He shouted to the tavernkeeper to bring him weak ale, before gradually climbing to his feet, standing and stretching, feeling the cool morning air wash over his bare body. He dragged his cloak about him like a robe, pulling it tight over his chest. Although there was a fine wisping of smoke up in the eaves, the room was brighter than on the previous afternoon because the window in the eastern wall caught the early sun. It made the room appear less foreboding than it had during the night.

He shivered again at the memory of Baldwin's words. 'Vampires!' he muttered. 'Stuff to scare children!'

Glancing at his friend, Simon saw to his surprise that Baldwin was not yet up. He lay on his bench, idly stroking Aylmer's head, staring up at the ceiling.

Breaking into his thoughts, Simon asked, 'Did you sleep all right?'

Baldwin turned his head just a little so that he could see his friend, and a faint smile eased the solemnity of his appearance. 'Not too badly,' he said. 'I was troubled by a dream, but no matter. It is daylight now. Soon we shall have helped the good Coroner with his inquest and be on our way.'

'Quite right!' Coroner Roger agreed, standing naked in front of the feeble fire and warming his hands. 'Ah good, it looks as though we have pleasant clear weather for it, too. What would you say to a jug of wine and some good bread and pottage, Sir Baldwin?'

Trying to prevent his nausea showing at the thought of food, Simon threw off his cloak and stood, shivering as he pulled on hose, shirt and tunic. By the time he was done, Baldwin and Coroner Roger were both sitting waiting for their meal, chatting happily about the weather, Baldwin sipping water while the Coroner slurped at a jug of ale. Simon winced, not only from the thought of eating food before viewing a corpse, but also from the noise. It was unnerving to see a man like the Coroner who, albeit some years older than him, was as full of bounce and energy as a youngster.

Simon took his pot of ale to the door, leaning on the jamb. 'What do you think about this story of a Purveyor going missing?'

Coroner Roger cocked an eye at him. 'You think there's anything new in that? The man who can tax an area and take their food is always unpopular.'

'No body was presented,' Baldwin said.

'True, so I'll have to see whether I can arrange a suitable fine.' Coroner Roger was quiet for a short while, thinking. 'What do you suggest, Sir Baldwin? I can see you're not happy.'

'I would recommend that you send someone to find the new Purveyor. Perhaps he has some record to show that Houndestail was mistaken. It is possible that the last Purveyor became ill and resigned his post.'

'Aye, and perhaps there's no record,' the Coroner growled. 'Which might indicate that the man died around here. It's a shame: if it weren't a King's Officer, I'd just forget about it. A murder committed maybe seven years ago – what chance is there of finding out anything useful?'

'Perhaps none,' Baldwin admitted, 'but we may find that there is a dead Purveyor as well. If more people have been killed here, we should be aware. It could have a bearing on this girl's death.'

'Very well,' the Coroner said.

'And what of this so-called curse?' Simon wanted to know.

'Forget it,' Coroner Roger said with conviction. 'Like you said last night, Bailiff, peasants will swallow the most stupid of stories.'

Their debate was cut short by the entrance of Jeanne and Petronilla, and soon afterwards food arrived. There was a large loaf of bread which the Coroner tore apart with his bare hands, and a platter of cold roasted meats. Waving the flies from it, Coroner Roger cut off a thick slice of cold pork and shoved it into his mouth. Simon watched him for a moment or two, but when the Coroner went on to spear a large yellow slab of fat, licking his lips, Simon felt his belly rebel. Muttering that he was going outside to clear his head, he left the others to break their fast.

All was bright and clear. Northwards he heard people in the fields, the rattling of tools, animals complaining as they were harnessed, chickens clucking and calling. He inhaled deeply, noticing the clean scent of cow's muck, the grassy odours of horse dung, the fresh tang of cut grass. It was a glorious morning, and his head was already beginning to feel a little better.

And yet something was missing. His mind was working slowly today, but he was sure that in and among the smells and noises of the little vill as it began to prepare for the new day, one specific sound was lacking. It took him some time to work out what it was. In fact, he had meandered around the huge patch of mud in the road outside the cemetery, and was up at the spring, drinking, before light dawned.

He stood up, shaking the water from his hands, and gazed about him with astonishment. To the north he could see labourers in the strip fields, bent over as they tugged tiny weeds from the rows of wheat and oats, or hoeing between rows of peas and beans in the gardens; he saw a girl methodically scattering grain for chickens in a yard; he saw a woman sitting at her door with a knife, cutting leaves for a pottage; he saw peasants heading for the door of the chapel to attend the first Mass. People everywhere, yet not one spoke.

It was incredible. The place could have been under anathema, despairing because their souls would be lost under the papal ban. Their demeanour would certainly have suited such a terrible fate, he thought as he watched them going about their business. No one chatted or laughed. All walked as though bent under an intolerable weight, and that was particularly the case when they caught sight of him. The women averted their faces, or raised their hands to hide themselves from him.

He remembered Houndestail's words: 'It's Athelhard's curse again!' and he gave a convulsive shudder.

Chapter Eight

Personally Joan thought that the inquest was a good idea. It meant that people had other things on their minds rather than looking into *her* affairs, and while all the vill were being told how much they would be fined for discovering the body, she and Emma could disappear.

Emma was panting already, and they weren't halfway up the hill yet. This track, which led straight to the moors, rose up from the vill and then turned right. It was steep, if not quite so stiff as the climb of the sticklepath itself, but it was quieter, and with the trees all about it was better hidden too. In fact, as Joan toiled upwards, she knew that by the time Emma and she broke out through the trees onto the moor itself, the whole vill would be up at the road and watching the inquest.

It was a shame, she reflected, staring back the way they had come. She would have quite liked to see the body dug up, but her mother Nicole had made it quite clear that if Joan showed her face down there, she would skin her alive. In preference Joan had persuaded Emma to walk up and see their old friend Serlo Warrener.

He was a curious fellow, Serlo. Short and bent, with a shock of brown hair that was never combed or untangled, he had deepset eyes which twinkled above his thick moustache and beard. Invariably dressed in a much-patched and worn fustian tunic of faded green, he would appear in sheepskins when the weather deteriorated, with boots made of the same plentiful material. Consequently he had a distinctive, musty odour, as Nicole once put it in her delicate way. Joan had laughed aloud when her father had growled, 'If you mean he stinks like a pig, say so, woman!' Her amusement had earned Joan a clip around the ear.

Many people didn't like Serlo at all, nor trust him. He was friendly with Mad Meg, and that was enough to put them off. Privately Joan thought that her mother was scared of him, but he wasn't scary to Emma and her, of course. They could see he enjoyed their company, with his funny smile and his fluttering hands, his high-pitched laugh and rumbling voice, but he was always reticent in front of adults.

They were at the top of the steeper part now, almost through the trees. As they came into the light, they turned left at the heather-covered hillside, and then right, towards Belstone.

This part was always quiet. There were no miners here on the northern face of the moor. The nearest miners were over at Ivy Tor, near where Vin's parents had lived. Here the only other creatures were the sheep and cattle which were pastured according to the ancient rights of the tenants of the forest, and the deer which belonged to the King himself.

There was also the warren. It lay on the path to Belstone, just past the soggy area where the streams so often overflowed their banks and swept down over the top of the grassed plains. The two girls sprang from boulder to boulder, giggling as they went, playing their usual game, but then Joan slipped on a moss-covered rock and fell with a squeak, straight into the black peat-rich soil.

'You'll get a right thrashing for that,' Emma said unsympathetically.

Joan shrugged. 'It'll wash out. I'll rinse the mud off in the river before we go back.'

'Ugh! It'll be freezing in the water today,' Emma said with a grimace. She turned and jumped to the next rock, her bare feet gripping the stone with the unconscious skill of long practice.

'I'll live,' Joan said. She wasn't looking forward to stripping and washing her garment, still less to putting it on again afterwards, but there was nothing else for it.

The hut stood a few yards below the warren on the side of the hill. It was a short distance from where Joan had fallen, and the two girls made their way to it without further mishap, walking around the stone-built warren on their way. The warren was quite large. Some three yards wide and ten or so yards long, it was built of good moorstone like any of the walls, but every few yards, gaps in the stonework made doorways for the rabbits to enter. To keep it warm in winter and cool in summer it was covered with turves.

Serlo had once told Joan that warrens had to be built all over the country to protect rabbits, because they weren't clever beasts and couldn't hide or run away from faster creatures. Martens and stoats, weasels and foxes could all hunt the slow and rather dim creatures in the open, while smaller predators would ferret down into the warrens as well. But at least when there was a decent warren like Serlo's, they could be protected. Serlo maintained a wall around the warren, with small stone traps installed in the angles. Here, if a weasel or marten should try to gain access, they would trip a lever which would release slate shutters in front and behind. Serlo checked his traps daily, with a large stone hammer to despatch the captured thieves.

The wall itself was a trophy display. Hanging from it, in various stages of decomposition, were many smaller carnivores, as well as magpies, jays, crows and rooks. There was even one skeletal buzzard. All were animals which had tried, or might have tried, to eat one of Serlo's rabbits. In the vill there were rumours that Serlo had killed men who had tried to break into his beloved warren. Even children, so people whispered. Joan thought the rumours silly.

His home was a circular hut with a thick thatch roof. The two girls walked straight inside, expecting to find him, but to their surprise, there was no sign of him. They sat and waited for some while, but then, as Joan felt the mud drying on her clothes, they carried on down into the valley to the river at the bottom. Quickly stripping, Joan shivered as she plunged her tunic into the water, rubbing it against the rocks at the edge until she was satisfied that it was clean enough. Then, thankfully, the sun came out, and she draped it over a bush, squatting naked on a rock while Emma lay back chewing a long stem of grass with her head on her hands.

'Where do you think Serlo could have gone?' Emma asked after a while.

'How should I know?'

'Do you think he went along to watch the inquest?'

'P'raps.'

'He's never asked to the juries in the vill, is he?' Emma frowned. 'Why not?'

'Well, he isn't from the vill, is he? He's from . . . the forest, I suppose.'

'He's so close, though. It seems odd.'

'People just feel uncomfortable with him around,' Joan said. She felt her tunic. Still wet.

'He's always nice to us.'

'So? That doesn't make other people like him,' Joan responded, thinking about the priest again. She shouldn't dislike him, she knew, because he was the man who could save souls or destroy them. He had the power. At least, that was what she thought he had said.

Emma was frowning now. 'Why shouldn't they like him, though? He's always kind. I'll never forget how he helped my mummy when I was little.'

'It's his back: all twisted like that. I think it makes people scared.'

'He can't help that,' Emma said.

'No. But it scares people,' Joan repeated.

'Does it?'

The girls sprang up like startled deer and spun around. Behind them, standing a short distance away, was Drogo the Forester. 'What are you doing here, girls?'

Joan flushed as he eyed her all over. She snatched her tunic from the bush and put it on. 'We were just talking about Serlo,' she said defensively.

'Where is the lazy whoreson? I was looking for him myself.'

'We don't know. Maybe he's gone to the inquest,' Emma said, noticing that Joan was red-faced with resentment.

'They're holding it today?' Drogo rumbled. His manner was pensive, as though he was considering other things while he spoke. 'That girl – poor thing.'

'We found her,' Emma said proudly. 'We went up to the hole in the wall and we found her.'

'My, wasn't that clever of you,' Drogo sneered. 'And then you pissed yourself and ran all the way home. You're no better than your mother, are you?'

Emma flushed hotly. She had never been able to counter an adult's scorn.

Seeing her wilt, Joan angrily stood up to Drogo. 'At least we found her. It's more than you and all your men were able to do, isn't it?'

He turned and stared at her. 'We did all we could, girl.'

'And it wasn't enough,' Joan stated contemptuously. 'If we weren't so young, we'd be down there talking to the Coroner. Why aren't you there?'

'I have other things to do.' Drogo's face was unreadable.

'You should be there with the others, shouldn't you? I thought all the men from the vill had to go.'

'I'm not from the vill. I live in South Zeal.'

'Oh!' She was silent for a moment, and then added more quietly, 'They'll be able to bury her after this. At last.'

He shot her a look. 'Really? Let's hope they can give her poor soul rest, then.' Turning abruptly, he stalked back up the hill towards Serlo's home, leaving the girls gazing after him with surprise.

Emma sniffed. 'What do you think he meant by that?'

'I don't care,' Joan said. 'Let's get back down to the vill.' She shivered. 'I don't like this. Something feels wrong. I hope Serlo's all right.'

As an inquest, Baldwin could not feel that the gathering on the sticklepath was particularly helpful.

While Coroner Roger ate there was a slow movement of people towards the inn, and Baldwin was aware of an increasing number of villeins and serfs gathering in the hall about them. Ill-kempt and undernourished, they were an unprepossessing lot, and their sullen, anxious looks made Baldwin study them more carefully. There was more to this whole matter than a girl's death, he felt.

In truth, he had not given the inquest much thought. As he had said to Jeanne on the day the messenger arrived, he had no doubt that the murderer would be found. The fact that there was a rumour of cannibalism did not affect him. There had been plenty of suspected cannibals during the famine, and some were genuine, although most were simply unfortunates disliked by their neighbours. More often than not, it was their accusers who were thrown into Exeter Gaol or fined for lying.

Eating other humans was repellent to all but the insane. There was no doubt about that, of course, and yet . . . and yet sometimes a person could be in such appalling straits that there was no apparent alternative. Baldwin had heard examples of cannibalism during sieges, when all other foods were exhausted; more recently there had been reported cases during the famine. As people lost everything, as their crops wilted, their animals expired from lack of feed, as children swelled from malnutrition, it was not surprising that they should turn to the only food available: other men and women.

Baldwin had heard of such cases, yes – but not recently.

When the Coroner stood and gazed about him imperiously, the whole room appeared to shuffle and move, all avoiding direct eye-contact. Baldwin saw young boys nervously casting their attention to the floor, while older men stared at the wall behind him. It was not unusual for villagers to feel bitter at the arrival of officials, he reminded himself, and turned back to his pot of watered wine, smiling to his wife.

Jeanne acknowledged his gesture, but she couldn't help gazing at the people collected before them, and at one in particular.

He was the only man who appeared not to be intimidated by the presence of the Coroner. Heavily built, he was fleshy of face, his jowls already blue with fresh beard, although he looked as though he had shaved that morning, from the two small cuts she could see which still bled beneath his right ear. His eyes were small, almost hidden in the folds of skin beneath his broad forehead, and his hair was a sparse horseshoe between ears and a bald pate, although unlike so many men she had seen, the dome of his skull wasn't shiny; it was dull, with strands of individual hair sprouting. For some reason Jeanne took an immediate dislike to him.

'Coroner, I am Alexander de Belston,' he said in a low, deep voice. It was the sort of voice that inspired confidence, and his slow, respectful manner created an instant hush in the room. 'I am Reeve of the vill under the authority of the Baron of Oakhampton, my Lord Hugh de Courtenay.'

'I am Coroner Roger de Gidleigh,' Roger replied with equal formality and gravity. Jeanne saw that he had lowered his head and was giving the Reeve a measuring look quite unlike his normal good-humoured grin. Then she realised that the Coroner had, like her, been unfavourably impressed by the Reeve. 'Would you lead the way for the jury and witnesses?'

'Of course, my Lord. Please follow me.'

Baldwin rose and held out his hand for Jeanne. She took it and walked at his side immediately behind the Coroner and the Reeve, and was unaccountably glad to hear the solid footsteps of Simon and Edgar behind her, and to feel Aylmer at her side.

Outside it was already warm, the sunshine all but blinding as they made their way up the roadway. The air was clean and fresh, with the tang of woodsmoke and cooking, but there was that strange silence again. Even the local dogs had stopped barking, she noticed, and the few miserable-looking mutts which were visible weren't foraging, but slunk quietly out of the way of the throng.

It was a dismal group which congregated about the wall with the tumbled rocks all around, and although he didn't expect them to be singing and dancing in these sad circumstances, Coroner Roger was surprised at the lack of noise here. It was as though all the folk waiting were drained, exhausted. He had seen people like this during the worst stages of the famine, but not since.

It must be due to the age of the victim, he thought. The destruction of children always seemed more poignant than the death of an adult.

'The body is in there,' the Reeve said helpfully. 'Two girls saw the wall had collapsed, and noticed some material inside. They prodded at it and it tore, and the skull fell out. Naturally they ran screaming.'

The Coroner crouched and touched the cloth which had attracted the girls. 'This is no good,' he muttered. 'Baldwin, what do you think?'

'If you try to pull her out you will damage her corpse and probably bring the wall down as well.'

'Quite right! We shall have to dig, as I suspected.'

The Coroner clambered over the wall and helped the Reeve to follow. Baldwin left Jeanne with Edgar and went to join him. He knew Simon would prefer not to see the corpse: the Bailiff had never fully appreciated the importance of the little signals which a body could give to an investigator.

A few flies were buzzing about the place as the Reeve motioned to a man with a long shovel. Flies, Baldwin knew, were the inevitable partners to death. On a warm day, flies could congregate in moments, laying their foul eggs on open wounds and quickly infesting a corpse with maggots. Baldwin loathed and detested flies. He had seen too many in Acre during the siege. As people fell dead in the streets, struck by the massive stone missiles from the Saracen artillery, swarms would suddenly appear, smothering their faces and feasting on the blood.

But flies liked fresh meat, he reminded himself, and this corpse was old. Looking about him, he saw that, in fact, the flies were busy seeking food elsewhere.

The man with the shovel was working hard with the regular action of someone used to manual labour. His broad wooden blade had been tipped with a sharp steel edge, and it cut through the smaller roots which lay under the surface of the turf as he stood on the footrest carved into the right side, thrusting the blade deep into the soil, then levering it up and away, shovelling it into a neat heap behind him.

'Once the body was discovered, we decided not to dig it up,' the Reeve said pompously. 'It would have served no purpose and we didn't want to disturb the remains until you arrived.'

Baldwin had already taken a dislike to this man. He didn't know why, for most Reeves were pleasant enough, and he had not yet had time to learn anything about this fellow which could give him cause for dislike, but there it was. As Alexander de Belston peered down into the growing hole, he started picking his nose, and the act grated on Baldwin. It was an insult to the body. There was a languid tone to his voice as well, as though Alexander was trying to show the Coroner that matters such as this were rather beneath him. He did appear self-important, certainly. It was there in the way he sighed as he glanced up at the sun, estimating the time, and in the frown that passed over his face when a child in the silent crowd down in the lane spoke up and complained of thirst.

Baldwin studied the ground.

Standing here on the slope, he could appreciate that the wall was only low, some two feet high, when viewed from this side. Of course, from the roadway, the wall was quite high, almost the height of a man. He wondered whether this fact had any relevance.

'God's teeth!' the peasant with the shovel swore, wincing.

Simon turned away from the melancholy scene.

He was down on the road with the crowd which had straggled up here. The poorest seemed to stick together, like a herd of cattle seeking protection from a dog, their status apparent from their threadbare clothing and drawn features. Near them were some twenty men and boys in slightly better clothes: wealthier farmers and franklins. These were the fellows who owned their own land, who didn't have to literally slave in the lord's strips. The labour of a villein's body was owned by his master, and the villein must leave his own crops to rot when he was called to his lord's harvest.

Looking over this lot, he reckoned that the men of Sticklepath looked less bovine than most. It was strange: in some towns and cities, he had heard that the lowest peasants could swagger and boast like franklins, but usually in the smaller hamlets folk knew their place, and would keep away from the likes of Simon and Baldwin. Here, however, he was conscious that men and women alike met his gaze with truculence. It was slightly alarming. This lot could become a mob, he thought, and unconsciously he tapped the hilt of his sword.

Ivo was there, too. His long face with its narrow nose was oddly intent as he stared up at the men working above the wall. However, Ivo was not thinking of the inquest, nor even of the child who was being exhumed.

There were so many children in Sticklepath, and this one had already been replaced. Peasants in this benighted vill bred like lecherous pigs, rolling and rutting in the dirt; it was no surprise the place was overrun with snot-nosed brats.

As the man cried and dropped his shovel, Ivo glanced up towards him. He knew well enough that this was a dangerous moment for the Reeve and Drogo, for he had seen them burying the body near here; if it turned up now, his hold over the Reeve would be ended. He shrugged. Oh well.

A small boy ran down the lane, narrowly missing Ivo as he passed, and the man pursed his lips. Illegitimate spawn of a sow and a hog! Next time the little sodomite tried that, he'd get a boot up his arse. See how *he* liked sprawling in the dirt.

Ivo loathed children. Always had. Mother had told him that he would love his own, but thank Christ there was no risk of that. His wife was barren, useless cow. Shame he'd ever married her. She was only ever a drain upon his purse, no good as a bedfellow or housekeeper. Couldn't manage a servant to save her life.

It was as he was thinking of his wife that he saw *her* again, and felt his heart flutter: Nicky.

She had a natural grace about her, an elegance that was without comparison in this dump; it must be her French blood, Ivo thought. He had often heard it said that Frenchwomen had more style and grace than their English counterparts, and Nicky proved it. She was gorgeous. He wanted to take her in his arms and kiss her, strip her naked and lay her on his bed.

Caution made him glance about, looking for her husband, his brother, Thomas Garde. Tom was a jealous git at the best of times, and he hated Ivo. Jealousy, Ivo thought smugly. Here he was, Manciple to the nuns at Canonsleigh, and Thomas no better then a peasant. If Ivo could, he'd get rid of Thomas, permanently. That would give him a chance to have a proper go at Nicky, without fear of interference. All he need do was think up the right plan . . . Of course, knowing Thomas's temper, any attempt to trap him would carry certain risks. He'd have to be very careful.

It occurred to him that he should use Tom's well-known temper against him – get him convicted of breaking the peace or something. Nicky would have to ask him for help then, and he could seduce her. Ivo groaned silently. It was a delicious thought.

Then he remembered his malicious comment the night before, to Sir Baldwin's manservant at the inn. He had merely thrown out the suggestion that his brother could have been responsible for the recently discovered murder in order to drop Thomas in the shit. No man liked to be interrogated like a felon, especially someone as fiery-natured as Thomas Garde. Ivo sniggered nastily.

If, however, Ivo was somehow able to implicate him properly – Ivo might yet be grappling with his widow before too long.

Looking about him, he was relieved to see no sign of his brother, although he must be there somewhere. The only man he noticed was Bailiff Puttock, who was watching him closely. Ivo saw his gaze go to Nicky, as though puzzled by Ivo's smouldering looks.

Ivo shrugged. He wasn't the only man to show an interest in his sister-in-law. Finally taking an interest in the proceedings, he glanced back at the grave, and then a frown passed over his face as he heard people mention the name Aline and speak in hushed terms of a girl's corpse.

'But what happened to *him*?' he said in astonishment.

Chapter Nine

When the peasant digging gave a shocked curse, Baldwin immediately peered into the grave. The man had exposed the ribs of a skeleton. As Drogo had suggested, this must be an old corpse.

Baldwin looked up and noticed the three men who had been with Drogo at the inn when he arrived. He nudged the Reeve and pointed. 'Who are they?'

'Drogo le Criur's men, the Foresters. Young Vin, Adam Thorne is the man with the limp and the other one is Peter atte Moor.'

'Tell them to come here,' ordered Coroner Roger. 'They can help this fellow instead of gawping.'

Vincent looked as though he might be sick when he saw the blackened bones protruding from the grave. Even Adam crossed himself as he limped over to it, a sad-looking man with heavily lidded eyes, but it was Peter atte Moor's behaviour which struck Baldwin most: he sprang up onto the wall and stood gazing down into the hole almost hungrily. When the three men were in the grave, they began to tug gently at the fabric and somehow managed to lift the bones from the clinging soil.

'Hurry up!' the Reeve called.

Baldwin noted that Alexander de Belston was no longer so languid. In fact, he looked very tense. He appeared almost stunned – but desperate to get the bones out of the grave.

By some miracle the material held until they had the headless corpse out of the hole and were standing before the Coroner; then there was a tearing sound and the cloth ripped, spilling the discoloured bones in a heap at Roger's feet.

'Not an adult, then,' he said thoughtfully.

'No, sir. I think it's a young girl who disappeared a few years ago,' the Reeve answered.

'I see,' Coroner Roger said quietly.

The Reeve's voice was convincing, and so was the fact that no one in the crowd saw fit to dispute his words. However, there was something that interested Baldwin. 'You saw that there was a body and left it covered?'

'What else could it be when we found the skull, *Keeper*? Yes, I set a guard over it day and night. We are law-abiding folk here.'

Baldwin smiled suavely. The 'Keeper' had almost been spat out, as though the Reeve held men like him in low esteem.

Alexander beckoned and one of his men came forward with the skull wrapped in a cloth. He set it down with the bones as though hoping the body might reassemble itself.

Coroner Roger glanced at the Parson, Gervase Colbrook, who was licking his lips and staring at the skeleton. Feeling the Coroner's eyes on him, he picked up a reed and dipped it in his ink, ready to take down the details.

'All right! Silence! Shut that brat up there!' bawled Roger. 'I'm the King's Coroner and this is the inquest into the death of this child. Does anybody know who it was?'

'Swetricus,' the Reeve called. 'Come forward, man.'

Baldwin watched as a large man shoved his way to the front of the crowd and stood before them all, his head bowed. The knight recognised the shambling gait, the hang-dog stance. Swet's demeanour was so like those of Baldwin's comrades after the destruction of their Order that he felt a pang pull at his heart.

'This is Swetricus, Coroner.'

'What do you know of this, good fellow?' Coroner Roger asked gently.

'I recognise the cloth. It's like Aline's. My daughter.'

The Coroner nodded. Swetricus had a steady, deep voice, but there was a slight tremble in it as his eyes slid down to view the pile of bones that might have been his daughter. 'When did you last see her?'

Swetricus looked at Alexander with a pleading expression. 'Four years ago.'

'I see. What happened to her?' Coroner Roger glanced down at the corpse again, wondering how someone could want to hurt a pathetic little bundle like this.

'Sir, I don't know. It was the middle of summer. I was out in the fields. She'd been there with her sisters that morn. First I knew was that night, when she didn't come home.'

'Did you search for her?'

'Yes.'

'Speak up, you dull-witted son of a whore!' Alexander grated. 'The Coroner doesn't have all day for you to order your brains!'

'Just answer the question,' the Coroner said, with a long, cold look at the Reeve.

'The Hue was raised. Didn't find nothing.'

'Really?' The Coroner's voice was quieter. 'How old was she?'

'Must have been eleven. Maybe twelve.'

That was a relief, Roger thought to himself. So often a father or mother had no idea how old their offspring were. 'Did she have a boyfriend?'

'No.'

'She was buried wrapped in that material. Is that how her body was discovered?'

'As I said, we didn't uncover all of her,' the Reeve said. 'When those wenches Joan and Emma tugged at the scrap of cloth, visible where the wall had crumbled, the skull fell out. There didn't seem any point in trying to get at the rest of the body without an official being present, and I didn't want it to be disturbed by wild animals, so we took the head to protect it and left the rest.'

'Who was the First Finder?' the Coroner called, and Miles Houndestail stepped forward. He answered Coroner Roger's questions clearly, telling how he had seen the two girls as they discovered the skull, how he had returned to the vill with Joan, and raised the Hue and Cry, contacting the Reeve and the nearest four houses as the law required. He had insisted that the Reeve should send for the Coroner.

Belston himself was silent. Of the two villagers, Baldwin considered that the Reeve looked even more depressed than Swetricus. The latter had lost his daughter, true, but now at least he knew what had happened to her. The Reeve, on the other hand, was responsible for the fines which would be imposed. And they would hurt his pocket considerably.

Yet there was another point. 'I have heard talk of cannibalism,' Sir Baldwin said strongly, and the watching crowd gasped. 'Could this poor child not merely have been raped and then silenced?'

The Reeve turned to the Coroner as though Baldwin had not spoken. 'Everyone was hungry. You remember the famine. It was just natural to assume the worst.'

Liar, Baldwin thought. 'May I take a look?' he asked.

Receiving the assent of the Coroner, he sprang lightly into the makeshift grave, where he crouched and studied the ground upon which the girl had lain. There were more pieces of material at the foot, and he saw a fresh piece of bone. Picking it up, he weighed it in his hand a moment, reflecting as he peered about him. In all cases where there was the possibility of murder having been done, he liked to see the bodies because, as he so often told Simon, the body of a dead person could tell the inquirer so much. Sometimes it was the type of wound which might have killed the victim, sometimes the position of the body, or the marks of blood. There was often something which the intelligent researcher could learn. Rarely, however, was the evidence so prominent as this. He bent and picked up a slender loop of leather, much decayed and soiled, but recognisable.

'A thong,' he said, holding it up, 'such as a traveller might use to bind a tunic or tie a roll to a saddle.'

'We have travellers coming past here all the time,' Alexander said dismissively. 'I have no doubt this evil murderer killed her on a whim as he passed through the vill.'

'Perhaps,' Baldwin said. It was a possibility, he knew. Except . . . 'Did no one notice that the field had been dug up?'

'Eh? Oh, when she was buried, you mean? No. This wall is often collapsing. It did so two or three years before Aline disappeared. This last time, we dug back into this ground a couple of feet, built the wall, then infilled. It's worked until now.'

'I expect it is the steepness of the lane,' Baldwin acknowledged. 'So whoever buried her so shallowly must have done so shortly after the wall was rebuilt, or you would have found her. Someone came up here, either with her already dead, or walked here with her. He could dig down and bury her, and then cover her without anyone noticing . . .'

'Yes,' Alexander agreed. His face had eased slightly, as though glad to find that there was a simple explanation.

'. . . probably,' Baldwin finished. He passed the thong to Coroner Roger and climbed out of the hole. 'I am still surprised that a grave wasn't noticed. You can always see where a body has been interred in a cemetery.'

'I don't know. I expect it was just some tranter or tinker,' the Reeve said, and there was almost a note of hope in his voice. 'Perhaps no one came here for a while afterwards.'

'A traveller who didn't know this area – some tranter or pilgrim who was unused to building walls?' Baldwin mused. 'Does it sound credible to you? Some fellow who wasn't aware that the wall had only recently fallen, who didn't know that the soil would be easy to dig up – does it seem likely that they would choose this spot? Surely this was done by someone who lived here, someone who knew about this wall falling, someone who could come here at night and bury her.'

'How long would it have taken a man to bury her?' the Reeve wondered.

'The same time for a local man as for a traveller,' Baldwin said drily, 'but a local man would have known where to lay his hands on a shovel. A traveller probably would not.'

Alexander looked devastated. 'This is terrible!'

'And a man who had friends to help him might bury the girl still faster.'

'What do you mean?'

'Just what I said.'

'No one here could do such a thing,' he choked.

'Really?' Baldwin looked at him steadily. 'Tell me, Reeve, what is all this talk of cannibalism?'

Alexander felt as though the ground was moving beneath his feet. 'I – I . . . Well, what else could it be?'

'Almost anything!' Baldwin snapped, allowing a little of his impatience to show. 'I would have said it could have been rape, anger, perhaps even an accident that someone was afraid to admit. The very last thing I would have thought of would be cannibalism. This body has no flesh on it: any evidence disappeared long ago, so why did your mind turn to it, Reeve?'

Alexander opened his mouth but no sound came. He frowned at the body, then down at his feet before looking towards Swetricus and the villagers as though seeking advice or reassurance. 'I . . .' He broke off helplessly, and it was Miles Houndestail who answered for him. Coroner Roger beckoned him forward and he stood at the Reeve's side.

'Because they had already had one,' he stated firmly.

'One *what*?' the Reeve demanded irritably.

'A case of cannibalism.'

Peter could only hold his face still with an effort. He had never cared for that kid Aline, but he had known her dad Swetricus for years.

Swet and he had worked together in the fields as children, and when they grew older, they married within a few months of each other, before both losing their wives during the famine. The only difference was, Swet still had his family.

Peter tried to keep his bitterness at bay, but it was hard, so hard. His wife had died, and then Denise was gone. Ever after he suffered from the torments of loneliness, but Swet still had his other three girls. Aline and his wife might have died, but Swet hardly needed them, did he? His life was unchanged, and he could go and enjoy the use of other women. Peter couldn't. Somehow they never attracted him, or if they did, as with the whore he'd bought in Exeter two years ago, he could not manage the act.

At the time, he had been ashamed at first. She was just some cheap slattern from a tavern, and she'd taken him to a room at the rear, where a worn and malodorous palliasse showed that she shared the place with other girls.

He had grabbed her, his blood inflamed by ale, and she had responded eagerly, thrusting her hips at his while she slobbered over his face, whining like a bitch on heat, moaning and pleading that he should satisfy her. He wanted to, God in Heaven, how he wanted to.

The light was poor, and with the ale coursing through his veins, he almost imagined her to be his wife when they married: young, slender and supple. He closed his eyes as he kissed her, and he was once more a young man and she his twelve-year-old sweetheart.

But then the whore had shoved her hand at his cods, speaking quietly and filthily about what she wanted him to do for her, what she would do for him, and as she spoke, his vision slipped away, along with his erection. She wanted him, badly – or so she kept telling him – but he couldn't do anything.

That was when the anger took hold of him. She wasn't his wife, she was counterfeit. Just another woman trying to get her hand on his cods and then into his purse. That was all she wanted, his money.

He had shoved her from him, the bitch. Bitch! Yes, he'd thrust her away, and she'd protested, just like they all did. Claimed he'd torn her tunic, wanted money. Told him he was a eunuch, that maybe he'd prefer a boy – and that was when he bunched his fists and went for her.

Afterwards, he found himself wandering the streets of Exeter with the money from *her* purse in his hand. He went to the bridge and stared at the coins, for a while, unsure where they'd come from, and as the memory came back, he had held them out over the water and let them fall slowly, one by one, into the cleansing waters of the Exe. They fell with the small drips of blood where one of her teeth had broken on his knuckle.

From that day he had never returned to Exeter. Women weren't for him. He remembered his wife as she had been when she was young, and there was no one who could compare with that memory. He sometimes lusted after young girls, but only because they reminded him of his wife. And it made him jealous that other men should own such perfect youth. *He* never could again. Not after his crime.

After hearing Miles Houndestail's words, Coroner Roger adjourned the inquest, telling the jury to repair to the inn. The girl's remains were to be taken to the chapel, and given into the Parson's care.

As the crowd began to disperse, Baldwin suddenly caught his breath. There, farther up the hill, was the dwarf-like man he had seen yesterday talking to the tall guard by the wall, and with him was the hooded figure Baldwin had seen in the clearing. Both stood silently watching, outsiders who were plainly not included in the jury.

'Who are they?' Baldwin asked the Reeve.

'That small fellow is Serlo the Warrener, and the one in the hood is Mad Meg. She's simple.'

The Reeve evidently considered their conversation to be over, for he turned to follow the Coroner. Glancing back, Baldwin saw the pair drift away among the trees. Somehow he felt sure that they were going to the clearing and he was tempted to follow them, but knew he couldn't. He must go with Roger and the others.

Entering the inn, he saw Coroner Roger was already sitting with a jug of ale in his fist. A few workers strolled in, as did one weary traveller, but one glance at the Coroner's face and the jury standing all about, persuaded them to sit elsewhere. Baldwin thought Roger looked close to exploding, his features were so red, and he saw Jeanne throw him an anxious look. She took her seat at Baldwin's side, and Edgar took his place behind them while Aylmer sat at Baldwin's knee.

Reeve Alexander appeared a few moment later and the Coroner eyed him with a thunderous expression. He did not invite Alexander to sit, but made him stand in front of the jury, next to Miles Houndestail.

'Master Houndestail, you have said that there might have been another case of cannibalism. Why do you suggest that?'

'I don't live here, sir. It's not personal knowledge,' Miles said. 'But when I reported the skull, I heard people say, "Not another child eaten!" That is why I thought fit to tell you about it.'

Alexander stood with his head hanging, his cocksure posture quite forgotten.

'Reeve Alexander,' Coroner Roger said gravely, 'we have heard that you had another case of cannibalism here. I do not recall any such case. When was this reported?'

'Perhaps it was before your time as Coroner?'

'Perhaps, yet I have been Coroner for more than eight years and in that time I have always discussed strange cases with my colleagues. I think that if they were to have come here and learned of cannibalism, they would have mentioned it to me. What do you think?'

'They might,' the Reeve stammered, 'but – but if there were many deaths at the same time, they might have forgotten about it.'

'You lying son of a Winchester whore!' Coroner Roger burst out. 'You open your mouth and spew out untruth! When was this body found?'

'It was so long ago . . .'

'Rack your brain, before I have you gaoled.'

'I swear, Coroner, it was so long . . .'

'Perhaps I can prompt your memory, then,' Coroner Roger said, his voice dripping with sarcasm. 'After all, I have all the rolls recording every reported death for the last many years. Tell me, do you think it might have been last year? Five years ago? I don't recall that many deaths being reported from over here, but I dare say my own memory is playing me false.'

Alexander looked about him as though seeking an escape. 'My Lord Coroner, if I could have a few moments to consider, to ask other men here when they recall it and—'

'Enough!' Sir Roger's patience finally ran out. He turned to Baldwin and brought the flat of his hand down onto the table-top to cut off the Reeve. 'Sir Baldwin, I want this man held. Could you instruct your man-at-arms to take him into custody and escort him and me to Exeter? We'll see what the justice thinks of his action. "Long ago", my arse!'

'My Lord, please, I don't mean to try your patience,' Alexander said hurriedly as Edgar stepped forward. The Reeve had paled, as though he was ready to fall to his knees and beg for his continued freedom, but he knew he must speak swiftly for Coroner Roger's temper would brook no delay.

'Then speak out, you whore's kitling!'

'It was at the height of the famine,' Alexander began painfully.

'*What?* You mean . . .' The Coroner was lost for words for a space. 'Christ's balls, you mean you kept secret a death that happened seven years ago?'

'What else could we do?' the Reeve returned shrilly. 'The whole county was being devastated, people falling over almost daily. We couldn't afford to send someone to fetch the Coroner, and we couldn't afford to be fined. What would you have done in our position?'

Roger clenched his fist and slammed it down on the table before him, making the table-top slip sideways on its trestles.

'Don't give me that, you shit! You know full well that it's the duty of all to report any dead body as soon as it's found. Your duty was to report the body to me, to *me*! Why didn't you?'

Alexander's face darkened and he lost his fear. 'Have you forgotten what it was like here seven years ago? We had half the grain we'd expected and then the animals began to die. Horses got rot in their legs and so did the cattle, with the rain and the mud. The sheep got blowflies and *they* all started to die, eaten from inside by maggots. Our children were fading away, growing weaker daily, and there was nothing we could do about it. *Nothing!*' His voice hoarsened. 'I lost two boys, two good, healthy, strapping sons, just because there wasn't enough food for them. When there's a famine, the children die that bit faster; they were falling like stuck pigs. Don't you remember?'

Simon took a gulp of his wine. 'We all remember, Reeve, but why didn't you report it?'

'How many deaths *were* reported? When there are so many bodies, you can't expect people to stick to the normal rules.'

'Such as reporting murder – or cannibalism, I suppose,' the Coroner sneered.

'Do not be too hard,' Baldwin said quietly. 'Extremes can lead to people behaving foolishly.'

'It hardly sounds convincing to me,' Coroner Roger said grimly. 'How could any man resort to cannibalism?'

'You have not lived through a siege, Coroner,' Baldwin said, watching the Reeve.

'No. So?'

'I promise you, when a man or woman is starving, they will do things that would have seemed unimaginable only a short while before. Imagine that you have no food; that you have not eaten for days; that you have no money; that you have no means of obtaining it; that the cost of food is in any case prohibitive. You have not eaten more than a mouthful of grain a day for three weeks, that you have only rancid butter, no meat, no clean water, no ale or wine. Try to imagine how you would feel after three weeks of that. Then picture your children fading away before your eyes; your wife has perhaps died, and you are still having to work. You have no expectation of long life, this is a means of surviving for a short while. It is foul to think of eating a man, but is it worse than death? The boundaries of fear can become blurred.'

Coroner Roger was about to snort and utter a sarcastic comment, but one look at Baldwin's face stopped it. 'You speak from experience?'

'I have never eaten a man,' Baldwin said, 'but I know how terrible a siege can be, and what is famine if not a siege against the whole of mankind?'

Coroner Roger thanked Sir Baldwin, then turned to stare sternly at the Reeve.

'Normal rules, eh? I shall be sure to report your advice to the King,' he remarked caustically, 'but for now, Reeve, you can make amends by telling us all about it. And don't leave anything out, because if I find you've been lying to me, I swear I'll have you gaoled in Exeter for perjury and waiting for the next Sheriff's Tourn, and that will be a good year from now.'

Alexander felt his belly sinking still further. It had been hard enough before, but he knew that he must tell the Coroner at least a few of the facts. He closed his eyes and felt himself swaying on his feet. 'Very well.' He sighed, opened his eyes and motioned towards a stool. 'But may I at least be seated?'

The Coroner nodded, and Alexander sat primly on the edge like a woman who feared dirtying her skirts.

'I can remember that day perfectly. We had just buried my youngest son and we were out in the churchyard watching the men shovel the soil over his poor little body . . .'

'How did he die?' Coroner Roger demanded.

'Like my second son, from starvation – early in the year, after Candlemass. We had nothing to eat. The crops had failed, the animals died, and wheat was eight times its usual price. What could we do? Even salt cost too much, so the dead animals we had couldn't be butchered and salted. The meat rotted quickly and had to be thrown away. We all starved together, men, women and children. Not a dog or a cat lived, all were eaten. I can remember finding a rat,' he said, almost to himself. 'We were grateful and ate it in a stew.'

Coroner Roger curled his lip and Simon grimaced. Baldwin, who had lived through the desperate siege of Acre, nodded understandingly. 'They can be tough.'

Alexander shot him a look, expecting sarcasm, and was somewhat confused to see Baldwin was serious.

'Yes, well,' he continued haltingly, 'it was a difficult time. My wife and I waited to see the last spadefuls fall on our son's grave, and then made our way back homewards through the rain. It fell all the time in those years, from the seventh year of our King's reign to the tenth. Miserable, constant rain. The river flooded out the vill for weeks on end. All the crops – *ruined*! Three lads from the village were drowned in the four months after Christmas the following year. You can't imagine what it was like.

'While we walked home, we were told that a body had been found up on the moor. I hurried there immediately, because sometimes a man might think that someone is dead, when they are only wounded. On the moor, people can become so chilled that they seem to have died. So I went up there to see whether he was alive or dead.'

He paused at the memory, and glanced about him, looking for the Foresters, but none were in sight. Taking a deep breath, he continued, 'It was one of the girls from the vill here, little Denise, Peter atte Moor's daughter. She was only ten years old or so. Such a short life.'

'Murdered?' Coroner Roger asked. He was quieter now that the story was finally being told.

'Throttled. A leather thong was still about her neck, just like the one in the grave,' Alexander admitted. 'But we never found all of her. Her thighs, her arms, were missing.'

Simon's stomach lurched and he unwillingly recalled Baldwin's stories of the night before.

'She had been flayed.'

The jury shuffled their feet and Simon rasped, 'Who could do such a thing?'

'Many, Simon,' Baldwin said gently. 'I know it is difficult to imagine, but if a man's family is starving, he will go to extremes to save them from death. There were stories of this happening in Kent during the famine, I recall.'

Simon glanced at Houndestail. He felt queasy at the thought of hearing the details, but seeing Houndestail reminded him of the other thing the Pardoner had said. Although he wasn't sure he wanted to know the answer, he cleared his throat. 'And what of the curse? This curse of Athelhard, whoever he might be.'

'That's just superstition,' Reeve Alexander said, but he had blenched.

'What is this superstition?' Baldwin asked smoothly.

'If a child dies here, it's said to be Athelhard's curse, but there's nothing to it. It's a local thing,' Reeve Alexander said firmly. 'So many travellers come through here. If one of them does something and flees, people blame Athelhard, a fictional character.'

Baldwin, watching him closely, was unconvinced, but since Simon had asked the question, and the Reeve seemed to have recovered from his shock, he thought it better to leave the matter for the present.

'Did you raise the Hue?' Simon asked.

'Of course we did! Her father was a Forester, we could hardly ignore the process of law. I had men hunting all over,' Alexander said. He felt sick having to recall the murder scene. 'There was nothing to be learned. No one knew who had done it and our worst trouble was, there had been several travellers at that time, all passing along the Cornwall road. Any one of them could have been the murderer, killing her and then keeping pieces of her in his scrip.'

He had no need to continue. Simon felt near to vomiting, and even the Coroner was still, considering this fresh evidence of the evil of men. Only Baldwin appeared to be studying him pensively. The knight nodded as though to himself. 'And of course, afterwards you decided to report the matter, but it was already some little while since the girl had been found . . .'

Alexander looked at him as his voice trailed away. 'There was nothing to be done. As I said, there had been many people along our road, and any one of them could have been Denise's killer. In the end, we merely buried her, and hoped that her murderer had moved on or else had met his retribution on the road.'

Baldwin nodded. 'Yet you knew that would be illegal. Surely you had some other reason to want to hide her?'

Alexander threw his hands wide in a gesture of openness. 'Sir Baldwin, my Lord Coroner, what would *you* do if the daughter of one of your friends had been not only murdered, but violated in that sort of way? How would you feel if she had been *your* daughter? For my part, I saw her body on the same day that I buried one of my own sons and I tell you, it is difficult, terribly difficult, to lose a child. I knew this, I know it today; I had to tell Peter that his girl was dead, I had to show him her remains, so that he could see what had happened to her. My God! By Christ's own wounds, I swear I couldn't bear to see him hurt more. The idea that someone could eat your child was so hideous, so appalling, that I wanted to do anything I could to save him any further upset.'

'I see,' Simon said, and he did. It was only three years since he had buried his own son. He found himself in sympathy with the Reeve. 'So you hid her body.'

'Had she been molested?' Baldwin asked, then when the man looked blank: 'Raped?'

'I wouldn't know,' Alexander confessed.

'Which brings us neatly to the present,' Baldwin said, 'and this latest body.'

'It is awful,' Alexander said. 'I'd hoped Denise was the sole victim.'

The Coroner looked at him. 'Did you hide her too?'

'No!' Alexander protested. 'Poor Swet, he's lost his wife, he's lost poor Aline, and he has three other daughters to try to bring up.'

'Quite so,' the Coroner said. 'But you attempted to keep the murder and the cannibalism from the King's Coroner. That will mean a significant fine, Reeve. A very significant fine.'

Alexander hung his head as the Coroner spoke at length about the importance of all sudden deaths being reported. 'However,' he finished, 'I can understand that you might be reluctant to bruit news of this kind abroad. For that reason I won't impose a fine right now. I shall have to think about it and consider the level to be paid.'

'Thank you, my Lord Coroner,' Alexander said. 'I didn't do it to defraud the King, only to prevent further misery to a good, hard-working man.'

'It wasn't your choice to make!' the Coroner snapped. 'Still, that's all I shall say for now. You can leave us.'

'Just one more thing before you go,' Baldwin said. 'When did Aline disappear?'

'I believe it was close to the feast day of Saint Bartholomew.'

'Oh, late in the year, then. After harvest.'

Alexander nodded, but as Baldwin leaned forward and tilted his head to one side like an expectant hound, he had a premonition that the knight had learned more than Alexander wanted him to.

'The length of time between the deaths of Aline and Denise shows that they couldn't have been killed by some traveller. You say this Denise died during the famine? That was the eighth year of the King's reign, while this poor child died four years ago – that is, the eleventh year of his reign. Two and a half years apart, Reeve. This was not done by a traveller. The murderer lives *here*. And he may still be alive!'

Chapter Ten

Alexander de Belston reached his house in a towering rage. It was ridiculous that he should have been made to feel guilty. It was the Coroner pandering to his own vanity, craven arse that he was! And to make himself feel important he was going to fine Alexander.

He kicked the door shut and strode through to his hall. At his table, he saw his maid Cecilia bending over a visitor, and stopped dead when he saw that it was Drogo le Criur.

'What are you doing here?' he demanded.

The leader of the Foresters leaned back in Alexander's own chair and put his boot on Alexander's table, all the while holding the Reeve's gaze. 'I just wanted to know if you were all right, Alex. We wouldn't want to learn you'd confessed to something silly and implicated other people.'

'Oh, wouldn't we?' Alexander sneered, but as he spoke he was aware of someone behind him. He made to turn his head, but before he could, he felt the prick of a knife at his neck.

'It's all right, Peter,' Drogo said. 'There's no need to hurt him. Not yet.'

Alexander's heart was thudding painfully like a drum being beaten too hard. 'What do you want?' He walked a little unsteadily to a bench against a wall, content in the knowledge that nobody could stand behind him. 'I've done nothing to make you distrust me.'

'Nope,' Drogo said. 'And nor shall you, Alex, old friend, because if I'm accused, I'll make sure that you get strung up with me.'

Cecilia stood nervously at Drogo's side with a tray of bread and wine. The Forester appeared to notice her for the first time, and reached out to take a pot and a hunk of bread, which he dipped into the wine, sucking it. 'This is good wine, Alex. You do yourself very well, don't you? No, we only wanted to talk to you and make sure that you weren't considering chopping any of us in to save your own neck.'

'I hadn't even thought of it,' Alexander said, motioning his servant over. He took a pot from her and waved her from the room. 'I have other problems. This Coroner will want someone to be the guilty party. He'll not leave until he thinks he's got the murderer.'

'Like who?'

'I don't want to see any man from here hanged. It would only mean a feud between one family and another. You've seen that as often as I have. A juror accuses a man, and that fellow's family try to avenge him as soon as his body's stopped dancing on the rope. I don't want that. A blood feud would only cause more trouble.'

'Aye. True enough.' Drogo spat onto the rushes. 'We need to find someone we can blame. The Coroner won't be satisfied without a felon.'

'No, he'll want someone.'

'Well, don't think of offering him me or my men, because if you do—'

'Before you start threatening me, remember we stand together, Drogo.'

'And don't *you* forget,' said Drogo, 'that if I'm caught, I'll know who's responsible, and I'll see you die before me, Reeve!'

He was leaning forward now, and in his eyes Alexander saw a terrible determination. Drogo was close to the end of his tether. He looked like a man who was staring over a precipice into Hell.

Simon left the inn to go and relieve himself behind a tree. As he peed, he considered all he had seen that morning, and had to confess to himself that he had shown a complete lack of spirit. At the first sight of a corpse, he had scuttled to Jeanne's side.

Not that he was ashamed of his queasiness in the presence of sudden death – especially when the body had been left to putrefy. The sight of a worm- and maggot-infested corpse was enough to turn anyone's stomach.

With that merry thought, he returned to the inn. The room was gradually emptying as people left, some gazing curiously at the men in the corner, but most looking away. Adam Thorne and Vincent were talking earnestly to William the Taverner, who ducked his head and left them as soon as he saw Simon.

The Coroner's foul temper had returned as soon as Alexander had left, and now he was trying to assess how much to fine the Reeve and the vill for their gross irresponsibility in evading their legal duties.

Jeanne was still in her seat. 'Like you I have no interest in seeking answers to questions which were posed so many years ago,' she said when Simon drew near. 'I feel great sympathy for the girl, but that is all. May her soul rest peacefully.'

Simon would have prefered to remain drinking wine with her, but when Baldwin and the Coroner walked from the room, he trailed behind them.

'It's ridiculous, man like him, playing with the law,' the Coroner fumed. 'I have children too, but that doesn't mean I'd flout my responsibilities. God's blood, but I'd like to have him gaoled for his stupidity!'

'Do you wish to arrest him now?' Baldwin enquired mildly, patting Aylmer's head.

'You know I don't! It's just that the man was intolerably smug and that grates on my nerves. Cretinous idiot! As though he could have got away with it.'

'He almost did,' Simon pointed out. 'If that fellow Houndestail hadn't given the game away, we'd have been none the wiser. Obviously Alexander didn't mean anyone to hear that this was a case of cannibalism.'

Baldwin said, 'That I find quite curious. Almost as odd as the two girls' deaths.'

'Yes,' the Coroner said. 'But it's plain that there's one man who has committed two murders and we have to find him if we can.'

'Only a madman could eat a child,' Simon stated with conviction.

'Certainly someone driven to extreme measures,' Baldwin said.

They were in the roadway, and in all directions the peasants could be seen heading back towards their fields. Felicia and Gunilda were at the top of the road near the mill; Joan was running past, chased by a giggling Emma. A steady ringing told that the farriers were back at work, and the low grumbling spoke of the mill's wheel turning. The place was returning to normal.

One group were apparently not returning to work. Ahead, leaning against the wall of a house, were Adam and Vincent. As the two girls rushed past him, Vincent caught hold of Emma, making her scream with delight as he tickled her, making her torn apron fly up in the air as he threw her up once, twice, thrice, and then set her down again and watched her pelt off after Joan once more.

When he saw the men approach, Vin's face turned suddenly grim. At his side, leaning against the Reeve's house and evidently unbothered by their appearance, was Adam, who greeted them, 'Inquest all done, then?'

'Your name is Adam?' Baldwin responded.

'Adam Thorne, master. Yes. This is my friend Vin.'

'Were you both Foresters when the children were killed?'

'Yes I was. Although Vin was only a lad then. I can remember Peter's girl being found, and then I can remember Swet's concern when his own girl disappeared. It was a terrible time.'

'Peter atte Moor was the father of the girl named Denise?'

'Yes. Swet's maid was third to disappear.'

Simon said sharply, 'Third? We have only been told of two.'

'Ah! You should speak to the Reeve again, master. Perhaps he forgot little Mary. Her parents died a while ago, so it wouldn't be surprising, I suppose.'

Baldwin noted that. Another dead child. 'How old was she?'

'Same as the others, about ten or so, I think.'

'Were there any travellers who were in the vill prior to each of these girls going missing?' the Coroner demanded.

Adam shook his head. 'No, there were few travellers then. Not enough food to go round.'

Vin nodded to each of Adam's responses. He hated the interrogation, but he daren't leave while they were talking, in case Adam gave something away. It was bad enough that Adam disliked Vin and might make some sly remark behind his back, about Vin always hating girls or something, but worse was the fact that Adam treated him as though he was soft in the head, the bastard.

'Do you have any idea who could have wanted to kill these children?' Coroner Roger asked.

Adam threw a sideways look at Vin, and there was a slight smile on his face as he opened his mouth.

Vin gabbled his words: 'You already know!'

Baldwin blinked with surprise. 'We do?'

'It was a vampire, that's what it was! A *sanguisuga*!'

Simon blenched, and the Coroner made a quick movement of his hand to ward off evil, but while Adam laughed, Baldwin merely looked intrigued.

'Vampire? How did you know we spoke of such things?'

'They've been talking to William Taverner,' Simon said. 'He must have overheard us last night.'

'Yes. And Vin likes to imagine things like that,' Adam said dismissively. 'Spends half his time daydreaming. There's no vampires here in Sticklepath.'

'But there are rapists,' Baldwin said. 'What of this Samson?'

'Rumours, nothing more,' Adam said comfortably. 'If I had any proof, I'd kill him myself. He's a wife-beater, for sure, but a murderer? No. I expect the murderer was someone who hated the vill.'

As he spoke, Baldwin, who was watching him closely, saw a brief concentration in his expression. It was as though he had realised someone might have had a motive after all. 'Such as whom?' he asked.

'I was only thinking that Ivo Bel has always hated this place, mainly because he can't stand Thomas Garde, and he was here, I think, when Denise and Aline died. But again, there's no proof.'

'Where were you when the girls were killed?' Baldwin said pointedly.

'Me?' Adam shrugged. 'When Denise died, I was with Peter, her father. We were in South Zeal at the tavern, drinking with Drogo.'

'What of you?' Baldwin said, turning to Vincent.

'I was on the moor. I lived up near Ivy Tor Water, with my father. My mother died when I was young and my father was a miner, a friend of Drogo's, and when Denise died I was there with my father.'

'And he can confirm that?'

'No. He died years ago. Anyway, when Aline disappeared I was a fully-fledged Forester. I was with Drogo that night. I remember it clearly.'

'You have a good memory,' Baldwin said drily. 'What of this third girl? What happened to her?'

'Mary was an orphan. No one knew when she disappeared. I expect I was on the moors.'

'So you have no alibi for the deaths, apart from Aline's?'

'I . . .' Vin's face reflected his confusion.

'Don't be hard on the boy,' said Adam.

'It's a long time ago,' Vin said, trying to remember, but his mind kept returning to that other night, when the Purveyor had been killed.

'Very well,' said Coroner Roger. 'In the meantime, do you have any other suspicions as to who might have killed the children?'

There was a long silence, then Adam spoke.

'That's for you to find out, Coroner, isn't it?' he said with a cold smile.

* * *

The three left Adam and Vin a short time later, walking slowly on up the main roadway.

'Vampires, my arse!' Coroner Roger said.

'The wall between the hall and the tavernkeeper's room is thin,' Baldwin said, 'and I've never known an innkeeper yet who could keep his mouth shut.'

'Yes,' Simon said, 'that must be it.'

'Hey! That's Miles Houndestail, isn't it?' Coroner Roger said, peering ahead intently.

'Looks like him,' Simon said.

'I want to talk to him.'

'Do you think he can tell you any more?' Baldwin asked doubtfully.

'As you suggested, I want to send someone to find out whether there was ever news of this Purveyor. That's another ruddy missing person on our hands!'

Simon decided to leave them to their investigation. For his part, the murders were too long past to interest him; he couldn't believe that they would discover the murderer, and after the excitement of the tournament he wanted rest. What's more, he found the mention of vampires repellent. He knew such creatures existed, for men were daily warned of demons by priests, but to hear that a *sanguisuga* might actually be responsible for the deaths here was unnerving.

He strolled over to the spring at the foot of the sticklepath. Here, a narrow way led along the valley towards Belstone, and he idly walked down it, whistling tunelessly.

The sun was already high overhead and Simon could feel the heat seeping into him. In the bright sunshine it was hard to imagine the tale which Alexander had told of torrential rains and famine, yet Simon clearly recalled those terrible years. Down here, he thought, if the river were to flood, it would wash all along this valley, and then thunder into the vill and fields beyond.

He had reached the end of the flat section, where the ground became boggy and marshy. After this he remembered the path curled upwards, following the track of a spring, climbing away from the river, and then heading as straight as a ruler for Belstone. Rather than take that route, he sat on a convenient boulder and selected a smooth, flat stone, sending it spinning on the water. The river here was very fast and narrow, and his stone bounced once, then clattered onto the rock wall on the opposite bank.

So intent was he on his game that he didn't notice the two at first. It was only when he glanced over his shoulder that he saw them.

They were approaching from Belstone, two young girls of maybe ten years or so. One was chubby, with a freckled, cheerful face and reddish hair, while the other was taller and more slender, with a heart-shaped face and regular, pleasant features. For some reason her dress was damp and badly stained. Simon recognised the shorter one as the girl Vincent had tickled earlier on.

They stopped when they saw him watching them, the chubbier one looking about with a quick anxiety, though the taller of the two appeared unconcerned. She studied Simon with a gravity he had not known in a young girl before. 'You're a stranger.'

'Not in my home I'm not.'

'Where is your home?'

'Lydford, in the castle.'

She looked surprised. 'I thought that was where the people were sent to gaol. Are you a prisoner?'

'No!' he laughed. 'I am the Bailiff. Sometimes I have to put people into the gaol, but I never stay there myself. Who are you?'

'I am Joan Garde, and this is my friend, Emma. We have been trying to see our friend Serlo.'

'Is he a miner?'

'No, he looks after the warrens.'

'On the moors?'

'Yes. He protects the warrens for Lord Hugh.'

Simon nodded. The girl's face was as solemn as her manner.

Perhaps she considered that this was the fitting way in which to address a Bailiff. All Simon knew was that it was novel to be treated with such respect. It was considerably more pleasing than the abuse he was used to receiving on the moors.

'Where are you going now?' he asked.

'Home. He wasn't at his hut. Maybe he was at the inquest.'

Emma peered at him with interest too, and Simon suddenly recalled Houndestail saying that two girls had found the body. 'Were you the two that found the skull?'

'Yes. It plopped out and rolled away,' Joan said.

'Ugh! It was horrible,' Emma added, with a grimace of disgust. 'It came right at me, and just sat there staring at me. Horrible.'

'She was sick.'

'I was *not*!'

'She was, and she peed herself. *I* stayed up there with Master Houndestail.'

'Have you seen him here often?' Simon asked. He only had Miles's word about his infrequent visits to the vill. The girls wanted to return, so he fell into step beside them.

'I think I saw him once,' Joan said doubtfully, 'but I was very young then.'

Emma interrupted. 'I ran to get help, and soon everyone was up on the road.'

'Were there many travellers here that day?' Simon wondered.

Joan answered. 'Only Master Houndestail and Ivo Bel. I don't like him.'

'Why not?'

'Well, he's my uncle, but he's never acted like one. My father has been very poor, but Master Bel wouldn't help him.'

'What of your parents?' Simon said to Emma.

She reddened. 'My father is dead, and my mother was away.'

Her tone was defensive, and Simon wondered whether her mother had a reputation – perhaps she was a whore. Rather than upset her further, he nodded to Joan. 'It's a shame when brothers fall out.'

'They just had an argument, I think, and now they won't talk.'

'What did they argue about?' Simon said, idly spinning another stone.

'Serlo said it was about the vampire,' Emma said.

'Father says there never was a vampire,' Joan sneered.

Simon had been picking up another stone, but it fell through his fingers. 'What do you mean, vampire?'

'It's nothing,' Joan said scathingly. 'Vampires aren't real. I asked my mother.'

'This Serlo – what did he tell you?'

Emma looked at Joan, suddenly nervous in the face of Simon's interest. 'He just said that a girl had been killed, but not by a vampire.'

Joan said, 'Parson Gervase says that there never was one here.'

'My mother was very upset when I asked about them,' Emma said in a small voice. 'My uncle wasn't a vampire, she said.'

They were nearing the main sticklepath, and Simon opened his mouth to ask more, when he heard a yell. It came from the right, down near the river, and he immediately pelted off in that direction. There was a shrill scream, then a woman's voice shouting for help, then the loud roar of a man's voice raised again in horror, and what sounded like pain.

It was the mill. Splashing through muddy puddles, he sent jets of filthy water in every direction, and then he was on grass at the rear of the mill's building, and he could see her. A woman standing near the leat, her hands clenched at her cheeks, but still she gave vent to her shock.

Simon took it all in at a glance. In the water was a man's body, and even as Simon ran to it, it was sucked under, the massive wooden paddles of the wheel clubbing it remorselessly with the sound of damp cloth being pounded clean in a tub, leaving only a feather of reddened water streaming away from the wheel, and then the foam at its base turned crimson.

Chapter Eleven

Reeve Alexander sat in his hall for a long time after Drogo had left. He heard the Forester greet his men outside, their laughter, then the sound of their booted feet fading away in the distance. He was just about to shout for his maid and a fresh jug of wine, when he heard more steps in the screens.

'Who the devil is it now?' he wondered aloud, grimly staring at the gap which gave onto the passage. Then: 'Ivo? What do *you* want?'

Bel walked in smiling and went straight to Alexander's table, taking his seat at the end. 'Hello, Reeve. I was surprised at the inquest today. Were you?'

'What do you mean?'

'The skeleton. Hadn't it shrunk?'

'If you want to talk in riddles, man, bugger off. I'm not in the mood for stupidity today.'

'Very well. I shall speak to the Coroner instead then, or the Keeper. It's nothing to me. I was just wondering how that girl could have been found in that grave today.'

'You're drunk!'

The smile vanished from Bel's face. 'I'll take no more shit from you, Reeve, and that's your only warning. You've accused me of stupidity and drunkenness; now I'll accuse you of murder.'

Alexander sputtered angrily. 'Murder! You primping sodomite! Get out of here! You have the nerve, the ballocks to come in here and accuse me, the Reeve, of—'

'Cool yourself, Reeve. I saw you – you and the good Forester – both walking up the hill with a man's body and a shovel. Yes, I watched you, both of you, digging a hole, throwing the man into the pit, covering him and returning to the vill. Do you remember that night?'

Reeve Alexander kept his face neutral. 'You were dreaming.'

'That's better. A measured response. Yes, I am happier with that. Now, I return to my first question: how did the man's body become a girl's? Interesting. Perhaps one of the men who buried the man also buried the girl – and that would mean that one of you was also the vampire, wouldn't it?'

'Perhaps it was the man who watched the burial who was the murderer?' Alexander said coldly.

'Perhaps.' Bel sat back easily and picked at a sliver of meat between his teeth. 'But if all I wanted to do was see you hanged, I'd have gone to see the Coroner, wouldn't I?'

'So what do you want with me?' Alexander demanded. This shit could see him dumped in gaol with what he knew.

Bel leaned forward, his long face staring intently at the Reeve's. 'What I want is to see that the felon is caught,' he said quietly. 'And we know who the culprit is, don't we? That nasty fellow, Thomas Garde.'

'But he's your brother!' Alexander protested.

Bel ignored him. 'I want him accused, I want him imprisoned, and I want him dead.'

'I can't do that. I have no authority.'

'You are the Reeve.' Bel stood, dropping a purse of coins on the table. 'There you are. Plenty to cover the cost of someone who suddenly remembers seeing Thomas killing the girls.'

Alexander groaned and cast a look at the wall in a gesture of theatrical disbelief. 'Bel, even if I wanted to, Thomas wasn't here when the first two died. He was still living in France.'

'Where there's a will . . .' Ivo patted the purse. 'I would hate the Coroner to come to the conclusion that *you* had done it. Oh, and I'd be grateful if you could talk to William Taverner. I believe he has been thinking of telling me to leave his inn and I don't want that. Right! Well, I'm glad the murders are resolved at last.

It'll be a weight off your mind, I know.'

Chuckling to himself, he walked from the room, Alexander's eyes following him to the screens. When the door shut behind him, the Reeve picked up the purse and weighed it in his hands, shouting for wine.

By the time Cecilia rushed in, her master was sitting shaking with silent mirth, and when he saw her pour his wine, he began to laugh out loud, tears falling from his eyes.

Not only had he been given a felon, someone to be convicted, handed to him on a plate, he had even been given the money to pay for his conviction! It was only a shame that Thomas couldn't actually have done the murders.

But, as Alexander reflected, wiping the tears from his eyes, you couldn't have everything.

Coroner Roger stood at the foot of the millstream and watched grimly as four peasants manhandled the body from the water. One day only had he been here – and now he had not only Aline's death to sort out, but also those of Denise, Ansel the King's Purveyor, and now another dead man to cater for as well.

There was nothing suspicious about this last death. Simon had already learned that the victim was Samson atte Mill, the screaming woman his wife Gunilda, and the younger woman with her their daughter Felicia. Coroner Roger knew plenty of cases where a miller had fallen into his own gears or millpond. Death from the paddles of his own mill was a common end for a miller. It was good to know that Sir Baldwin was at his side, for the knight was an excellent questioner, and yet Sir Baldwin remained mute as he watched. It served to confirm the Coroner's opinion that the case was a simple matter.

The Parson was already at the side of the water, mumbling his words like a good priest, although it sounded as though he was slurring most of them. He was clearly drunk. It was a miracle he could stand without toppling. Roger looked meaningfully at

Simon, who nodded resignedly, taking Gervase's scrip and setting out ink and reeds and paper.

As the body was dragged from the water, the witnesses peered with interest. There was a dry retching and a boy of some twelve years fell to his knees and spewed. It wasn't a surprise. Not many lads his age would have seen a man so mutilated.

The left side of the miller's face was fine, but the right was a bloody mess. A long flap of skin had been peeled away from his scalp, like a skinned sheep's head, and now dangled above his ear. Coroner Roger gave him a cursory once-over, but it was clear enough that the man was dead. There was no sign of movement at his breast, no breath, and his eyes were still and unfocused.

'I am Coroner to the King, and I declare that this inquest into the death of . . .' he glanced enquiringly towards Simon, who called clearly: 'Samson atte Mill.'

'. . . Samson atte Mille, is opened. Are all the men of over twelve years here?'

The Reeve stepped forward reluctantly. 'They are all here, but couldn't this wait until you decide the matter of Aline, daughter of Swetricus? We have our work in the fields to get on with and—'

'Bearing in mind I have yet to decide on the fine to impose on you for concealing the death of Denise, daughter of Peter atte Moor, I'm surprised at your suggestion that I should delay this inquest,' Coroner Roger thundered, and was glad to see that the Reeve bowed his head, abashed. Good, he thought. Just wait until I question you about Mary as well, you lying turd! 'Now, who was the Finder?'

'Samson's wife, Gunilda,' Alexander said more quietly. He cast Roger a pleading look, as if to beg that the Coroner would not be too harsh with the woman.

Coroner Roger made no sign that he had seen Alexander's expression, but he didn't miss its significance. He had no wish to make the woman suffer. 'Mistress Gunilda, would you come forward?'

She could only walk supported by two other women, and as

she was taken through her evidence, she turned regularly to them, weeping. The Coroner was calm and almost gentle with her. At his side, scribbling odd notes on the parchment, Simon thought he was seeing a new side to Roger, a more kindly aspect. Simon knew him to be a good companion in a tavern, an astute questioner who was keen to ensure not only that justice was seen to be done, but also that any infractions of the law were spotted so that fines could be levied, but seeing him cautiously question the widow of a man while her husband's corpse lay before her, Simon thought the Coroner behaved with great sensitivity.

Gunilda was not a prepossessing sight. Short and sturdy, her peasant stock was plain in the squareness of her face, the coarseness of her features, the large, masculine hands. Yet for all that, she showed little of a serf's fortitude. Instead her frame was racked with sobs as the Coroner prised from her the details of her man's death. There was a bruise at the side of her face, an angry, painful-looking mark.

One of the women upon whom she leaned was the one Bel had been watching at the inquest earlier. She appeared anxious for the feelings of Gunilda, giving the Coroner a pleading look when she thought his questions too pointed or unsympathetic. It made Simon warm to her.

Samson had been worried about a grumbling from the main axle of the wheel for some weeks, Gunilda said, but he hadn't bothered to do anything about it because there wasn't much work coming in yet, not until the grain was harvested. Now, with the harvest soon to begin, he had decided to get on with the maintenance.

'He was working on the machine?' Coroner Roger asked.

With much wailing and many declarations that he ought not to have done so with the wheel still turning, but should have stopped the water at the sluice first, Gunilda agreed that he was. 'I wouldn't have thought he'd fall. I saw him lean over to reach the bearings with his hand full of grease. Then . . .'

'How did he reach it?' Roger asked, glancing at the wheel. It was massive, at least five feet in diameter, far too big for a man to reach over.

'From that window,' she said, pointing. There was a small hole in the wall with no shutter to close it, almost concealed behind the wheel itself. 'He leaned out, and he was slapping the grease onto the axle when he slipped.' There were more tears, but then she sniffed hard. 'He tried to reach up with his hand to save himself, but it was filled with grease, and he couldn't hold himself. He . . . he fell, and I saw the wheel come around and . . .'

'That's enough, mistress. I am sorry about your loss,' the Coroner said. 'Has anyone anything else to add?'

Simon cast an eye over the waiting people, but there was no movement. Nobody stepped forward to speak. Baldwin was silent, although Simon saw his attention was fixed on the woman with faint puzzlement.

'Was no one else near when he fell?' the Coroner asked again. 'No? In that case I shall declare that I am certain that there was no crime here. Misadventure. How much is the wheel worth?'

The men before him shuffled their feet and looked at each other, and then Alexander, with a face like a man who had bitten into a crabapple thinking it was a pear, suggested, 'Perhaps tuppence? It's a very old wheel.'

Simon kept his face blank, and when he glanced about him, he saw that Baldwin was studiously avoiding his eye, and Simon knew he too was close to laughter. The amount was derisory: utterly unrealistic.

'Would you say so?' the Coroner asked jovially. 'But surely not! Look at it, the wood in places is still quite green, isn't it? Fresh timbers, I'd think. Do you really mean to tell me that this magnificent wheel is ancient?'

'Perhaps it is not terribly old,' the Reeve amended. 'But then it can only be worth a little more. It is not a very large wheel.'

'Eight pennies, and think yourself lucky I don't de- mand a shilling,' Coroner Roger said, losing interest in the process of haggling. 'Does the jury agree?'

There was grumbling and several black looks, but the noise died when the Reeve gloomily nodded his head.

'Good. I am glad that at least this has been cleared up,' Coroner Roger said. He shot a look at the drunken priest. 'I would suggest that he be buried as soon as possible, in this heat.'

It was as the crowd parted, slouching off back to the fields and gardens, that Simon saw her again. Nicole Garde had left the grieving miller's wife, and now held Joan by the hand. Baldwin and the Coroner had already set off back to the vill's inn, but Simon wandered over to speak to them.

'Hello again,' he said.

Joan peered up at him expressionlessly.

'Sir?' Nicole said.

'I am called Simon Puttock, my lady. I met your daughter near the river earlier.'

Nicole gave her daughter a long, steady stare. 'I thought I told you never to talk to strangers on the roadway, did I not? Ah, you never use the brains you were born with!'

'Is something wrong, Nicky?'

Simon found himself being confronted by a tall man with sparse dark hair and a narrow, suspicious face. He was reminded of Ivo Bel. Both men had long faces, the same nose, and deepset, rather intense eyes, but there the similarity ended. This man looked like he had a more open, genial temperament. Unless, apparently, he found another man talking to his wife. He snarled, 'Who are you?'

'Please, Thomas, do not be concerned. Our daughter was talking to him, up on those moors.'

'I wasn't on the moors,' Joan protested.

'Enough!' she said, giving her daughter a shake. 'You spoke – it is enough. You should not, and that you know.'

'I didn't see her on the moor,' Simon explained, pointing. 'It was on the road here, and she didn't talk to me – *I* spoke to her.'

'Oh, yes? And why'd you want to do that, then?' the man asked suspiciously.

'You are Bel, aren't you?' Simon stated.

He had intended to throw the man off-balance, and was pleased that his ploy worked. The fellow's eyes narrowed, and there was a fresh wariness about him.

'That was my name once; no more.'

'What name do you use now?'

'I am called Thomas Garde, and this is my wife Nicole – and now you know who we are, who are you, and why are you so interested in us?'

'I am Bailiff of Lydford Castle, and I'm here to help the Coroner. When I saw your daughter, I asked her about finding the body. That is all – apart from your brother.'

'What about him?'

Simon surveyed him with interest. It was obvious that he had touched a raw nerve, because Thomas's face blanched and he cast a quick look at his wife. 'Nothing, except that he is here.'

'Is this true?' Thomas demanded of his wife. 'Is he here?'

'Yes,' she nodded, her face downcast. 'I did not want to tell you this. I did not think it was necessary to worry you.'

'I haven't seen him. Where's he staying?'

Simon said mildly, 'I don't see why you should be so bothered about him being here.'

'That's none of your business,' Thomas snapped.

'I'm helping the Coroner. I can make sure it's *his* business, if you want.'

Thomas scowled, and he would have spoken, but his wife touched his arm. She looked up at him appealingly, and he gave an exasperated snort. 'Oh, very well, Nicky!'

'My husband married me when we were in France,' Nicole said.

'I had noticed your accent,' Simon said with a half bow to her. She returned his smile, but weakly, as though there was little enough to smile about.

Thomas took up their story. 'At the time I was in the service of a nobleman in Gascony, but he died and his son had no place for me in his household. Still, we parted on good terms, and he gave me a purse to remember his father. With it I bought a little parcel of land here and our pigs. All my father's property fell to my brother. I had nothing.'

'I see. And that caused friction between you and your brother?'

'No. Ivo took everything, but he still wasn't satisfied. He's a grasping, selfish man who has always taken what he desired. When I returned from France with my wife, he tried to persuade her to leave me and become his whore. He couldn't believe I could give her a life to compare with living with him as his prostitute.'

'It was brave of you to leave your home and come all the way here, my Lady,' Simon said.

'It was not so very hard.'

'I will find my brother,' Thomas said. 'he must be at the inn. Nicky, go back to the house. If he turns up, tell him to leave. I don't want him pestering you again.'

'Yes, Husband.'

Thomas looked as though he was going to say more to Simon, but after studying him balefully for a while, he spun on his heel and marched through the mud towards the inn.

Nicole sighed. 'He is a good man, but his brother offended him greatly, I think.'

'I can quite understand your husband's feelings,' Simon said. 'What's that?'

There was a howling from some sheds at the edge of the cemetery. Nicole barely glanced towards them. 'Samson's hounds. They are mourning their master's death.'

'Let's get away from this miserable place,' Simon muttered.

'You see,' the Frenchwoman continued as they left the mill, 'it was not so very easy for Thomas to marry me.' She let go of her daughter's hand. 'Emma is over there, why don't you go to her?'

'I played with her all afternoon,' Joan protested.

'And morning, too. You think I don't guess? Now, go!'

Once her daughter was out of earshot, Nicole continued quietly, 'You see, where I lived, my father was the executioner. The people of the town loathed him. And me.'

'I see!' Simon breathed. No one wanted to continue the line of a murderous bastard like an official executioner, nor would anybody want to sleep with a woman born to such a man. Well, Simon wouldn't, anyway. It was repugnant.

She caught his tone; she must be used to hearing revulsion in people's voices. 'Thomas was the only man who treated me like a woman. He did not care, you see, what other men said. All he cared about was that he loved me, and that I loved *him*. That was all. I could never betray his trust in me. His love. That was why I was so shocked when Ivo asked me to leave Thomas for him.'

'I don't know that it is so surprising,' Simon said gallantly.

'It was so confusing. Ivo was staying with us, and he made me his offer while Tom was working.' She gave a snort and wouldn't meet Simon's eye as she said, 'He wanted to buy me, like a milch cow or a dog. It was a simple transaction. And he had no thought for his brother, whom he would be betraying – whom he asked *me* to betray! No, he just expected me to fall at his feet and agree because he had money.'

'You refused.'

'Of course. I was married to a good man who loved me, and this other offered to *buy* me. It was contemptible.'

'Your daughter told me that the Warrener said they argued about vampires,' Simon said tentatively.

'Vampires?' she repeated, shooting him an amused glance. 'I expect Serlo thought it was kinder to scare Joan than tell her that her uncle wanted to steal her mother.'

Simon sighed. 'Yes, of course.'

Her humour faded. 'The worst of it is, now I think Ivo hates Tom so much, he would do anything to destroy him and win me.'

Chapter Twelve

Thomas marched into the tavern and looked round, glowering. When the taverner appeared in the doorway, he rapped his knuckles on the table-top to attract the man, then called for a jug of ale. Once it arrived, he held Taverner's wrist.

'Will, you wouldn't hide something from me, would you?'

'Like what?'

'Someone tells me you've been putting up a man I know – Ivo Bel.'

'Of course. He's been here a few days. So?'

Thomas wanted to reach up and grab Will's tunic, yank him down and beat his face into the wood of his table. 'I wanted to be told if he arrived here.'

'Tom, whatever there is between you two, it's nothing to do with me. I run an inn and I'll offer rooms to any traveller.'

'That's an end to it, is it?' Thomas said, feeling the anger coursing through his body. 'Do you want me to make it your problem?'

The innkeeper sighed. 'If you do, you'll only make life difficult for yourself, Tom Garde. You'll have the Reeve on your back.'

'The Reeve, my arse! It's got nothing to do with him.'

'Alexander came by today, before going to Samson's inquest, and asked me to let Ivo stay on. So if you're not happy about it, you speak to him.'

'You could have told him to go to the inn at South Zeal, you bastard. You could have told me he was here, you could have warned me and my wife, couldn't you?'

'Tom, let go of my hand.' His voice was cold, and Thomas

immediately released him. None of this was the innkeeper's fault.

Thomas sipped his ale. 'This inquest – what good is it doing? How can anyone hope to find what happened to Aline after so many years?'

'God knows. You were here when she disappeared, weren't you?'

'Yes. We came here just after the famine, about the same time Peter's daughter was killed. Terrible business, that. I wouldn't wish it on anyone.'

'No,' the taverner agreed.

'And now Ivo is here again, curse him,' Thomas sighed.

'Yeah, well. You leave him be. He'll soon push off. What's the point of punching him and getting a fine? If you're that keen to lose money, give it to me. At least I'll spend it wisely, which is more than I can say for some around here.'

Thomas managed a wry grin, and by the time he was halfway through his drink, his mood had improved to the extent that he could chuckle at some of the taverner's sallies.

'All right, Will, I'll leave him for now, but you tell him that if I find him anywhere near my wife, I'll kick his teeth so far down his throat, he'll have to stick his food up his arse to chew on it.'

Nicole's words haunted Simon for the rest of the day, and it was with relief that he saw the last of the drinkers leave the inn so that he, Baldwin and Coroner Roger could settle down to sleep.

'You're quiet, Simon,' Baldwin yawned.

'Yes, well, there's been a lot to absorb today,' Simon said.

'Too many corpses,' Coroner Roger grunted in agreement.

'You spoke to Houndestail?' Simon asked. He had forgotten in the emotion of Samson's inquest.

'Yes. For a fee he agreed to go back to Exeter, the tight-fisted, thieving son of a moorland horse-dealer! Still, it will be good to see whether there was any record of the Purveyor's death.'

'Tomorrow I suppose the funerals will go ahead?' Baldwin asked.

'Yes, the miller's and the girl's bones.' Sir Roger sighed heavily. 'Mind, with that priest, it's a gamble. I hope he does not get them confused. He was so drunk today it's a miracle he could remember his Offices.'

'What did you think of the story about vampires?' Simon asked reluctantly.

'It was nonsense!' Baldwin stated bluntly. 'Purest nonsense. A story to scare a child.'

'But your friend, the man who wrote that book . . .'

'William of Newburgh died over a hundred years ago.'

'So how did the folk here know of such things? Why should men mention them?'

'Simon, are you really asking me to guess at the workings of the minds of the local peasants? Dear Heaven, just go to sleep.'

Coroner Roger chuckled quietly. 'If you will tell these stories, Keeper, what do you expect? Simon is concerned that someone might come and cut out his liver tonight.'

As he spoke, a mournful howl shivered on the wind, then a second.

'What the devil?' Roger demanded. 'Wolves?'

Simon explained, 'I think it's the miller's hounds. They started earlier on.'

'Wonderful! At least he'll soon be in the ground and out of the way!' Roger said unsympathetically, rolled over, and was soon snoring.

'Baldwin?' Simon asked a few moments later, but Baldwin was either asleep or pretending to be. He had turned the cold shoulder to Simon, and the Bailiff was left staring up at the ceiling, starting at every creak and groan of the building. No matter how he tried to stop thinking of vampires, in his mind's eye he could see the cemetery fringed with its pollarded trees, and figures moving among them.

*   *   *

Next morning, after Mass, Simon joined the funeral parties at the graves of the miller and Aline; a doleful pair of ceremonies, but that of the girl's bones was strangely touching. Her father Swetricus was there, with his three other daughters, aged from twelve up to sixteen years old, all weeping unaffectedly. The girl had been dead these four years past, and yet from looking at her sisters, Simon thought, one could believe that she had died only days before.

The ceremony at Samson's graveside was not improved by the behaviour of the priest, who was already drunk at this early hour of the morning. His voice was a low mumble, his hands shook as though he had the ague, and Simon felt disgusted that he could so demean the service. Matters were not helped by the steady howling of Samson's dogs; nor by the sudden shriek as they all approached Samson's grave.

'No, no! I won't have him put in his grave without a coffin. He must be done properly!'

Simon turned to see Gunilda, Samson's wife, their daughter beside her.

'There's no time to build a coffin, mistress,' one man said. There was a hint of exasperation in his voice, from which Simon guessed that she, like her husband, was not very popular in the vill.

Still, they humoured her. Two men went off to the mill, and soon returned with some long timbers.

'We can put him under this. That will have to do.'

She sniffed, then sobbed again, her daughter wailing at her side, and the grave was dug with the howling of the hounds throbbing in the background.

Simon watched as a rough board was fashioned from the timbers, two men lashing them together with thongs, and then the funeral continued, the priest looking annoyed that it had taken so long to get things done. When the men were finished, the priest moved to the head of the corpse and swayed gently as he sprinkled it with holy water from a sprig of hyssop. Simon recalled that the ceremony came from Psalm 51, which said, 'Purge me with hyssop, and I shall be clean; wash me and I shall be whiter than snow.' As usual there were the solemn Latin phrases, but Simon was sure that the priest missed out a few words. He wasn't certain, because it was some time since he had learned Latin, and weeks since he last attended a funeral, but one thing he did know – the priest, in his hurry to get away, was rattling through the service faster than he should.

The body was wrapped in a winding-sheet which was brown and stained, as though it had already lain some months in a grave. At the head Simon could see the blood still leaking from the scalp wound.

Simon felt sad on behalf of the dead man. To his eye it was disrespectful to put the miller in his grave in this way: hastily, without preparation, wrapped in a soiled shroud, the priest drunk. He watched sombrely as men picked up the corpse and set it down in the grave. One of them placed some large rocks at either side of Samson for the lid to rest on. He may not have a proper coffin, but at least his body wouldn't be crushed. He would have some dignity in death. The boards were passed down and set over the body and then, while the priest intoned more doggerel and flailed about with his sprig, dashing water into the grave but over many of the congregation as well, the two men began to shovel soil back into the hole.

It was a grim scene, made still more bleak and unpleasant by the cross in the middle of the cemetery, which appeared to have chosen this moment to droop. The cross arm had slipped from the horizontal, and as Simon looked at it, he could see that the wood was rotted by the wind and rain which lashed at the vill.

He felt a sudden unpleasant sensation. The sight was one of utter melancholy, and seeing the men up to their shins in wet soil, women wailing, the priest quivering and looking ready to puke, the crooked cross standing out above them all, Simon felt a trickle of ice run down his spine. He shivered, filled with foreboding.

Somehow he felt sure that this was not an end, that even the formal inquest tomorrow would not bring his visit to Sticklepath to a close, and depression overwhelmed him.

The party at the side of the grave watched as the diggers finished their work and stood back, one of them with his shovel over his shoulder, the other leaning on his. The two wailing women covered their faces. Slowly, in dribs and drabs, the crowd began to move away, only a few remaining to console the widow and daughter. Soon even this last remnant started to make their way to the mill, whose wheel could still be heard rumbling like far-distant thunder.

That last picture would remain with him: the mourners helping each other through the mud towards the machine which had caused their loss. And that sound of thunder grumbling far away.

Drogo yawned, leaned against the oak and scratched at his ear. There was a bite there from the midges last night, and it itched like the devil.

He was tired, so very tired. The long sleepless nights, the constant fear that the Coroner might notice something amiss – all had taken their toll. All those children. Denise, Aline, and Mary, the disobedient little brats.

Leaving the tree, he slumped down and picked up his skin. It was made from a kid goat, stitched into the form of an animal, and it held a few pints of water, enough to permit a man to survive even if he got lost out on the moors. Not that Drogo was worried about survival.

He had often thought about death but never before had it seemed so appealing. Now he looked upon it as a long rest. There had been times, especially during the famine, when he had done everything he could to survive, but what was the point? His woman was dead, and with her, all love had shrivelled. There was nothing left for anyone else. He had once had a daughter, but she was dead now, and all he felt for other men was an intense, burning jealousy that they should still have what he missed so badly, so desperately. The death of his little Isabelle was a terrible agony, and he couldn't do a thing about it. While he lived, that pain would be there.

He hated the others, men whose daughters were still alive. Sweet, pretty things, who could cuddle up to their father, snuggle beneath the blankets on a cold winter's evening. None of them truly understood. All thought they did, but none of them could.

Staring out over the bleak wasteland that was the valley from Cosdon to Steeperton, over the Taw Marsh, he felt his face twist once more into his habitual grimace. Now he only had his son. He couldn't lose him too. He wouldn't.

But questioning from strong men like the Coroner could scare people, especially feeble cretins like the Parson. He was terrified, a drunk, because he had led the vill to murder Athelhard. If he hadn't told them Meg's story, they wouldn't have killed her brother.

Drogo sniffed, sipped more water, then shouldered his skin. He must speak to that moron Gervase, and the sooner the better, before he could blab to anyone.

After the funeral Simon walked up the steep pathway to the hole in the wall where the skull had been found, and stared at it for a few moments, peering inside. Now that Aline's body had been removed, he could see that there were still scraps of material, some red, some brown-stained, some almost black, lying on the floor of the grave.

It was a nasty, mean little hole in which to secrete a poor young girl. How someone could seek to end a life was incomprehensible, but then to stuff the child's body into this grave was another act of cruelty that Simon could never hope to understand.

Another short life ended unnecessarily. Only one day in this place and already he had learned of five deaths, if he included the Purveyor's, Samson's he had been close enough almost to witness, the poor fellow. The idea of being mashed up in his machine was somehow repulsive, almost an act of betrayal. There was something obscene about a machine which was designed to serve men crushing the life from one of them.

Looking up, he realised that it was almost midday. No wonder his belly felt empty. Glad to be leaving the road, he bent his steps towards the inn. He found Baldwin sitting with his wife on a bench.

'Simon, sit with us and drink to the warm weather!' Baldwin exclaimed, bellowing for ale.

'It's good to feel the sun on your face again, isn't it?' Simon agreed.

'Where have you been? Sir Roger and I went to question the peasants to find out whether any of them remembered the Purveyor, or whether they could shed light on this girl Denise's death. We looked for you, but you had gone.'

'I went to watch the funerals, then looked at the hole again.' He frowned. 'There are scraps of cloth still in there. Some looked different from her winding-sheet.'

'Oh?' Baldwin was interested. That was something he had missed. 'The Coroner's gone to speak to people in South Zeal to see whether they know anything of the Purveyor, so I doubt we'll see him again today.'

'I assume you learned nothing new?'

'If we wish to find out anything, it must be without the help of the local population.' Baldwin grimaced. 'There seems to be nothing that any of them can tell us.'

'If Houndestail is right about the Purveyor dying, that would explain them keeping quiet,' Simon said. He recalled his conversation with the two girls. 'There is one who might know something: the Warrener, Serlo. He lives up on the moor, according to the girl Joan.'

The innkeeper arrived as he spoke, depositing a large jug of ale before him, and Simon asked him, 'Where does Serlo Warrener live?'

'Up on the side of the moor behind the vill,' William said. 'But it's a good climb up the hill.'

'We can manage, I am sure,' Simon said.

'Tell me, Taverner,' Baldwin said. 'What do you know of vampires?'

'Me?' The man shook his head vigorously. 'Nothing! I don't know nothing about them. You ask the others about them.'

He hurried away, and Baldwin smiled at Simon. 'Everyone is *so* helpful here,' he murmured. 'What would he say were I to ask about the curse, do you think?'

Soon they were on their way. Baldwin had patiently listened to his wife's protestations as she pointed out that he should be resting, but then he politely overruled her and called to Aylmer.

'Jeanne will fret,' he said, with the nearest to impatience Simon had ever heard in his voice when discussing his wife. 'She has this ridiculous fear that the moors are dangerous for me.'

'You are sure that they are not?'

'Not you as well, Simon!' Baldwin exclaimed.

Baldwin and Simon crossed the pasture behind the tavern and forded the river, then followed the riverbank on an old trackway among tall trees. After a half mile, they were out of the woods and their left flank was bounded by ferns and furze. They saw the path of which the innkeeper had spoken. Here they turned off and began to climb, a steep ascent at the side of a stream.

They walked in companionable silence for a while, and then Simon said, 'Women can sometimes be right when they fear for their man's safety.'

'Superstition!' Baldwin spat. 'It is all about us here. The people fear vampires or the discovery of a Purveyor, and at least the second is likely. The taxes which Roger will impose on them all will be enormous, let alone the punishment to be meted out to the killers.'

They had reached the top of the slope and it now became

shallower. Baldwin stood and rested his hands on his hips, staring back.

Behind them the vill was concealed by the curve of the hill. There was a constant noise of water, but over all there was the whistle of wind in their ears. 'Look at all this,' Baldwin said, flinging an arm in the general direction of the scene. 'Beautiful! Clean, unsullied land, ready to be farmed and improved by men. This is the fourteenth century since the birth of Christ, and Jeanne and you would have me believe in some spirit of the moor that seeks my death! Ludicrous!'

'There is something here.'

'From the time that the first people came here,' Baldwin said, 'when Brutus escaped from Troy and defeated the giants who lived here, the moors have been Christian.'

'I know my history too, Baldwin. But if that is so, what of the vampires?'

'Stories to scare children.'

'They seem to have upset several people here. Could it have caused the strange atmosphere?'

'Fools, the lot of them. Vampires, indeed!'

'It was you who told me of them,' Simon pointed out.

'Yes, well.' Baldwin was reluctant to confess that it was a joke which had turned sour. He said lamely, 'I thought you would be interested, that was all.'

They had reached a thin track, little more than a sheep's path, and turned along it. The ground was soon boggy, and their boots grew stained from the peat-laden soil as they marched along a stretch which passed through a series of streams, each glinting and sparkling in the sunlight. Aylmer chased after a rabbit, exulting in his freedom and the space.

'Look at it, Simon! How could anyone think that this place was in any way cursed?'

'You are seeing it on a clear bright day, Baldwin. I've been on the moors in rain and snow. It gives you a different perspective.'

'Perhaps. Look! That must be the place,' Baldwin said, pointing to the long, low shape of the warren and the circular hut beyond.

They trudged on, but suddenly a cloud passed over the sun and blotted out the light. In an instant, the pretty streams became dull lead, the air was chilled, and Simon felt a shiver rack his frame. Baldwin said nothing, but Simon wondered whether the spirit of the moors had been offended by his levity.

'What an unpleasant little shack,' Baldwin said.

Looking at the corpses of magpies and crows dangling on the wall of the warren, Simon had to agree. It lent a chilling feel to the place. Simon stood gazing about him while Baldwin beat upon the door.

There was the huge mass of Cosdon Hill south and east, while westwards he could see the tiny hamlet of Belstone, and directly south there was the valley of the Taw, but as he looked that way, he felt his trepidation increase.

'Baldwin?'

'No one here. What is it?'

'Look.'

'A mist?' Baldwin said. He shrugged.

Then it was on them. There was no sun, no rain, only an all-enveloping greyness.

Baldwin was astonished how quickly he lost all sense of direction. He could still see at least five yards around him, but beyond that was only fog. To his amazement, he could not even tell which way was up and which way was down. It was quite alarming, and yet stimulating as well. Not fearsome at all, he thought.

'CHRIST JESUS!' Simon bellowed suddenly.

'Gracious God, what is it?' Baldwin demanded, startled out of his reverie, his hand flashing to his sword hilt as he leaped away, seeking danger.

Simon was glowering down at Aylmer's enquiring face. 'Your damned dog just thrust his nose in my hand.'

'A cold, wet, *ghostly* nose, eh, Simon? Perhaps that will show you something about the power of superstition.'

Simon held his tongue, merely wiped his hand on his tunic while he stared balefully at the dog. If he had ever before doubted that a dog could laugh, he never would again. 'Bastard hound,' he muttered and Aylmer's mouth opened as though in a broad grin.

'Does this often happen?' Baldwin asked, peering into the mist. 'Where should we go?'

'Follow the sound of water. If we can get to the river, we can follow it away from the moor. No rivers flow into the moor, they all flow away.'

It made sense, Baldwin thought. 'Which way is it?'

'Down there,' Simon pointed.

Baldwin took the lead, walking away from the hut, but before he had gone a couple of yards, he stopped dead. There was an indistinct figure ahead of them in the mist, a darker shape which made Baldwin hesitate. For a second time, his hand went to his sword. 'Hello? Who is that?'

'What're you doing here?' came a surly reply, and Serlo stepped forward out of the gloom.

Chapter Thirteen

Baldwin felt an enormous relief, and let his hand fall away from his sword again. 'Where have you been?' he demanded a little harshly.

Over his shoulder, Serlo carried a small bag. He patted it now, staring at the two men suspiciously. 'Provisions. A man is allowed to buy food. What are you doing up here?'

Earlier when Baldwin had seen the Warrener, he had thought Serlo was very short; closer, he could see that the man was badly deformed. His back was twisted, and although his legs were the size of an ordinary man's, the curvature of his spine made him appear short. His head had a thick mat of hair that sprouted under his faded green cap, and his beard was every bit as bushy and bristling as Baldwin remembered, while his eyes were as bright and intense as a wren's. Though he wore the torn and patched clothing of the lowest of peasants, there was a sharpness about his face which pointed to keen intelligence. Baldwin had never subscribed to the opinion, so often expressed by noblemen and others, that the meaner the peasant, the poorer his brain. However, intelligence was no guarantee of hospitality.

'What do you want here?' Serlo repeated.

'I am the Keeper of the King's Peace, Sir Baldwin Furnshill, and this is my friend Simon Puttock.'

'You're not the Keeper around here, the man from Oakie.'

'Oakie?'

Simon interrupted smoothly, 'It's what the locals call Oakhampton, Baldwin.'

'Ah, I see. No, I'm not. Simon Puttock here is Bailiff of Lydford Castle, friend,' Baldwin added.

'Oh.'

'As such,' Simon said, 'I have authority over the moors. And you are Serlo the Warrener?'

'Yes.'

Simon nodded dubiously. 'The friend of Emma and Joan. I have heard a little about you.'

'Yeah, well. What of it?'

'Where were you when the inquest was being held into the death of Aline, the girl found in the wall?'

'I'm not a villager there. Different parish,' Serlo said defensively.

'True. Yet you weren't up at your warren either,' Simon noted.

'How do you know?'

'I spoke to Joan and Emma after the inquest. They said you weren't about.'

'So? I was out on the moors.'

Baldwin said, 'I recall seeing you on the night before the inquest. You were there, where the body was found, weren't you?'

'I was talking to Henry Batyn. He'd been told to guard the body until the Coroner arrived,' Serlo explained, 'but none of the lazy buggers in the vill thought of taking him ale or anything, so I gave him some.'

'I see. Did you know the girl?'

'Who, Aline?' Serlo asked. 'Of course.'

Simon thought that he looked as though he was considering lying, and was instantly on his guard, listening for the subtle changes in tone that would show the Warrener was inventing, but Baldwin, watching his eyes, saw no guile or deceit. Serlo didn't look away or shuffle his feet, he met Baldwin's gaze steadily. Baldwin made a beckoning gesture with his fingers, and Serlo shrugged.

'I knew her as well as any, I suppose. A pretty maid, with a sweet nature to go with her looks. Her father never could see it. Kept telling her she was ugly, poor lass. Slim, she was, and long-bodied. Near as tall as me, I'd guess, with hair like ripened wheat, and eyes as blue as clean water under a clear sky. She used to visit me up at the warren of a day, and chat to me. Lots of the youngsters do.'

Baldwin said, 'What of Denise?'

'Poor Peter's maid? That was a bit before. I think she died in the first year of the famine. She was as lively as a hawk, she was. Auburn hair and dark, dark eyes. Born before our King's crowning. King Edward took his crown from Edward his father fifteen years ago, didn't he? I think she must have been ten or eleven when the famine struck.'

Baldwin glanced at Simon. 'Same age as Aline.'

'Yes,' Simon said doubtfully. He didn't trust men who were so twisted and deformed. Someone in so foul a condition must have done something to deserve it.

Baldwin had known many cripples from his sojourn in Acre, and thought disability to be irrelevant. He had the belief that men's souls were their own, unaffected by their outward appearance; though he knew some could grow bitter as a result of wounds, there were others who showed a saintly patience. Listening to Serlo, he felt the Warrener was trustworthy, an impression which was validated by Aylmer. Baldwin respected the judgement of his dog, and Aylmer was now leaning against Serlo while the Warrener scratched his flanks.

'I reckon so,' Serlo agreed. 'Everyone thought she'd run away.'

It was odd to be questioned by this tall, grave man. Usually a knight was a source of fear to be avoided, especially one who was a Keeper. Keepers of the King's Peace were as corrupt as Coroners and Sheriffs; worse, they were often more greedy about getting cash from people because they received no official compensation for their efforts, whereas the others did at least get a salary.

This one looked different. His dark eyes held an inner calmness, like one of the monks at Tavistock, as if he was content with himself and knew his faults – a rare trait among his sort. Most knights thought their strength made them better than other men – the arrogant pricks! – but this one looked as if he was capable of understanding the life of an ordinary churl. He even understood Serlo, if that expression of benign sympathy meant anything.

Serlo was in two minds whether to trust him. Caution was so firmly ingrained in him that it was impossible to throw it from him like a cloak, to be donned or doffed as the mood took him.

When Baldwin next spoke, his question didn't surprise Serlo. 'Did you know of other girls who died?'

The Warrener snorted. 'There are loads of girls about here. And many die.'

'What do you mean?' Simon snapped. 'How do they die?'

'The same as anywhere else, Bailiff. How do you think? Some get kicked by cattle or horses, some fall into bogs. There are many of those on the moors. One drowned in the Taw last year. Some get run down by accident, and some even get raped and killed, just because they have a beautiful body to a man who's fired with lust. There are all sorts of ways for a young girl to die.'

'You know how Denise and Aline died, don't you?' Baldwin said.

'I reckon.' In his mind's eye Serlo could see again that broken and mutilated body.

'So – *were* there others?' Baldwin persisted.

'Some, I think.'

'By God's own bones, you're lying!' Simon burst out. 'You mean to tell us that none of the people who visit you gossip? You've heard them talking, man! Especially the girls, like Joan and Emma.'

'What if I have?'

Baldwin set his head on one side. He still wore an expression of sympathy, but now it was mingled with sadness. 'We have heard that at least one other girl died in a similar way – an orphan called Mary. You are friends with so many of the vill's girls, and I dare say that others have felt as trusting of you beforehand, haven't they? Did Denise and Aline drop by the warren when they were bored or worried? Did Mary come to talk things through with an adult who was sympathetic?'

Serlo scowled at him. 'Are you accusing me? Just because some kids like to visit me, that doesn't mean that I kill them.'

'No, but if you are reluctant to talk about children who have died, when they have been along to see you, it puts you under suspicion when the reason for their visit might have been entirely innocent – and when you were innocent too, of course.'

Serlo wasn't fooled by Sir Baldwin's suave tone. There was steel in that voice. The knight was angry that a man should have killed these girls. It was there in his eyes. If he thought for a moment that Serlo was truly guilty of the murders, Serlo knew that Sir Baldwin would personally seek him out and decapitate him in vengeance. With that realisation, Serlo felt a shiver pass through him.

He explained, 'The girls would often come by to see what I was doing. They liked to watch the rabbits and help me kill the animals which came to take them. There was nothing more to it than that.'

'Denise and Aline used to come by and see you?'

'Yes.'

'And in the same way, Joan and Emma have done so more recently?'

'Yes. They enjoy a chat. I am different from the adults down there in their vill. Always have been. They feel they can trust me.'

'Why?'

Hearing Simon's harsh sneer, Serlo faced him. In his eyes Serlo could see the distaste for someone . . . some*thing* which was so damaged and ugly. It was a look Serlo had seen every day for many years. It made the blood rise in the Warrener's heart, and he felt anger begin to flood his veins.

To his surprise he saw that the knight didn't wear the same expression. Like a monk, his face held only compassion, as though he knew what it was to be reviled and persecuted. The fury which had been threatening to engulf Serlo receded. His bitterness became sadness, and his voice lost its harshness as he felt his frame sag.

'You can't understand, Master Bailiff. You are whole and strong, powerful. When little girls from a peasant's home look at you, they see a man of authority and strength, tall and imposing. Look at me! I'm only a little taller than a child. Their parents all gaze upon me with horror and loathing, but the children just see another person and they are happy to come and chat to me, because I'm an outsider, and I can talk to them on their own level.'

Simon, whose own daughter was growing more fractious as she learned to enjoy the company of youths rather than the young ladies of her own age whom he considered eminently more suitable for her, viewed him askance, wondering how any attractive young girl could crave his company.

'They were such pretty little things, all of them,' Serlo said without thinking, the sadness filling his voice.

Simon wondered about the man's sex-drive. There were stories of men whose natural strength was constricted in one way who developed astounding powers in others. Lepers were believed to be as lecherous as sparrows, for example. Could this man have a ferocious sexual desire which made him rape and murder young girls?

Serlo saw his quizzical expression. 'You wonder whether I could have taken them, Bailiff? Maybe I lured them up to my warren and had my wicked way with them, and then took them to the vill or out to the moors to kill them and silence them for ever. A nice thought, but no, I couldn't.'

'Your injury?' Baldwin guessed.

'An ox. He tossed me high in the air and then gored me and stamped on me a few times to make sure. That's why I look like this. And that's why I couldn't have taken them.'

'Why?' asked Simon.

'I'm a eunuch.'

Simon blenched with the very thought, but Baldwin simply nodded. 'I see. Now, the girls Denise and Aline. Is there anything you can tell us which might help us learn who their killer could have been?'

'You are asking about deaths spread over the last seven or eight years. How should I know?'

'You should wish to help us.'

'Because you're the King's men?' Serlo sneered.

'No,' Baldwin said thoughtfully, 'because their killer could still be alive and might kill again. They were friends to you. Surely you would like to bring their murderer to justice?'

'Maybe.'

Baldwin smiled at his grudging tone. 'Then just answer a few more questions, Serlo. For example, who was in the vill all through this period?'

'Most of the men who are there now. Thomas Garde, he wasn't, but almost all the others were.'

'Including the Reeve?'

'Yes. He was here during the famine. He moved here from Belstone . . . oh, eight years or more ago.'

'I see. So he could have captured any of them. Do you have any idea where Denise was last seen?'

'I heard that she was seen by Drogo the Forester walking up to the moor. She loved it up here. I often used to see her up near Ivy Tor Water, or up at the top of the hill.'

'What about Aline – do you know where she was last seen?'

'In the vill, I think. No one admitted seeing her leave the place,' Serlo said, watching him from under beetling brows. 'Are you serious about finding the murderer of these girls, then? Really serious?'

Baldwin contemplated him for a moment, and then very slowly, he drew his sword and lifted it, point down, until the hilt was before him. 'By the cross, I declare I am determined to find the murderer or murderers of these three young girls,' he said, and kissed the hilt.

Serlo grimaced. 'Very well. I believe you. Look, Samson was a vicious bastard. He enjoyed hurting people, but he was also nasty in other ways. I know he scared all the girls in the vill, but some he scared worse than others.'

'In what way?' Baldwin asked.

'I think he raped them, but made them too fearful to tell anyone. Even with me they were quiet.'

'So now he is dead you think that the killings are over?'

Serlo looked at him with those bird-bright eyes. 'My Christ, but I hope so!'

They left him not long afterwards, and made their way carefully through the mist towards the growing noise of the river. Then, in a moment, the greyness had gone, and they were instantaneously warmed by the bright sunlight.

'How peculiar,' Baldwin said.

'That's what happens when you mock the moors,' Simon said seriously.

They had reached a broad curve of the river, at which there was a deep ford. The two removed their boots to cross it, and sat on a rock at the far side to put them on again. While they were there, they heard steps, and Vin appeared, coming from the same direction as them.

'Keeper . . . Bailiff . . .'

'You look surprised,' Baldwin said.

'I didn't expect to meet anyone up here.'

'It was not fear that we could be vampires?' Baldwin snorted.

'You can't live up here without being aware of them. There have been too many deaths.'

'Do you believe in such nonsense?' Baldwin asked.

Vin gave a half shrug. 'I think a man can be called many things.'

'Have you got any idea who could have been responsible?'
Simon asked.

'Whoever did it would have to hate the people he murdered.
Killing little girls . . . I only know one man who could have done
that: Samson. He was always a violent, dangerous man with his
brain in his cods, and preferred young girls to his wife, if the tales
are true. I've heard he raped his daughter and others. Perhaps he
sought to keep them quiet afterwards.'

'Wouldn't someone have cut off his tarse if that was common
knowledge?' Simon scoffed.

'Samson was a dangerous man,' Vin said simply. 'Even an
angry father would have thought twice before accusing him.
Perhaps his secret has died with him.'

'Where was he when the girls died?' Baldwin asked. 'Do you
know?'

'Yes. Denise and Aline both disappeared when Samson was at
the mill. We were up on the moors at the time. It was only when
we came back that we heard about the Hue and Cry. I was with
Drogo on his bailiwick because I was still new.'

'You were with Drogo all the time?'

'More or less. We went on separate patrols occasionally.'

'Tell me, where was Denise found?' Baldwin asked.

'Up there.' Vin pointed over beyond Serlo's house. 'Down
towards Sticklepath. I remember coming back from Drogo's
bailiwick one day and finding the Hue and Cry waiting with her
body. No one had passed me going up to the moors, though.'

'What of this girl Mary?' Simon asked. 'Was she buried like
Aline?'

'No. She was out near the river, strangled like the others. And
cut about.'

'Why should Aline be treated differently and buried?' Baldwin
asked. 'Is there anyone you suspect of her murder?'

Vin was thoughtful. 'Peter has been a bit unbalanced since his
own daughter died. I doubt he could attack any children, unless

he's like Drogo and jealous of their fathers. Adam's all right, but he keeps himself to himself.'

'Drogo?' Simon queried.

'Nothing,' Vin said, but on being pressed, he reluctantly imparted: 'He can be a bit jealous of men in the vill who still have their daughters.'

'Why were you up here today?' Simon asked.

'My parents used to live up there on the high moor, out near the Taw Marsh. I go there now and again to sit and remember them. They both died up there.'

'It's unforgiving, the moor,' Simon said.

'It is a hard land,' Vin agreed.

Returning to the inn, there was no news of the Coroner, and Baldwin walked through to sit with Jeanne. Simon remained in the tavern with a jug of wine, but when the jug was empty, rather than remain and doze, he wandered outside and sat on a bench in the fresh air.

Although it was still daytime, the sun was low enough to leave the vill in twilight. He shivered, remembering the cloud settling on them, and felt another cloud settling on him like a cloak of sadness, a morbid conviction that here in the vill was an evil spirit, a demonic presence that could infect and pollute the whole parish.

Baldwin couldn't understand; he was no moorman. Simon had grown up with the moors nearby, and had lived the last few years out at Lydford. He knew that there was a spirit on the moor, a spirit which would protect it against men, and men only roused that spirit to anger if they were ignorant or stupid. The mist had been a warning.

He was cold. Standing, he decided to clear his head with a brisk walk and set off westwards towards the sticklepath. He marched along the roadway until he reached an enormous puddle near the chapel. Circling it, he walked nearer the chapel itself, following the line of the cemetery's fencing going under the branches of the pollarded trees which stood there. It was then that he heard it.

At first he thought it was the breeze soughing through the branches above him, but then there was a prickling at his scalp, as though he knew that this was no wind but something unearthly. He carried on, past the trees, and it was then that the sound came towards him without interference, a distinct, mournful cry; half that of an animal in deep pain, half that of a soul in torment.

Simon felt his eyes widen, his hair stand on end; he was filled with a terror so all-encompassing that he could not move. All his attention was focused on the sound that drifted to him, quiet, but unutterably sad.

It was like a voice whispering, cursing, begging, threatening – a spirit's voice, a ghost's voice – and even as they heard it, Samson's dogs began to howl.

Chapter Fourteen

Vincent Yunghe felt scared. He had made his way back from the river and met Drogo and the others at the inn, but every time he looked up he found himself staring into Drogo's eyes, as if the leader of the Foresters was wondering whether Vin would turn him in.

Drogo le Criur was dressed in older green clothes today, with a stout leather jerkin to protect his torso from brambles and thorns, and his knife and horn at his belt.

Vincent swallowed uneasily. It would serve Drogo right if he told everyone the truth – that Drogo was never at his bailiwick when he was supposed to be on duty, that he was jealous of all the fathers who had little girls of eleven or so, the age at which Drogo's daughter Isabelle had died, but the words wouldn't come.

It was true. Drogo was rarely at his post when he should be. Hadn't anyone else noticed? He was always making the excuse that he had to go and walk about to see that no cutpurse or felon was robbing someone, but Vin doubted that. He was away too often.

His eyes met Drogo's again, and he felt his spirit quail. The man was his friend. He had taken him under his wing when Vin's father had died, when no one else wanted to know. How could he betray that loyalty and friendship? He couldn't.

This time it was Drogo who looked away, and Vin blinked. He suddenly wondered whether the Forester held the same doubts about *him*. After all, Drogo knew that he wasn't with him when the girls had died. Still, he had always demonstrated that curious, twisted loyalty towards him, much more than even the son of a friend deserved.

Drogo knocked back the last of his drink and stood. Adam rose with him, slapping Vin's shoulder. 'Come on, boy! We have work to do.' He gazed about him at the villagers drinking and eating. 'Look at them,' he grunted. 'Now Samson's dead, they feel free to eat and drink and be happy because the ogre from the mill's gone for good. So many thought he was the murderer, but not one dared accuse him. Not a single one. Fucking peasants! I've pissed stronger streaks than this lot. None of them realise that Samson's *soul* hasn't gone, though, do they?' He came to with a visible shiver. 'What are you gawping at, boy?' he snapped. 'Get moving before Drogo loses his patience with you.'

He rolled away, the crippled leg impeding his progress, and Vincent spat angrily. Adam knew well that he hated being called 'boy'. He was no mean, feeble youth, he was a man, in every sense.

Walking away, he found himself meeting the sad gaze of Felicia. She sat at the back of the tavern with her mother, and as she caught his look, she gave a weak smile.

Vin felt as though she had stabbed his heart. He had grown up with her, made love with her, and then deserted her immediately afterwards from terror of her father. That was hardly the action of an adult. If he had the courage of his conviction, he would have returned to her later, maybe even offered to marry her. At least he could have rattled her again.

There was still time. Samson was gone, rot his soul! But Felicia was still here, and maybe even more lonely than before. It should be easy to persuade her to see him. If he could get close to her, surely she'd submit to him again, as she had that day by the river, the day Ansel had died.

Gervase was in his cottage when Simon strode past, and the priest looked about him blearily as the splashing of the Bailiff's feet in puddles disappeared up towards the village. He had never forgotten his roots, Gervase hadn't. No, he could still bring to mind the tatty little vill where he'd been born, the great barn owned by the Bishop just outside, where the cathedral's crops were stored after harvest, dwarfing the peasants' own meagre supplies.

Gervase had been born into a poor family, but that didn't mean they weren't proud. His father was never so pleased with him as on that day when the Bishop's man had claimed him. All because Gervase had been blessed with a pretty voice as a youngster, and the ability to memorise songs. That was all they wanted in those days. They didn't expect a chorister to be able to learn Latin and French, only to sing in tune with other boys and behave in the cloister. And for that, he was to have a new life at the age of six, taken away from his home and dropped down into the midst of the great bustling city of Exeter.

If he had worked more assiduously, perhaps he would have been able to make more of a mark, he thought as he poured a fresh beaker of ale. The wine was all gone. More and more often lately he had been prone to thinking of what might have been possible, now he was approaching forty years, especially when he was in his cups. Not that he was often dry since the discovery of Aline's grave. Poor little lass.

It hurt. God's body, but it hurt! He hadn't wanted to harm anyone, had never wished to see a man cut down and burned without being shriven, but he had. It was him, him and his damned stupidity, which had sealed the execution, and he had given up the man's soul to the devil. All he had to do was take the confession and give him Absolution, but he hadn't.

Sniffing, he finished his beaker and set it down on the table, then he pulled his robe about him. A Parson had duties to his flock. Gervase walked out into the warm evening air and set off towards the chapel. Hearing the dogs howling, he reflected that it was good to witness creatures demonstrating loyalty to their fallen master.

Sticklepath was a nice little place. If it hadn't been stained with blood, he would have been very happy here. After his years in Exeter, it was a shock to be dumped in so squalid a mud-filled parish, but he was glad of a post of any sort. So many of his friends were doomed to be forced out of Holy Orders, luckier ones taking clerical posts, others reduced to menial chores about the city's churches, that he knew he was fortunate.

For a Parson, Sticklepath was better than places like Belstone. Folk were odd up there, he thought and burped. After all, Belstone was cut off from civilisation. No road to speak of. Whenever it snowed, no one could get up there. And the wind, God's teeth, how it howled up there! Like the hounds of hell.

Hang on, he thought, Alexander came from Belstone. But there was nothing to suggest that the Reeve was mad. Not like Samson. Parson Gervase had heard his confession.

'An evil, evil man,' he said to himself.

The ale was making itself felt. At the cemetery's wall, Gervase lifted his robe and pissed against one of the pollarded trees. Resettling his hose and tunic, he suddenly stopped. He was sure he could taste the change on the wind. More rain, he told himself gloomily. Always more rain. Unless it was snow.

He reached the chapel's door and gave an elaborate reverence. It was hard to remember which day of the week it was, and if he weren't reminded by travellers, he would have the day wrong more often than he already did, often missing fast days. He was fallible.

At the altar he prostrated himself, arms outstretched in imitation of the crucifixion. The position was looked upon as an affectation or, worse, proof of ill-education, but he didn't care. He was before God, and other men didn't matter.

'Glad you deigned to drop in, Gervey.'

He didn't need to turn his head. 'What are you doing in here? You pollute the air of my chapel.'

Drogo laughed quietly. 'More than your drunken breath, you mean? Be fair, old shriver, and look to yourself before you insult

me. What is it – pull the plank out of your own eye before seeking
the splinter in mine?'

'What do you want? I am here to perform my holy ritual, and
you offend God by delaying me.'

'Gervase, there is a Coroner here in the vill. I don't want him
reopening old wounds that he can't possibly do anything about.
There's no point in getting him involved.'

'You threaten me? You come to God's house and threaten one
of His own priests? You are a blasphemous dog, Drogo.'

'Aye, I dare say you've the right of it.' The Forester nodded
agreeably.

'Damn you! You think I compliment you, you son of a whore!
You whore's shite, you turd of a festering snake, you worm,
you—'

'Most interesting, Parson, but I have work to be getting on
with. You may not have noticed, but we Foresters have duties to
attend to, and we tend to be at them more regularly than some.'

'You insult me in my own chapel, you devil? Be gone at once!
You suggest that I am drunk? If I am, whose fault is it, eh?'
Gervase's voice rose in anger. 'You forget who caused me to fall?
Who made me what I am today, eh? *You*. You used me, and you
made me a monster. You alone.'

Drogo stood and gave an elaborate yawn. 'So we are back to
that, are we? Well, you have been blaming me for many a long
year, and I doubt not that you'll continue to do so, even though it
wasn't me but Samson.'

'You'd blame the misguided fool now he lies in his own grave?
Hypocrite!'

'It was Samson started the attack on Athelhard.'

'You were there, you with your men, and you should have
prevented it. You are a King's man, Forester, and you failed to stop
the murder.'

'Gervey, it was your preaching that caused the vill to kill him.
Don't forget your own guilt.'

'At least I tried to persuade people out of their crime!' Gervase spat.

'Yes. Still, it'd be better not to mention it to the Coroner or his friends. Secrets like that are better kept hidden.'

'You come here to protect yourself?'

'What I have told you was under the seal of the confessional. You broke your vows once, you wouldn't want to do it again, would you?'

'You are worse than a blasphemer, you are a heretic as well.'

'Ah, Christ's blood, man! Do you honestly think you can blame me for that? Athelhard died because of your words, not mine, so don't try to put the blame onto me.'

'I know.' Gervase felt his rage dissolve, washed away by his guilt. It was true – it was his fault Athelhard had died. 'I preached against him and fired the men here with hatred. I guaranteed his death. I sealed his death warrant and provided the rope.'

'If you want to wallow in it, carry on. I have better things to be doing,' Drogo said dismissively as he walked to the door. When he had pulled it open, he glanced back at Gervase. 'You know, I would not have you taking all the responsibility for Athelhard's death. He was a hard man, and he died a hard man's way. But it wasn't you alone. We all knew he was guilty.'

'But he wasn't, was he? He was innocent.'

'He was foreign. It's no surprise we thought it must be him. Who else could it have been? Poor Denise. She was such a pretty little maid. And then we found her . . . like that. Who else could have done it?'

'Who else could have eaten her, you mean?'

'If you must have it so, yes. Athelhard was well fed, and Meg described the meal he gave her.'

'She told me he had bought it from a traveller. A joint of pork.'

'No one saw this meat. It's no surprise all thought he killed Denise to feed himself and his sister.'

His defensive tone of voice made Gervase sneer. 'Oh yes, and then it was but a short step to thinking him a vampire!'

'It was your preaching did that.'

'I know,' Gervase said desperately. 'I didn't think what I was saying.'

'What does it matter? A man who can eat others has to be possessed.'

Gervase brought his fist down on the altar. 'But he didn't do it, did he? That's the whole point!'

'We don't know that for certain,' Drogo said uneasily.

'Oh no? Not even when we found the body of Mary two months after Athelhard had been slaughtered outside his home?'

'You were partly to blame for Athelhard's death. Don't put all the responsibility onto me, priest.'

'And Aline, too.' The priest's bleary eyes turned back to the altar for a moment. 'Why was she buried?'

'Eh?'

'Aline was buried. Why was that? The others were left out in the open.'

'Who can tell? Maybe the killer wanted to punish her father. Or her,' Drogo said.

'And Mary and Aline both died *after* Athelhard. So he couldn't have been the murderer.'

'You think what you like, Gervey. For me, I think he was desperate and sought anything to eat. He killed and ate Denise all right. Local men would have begged food from their neighbours, but a stranger like him? He couldn't. It was only to save his sister's feelings that he told her it was pork.'

Gervase snapped, 'And I suppose he returned from the grave to eat Mary? And Aline too?'

'If he was a vampire . . .'

'Oh, but you saw to that, didn't you? You let Peter cut out his heart and throw it into the flames. No vampire could return after that.'

'Then maybe we released the demon and it infested another

man?' Drogo said with a chilly horror.

'Or it was never him in the first place!' Gervase shrieked.

Drogo sighed heavily. 'Christ, I've had enough of this. You carry on blaming yourself if you want, but I have work to be getting on with,' he said, drawing the door wide and striding outside.

Fool of a priest! He was close to shitting himself with righteous indignation every time they spoke, seeking to offload a little of his guilt on someone else. Thank God he hadn't questioned Drogo's presence in the chapel. The Forester didn't want to have to admit that he was there to ask for forgiveness. To beg for understanding. It wasn't that he hated the girls – he might be jealous of the parents, but he didn't hate the girls. Still, God knew his feelings.

Drogo could remember the day of Athelhard's death. Doubted he'd ever be able to forget it. That morning at Mass, Gervase had begged them to pray for the dead girl, weeping at the altar as he told the congregation about Denise.

Not that there were dramatic demonstrations of grief at the time, apart from the Parson's. Even the girl's father was too far gone for grief. Peter atte Moor was white-faced, with the tears streaming down his face, and Drogo had been moved to put his hand on his man's arm in a mute expression of sympathy. Exhausted, Peter was too hungry to cry properly.

That was the point. Everyone in the vill was starving. The children's faces were shrunken and distorted, their eyes tearful and pleading. The famine had struck the year before, due to the rain, the accursed rain that still fell outside even as Gervase held his hands aloft and begged Him to help them, to save them all from death. But He was too busy.

It was difficult to remember exactly when the congregation had realised who was guilty. The Parson wasn't happy about it at first, but he knew, just as they all did, that no local man could have done this terrible thing, cutting up Denise like a side of pork. Not even one of the folk from South Zeal would have done that. They were weird up there, but not to that extent. No, it had to be a stranger.

They had gone up to the edge of Sticklepath, all the men of the vill, the hunters with their bows, the peasants with their billhooks and staffs, and there, at Athelhard's property, they had stalked and killed him.

Drogo was by the graveyard now. Samson's dogs were howling, over in the kennels at the far side of the cemetery. They were loyal hounds. He could hear nothing over their racket, was unaware of the low moaning that shivered on the breeze. Deep in his thoughts, he was aware only of a chill, a melancholy which affected even him, and he resolutely jerked his shoulders to ease the stiffness as he made his way home.

There was nothing, he told himself. Nothing.

Simon entered the inn with relief. He hesitated in the screens to catch his breath, but as he felt his heartbeat return to normal, he began to rationalise what had happened to him.

It was the effect of the mist on the moor, that was why he was so jumpy. If there had been a ghost, he would have seen something. Apparitions *appeared*. It wasn't logical to worry about a sound.

Logical! Logic was a word Simon had grown to detest when he was schooled by the Canons at Crediton. They taught him philosophy, grammar and logic, or tried to, but Simon, who could pick up and comprehend Latin easily, who could write and read with facility, found logic impossible. It was partly this that persuaded him he had no vocation for the priesthood. Not that he minded. He was happy to aim at becoming the steward to his Lord Hugh de Courtenay, as his father had been.

Baldwin would treat any suggestion that there had been a ghost crying to him with amused contempt, and Simon wasn't prepared to leave himself open to an accusation of credulity. Instead he took a deep breath, then walked into the inn.

Coroner Roger glanced up as he entered. 'Good Christ, man, you look as though you've seen a ghost!'

'No!' Simon said, perhaps a little louder and more emphatically than was necessary, for several people in the room looked up. He repeated his denial more quietly. 'No, but I feel in sore need of a pint of wine. Is the taverner about?'

'His daughter is,' Coroner Roger said, and bellowed, '*Martha! Baldwin's* with Jeanne and they'll be coming here for some supper. God knows what the cook will produce, but I suppose needs must . . .'

'Did you have any luck in South Zeal?' Simon asked, taking a large pot.

'No. No one there knows anything. The lot of them could have had their tongues ripped out and it wouldn't have made a difference,' the Coroner said gloomily. 'What I am supposed to do when confronted with useless, silent halfwits, I do not know.'

'You are supposed to continue questioning them, Coroner,' Baldwin said, entering with Jeanne. He grinned at Roger, then gave Simon a speculative glance. 'Are you all right? You look a bit pale.'

'I'm fine,' Simon said, moving to make space for Jeanne. 'How are you, my Lady?'

She smiled at his enquiry. 'I am well. This is a terribly depressing place, though.'

'The whole vill is silent. Someone must know something,' Baldwin said. 'I cannot believe that every peasant here is determined to hold his tongue out of fear of our rank, yet they are resolute in their dumbness.'

'It is almost as though the whole vill shares in a secret,' Jeanne said.

'Maybe they've moved a parish boundary and fear someone will notice,' Simon scoffed.

Baldwin mused. 'The messenger's suggestion of cannibalism was an embarrassment to the Reeve. Also, the Reeve had little

choice in sending for the Coroner, do not forget, because Miles
Houndestail was with the two girls when Aline's body was
discovered. What if other deaths were not reported and the whole
vill knew? Surely everyone would keep silent on the matter. Just
as they are.'

'You suggest that there might be more dead?' Coroner Roger
said, appalled.

'There could be another reason for their silence,' Simon
suggested.

'Name it!'

'You don't believe in them, but what if the people thought that
there was a vampire?'

'Oh, so we are back to vampires!' Baldwin scoffed.

'You don't believe in ghosts?' the Coroner asked.

Baldwin considered. 'Demons can certainly reinvigorate a
dead body. That is why the dead must be protected, so that
demons do not take corpses and animate them to scare people,
but I find stories of vicious ghosts persecuting an area entirely
unbelievable.'

'The dead can return,' Jeanne said quietly. 'I remember many
stories from when I lived in France.'

'Come, Baldwin,' Simon said. 'Put aside your prejudice for a
moment and look at it from the perspective of the people here. If
they feared a vampire, they would surely hide the fact. They
might even seek to conceal his victims, from shame.'

'True enough,' Baldwin agreed.

'And they would have attacked any man who they thought
could have been the vampire!' Jeanne declared.

'You mean the Purveyor?' Baldwin asked. 'I think he died
some time before the girls.'

Simon stared at Jeanne. 'But what if there was someone else,
someone they thought was the vampire, and they killed him?'

Jeanne nodded. 'And then they realised it couldn't have been
him. That would be a secret worth keeping.'

Baldwin was non-committal. 'Perhaps. It makes more sense than a real vampire, anyway. Yet even as he spoke, he saw in his mind's eye that figure of his nightmare, the figure at the tree, and he shuddered. This vill was making even him become superstitious. He thrust the thought aside as Jeanne spoke.'

'Are you all right, Simon?' Jeanne asked.

Simon looked at her, but he thought that at the edge of his hearing he could pick up that curious, low moan once more. 'I . . . I don't know.'

Chapter Fifteen

Long after Drogo had gone, Gervase tidied up the altar and swept the floor. At the door, he bowed, making the sign of the cross, and then changed his mind, walking to the altar and praying for strength. Drogo's words had reminded him that he was not solely guilty. 'If You would help me, Lord God, I could become a sober, useful priest again,' he begged.

Later, pulling the door shut behind him, he noticed that the cross in the cemetery was damaged. His first test, he thought. He stepped over the low mounds where bodies had been laid to rest, and touched the cross member gingerly. Only four years ago he had paid a carpenter to make this, and already the wood was rotten. The churl must have knocked it up from any old stuff. He would get a piece of Gervase's mind next time they met. In the meantime he would have to get a new one made.

The hounds were still howling. It was a miserable sound, as though dead souls were calling to the living, desperate to rejoin their families and friends, he thought. Strange that an animal could form so close an attachment to his owner, but oddly comforting, too. Even a man like Samson, a fellow universally disliked, was mourned by his own creatures.

A breeze passed over the tree tops and Gervase shivered. His robes felt thin. Perhaps it was his age, he thought. He never felt warm these days; even his spiced wine failed to remove the chill from his bones.

He was about to walk to the gateway once more when there was a pause in the howling and he heard a low, coughing moan. He spun sharply on his heel, but there was no one there. Frowning, he peered into the murk, but saw nothing out of the ordinary.

At the low groaning he made the sign of the cross once more, murmuring a *Pater Noster* to give himself courage. Stiffening his resolve, he stepped forward boldly. 'Drogo, is that you?' he demanded.

The only answer was a sobbing wail which seemed to come from the earth at his very feet.

Uttering a choking cry, the Parson leaped back and, looking down, he saw he was standing on Samson's grave. A breeze caught at the cross, and it squeaked and groaned, and Gervase gave a great sigh of relief: it was only the cross. For a moment he had believed that a ghost was with him.

All was well. He walked from the cemetery along the roadway past the puddle. As he went, he saw Drogo. The Forester was up near the spring, watching the priest. At his side were Peter and Vincent, the latter with his air of faintly baffled seriousness which always reminded Gervase of a hound which had lost a scent, and Peter, looking joyless, as he had ever since the day they had found his daughter.

Gervase nodded to them, but Drogo and Peter made no response. It was as though he was too insignificant to merit acknowledgement. Vin lifted an apathetic hand, but allowed it to fall, and Gervase licked his lips nervously. He felt threatened by their grim features and silence.

He was glad to reach his little cottage and be able to pull the door to, shutting out their unsettling expressions.

Felicia could hear her mother muttering to herself, and the noise was disconcerting.

Samson had been a terrifying presence in the house, and both women had avoided him when they could, for otherwise they would earn a stripe or two from his rope-end, and Felicia couldn't count the number of times she had prayed that he would die, that he would leave them to have some sort of life of their own without having to pander to his whims and fancies. And then he tumbled through the window and was struck about the head by the wheel and their lives were changed.

Felicia found a fresh confidence, a sudden inrush as though she had drunk a gallon of wine. It was heady stuff, knowing that she need never fear being woken in the night by his rough hands forcing her thighs apart, that she could select a husband for herself, that she could choose to remain celibate, that she could join the nunnery if she wished. She need not take her father's views and prejudices into account.

The same was not true of Gunilda. She had been married to Samson for so many years that life without him was alarming. Samson had dealt with all the family finances, he had arranged for the deliveries of grain, he had kept the machinery working. Gunilda couldn't conceive of life without him. It was like trying to imagine life without air or fire or water.

He had been a lowering, grim old demon at the best of times, but he was solid and inflexible, something upon which Gunilda could depend. And now this firm, rocklike being was gone. With it she felt her life was also gone.

Felicia could vaguely comprehend this. The destruction of what had been to her a gaol, was to her mother the loss of a protective institution that shielded her from all risk or danger other than those represented by Samson. His brutality became for Gunilda a kind of certainty. Like a hound, she craved even a cruel master so long as there was someone for her to respect.

That might be good enough for her mother, but Felicia wanted more. She wanted her own husband, her own life, and now there was a possibility of both, she found herself growing irritable with the other woman. Gunilda should be sharing in her fierce joy, not whining like a beaten dog.

The knock on the door was a relief. Felicia went and peered through a crack in the badly fitted timbers. She felt her face go blank for a moment in surprise, then pulled the beam from the door and opened it.

'Vin? What do you want at this time of night?'

He tried to answer, but he was tongue-tied. Redfaced, he stammered that he was passing and wanted to see how she was.

Felicia felt an urge to laugh. She knew why he was here. Pausing only long enough to grab a rug, which she spread over her shoulders like a cloak, she walked with him up the trail alongside the river.

Neither spoke. Both knew what they would do when they returned to that quiet, peaceful glade by the river, and later, as Felicia gave herself up to the pleasure of Vin's hands and mouth on her body, as she felt the first ripplings pass through her, she offered up a prayer of thanks for the death of her father.

Simon slept only fitfully that night. There was a heaviness on him, as though a thunderstorm was brewing. He lay on his bench near the fire, resolutely avoiding any thoughts that could unsettle him further, such as skeletons, young girls eaten many years ago, and the sad, mournful sound he had heard earlier.

'Are you still awake?'

It was the Coroner who called quietly to him, and Simon gave a low grunt of acknowledgement. Soon Roger rose and walked to him, tugging a blanket over his naked body. He sat on the floor near Simon's bench, staring at the fire. The Coroner reached to the pile of spare logs and quietly dropped one onto the embers. It sent up a small cloud of sparks which twinkled and flared in the darkness, and Simon was surprised to see that the Coroner looked drawn and tired.

'Are you all right, Roger?'

'As well as can be expected. But I don't like Baldwin's suggestion that more people may have been killed.'

'You're well enough used to investigating such things, aren't you?' Simon asked in surprise. The Coroner had always seemed calm and unflappable in the past, even when a murderer struck more than once.

'I'm not worried about death,' Roger said, 'but I fear that a man who could have killed like this, who was not caught, will strike again. It's terrible to kill a girl, but to *eat* her as well?' He shook his head uncomprehendingly. 'That is the act of a genuinely evil man. A devil.'

Simon was unwilling to discuss such matters in the dark. 'I felt terribly sorry for that woman at the mill yesterday.'

'It's all too common. I often see millers who've fallen into their machinery. Only last month I had an inquest on a mill's assistant who fell into the cogs while trying to grease them. He was horribly chewed up. The miller himself was terrified that he would be held responsible, so he fled to St Mary's and claimed sanctuary. He refused to come out, fearing for his life, and the bailiffs had to allow him to abjure the realm. He left for France. When we held the inquest, no one thought he was responsible. If he'd given himself up, he'd have been fine, but he didn't trust the jury to declare him innocent.'

'Why should he doubt their integrity?'

'He was a newcomer. Been living there seven years. If he'd been born and raised in the town, he'd have known he was safe, but you know how it is. If you're not born and bred in a town, you're never fully accepted.'

'So the poor devil ran?'

'Daft bugger. Yes.' The Coroner shook his head. 'He was distraught and couldn't see reason, but it was plain as the nose on my face that the assistant died from misadventure; nothing more. And now, since the bailiffs allowed him to abjure, he has lost all his chattels even though he's innocent, and we must seek his pardon from the King. And he may never even hear of it.'

Simon was sitting up now, and puffed out his cheeks in commiseration at the miller's loss. Home, friends, work, everything. 'And even if he gets his pardon, he'll never be able to recover all his chattels or take up his work at his mill again?'

'No. The fact that he abjured means he's lost all.'

Simon stood and covered himself with a cloak, then walked to the buttery. Drawing off two jugs of ale, he returned and passed one to the Coroner. 'It's sad, but it's the law.'

'Sometimes the law can make life difficult. Just think, there could be a murderer about still, and if there is, he might kill again – all because the vill didn't want to run the risk of penalties. If I didn't have to levy fines on them for breaking the King's Peace, they might have reported the murders and then we could have caught the man responsible.'

Simon frowned. 'Since it means they still have a murderer in their midst, I'm surprised that they didn't try to seek help.'

'Or hang the bastard.'

'Yes.' Simon took a long draught and stared at the fire. It was a good, strong ale, and he could feel it calming his frayed nerves. The noise, whatever it was, had scared him more than he liked to admit, and it was good to keep his mind occupied on other subjects. 'Why would they not have tried to find the killer?'

The Coroner sniffed and spat into the flames. 'Christ knows. Maybe they knew who it was, and didn't want to arrest him. Say it was Alexander. How many of the villagers would dare to denounce their Reeve? Not many, I'd swear.'

Simon stared at him aghast. 'You don't honestly believe they'd leave a murderer – maybe a vampire – in their midst, knowing what he had done?'

'Unless they thought the killer couldn't be killed. Like a vampire, eh?'

'Aargh!' Baldwin grunted disgustedly, rising and joining them. 'You two make enough noise to raise the dead! What do you mean, "like a vampire" forsooth! They are creatures of fable, no more.'

'But perhaps the people here believed in them,' Simon said.

'You think so?' the Coroner queried.

Simon was frowning. 'What of motive? Did the killer seek children only when he was hungry?'

'Or is he keen on any living flesh at night?' Baldwin asked facetiously.

'Oh, shut up!' Simon said, noting that the dogs had stopped howling.

'Well, it's ridiculous.'

'A vampire seems more believable to me than that a man should turn to cannibalism,' the Coroner murmured. He stared into the fire for a while, then threw his hands into the air. 'Ach! Finish my ale for me, Simon. My head tells me it's time to close my eyes and dream pleasant dreams of young nymphs and houris tempting me to join them in a land where my wife doesn't exist.'

'How is your Lady?'

Sir Roger threw Baldwin a disgruntled look. 'As fit and healthy as a woman half her age, God rot her! She'll outlive me, once she's made my life as miserable as she knows how. Faugh! Why did you have to ask me about *her*? Now you've got my mind working on that track, instead of nubile girls writhing and moaning against me in pleasure, I'll dream of my wife moaning *at* me! Here, give me back that ale. I need it now!'

He drained his jug, setting it empty on the floor, before yawning and walking slowly back to his bench, covering himself with his thick blanket and almost instantly snoring. Baldwin wandered back to his bed and soon he was breathing regularly.

Simon lay down, grinning to himself. In the Coroner's words about his wife there was no unkindness, only genuine affection.

There was a creak as a shutter moved in its runners, then a door rattled as a light gust of wind caught it. Simon closed his eyes, but all he could see was the cemetery, with that menacing, drooping cross.

And he could hear that cry, calling to his very soul.

As the Bailiff walked out into the bright sunshine, he found it hard to believe that he could have been so alarmed last night. The sun was gradually driving off the thin mist which enveloped the vill, and when he glanced westwards, he could see that the long spur of land up which the sticklepath climbed had already cleared, and was lighted with a splendid golden hue which made the grass and furze gleam like emerald.

Looking about him, he could have laughed aloud to think of his pitiable trepidation by the cemetery. The noise must have been nothing more than the wind in the trees, or the creaking of an old branch dangling from a bough.

He could scoff at his foolishness. Indeed it was almost tempting to tell Baldwin – but perhaps not. It was the sort of tale which his old friend would find amusing. Although Baldwin could be the soul of discretion and sympathy, he could also be unsubtle – and hearing further evidence of Simon's superstitious nature would not make Baldwin shine in his best light.

Men and women were leaving the chapel, he noticed. The vill's folk were a dull, ungracious lot, in his opinion. Still, the place should cheer up before long, now Samson was dead.

It was a point he had not considered yesterday, but it was important. Almost everyone they had spoken to expressed the opinion that the killer was almost certainly Samson. For one thing, no one else was so violent. Also, the miller was thought to be a rapist not only of other men's daughters, but of his own. Samson had been a brutal man, but now he could terrorise the neighbourhood no more.

With this pleasing reflection, Simon set off towards the river, and meandered along the bank. In this way, he came across Ivo Bel, who was sitting propped up against an oak tree. Simon was about to turn and make good his escape, when Bel looked up and noticed him.

'Bailiff Puttock,' he said. 'You slept well?'

Simon answered truthfully enough that once he had managed to find sleep, he had slept soundly.

'Ah, I suffer from the same problem. So often in a new place, I find I cannot relax. The fear of thieves, the discomfort of a

strange berth, the draughts, the noise of other men's snoring . . .
Travel is a hard life. It is better to be stable, to remain in one's
home.'

'You are married?'

'Yes, but my wife is a foul wench. I should never have wedded
her. A man in my position shouldn't give himself to the first
woman he meets, but still, we can all make foolish mistakes when
we are young, can we not?'

'Oh, yes,' Simon muttered. There was genuine dislike in Ivo's
voice as he spoke of his wife. The Coroner was just as rude about
his Lady, but he was not being serious. Simon had the impression
that he would be desolate if anything ever happened to his wife.
That was not the case with Ivo.

'My brother is fortunate with his wife,' Ivo continued. 'She is
a lovely thing, little Nicole.'

'Yes,' Simon agreed politely.

'He met her in France, you know. Over there he had been a
soldier, but then he returned here when he had married.'

'They married over there?'

'She was saved by him,' Ivo said. He cast a sidelong look at
Simon. He was disappointed with the lethargic pace of Alexander's
action against his brother and this, he thought, was an excellent
opportunity to lay the groundwork for Thomas's destruction.

'Nicole was the daughter of the local executioner, who was
proved guilty of rape and murder. The drunken fool beat a woman
and took her by force. If he'd killed her, he would have gone free,
but she lived long enough to accuse him. The townspeople held a
court and hanged him. They left his body where he had committed
his crime to show felons they weren't tolerated, but then some
hotheads turned on his family. They beat his widow and sought
Nicole, but she was saved by my brother. He took her to the
church and sealed their marriage in front of the priest, and then
held her under his personal protection. He had to beat off a couple
of local boys, and thereafter the villagers left them alone.'

'Why should they attack her anyway? She was hardly to blame for her father's position.'

'You know how foolish some people can be, especially the superstitious, Bailiff. They thought she was a witch, that she routinely communed with spirits and demons. After all, to a dimwitted villager, anyone associated with an executioner must be morbid.'

'Your brother was lucky. He could have been attacked by a whole village.'

This, Ivo thought, was the opening. 'You haven't seen Tom when the red mist comes down, Bailiff. When he is in a mood to fight, nothing can stop him but his own or his opponent's death. The villagers would have seen that soon enough.'

'He doesn't give that appearance.'

'You have not seen him enraged, my friend. When he is thwarted, he is like a mad bull.'

Simon wasn't interested. 'Your brother brought his wife and child here and the villagers accepted her because she was married to a man from the area?'

'My brother is not of this area. We are both foreigners, Bailiff. We come from the north, up near Exmoor. No, I moved because my position was offered to me and it suited me; Thomas, my brother, came here because he heard of Sticklepath from me. Before the famine, that would have been.'

'And he felt this vill would suit him?'

'Yes. There is good soil here, and he would be away from trouble. Of course there was always Samson, who had a similar temper to Thomas, but I thought that my brother could avoid him.' Ivo leaned back against the tree. 'You can see why they wanted to stay. This place can grow on you, and he had good land, good trade, and a good woman to warm his bed for him. He lacks for nothing so long as he keeps his temper under control.'

Simon chatted a little longer, to appear polite, but soon he made his excuses, and went back towards the inn.

Ivo watched him go, his smile disappearing. He was only hanging around here because Nicky was here, and he wanted her, but it was impossible even to speak to her while Thomas was in the way, the bastard!

Ivo had always hated him. The fit, healthy one, the one who could enjoy himself, who could do as he wanted, who bedded any woman he fancied. Thomas had an easy time of it, while Ivo, the eldest, must learn his letters and marry the woman his father chose. It was necessary, his father had said. It tied their failing, bankrupt manor to a larger one a mile away. That place had no sons, only one daughter, and her dowry was the manor itself.

But she was a cow, ugly and slow-witted. Thomas had a loving, loyal wife, while Ivo was stuck with *her*. Oh fine, Ivo also had his estates, two of them, but both had been devastated by famine and murrains. He depended upon his income as Manciple to keep both solvent. His entire life had been spent maintaining the family's interests, while Thomas flitted from England to France, playing soldier boys and bringing a fancy French wife back with him. It was unfair!

Ivo wanted Nicole, and his conversation with Simon had given him an idea. It would take a certain effort to make Thomas angry enough for it to succeed, but Ivo had managed when they were children and with some luck he could do it again. And that might just seal his younger brother's fate.

Chapter Sixteen

Alexander took a deep breath and gazed about him. The morning's mist was burning off as the labourers toiled in the fields.

They were as easily guided as oxen, he sometimes thought. He had risen through the ranks of peasantry himself, and was still owned by Lord Hugh de Courtenay, but there the similarity with his neighbours ended. Alexander had his own house, which possessed six rooms as well as the hall. That meant wealth in any man's terms, and then when you learned that he owned two horses and a full team of oxen as well, not forgetting his flocks . . . well! You realised you had to tread carefully in his presence. People respected him. They had to.

Except a Coroner and Keeper wouldn't. They were so much higher up the social scale that they need pay no attention to the likes of Alexander. Damn them both! It was at times like this that he missed the moderating influence of his wife. He still missed her dreadfully, and his boys. It was God's will, he knew, but it was a cruel fate that took them all when others lost nothing.

Not that all the dead were mourned. Samson wouldn't be. A rough, untutored thing, the miller. The tavern would be a safer place without him. Still, it was terrible to die like that, to be smashed underwater by the blades of his own wheel and drowned.

Alexander wondered whether the rumours of his assaults on young girls were true. Most people believed that he was guilty of incest with his own daughter, maybe even of raping young Aline, but at least no one had spoken to Swetricus of their suspicions. That was one feature of a vill which was vital, Alexander considered. Everyone knew everyone else's secrets, but they never discussed them. A man could be cuckolded by a neighbour, and no one would tell him, even though the whole vill knew of it. To tell him could do no good, just as it would have done no good to tell Swetricus that Samson could have violated his daughter. There was no evidence, only conjecture.

Still, even if Samson were the killer, he had paid for it in the manner of his own death, Alexander thought. The idea of water filling his lungs, of choking and retching, then the slamming shock of the paddles pounding into his head made the Reeve wince.

He set off along the back lane again, his eyes flitting hither and thither as he monitored the efforts of the men, women and children in the fields. Some would drop their tools and doze in the sun, or mount their women, or go to the pots of cider cooling in the river, if they didn't know he was there, keeping an eye on them.

He avoided the top of the lane. That was where *she* lived, Mad Meg, 'widow' of the Purveyor, and he had no desire to be accosted by her again. It was bad enough knowing the mad bitch was up there, without inviting her abuse.

These last days had been terrible. First that blasted girl's body turning up, then the admission that there had been others, and the questions about the Purveyor . . . at least that avenue appeared to have been forgotten. Neither the Coroner nor the Keeper had asked about Ansel since Samson's burial.

Alexander leaned on a gate, with an entirely unaccustomed wave of depression washing over him. Had he made a mistake? Perhaps he had. Maybe he should have sided with the Parson and sent for help when they suspected Athelhard might have been a vampire or cannibal. But at the time it seemed so obvious. Who else could have been the murderer? And then, when two more girls disappeared, Mary and Aline, they knew they had made a grievous mistake. Athelhard had been innocent.

'Who is it?' he demanded again. He clenched a fist in quick, futile anger, and slammed it down on the gate. But as always the answer evaded him, and he must return to his hall to catch up with his own work.

The path took him around the back of some little cottages, then through the yard of Thomas Garde, and so out to the road. Thomas regularly complained when people took this short-cut, but he was a foreigner; not someone whose opinions mattered.

Chickens strutted, self-important and stupid, their twitching heads turning this way and that as they attempted to spy out worms and grubs among the thick straw piled all over. Flies swarmed about the manure heap, and the pig was snuffling happily in a wooden trough near the door to the house. It was a scene of pastoral comfort, soothing to a man like Alexander, who enjoyed being reminded of his own roots in a house and yard much like this one. He stood still and gazed about him, a smile on his lips.

There were more flies at the stable, he noted. A thick swarm hung about one particular pile of straw – and then he saw the red pool leaking from beneath it which made his smile disappear and his face become fixed with horror. He ran to the stooks and pulled at them, tugging them away from the small, curled and bloody shape they concealed.

Emma's body.

'Who found her here?' the Coroner rasped as he took in the scene. He had arrived a few minutes after Simon and Baldwin, all three running as the Hue and Cry went up.

'It was me, sir.'

The Reeve was leaning on his staff like an old man now, his eyes sunken and bruised, his face drawn and anxious. For once, Coroner Roger thought, this was not a man who was scared of the fine he would soon have levied against him; this was a man who could see the ruination of his entire vill because of a crazed murderer.

'I was walking through here on my way home. I only came this way by chance.'

The Parson was at his side, swaying heavily, his face blotched and sweaty, swallowing and clearing his throat like a man who was about to be sick. Simon took one look at him and, removing Gervase's paper and reed from him, went and sat down near the Coroner. Parson Gervase shivered convulsively, and then, to Simon's relief, he staggered away from the hideous sight.

Simon himself felt shaken; exhaustion and nausea washed over him at this fresh corpse. With the death of Samson, they had all hoped that the murders were at an end, and now this poor child had also been slaughtered.

Vin and Serlo had hinted that Samson was probably the guilty man. So had Adam and even William the Taverner. Samson's death had seemed a suitable marker to show that the deaths were over, that the girls from the vill could live in peace and security. In his mind's eye he could see Emma chattering and laughing with Joan near the river, and was overwhelmed with a renewed grief.

The Coroner had no time to let his feelings get in the way. He was professional and businesslike as he cast an eye over the silent crowd. 'Where is her father?'

'Gone many years ago. He was the Purveyor: Ansel de Hocsenham. Her mother is mad. "Mad Meg" we call her. Emma often slept in the hay barns during the summer when the weather was mild, and stayed inside with friends during the winter.'

The Coroner grunted. He lifted his head and indicated two men standing nearby. 'You two! Come here and roll her over for the jury to see.'

Peter and Vin approached. They each grabbed a leg and an arm and lifted her from the stable floor. Vincent looked as though he was ready to throw up, but Peter had a certain eagerness about him. Almost a ghoulish excitement.

The jury was agog as the naked figure was hauled over and over before them. When her entire body had been displayed, Roger began measuring the wounds, calling out to Simon, who tried to concentrate on the paper and ignore the girl's body.

'A leather thong about her neck. The same form of ligature as that used on Aline. No stabs, but plenty of bruises, which means that the child was beaten before she died.'

Simon swallowed and concentrated on making his notes legible. Little Emma's death was rendered all the more horrific by his knowing her, if only vaguely.

'Whoever did it hacked at her thigh like a haunch of meat. Does any man here know who could have done this?' Coroner Roger called, and there was a short silence. 'Well?'

'It was him. Thomas must've done it. Why else would she be here?'

Simon peered in the direction of the voice but could not see who spoke. He let his gaze wander over the surrounding villagers. Ivo was standing near the back of the crowd, a sneer on his face as though he was delighted at this turn of events.

Nearer was the tall, dark-haired man who lived here, Ivo Bel's brother, Thomas Garde. Garde's frame was rocked by this accusation, and he licked his lips and swallowed like a man whose throat was blocked by a dry crust. It seemed as though he was incapable of speech, that shock had left him dumb.

About him men were staring at him with dawning horror. More than one had gripped his knife's hilt, and was watching Garde darkly.

'Speak, Garde!' the Coroner commanded.

'Sir, I had nothing to do with this child's death.'

Simon looked up to see Baldwin watching Nicole. She stood with her fist at her mouth while the questioning carried on, the Coroner's voice slow, grave and relentless, Garde's growing more highly pitched and with a slight tremor of passion as he rejected the accusation.

'Garde, the girl was found in your own yard,' Coroner Roger thundered at last. 'Who else could have put her there?'

Simon and Baldwin exchanged a glance and Baldwin nodded

to himself as Garde weakly shook his head. It was, Baldwin thought, one indication that Thomas might be telling the truth.

Baldwin felt a sudden rush pass through his body like a charge of strong wine. It felt as though his mind was being used again for the first time in weeks. Until now he had been directed witlessly by the melancholy atmosphere of the vill because the deaths were all so ancient and the likelihood of identifying the murderer so remote; however, now he had a recent murder to consider, he began to see the first indications of a pattern.

Of one thing he was convinced: no man would leave such proof of guilt in his own yard. Unless his wife and children were party to the murder, he would keep the body far away, and he would conceal it better than merely stuffing it under some sheaves. No, Baldwin was almost certain that someone else had planted it there. Presumably the true killer.

People suspected Garde because they wanted to. It was there in their eyes: the hatred of villagers for a stranger. For all that Garde had lived here for several years, he was still a foreigner. He hadn't been born here.

Baldwin noticed Roger cast him a quick look, and correctly interpreted it as an invitation. He muttered a command to Aylmer to stay where he was and walked to the Coroner's side, contemplating the accused man, at last seeking out Swetricus in the crowd. 'Your daughter went missing when?'

'Four years ago.'

'When did you arrive here, Garde?' Baldwin asked.

'I . . . think it was five years ago.'

His stammering did not affect his upright posture. He was a proud man, this Garde. Just like his brother, Baldwin thought to himself.

Simon was also thinking of Garde's brother, seeking out his face among the crowd. Bel had told him only that morning that Thomas Garde had arrived *before* the famine – and the only reason he could have had for lying was in order to put the blame for the murders of Denise and Mary onto Thomas. Simon felt his anger begin to simmer even as he grew convinced of Garde's innocence.

Baldwin continued, 'Do you recall the disappearance of Aline, Swetricus's daughter?'

'I do.'

Stiff now, wondering whether he was condemning himself, Baldwin noted, but not lying. It would be foolish were he to do so, of course, since the rest of the vill would know the truth.

'Before that where were you?'

'During the famine I was in France. That was where I met my wife. We married and had our daughter there.'

'It is important, of course,' Baldwin told them all. 'If he were here only *after* the famine, for example, he could not be guilty of the murder of Denise, could he? She died during the famine seven years ago.' He allowed his eyes to range over the men in the jury, to see whether his shot had struck home, and he saw that it had – but it had no effect. The men knew that if they didn't convict this stranger, the guilty man must be sought from their own ranks.

'Swetricus, what do you believe?'

Baldwin watched as the large man bowed his head. Swetricus cleared his throat. 'I think Samson might have killed some, but Aline and Emma . . . I think Thomas could have killed them.'

'There you are, Keeper. Thomas must be attached or gaoled,' said Alexander.

Baldwin stared long and hard at the Reeve. 'I think you know, or have a good idea, who was guilty, but you are trying to protect him. Or,' his eyes narrowed in a quick suspicion, 'or is it simpler? Was it you, Reeve? Did *you* commit these crimes?'

'No, I did not!'

'You seem insulted by the suggestion, but that could be a counterfeit emotion. Some men are good at play-acting. No matter, I will find out.'

'I have nothing to hide,' Alexander stated firmly.

'That is a lie in its own right,' Baldwin said. 'No man is that innocent.'

'How dare you speak to me—'

'We dare easily. You have lied about the death of Denise, and Mary too,' Coroner Roger said. 'Oh yes, Reeve, we have heard about Mary. Which makes us wonder whether you have told the truth at any point.'

Alexander rallied. 'Whether you like it or not, the body was here. I demand that Thomas Garde be amerced – arrested on suspicion of felony.'

'Nonsense!' Baldwin snapped.

'Quite,' said Coroner Roger. 'As First Finder, you must yourself be amerced, Reeve.'

As the Reeve reddened and swelled ready to explode, the Coroner raised his hand. 'I will adjourn this inquest. Reeve, I want the truth from you, or by Christ's own blood, I'll have you gaoled in Exeter until you learn to tell it!'

'Before you do, I declare that Samson was responsible for the earlier murders,' Alexander stated loudly. 'I believe that now he is dead, this man Thomas decided to punish the girl Emma for some insult or slight, and that is why her body is here.'

'What evidence do you have?' Baldwin demanded coldly.

'The evidence of my eyes, Keeper! The man is here, the body is in his stable. I demand that he be attached ready to attend the next court, and if he won't pay his surety, he must be sent to Exeter's gaol to await the Justices.'

Thomas threw a glance at his wife as he was led away by the Reeve under the guard of William Taverner and Henry Batyn.

It was a curious feeling, this deadness in his soul. For some time while he was standing before all these people, his friends and neighbours, he had felt threatened only by the Coroner and the tall, grave knight. Swetricus had helped accuse him, but Swet wasn't an evil man; he just naturally missed his daughter and sought anyone who could be her killer. Aline was his own, even if Swet had never much liked her. He was always telling the other men in the vill that she was a waste of good food, whenever he was in his cups. Too ugly to be married, even though everyone else thought she was nice-looking, and without the brains the Good Lord had given her, he grumbled that she would no doubt remain in Swet's house until he himself died, a permanent drain on his purse.

That all changed, of course, when she disappeared. Then she became the perfect daughter, the most loyal, the warmest in his bed, the little one who always brought him a warmed ale on a cold winter's day, or who kept his ale cool in the summer, dangling his firkin in the river. None of his other girls was so thoughtful or kindly, Swet would say, his eyes red and filled with tears. It was only natural that a father should feel that way about his daughter, though. Faults and misbehaviour were forgotten when a child died.

For his part, Thomas was wishing he had remained in France with Nicole. He had seen enough of the Justices' tourns before, to know how they proceeded. All the hundreds would meet to present their *veredicta*, their responses to the questions asked in the rolls: one referred to murders to be reported. And the case would be called before the Justices.

It was a speedy process. The accusation would be registered, and the man who appealed the guilt of the accused would be questioned, together with any witnesses he brought to support his case, and then the accused could give his reply, again with his supporters, and the matter would be put to the jury. The Justices didn't mind how the decision went, they were too busy looking at how much they could fine the vill, take from the guilty man, or fine the man appealing the murderer because of presenting his case wrongly. There were always good sums for the King from dispensing justice.

Thomas knew his own case would take little time. No one

would speak for him. He would be listened to, then the jury would speak, and immediately he would be taken outside and hanged. Just as Nicole's father had been. He was an outsider too.

They couldn't really have stayed in France. That was clear as soon as the old man was hanged. No one liked an executioner, but Nicole's father was detested still more because he was a drunk. Perhaps he hated ending young lives unnecessarily; for whatever reason he would drink wildly before attempting an execution. He was a bleary-looking man, with dribbling mouth and sagging eyes under a tousled thatch of grey hair, with large hands that looked too thick and unwieldy to tie a knot. And often they wouldn't. When Thomas first met him, he was begging the priest to help him, and when the priest refused, old man Garde had looked about him at the angry crowd with a fearful eye, like a horse shying from a flapping cloth in a hedge.

Thomas himself offered his help, not because he wanted to assist an executioner, but because he hated seeing the victims waiting, and he feared that the executioner would botch the job, leaving them to throttle too slowly, or mistying the knots so that the victims fell to the ground, and must wait while another noose was fashioned in order that they might go through the whole process again.

The thought of the poor devils' torment spurred Thomas on. He ducked under the polearms of the two nearest men-at-arms while they laughed – two of the waiting convicts had soiled themselves in their terror – and walked over to the pathetic executioner. Taking the slack rope, he swiftly fashioned a knot, English-style, with a large loop to allow the rope to travel quickly. At home he knew that the local executioner smothered it in a thick layer of rendered pig's fat to make it slip all the more easily, for any countryman disliked the thought of protracting death. Whether it was a hog, ox, rabbit or man, the slaughterman tried to make death as swift as possible.

Old man Garde bobbed his head and flapped his hands while

his mouth slobbered his gratitude, and then Thomas found himself helping move the four convicted men into a line. While they shivered, staring about them with the terror that only a man about to die can know, Thomas thrust the executioner from him and gently slipped the nooses over the men's heads. As they sobbed and prayed, one loudly declaring his innocence, another calling on the devil to hear his plea that the crowd should themselves be burned in Hell's fire for eternity, Thomas rested his hand on their shoulders and tried to calm them.

Not for long. The old man gave the signal, and the teams began to haul on the ropes, yanking the four high into the air; twisting and jerking, their legs kicking madly, bound hands tearing at the ropes that choked their lives away as their women and friends came and pulled on their legs, trying to end their suffering more speedily.

Later he heard of the executioner's own trial. Thomas felt no sympathy for him. Garde had tried to rape a woman and she had later died, living only long enough to point him out. Garde was hanged.

Thomas went to watch it. It wasn't often you got to see a hangman's end, and at least the old man went gamely, cursing his gaoler and executioner. Then Thomas saw men punching a woman and making for her daughter, shouting lewd obscenities and taunting her. One pulled down his hose and displayed his tarse, beckoning the terrified girl to him.

It was enough. Thomas saw red. He took his iron-shod staff and thrust it at the man's ballocks, then sprang to Nicole's side. With his staff he was able to beat back the crowd, and although a few hurled rocks in a lacklustre manner, Thomas bellowed to some men-at-arms for protection, and finally they grunted assent and stood between them and the mob.

Within a week Thomas and Nicole were wedded, and she soon fell pregnant with Joan. That was 1311, and for a while they were happy, but Thomas didn't want his daughter brought up in a vill where all pointed at them, saying, 'Her grandfather was the executioner.' No child of Thomas's should have to live with that. In 1317 he returned to England with his little family to make a home.

He had found things peaceful until Ivo had turned up, causing trouble, and then Swet's girl had gone missing. Many had looked at him askance, but nobody had actually accused him. Now of course he understood why. Everybody knew that there had already been two earlier deaths, long before he had arrived here – during the famine years, while he had been in France.

As he and his guard reached his house, he considered that again. No one had accused him before, even though he was a stranger; only today, when Emma's body had been found. Swetricus couldn't really believe him to be guilty, or he would have killed him long before the inquest. He was the sort of man who'd pick up a baulk of timber and beat to death any man who harmed one of his darling daughters, even if Aline hadn't been his darling before she died.

There was no money in the house. He knew that as well as the Reeve, but he did have chattels worth a few pence. After some consideration, he selected the large iron pot. He had little choice.

'I want cash,' Alexander said harshly.

'Take that and be damned!'

'If you threaten me, it won't make your position any better, *foreigner*!' Alexander taunted.

'Foreigner? I've lived here almost five years, man! I was born in Devon.'

'Ah, maybe you were, but you and your brother come from the north, don't you, not from here. Are you sure you have no cash?'

'No, I haven't. Now take that and go.'

Taverner had remained silent. Now he glanced at Batyn, and Thomas saw them exchange a look. Batyn he had always thought a fair and reasonable man, just as he had thought Swet all right in his own way. Now he wasn't sure of anything or anyone.

Batyn's voice was gentle. 'Come on, Reeve. Take the pot and be done.'

'I'll have the cash, or this fool can go to the gaol.'

'In that case, I'll buy it from you, Tom,' Batyn said. He reached into his purse and brought out a shilling or so in coins.

'No!' the Reeve protested. 'He should pay me now from his own money, or he will have to go to gaol in Exeter and wait for the Justices.'

'Why are you so determined to get me away from here?' Thomas demanded. 'What have I ever done to you that you should persecute me like this?'

'Take the money from Batyn if you must, and then give me the sixpence the Coroner commanded. And leave Swetricus alone. He learned what you were capable of when he saw Emma's body.'

'You can't think I could kill a little girl!'

'I don't know what you could do. You seem mad to me.' Alexander curled his lip as he looked about the room. Seeing a bowl next to the fire, he stalked to it and stirred it with the wooden spoon. 'What is this?'

'It is only pork, sir,' Nicole said quietly. She had followed the men into her home and now she stood at the doorway, her hands clasped at her apron, her eyes following the Reeve as he stalked about her room. 'From our pig.'

'How can I tell that?' Alexander asked, staring at the meat on the spoon with undisguised disgust. He had heard that human flesh looked and smelled much like pork.

'Taste it, sir. It is salted pork.'

He dropped the spoon back into the dish, shuddering as though it might in fact be part of Emma, held out his hand for the money, and counted it carefully before sniffing loudly as though disappointed, and marching out. Taverner walked after him, but Henry Batyn stood uneasily a moment.

'Tom, don't blame the Reeve too much. He has to get rid of the

Coroner and the other two before he can get the vill back to normal.'

'He knows I am innocent.'

'He has to get the matter sorted, that's all.'

Thomas dropped onto his stool and shivered. 'Henry, I helped you when your house was flooded, didn't I? I had you here, in my house, and let you and your wife sleep here until you could build another shelter. And you expect me to tolerate a Reeve who seeks to have me hanged?'

Batyn met his eye resolutely. 'There are ways to protect yourself. The Justices won't be here for ages, and you know that the church at Oakhampton is a sanctuary. You could make your way there for a market, and then abjure.'

'Why should I? I am innocent!'

'You think that matters?' Batyn expostulated, throwing his hands wide. 'Look, if you remain here, you'll be the obvious target. You have to go.'

'If I go, it'll be as good as an admission. I'll be remembered for all time as a vampire.'

'And if you stay, you'll be hanged and still be remembered as a vampire. Which is better? One way at least you live.'

'And what about Nicole and Joan? They will be reviled as the widow and child of a confessed man-eater. You would have that?'

Batyn looked away, unable to meet either Thomas's or Nicole's eyes. 'I could look after them, if you want.'

'In Sticklepath, where other children would victimise my daughter, where men would insult and rape my wife? No, Henry. I thank you, but no!'

'Thomas, you must do something. The alternative is death.'

'Take your pot.'

'I don't want it. Pay me back when you can,' Batyn said. He met Thomas's gaze. 'You must do something.'

Chapter Seventeen

Reeve Alexander was fuming as he walked away from Thomas's house. It was frustrating as hell to have to let the man go when he was the perfect suspect for the Coroner to choose. Why that cretin hadn't arrested him on the spot and had him taken away to Exeter's gaol was beyond him. Someone like Garde could be left there safely, waiting for his trial, if he should live to see it. After all, so many prisoners died of natural causes in gaol – from cold, illness, starvation, thirst – and wounds caused by other prisoners trying to rob them to buy food. Yes, gaol was the best place for him.

Sighing, he felt the weight of his office crushing him. He knew Thomas was innocent, but that meant nothing compared with Ivo's threat and bribe. Ivo had seen him burying the Purveyor's body that night in 1315, and although it was a long time ago, Alexander could be hanged if Ivo was to spread the story around.

What was Ivo's problem? Fine, so he hated his brother and fancied his sister-in-law, but why go to such trouble to destroy the one and possess the other?

More to the point, who had killed the girls? After all, if it wasn't Thomas, it was surely someone from the vill. It was confusing, because Alexander had believed the local stories that it must have been Samson. If there had been a shred of evidence, and if anyone in the vill had dared to stand and accuse him, Alexander would have seen him destroyed. But now Emma was dead. It was baffling.

The murders were committed by someone who was in the vill during the famine, someone who was in the place last night. That left it open to almost anyone, he acknowledged.

'Has my brother paid?'

'Ivo Bel,' the Reeve muttered under his breath. Then, 'Yes, Master Bel. I have his money.'

'Shit!' Bel swore. 'How did you come to let him get off?'

Alexander saw no reason to comment. He was reflecting on the fact that Ivo himself was always in the neighbourhood when one of the girls disappeared. He himself could be the murderer.

'My brother was always a violent man, you know,' Ivo said fussily. 'That was part of the reason why he had to leave home. He left England to go to France, but soon he had to return. I wonder why that was. He might have been forced to leave. After all, he was always getting into fights when he was a boy.'

Alexander stopped. Rebellion overwhelmed him. 'I can't put him in gaol for no reason, Bel. You've seen the Coroner – he won't listen to me.'

'My friend, I don't know what you mean!' Ivo said. 'I would never try to convict an innocent man. Especially my own beloved brother. No, but if Thomas were to get into a scrape . . .'

'I won't have fools causing fights here in my vill.'

'. . . and if he were crazed enough, I would think you'd have a good reason to believe him capable of killing poor Emma.'

'I won't gaol a man I've known for years just because you want his wife.'

'No. You'll do it for money and because you want your *life!*' Ivo hissed. 'I haven't forgotten that grave. Odd, isn't it? Just in the same place. Anyone would think *you* could have killed the girls!'

Alexander gaped. 'You can't seriously suppose . . .' Anger made him sputter.

'I accuse no one. I only hope my brother can contain himself, but you know what he's like. I should keep a close eye on him, Reeve. You don't want any more deaths, do you?'

He turned away and wandered off, whistling under his breath, while the Reeve stood staring after him. He hawked and spat into the road where Ivo had been standing.

If Ivo believed he could have been guilty, what chance was there that others wouldn't think the same?

Gervase woke with a pounding in his head and a sour taste in his mouth. As soon as he opened his eyes, he knew what was meant by light 'lancing' through a window. It felt as though he was stabbed with a white-hot point, and he snapped both eyes shut again, groaning to himself.

He had managed the Mass without difficulty, feeling light-headed and happy, and afterwards he had swept the chapel until the noise of Samson's dogs got to him. That and the dust. It rose in a fine, stifling cloud, a choking mist. And every time he coughed, he felt slightly worse. The hangover grew gently, almost imperceptibly as he worked. Then, of course, he'd been called to attend the inquest, and it was all he could do not to vomit at the sight of little Emma's ruined body. Poor, sweet little Emma, the last reminder of Ansel, the last reminder of Athelhard, too, in some ways.

Fortunately he made it back to his little home and sprawled upon his bed, an arm over his eyes, intending to catch a few moments' sleep before carrying on with his chores. He didn't mean to fall asleep, only to relax. Then he was sick and fell into a heavy doze.

It wasn't his fault. He had needed to drink more last night, to drown out the noise of the hounds, damn them! And that other noise still kept coming back to him, the wail like that of a soul in Purgatory.

The knocking came again, an insistent rapping on his plain, bare-timbered door, and he tugged the rough blanket up over his head, pretending he wasn't there, while fumes from last night's drinking rose to his nostrils. He had been sick again, he remembered, and acrid bile reeked from the rushes at the side of his palliasse. It was enough to make him want to puke again, and he rolled away to the other side of the bed.

'Parson, are you well?'

'Sweet Jesus, let me kick him just once in the cods, and I'll forswear all wine from now on,' Gervase muttered pleadingly from gritted teeth, adding more loudly, 'My son, I am suffering from a vile malady. Come back later, and I shall see you then.'

'Parson, this is Sir Baldwin Furnshill. I want to speak with you. Now.'

'Holy Mother, give me strength,' Gervase whispered, and let his legs slip over the edge. Soon he was upright, and he shivered as he unpegged the latch.

'What possible excuse can you have for interrupting an ill man? I was praying, Sir Knight, and you should not see fit to break in upon my meditations.'

Baldwin entered first, the Coroner following with interest, while the Bailiff stood blocking the doorway.

'Good Christ, Parson – were you puking all night?' Coroner Roger asked, his nose wrinkled at the noisome fumes.

'A passing sickness, that's all. What do you mean by breaking in upon me? Cannot even a priest count upon some peace in his own house? And what's that hound doing in here?'

'I hope you aren't missing your services?' Coroner Roger enquired, ignoring his questions.

'Didn't you hear me, Sir Knight? You can try to evade my questions if you wish, but by God, I shall keep asking them! What is the meaning of—'

It was as though the knight had no respect for a man of the cloth. To Gervase's astonishment, Baldwin walked out through the rear of his house, Aylmer trotting at his heel. 'Just where are you going?' Gervase shouted, and then winced as his head appeared to explode like one of those new-fangled cannons.

'If you want to speak to him, you'd better go on after him,' the Bailiff said helpfully.

'He's not of a mood to sit indoors,' the Coroner added.

Gervase was about to give a rude reply when the Bailiff

sniffed with a slow deliberation. 'You know, my master, Abbot
Champeaux of Tavistock, is always careful to protect his monks
from over-indulgence. Especially with wine and ale. I had thought
that the Bishop of Exeter was moderate in his drinking, too. I
must speak with him next time I meet him. He is a very pleasant
man, Walter Stapledon, isn't he?'

'I have only met him twice,' Gervase admitted warily. He was
unpleasantly aware that there was a sting in this conversation's
tail.

'Really? Oh, I meet him regularly. He often drops in on my
wife and me when he is travelling through Dartmoor.'

Gervase smiled without humour, but took the hint and walked
out to the open air. Baldwin was sitting, the presumptuous popinjay,
on Gervase's own favourite bench, the dog in front of him, and a
carelessly beckoning finger invited Gervase to join them. That
would mean either sitting at his side, a prospect too awful to
conceive of, or standing before him like a felon awaiting sentence.
Gervase pointedly walked to a seat at an angle from the knight,
sitting there with his back straight and as haughty an expression as
he could fit upon his features. It wasn't easy, with his hands wanting
to shake and his urge to vomit. Gervase had a dislike for knights
generally, but the sort of knight who could break down a man's
door, figuratively speaking, of course, or who would presume to
break in upon a man's pain when he might have drunk a little too
much the night before, was detestable. 'Well? I noticed you failed
to appear at Mass. Is this to apologise or atone?'

'I have nothing to atone for. What of you?'

Gervase was tempted to throw a tantrum, to stamp his feet,
declare his rage, insist that these rude bastards leave his home,
and then sink back once more onto his palliasse, out of this
hellish sun. Perhaps with a cup or two of wine to help him, he
thought. But one look at their faces told him that they wouldn't
listen to him. 'I have nothing to confess to a secular knight. I am
a man of God.'

'That is good,' Baldwin said. 'But perhaps we can discuss matters which do concern you. First, I believe that this chantry chapel of yours was given to you by the Lord Hugh de Courtenay. Is that correct?'

'What if it was? It's now in the hands of Holy Mother Church.'

'Yes. Except the Lord Hugh has an interest in it and I fear he would become most alarmed to learn that the very priest he had installed here was keeping secrets from him. Secrets which could affect him.'

Gervase felt his eyebrows rise. 'What are you talking about?'

'There is a secret in this vill which permeates the whole place. It is rooted in the soil, and it affects every man, woman and child in the place. You attended the inquest this morning, so you know that there has been another murder.'

'Murder?' Gervase felt his stomach shift at the word as though ready to fight free. The sweat broke out on his brow and the faint breeze chilled it like ice; God, but he needed a cup of wine.

'Oh, poor Emma,' he groaned. Sadly. 'She was such a sweet little thing!'

Simon interrupted. 'She wasn't only killed, priest.'

'She was eaten, too,' Coroner Roger said relentlessly. 'Just like the other three.'

Gervase stared at him blankly for a moment, but then his belly clenched and he had to bend over, throwing up over the foot of his robe.

The Frenchwoman could have wept to see her man so dejected and distrait. He looked as though everything he had striven for was suddenly gone; all his hopes, ambitions and dreams had been snatched from him in the space of one morning.

After Batyn had left, Thomas sat for a long time on his stool, and when he stirred, it was with an effort, as though his mind was far away. He looked up at his wife and smiled ruefully. 'It seems

I brought you from the dangers of your home only to set you down amid others just as deadly.'

'We are still alive, my love.'

'For now, Wife. For now.'

He reached up and caught her about the waist, pulling her to him so that his face was between her breasts, inhaling her fragrance, his cheeks surrounded by her softness. He closed his eyes as he felt her bend over him, her hands on his shoulders, her lips on his brow. 'Ah, my *chéri*, it will all be good. We shall survive this. No one who knows you could ever believe you guilty of anything so monstrous as killing the child. Our own daughter would never think it for a single instant.'

'Someone has accused me by leaving her body in our yard,' he said, his voice muffled.

'There is someone here who is mad. That is all. Soon he will be found and hanged.'

'Nicky, you must be ready to leave,' he said, withdrawing from her embrace and gazing up into her eyes.

'Nonsense! We have friends here,' she scolded mildly. 'They would not let us down.'

'This is England, Nick, not France. Here the powerful make the decisions and the peasants have to agree. If the Reeve decides it's in his interests to convict me, I'm dead. You heard Batyn just now. He was warning us. We have to go.'

'Perhaps your brother might help us?'

'Him?' Thomas gave a short laugh. 'Nicky, if you think Ivo would lift a finger to help me, you're mad.'

She frowned slightly at his words. 'What do you mean?'

'After he tried to tempt you from me last time, we argued. Well, we fought. I struck him down and told him that if I ever met him here in Sticklepath again, I'd kill him. There's no possibility that he'd try to save me.'

It was fortunate that Thomas was staring out through the open doorway as he said this, for otherwise he must have seen her face.

On it was printed a terrible resolution.

Ivo wouldn't help them because he was jealous of Tom, mainly jealous of Tom owning her, she thought. But perhaps Ivo would help save him if Nicole was his reward. If she offered to sleep with him, Ivo might be willing to forget his enmity.

Prison was a terrible place. When her father was alive, she had visited gaols with him, and she had no illusions about them. Gaols were filthy, festering places, filled with rats, lice, fleas and death. Men who went inside hale and strong came out wizened, pale and bent, or dead. Thomas was a man who loved the elements. He worked hard in wind and rain, and enjoyed labour in the open air. To throw him into a cell beneath a castle would destroy him as surely as a knife-thrust in the heart.

Compared with his safety, nothing mattered. If it would save him from gaol, Nicole would even submit to Ivo.

Gervase returned, wiping his mouth with his sleeve. 'I'm sorry, Lordings,' he gulped. 'I knew the poor child was dead, but to die and then be violated . . . and in such a way. My God! Only the arch-enemy of God could conceive of such a foul transgression. It's appalling.'

Baldwin eyed his ravaged features dispassionately. 'Perhaps, but I have less faith in human nature than you. I think that men are perfectly capable of such evil.'

'The poor child.'

'We have been told her father was Ansel de Hocsenham,' Simon commented.

'Yes,' Gervase swallowed. 'He's dead. He was a local fellow, Ansel, from out beyond South Zeal. He was a King's Purveyor, and often had to ride out over the country.'

'What happened to him?' Coroner Roger snapped.

'He rode off one day during the famine, and that was that. It was the year before the death of Peter atte Moor's daughter, Denise. Never turned up again.' Gervase wiped at his brow with the palm of his hand and shook his head. He stood and motioned vaguely towards the house. 'Would you care for some drink? I have some wine, a loaf. It would be sufficient for us, I am sure.'

'It is most kind of you,' Baldwin said with a gracious inclination of his head, 'but I am neither hungry nor thirsty.'

'I am,' said the Coroner hurriedly.

Gervase gave him a pale grin, then wandered back inside his house.

'Look at this place!' Baldwin said. 'What a miserable hovel. One room only, in which he must eat, work and sleep, and this little garden where he might be fortunate enough to grow some peas and beans, were he to bother trying.'

'If the river hadn't risen and washed them all away,' Simon agreed, eyeing the few straggling plants which had survived. 'But it's no worse than thousands of other parsons' dwellings up and down the country. And provided that he performs the daily Chantry, he will always have money and some food. Probably a new tunic each year, too.'

'And yet he seems relatively well educated,' Coroner Roger mused. 'Why should a man with a brain wish to come to a dump like this?'

'It isn't that bad,' Simon protested. 'And there's nothing wrong with a priest who wants to serve his community.'

'No,' the Coroner agreed, 'but there's something wrong with a man who invests all his wealth in wine and regularly drinks himself into a stupor.'

'Perhaps last night was a rare occurrence.'

'And perhaps I was born a Moor,' Baldwin said. 'Didn't you see the state of his rushes, couldn't you *smell* the vomit? It is days since he cleaned in there. No, this man has his own guilty secret.'

Gervase soon returned, bearing a jug in one fist, a platter with three irregular sized pots on it and a large loaf. He spoke a short prayer in thanks, then sat, pulling the loaf into chunks and pouring wine for them. Then he sat back, chewing and slurping.

'This Ansel. His wife doesn't live in the vill?' Coroner Roger prompted.

Gervase felt the cold grip of fear grasp at his bowels. 'They were not married. I fear he was one of those men who sought their pleasures here on earth instead of the enlightened attitude which looks to the life to come. No, he was not very religious.'

'In out of the way places, not many are,' Baldwin noted reasonably. 'Where is the mother, then?'

'Meg is touched, and more than a little insane since her brother died, God bless him, in a terrible fire in their cottage.' He studied the bread in his hand and bit off a chunk, chewing it dry. 'Meg saw him die and it addled her brains. People about here call her "Mad Meg" now.'

'*Where?*' Coroner Roger demanded, his patience run out.

'She inhabits a place in the wood out to the west of the vill. A small assart, which her brother worked for her.'

'She was local?' Simon pressed.

'Not really, no. She was from up aways, round Exbourne. She and her brother came here after he had fought with the King in France and made himself some money. When he came back, he used his money to buy the plot from Lord Hugh.'

'When would all this have been?' Baldwin enquired.

'He died in the famine. Shortly after Denise had been found.'

'After her man disappeared?' Coroner Roger asked.

'Yes. Ansel disappeared in 1315, while her brother died in 1316, just before Mary died.'

'Ah, Mary!' Simon said. 'We have heard a little about her. She was an orphan?'

Gervase bent his head in assent.

'Did she die the same way?' Baldwin demanded. 'Throttled and eaten?'

'May God take her to His breast and comfort her, yes,' the Parson said, closing his eyes as the vision rose before his eyes. 'The little child had her legs cut away, as though someone had . . .

as you would a haunch of venison. I can still see her poor little face. She was such a sweet, kindly little girl. No one deserves that sort of death. It was an obscene attack: a violation! Hideous.'

'You buried her?'

'Of course. And there is never a day I don't go out there and pray for her. I love children, just as Our Lord did, if you know your Gospels, Sir Knight.'

'Except you never reported her death, did you?' Coroner Roger rumbled.

Gervase looked away, but Baldwin was frowning. 'This brother. What was he named?'

Gervase felt the clamminess at his palms as he took up his cup and took a deep draught. It served to soothe his spirits, and as he put the cup back down, he could say without a tremor in his voice, 'Just some fellow called Athelhard.'

'And you say he too is dead? In a fire?'

'Yes.'

'An accident?'

'I can tell you no more. I'm bound by secrecy and the secrets are not mine to divulge. Only let me say that I may have inflamed them, and I am heartily sorry. I feel my guilt most terribly.'

'Damn this!' Coroner Roger roared with frustration. 'I need answers, Priest! Who can answer if you won't?'

'I *can't*. I am tied. Why not speak to Mad Meg – she may be able to help.'

'Is there nothing you can tell us?' Baldwin asked, his tone more gentle.

Gervase looked into his dark, intense eyes and found himself wavering. 'I can't tell you secrets told to me under the oaths of the confessional, Sir Knight. All I can say is, I heard that Athelhard shouted out a curse before he died. A terrible curse, one which still stalks the vill even now, six years later.'

Chapter Eighteen

'This is maddening. There is a secret in this vill, I am sure of it,' Baldwin said bitterly as they left the Parson's place. 'Look at that fellow's attitude in there. Did you see how he reacted when I asked about this man Athelhard? He almost chewed through his cup!'

'You're reading too much into it,' the Coroner protested. 'There may be some secret, but it's probably just that they've been holding back on some of their grain, trying to conceal it from Lord Hugh, or perhaps it's avoidance of the tithes or some other tax. There are always secrets in little vills like this. They have to struggle hard enough just to survive, God knows, and you can't blame them for keeping a bit back for themselves.'

'My Heavens! And this is the terror of Exeter talking?'

'There's no call for sarcasm. I'm only pointing out that there could be a perfectly innocent explanation.'

'Let us find this woman Meg and see what she thinks,' Baldwin decided.

'We need to talk to the other child as well,' said Simon. 'The girl called Joan, whom I saw returning from the moors on the day of the inquest.'

'Perhaps,' Baldwin said, 'but later. She can wait. Let's see this Meg first.'

'Very good,' Coroner Roger agreed, but as he spoke he stumbled on a dried rut, and his ankle turned painfully. 'Ach! Christ Jesus! My leg.'

'You cannot walk down the lane,' Baldwin observed.

'Christ's bones, trust this to happen.'

'Do you want me to help you back to the inn?' Simon asked.

'No. I can manage,' the Coroner said. 'Thanks all the same.' He pointed to a tree. 'Bring me a branch and I will be fine. I'll get back to the inn, you two go ahead without me.'

'If you're sure,' said Simon. The inn wasn't that far away, fortunately. He hurried to cut a stave.

Baldwin lent Roger his shoulder while they waited, but his thoughts were not with the Coroner. Since hearing that Mad Meg lived out at the western tip of the vill in her own assart, Baldwin had wanted to go there and talk to her. He felt a curious certainty that if he could visit the place with the level-headed Simon, he would be able to confront his dream head-on and reduce the potency of his fear. Somehow his dream had grown more virulent here, as though something in the vill associated itself with his own dark past and drew upon his own guilt and secrets. It was foolish thinking, immature and irrational, which irritated him beyond belief, but as Simon passed the stick to the Coroner, he felt relieved that he and Simon would continue alone.

Once Roger was gone, hobbling slowly back to the inn, the two approached the spring. Baldwin could not help his steps from faltering. A fine sweat broke out upon his forehead and back, but there was no heat. He felt stony cold as he stared down the track between the trees. Aylmer stopped at his side and looked up into his face.

Simon, of course, could see nothing. For all his superstition, he was quite insensitive. He peered down the trackway. 'You think this is the road, then?'

Baldwin said nothing, merely moved on along the track, his own sense of foreboding growing as he let himself slip under the shadow of the trees. He felt like Orpheus entering the Underworld.

Still in his garden, Gervase felt dread overwhelming him. He knew that the three men who had visited would not be content with half truths for long. The knight in particular had a peculiarly intent gaze, as though he could see right through a man's deceits to the filth and lies that had held him together all his life. Talking to him had been difficult, like confessing to a foul deed before a Bishop, but there had not been the slightest hint of Absolution at the end of it. He had not confessed with honesty, he had concealed more than he had admitted. It would remain on his conscience until somehow he let it out. And yet he couldn't.

He wanted to cry, to bawl his head off, to admit his crimes and receive some form of penance, but he knew that he must wear the mask of an ordinary village Parson. Only a few knew his guilt, and they knew because of their complicity.

If he could, he would give all his wealth, such as it was, to bring back that life. He was a sinner, for he had murdered. Doubly a sinner, for he had withheld the extreme unction and *viaticum.* He had knowingly condemned a man to Purgatory or Hell, thinking he was guilty of murder, but now the real killer had struck again.

The thought forced him to close his eyes and weep. It was unbearable, this guilt. Maddening and incurable. Perhaps he should travel to Exeter, confess his crimes to the Bishop, admit all that he had done and wait to hear what penance he would receive. At least then there would be an end to it, although he might well be condemned to a monastery hundreds of miles away, to spend the rest of his days in silence, without the solace even of sunlight playing on flowers, of the feeling of warmth on his back. Even the simple delight of standing in a summer's shower would be lost to him for ever.

He stood, feeling suddenly ancient, and walked through his house. Shutting the door behind him, he went over the road to his chapel and entered it, genuflecting to the altar, before which lay the body of young Emma. Two women sat beside her, and he recognised them as Gunilda and her daughter, Felicia. They were holding vigil. Gervase nodded to them, then approached the altar himself. He knelt, pressed his palms together in the modern way and begged for forgiveness.

It was unsatisfying. There was no relief for him in prayer. There never was, not since his realisation of his guilt. That recognition had so devastated him that his faith had suffered accordingly. Now he hardly knew the right words to use, as though God had taken them from him, as though God was Himself disgusted and wanted nothing more to do with him.

He heard steps and the door shutting. Looking over his shoulder he saw that Felicia had left, and now only Gunilda sat, rocking gently by the side of Emma's corpse.

'It's all right, Father,' she said. 'He'll not want any more.'

The woman was plainly losing her mind. Her sanity, which Gervase doubted had ever been better than fragile, was shattered. He tried to sound comforting. 'That's good.'

'You think I'm talking rubbish, don't you?' she smiled. 'But Samson won't come back now. This was the last one he fancied. He'll leave the others in peace.'

Gervase was tempted to point out that her husband was dead, but his tongue clove to his palate in sympathy at her ravings.

'He got Aline pregnant, you know. He loved her, I think. And Felicia, too, but she was lucky and miscarried. It would have been difficult for me if she'd gone to term. But Aline, she was scared. I think Samson thought she might go to her father. Swet would have been very angry if he'd learned that Samson had molested her, wouldn't he?'

Gervase felt his belly contract at her words. Surely she was wrong. She must have told someone if she had known about her man's raping of young girls. Nobody could stand by and permit such a heinous crime, could they?

He was grateful to be interrupted by Felicia returning. Patting Gunilda's hand, he stood. She hardly appeared to notice, as though she had already forgotten he was there, and he walked from the chapel, going into the cemetery to seek peace. The sun was lower in the west now, and he stood watching it move towards Tongue

End, musing on the evil that there was in the world. When he continued walking, his sandal was loose, and he irritably scuffed it against the ground. The sole came loose and he stamped his foot in anger. It was as if even his footwear was conspiring to make life difficult.

And it was then, as he stifled his cursing, that he heard the low, doleful wail coming from beneath him; from beneath the soil, from the grave itself, and he gave a short shriek of horror, walking backwards, his gaze fixed in terror at the ground.

The truth was forced upon him. God sought to punish him, the vill, everyone, for their evil: the curse was returned to life!

'No! God, please, no!' he whispered. At that moment the hounds began to howl again, and he felt his bowels loosen as though filled with water. A primeval horror rose and engulfed him, making him gibber, and then he turned and ran from that hideous place, over the road to the security of his own house and his wine.

Only later did he realise he had bolted past the open door to his chapel and the safety that the cross should have offered him, and that realisation made him weep still more bitterly. His soul was taken by demons, and now it must be tormented for all eternity in hellfire. Even the cross couldn't give him solace.

He was lost.

Thomas walked from his house with the feeling that everyone was watching him, although whenever he turned and peered at the houses all about him, he could see no one.

His sow, his pride and joy, was in her yard, enclosed by a solid wall and well-constructed hurdles which she could have pushed over if she had a will, but she was ever a calm, mild-mannered creature, and never bothered. Thomas walked to her and stood leaning on the wall a while, watching her as she snuffled her way through the thick straw piled high all about her. She at least looked unconcerned by accusations or possible trials. All she cared about was the next meal. It was a simple life, one which today Thomas could envy.

The body was gone. That was a blessing, although from the clouds of flies which rose and swarmed about the straw, there was still plenty of Emma's blood about the place. The corpse had been taken away and was even now probably being bathed and wrapped in her winding sheet. In this heat the vill would want her in her grave as quickly as possible, and since her father was long gone and her mother was insane, there was no need to worry about the family's wishes.

She was the last of her father's line. It was a poignant idea, that the youngest member of a family should die and be found in so undignified a manner, lying half concealed in an outbuilding. It made him consider Joan. If he were to be accused in court and convicted, for he had no faith in his neighbours after this morning's display, then what would happen to his little girl? On a busy road like this, there would be bound to be plenty of felons, draw-latches and thieves who would be interested in a girl like her.

Nicole would do all she could to protect their child, but her own life would become unbearable after Thomas had died. He had seen too many other widows in vills like this for him to harbour false hopes. It would only take one man to decide that she wanted him after he had spent an afternoon on the ale, for him to rape her. And soon the news would spread that she was 'begging for it, desperate, she was, without a man for so long. Give her one for me . . .' Oh yes, Thomas had heard it all before. There had been subtle variations on the same theme when he had married Nicky to protect her from the families of her father's victims.

Rape wasn't unknown. It was rarely appealed in court, for the woman must demonstrate that she had suffered, and that meant displaying her torn and bloodied garments, and stripping to prove that she had been evilly used. Not many women would willingly go through that.

He tried to force the ideas from his mind, walking out to the roadway again.

'So, brother, you may go to gaol soon.'

'Ivo!' Thomas breathed. 'Have you come to gloat?'

'No, not gloat. I merely wanted to see where the murderer lived. You know, I hadn't realised you could do something like that. Killing her, yes, raping her, of course, poor child. But eating her? That seems to have shocked even your neighbours here, surprisingly. I'd have thought that the folks here would be fairly stolid, but they seem perfectly stunned at your behaviour.'

'I've done nothing wrong. I never touched Emma.'

'Come, brother, you don't have to lie to me! Was she sweet and willing? Or did you have to force her?' Ivo asked. He held a long staff in his hand, and he leaned on it to smile lecherously at Thomas.

'By God's grace, shut up.'

'Threats again? That's one way of convincing everyone that you're innocent, I suppose, although I'd have thought it preferable to maintain a dignified calmness.'

'Be silent, Ivo!' Thomas noticed a movement out of the corner of his eye, and looked up to meet Joan's appalled gaze.

'Perhaps you think that I would be easy too, like that little girl? Is that it? I am only a clerk, when all is said and done. A Manciple has no military training, after all. I should be easy for a hulking great peasant like you to overwhelm. Just like a little girl. I hope you found her satisfying. It's a shame that your wife can't satisfy you any more, but I suppose even you learned that a hangman's daughter is not the tastiest morsel. Strange. She looked attractive enough when I first saw her and lay with her, but now I don't think I'd want to touch her with your staff, brother, let alone my own.'

Thomas forgot his daughter as the angry flush coloured his cheeks. 'You have never lain with my wife, you lying bastard!'

'Ah, she didn't want you to know. Perhaps the comparison did not favour you! But yes, I had her three times that first time I came through here after you returned from France. In the one day. You were out working, and – well, so was I in my own way. Ha! But she lacks a certain something, doesn't she? In the bed. Enthusiastic, but not satisfying.'

With a growl low in his throat, Thomas felt the rage wash over and smother him. It was enough. The taunts had served to flare his frustration and fear into flames of rage, and as he looked at Ivo, there was a red mist, as though there was a fine spray of blood between them. Thomas leaped for him, grabbing for Ivo's long robe, even as his brother gave a short squeak of alarm and bolted up the road.

Thomas didn't hesitate. He gave chase, reaching with his long arms for the flapping material before him, and as they reached the Reeve's house, he caught it. Snatching it quickly, he stopped his brother in his tracks.

Ivo scarcely knew what had happened to him. In an instant he had been halted by an immovable force that reached about his shoulders. He felt like a horse he had once seen, which had been pulling a heavy cart up a track, when a wheel had collapsed. The horse had been going along smartly, and the shock of suddenly halting had caused it to collapse in a heap on the track.

He didn't intend copying it. Thrusting an arm backwards, he let the cloth fall from him, then gripped his staff in that hand while letting the other sleeve loose. Before his brother could grab at him, he shot off again.

Thomas was caught off balance. He gazed blankly at the stuff in his hands for a moment before balling it and hurling it from him with a snarl and setting off again after his brother.

Ivo had a head start and made good use of it. He turned a corner past the inn and hared down into the pasture bounding the river. Ivo was already almost halfway along towards the river, and he cast a glance over his shoulder as Thomas started to catch up with him.

Ivo had wanted to rouse his brother, but he hadn't expected the mad bastard to take off so quickly. Thomas looked so slow, with his dim expression and dull eyes, Ivo had felt safe, but Thomas had managed to spring forward like some sort of cat as soon as his restraint was gone. Ivo had expected him to snap, but he had miscalculated, thinking he could lead Tom back up towards the Reeve's house where he could have him arrested for being a danger to all, but the speed of Tom's attack had thrown him completely. Instead he had run straight past the Reeve's place not daring to pause, and now he was in the open land behind the tavern. There was no one here, no one to whom he could appeal for help. As he ran he cursed his decision to taunt and insult Tom, but the idea had seemed too good. Little brother Tom was always swift to rise to the bait and Ivo wanted to show him to be dangerous so that he would be imprisoned – and then he could have a free hand with little Nicky.

Oh God, Nicky! She was so beautiful. A peach. She would grace any bed, with her calm eyes and rich, comfortable body. Her accent itself was enough to excite Ivo, with that soft, nasal French of hers. Ivo had fancied her with a chronic desire ever since that first time he had met her, when little brother Tom introduced them, and the desire hadn't gone away. He hadn't really slept with her, of course, that was a lie, but it seemed to have worked – rather too well.

He glanced over his shoulder, only to see that his brother was gaining on him. With a squeak of panic, Ivo tried to force himself forwards with a little more speed, but at his belly was the early cramp of a stitch, and his chest felt ready to explode. Little sparks flared and glowed in front of his eyes, and he could feel his feet growing heavier, as though there was lead in them. In a vain attempt to speed his flight, he threw away his staff, the only defence he had.

Perhaps it helped a little, but soon he could hear Thomas's stertorous breath behind him again and knew he must be caught.

Swiftly he darted right, back towards the chapel. He daren't look over his shoulder, but an explosive grunt told him all he needed to know: Tom had grabbed for him and missed. In doing so, he'd continued onwards, unable to turn to follow Ivo.

Ivo saw that there was a small group of men standing up near the cookshop by the tavern. He set his feet for them, praying that he might reach sanctuary with them.

'Stop, you evil shit!'

Tom's voice sounded as ragged and worn as that of a man who had run a ten-mile course, and it lent Ivo a fresh spurt of energy. In a few moments, he had broken in among the waiting men. 'He's gone mad!' he panted, gripping one man by the shoulder as he bent almost double. 'He wants to kill me! Call for the Reeve.'

'He taunted me! Told me he'd slept with my wife!' Thomas roared.

'Is that true, Bel?'

The flat, uncompromising tone was familiar. Ivo looked up into Henry Batyn's unsympathetic face. William Taverner stood at his side with Edgar, and all eyed him coldly while Ivo tried to gather his breath. 'Help me, save me!' he managed.

Batyn pushed Ivo from him, and watched Thomas approach, flexing his fists. 'It's not right for brothers to fight like this.'

Thomas grated, 'This is between us. If you don't like it, don't watch.'

'He wants to kill me!' Ivo squealed.

'He said that three times he cuckolded me! Would you tolerate that? I warned him, but he wouldn't shut up.'

'You'll be breaking the King's Peace,' Taverner said, but there was a tone of excitement in his voice.

'Leave us alone. We won't upset anyone else,' Thomas promised, trying to grab his brother again.

'Wait, both of you,' Batyn said, and ran lightly to his house. He soon reappeared, carrying two long staves. Throwing one to each, he stood back. 'If you're serious, use these. At least you're less likely to kill each other than you would be with knives.'

Ivo clutched his staff desperately. He hadn't used one in years
and wasn't sure he could remember how to – there was skill in
using the stances and defences. Thomas looked as though he
hadn't used one for an age either. He stood holding it in one hand
as though he was expecting to use it as a lance and was only
waiting for a horse to carry him. Then, to Ivo's faint surprise, he
set it down and began to take off his shirt, pulling it from him and
throwing it against the cookshop's wall. Finally he picked up his
staff and, holding it before him, he pointed it at Ivo and advanced
slowly.

He had no choice. Ivo grabbed his own staff and knocked away
Thomas's as it poked towards his face, then his belly, before
swinging in low at his legs. Ivo retreated, but almost fell when his
ankle turned on a loose stone.

Immediately Thomas swung back at his legs and Ivo felt the
material of his hose rip as a splinter caught. He roared as the blunt
end of the pole thudded into his thigh and then scraped all the
way down his leg, taking his woollen hose with it. It was all he
could do to stay on his feet.

'Sweet Jesus!' he whimpered.

'*He* won't save you,' Thomas hissed.

He thrust again, and Ivo felt the wood strike his breast. This
time he was slammed down onto his back, the breath knocked
from him, and he saw Edgar hold Thomas back until he was on
his feet again. As soon as he was up, Edgar stood back again and
Ivo saw the thick pole aiming at his face. He managed to block
the main blow, but it came down and thudded into his shoulder
and he cried out with the shock. Suddenly his hand felt weakened,
and he couldn't keep a firm hold of his own weapon.

With the next attack, his staff was knocked aside with contempt-
uous ease, and Ivo felt the same raking pain as the point tore
down his shirt, ruining it. He tried to retaliate, swinging his own
heavy staff at Thomas's head, but his blow was too puny and

Thomas merely swept the stave away with a swing of his forearms, and then gripped it in his fist and pulled.

Ivo's arms were outstretched, his pole useless at his fullest reach, and he was unbalanced. When he saw his brother yank on his staff, he realised he was too late. Thomas slid his hands along his stave, gripping it like a quarterstaff, and brought the butt around. Ivo tried to bring his own pole back to parry, but he was already too late, and at the last moment, as he saw Thomas's staff thrusting towards his nose, he closed his eyes.

There was nothing else he could do.

Chapter Nineteen

Baldwin shivered as they walked along the path. It was cold and miserable down here, as though they had left the summer weather and found themselves in a moorland winter. He almost expected to see snow at his feet when he glanced at his boots, but although there was the sound of crunching, it came from the leaves and twigs which lay all about, not from ice. The only other sound was Aylmer's panting.

'Are you all right, Baldwin?'

'Why should I not be?' he snapped. 'I am sorry, Simon. It is just that I have been here before.'

'Oh?' the Bailiff said unemotionally.

Baldwin didn't answer the unspoken question. To speak of his dream would be embarrassing, and he was in no mood for a confession, especially one of superstition.

They carried on down the lane. The woods were thick on their left, with the undergrowth making them appear impassable. Aylmer went and sniffed at various scents where animals had passed. Once more the dog appeared unconcerned.

'You're sure that she will be down here?' Simon asked.

Baldwin continued as though he hadn't heard. He could remember every stage of this path, even though he had only come down here the once. It was as though it was ingrained upon his memory; he could almost smell the place where he had seen the figure at the tree, and his feet unconsciously slowed as they approached.

'Wait!' he whispered. It was there, a tang of woodsmoke on the air, with a faint scent of burning flesh: sweet and slightly gamey.

It made Baldwin's stomach turn, reminding him too distinctly of the time when the pyres were lit and the living Templars were bound to their posts, praying, weeping, cursing and choking in the fumes as the flames licked higher and higher about their legs. Later, when the men were dead, this same odour lingered about the place.

Simon gave Baldwin a curious look. To his eyes, the knight was acting most peculiarly today, and never more so than now. Simon had never known his friend to give the slightest indication of nerves, especially when it came to his personal safety, so seeing him like this was unsettling, particularly when there was nothing for him to be anxious about. The place was clear.

He looked past Baldwin to Mad Meg's home. It looked much like any other assart, if more dilapidated and worn. There was a stone-walled cottage with new thatch on the roof sitting in its own clearing. In front was a fire with a trivet and pot standing over it, while chickens strolled and pecked at the dirt, one or two gazing at Aylmer with alarm.

There was nothing for the knight to be worried about, and Simon wondered what could have driven his friend to this state of concern. For there was no doubting Baldwin's anxiety as he stared at the scene.

'This is stupid,' he muttered.

'What is it, Baldwin?'

'I . . . When I walked here the other day, it reminded me of another time,' he said evasively. 'Yet now I can see nothing to make me feel panic.'

He didn't add that there was no sign of the figure he had seen standing at the tree. Instead he took a deep breath and climbed up over the wall, marching to the fire. 'Hello? Meg? Are you here?'

'No, she isn't.'

'Serlo!' Baldwin breathed. 'We thought to come and ask her a few questions.'

Serlo had been at the edge of the assart. Now he stepped

forward to tend the cooking fire. 'Why can't you leave her in peace?'

'Because the priest suggested we should talk to her,' Simon said.

'That drunken fool! So what if he does?'

Baldwin walked to Serlo's side. 'Have you heard about Emma?'

Serlo paled. 'Emma? What is it? My Christ! Is she dead?'

'The same as the others,' Baldwin said. 'I am sorry.'

Serlo stood. 'Come with me,' he said.

Joan clapped her hands in delight as soon as her father bolted after Ivo, and she felt a cruel thrill to see how close he came to catching her uncle. She hated Ivo. She had heard his taunts, and the viciousness of his words had torn at her.

Her mother would never have done such a thing. It was wicked even to suggest it. Ivo had just said it to be intentionally hurtful. As the men disappeared around the inn, she was tempted to follow and watch, but today it didn't seem right. Not with Emma dead.

It was hard to believe. Emma was such a part of her whole life, it was impossible to conceive of being without her. In one short year Joan had lost her worst enemy, old Ham when he drowned, and now she had lost her best friend. Poor Emma. Joan hoped she hadn't been put through much pain. Who could have dropped her in the yard like that?

She walked slowly along the road. It would have been fun to see her father pound Ivo into the ground, but not today. She was perpetually on the brink of tears, ready to weep at a moment's notice. Serlo would want to hear from her, and she was tempted to go on up to the warrens to talk to him, because he always listened and treated the girls like adults, not silly children, but the thought of climbing all the way up to his hut was daunting on her own.

Sitting on a rock at the side of the road, she felt the trickling of tears again. Poor Emma. She'd been a good friend.

There was a pattering of feet, then harsh shouts, and a curious, nasal voice bellowing. Looking up, she saw Ivo, a bloody rag held to his nose, while two men laughed at his side. Behind was her father, walking stiffly with William Taverner and Swetricus beside him. The little procession passed over the roadway and went into the Reeve's house. Intrigued, Joan stood up and crossed the road. She was just in time to hear her father shouting something, then the low rumble of Alexander's voice.

'Stick him in the cellar and lock him in. Don't let the murderous bastard escape.'

Jeanne's nagging fear hadn't left her, and hearing that Emma had died didn't help. She had tried to busy herself with the mundane tasks of feeding and changing Richalda, helping Petronilla remove the bedclothes and beat the sheets and rugs outside to remove as many bedbugs and lice as possible. Returning to the room, they set down the bedclothes and carried out the palliasse itself to be beaten. When that was done, they found that a dog with an incessant scratch had taken up residence in their blankets, and Petronilla had to kick the thing from the room so that they could take the blankets back outside to beat them again.

It wasn't easy for Jeanne to concentrate. She could sense a breathlessness in her that didn't come from the air outside. Rather it seemed to come from within her, a heaviness of spirit. She was convinced that there was some evil at work in the vill, and she looked down at her baby with a feeling of doom.

She had to get out of the chamber, so she took a walk to the tavern's hall. Edgar had returned after witnessing a small fight, he said, and he followed in her wake, ordering wine for her and standing nearby while she drank it.

The place was deserted. Earlier, men had come in for thin ale to keep them going through the morning, but now all were out in the fields, and none would return until the sun had sunk low in the sky. Jeanne's mood was not improved by the oppressive silence about her. Smoke from the damp logs in the fire made the place dingy and unwholesome, and she felt her spirits fall still further. This melancholy was a new experience for her. Even when she was younger and had been married to that jealous bully of a husband, Sir Ralph de Liddinstone, who had taken to insulting her before his friends and servants and then beating her because she could not bear him children, she had not felt this bad. She had been strong, and his treatment of her only raised in her a reciprocal contempt, then hatred. When he died she had felt some guilt, as though the strength of her own loathing could have contributed to his death, but that soon faded when she met Baldwin at Tavistock Abbey.

There were some ridiculous women who talked of love at first sight. Jeanne was not prepared to believe in such nonsense, for she was a modern woman, and knew that for all the chivalrous ideals, very few men or women behaved chastely, and the best excuse for drunken lechery was instant love. Jeanne was happier to call lust by its own name, but for all that when she had first met Sir Baldwin there had been something, a mutual attraction, as though both knew of the other's sufferings in the previous few years, she with her abhorrent husband, he with the persecution that followed on from the end of the Templars. She had felt as though she had at last met a man who could understand her.

It was this which made his cynicism about her impressions of danger all the more hurtful. She knew all too well that he was a resolutely logical man, but she would have hoped that he might have listened to her a little more closely.

'Edgar, I shall walk in the air a while,' she said. 'This room is choking me!'

'Very well.'

'You can go back to Petronilla.'

'I think I should remain with you, my Lady.'

She smiled up at him, shaking her head. 'There's no need, and you've had no time together since we got here. Go to her.'

He was reluctant, but after a little persuading, he agreed,

provided that she promised not to wander far.

It was an easy promise to make. The place was hardly welcoming, what with the mud and filth all about. Two dogs were fighting in a space between two cottages as she left the inn, although when they saw her, they slunk away into the shadows beneath a cart.

Sticklepath held nothing to attract her. The place was ugly and inhospitable. In fact, she regretted her decision to come here with Baldwin now. Although she would have hated to leave him to travel here alone, when he still hadn't recovered from his injuries, she was terrified that whatever was here might affect her daughter. Richalda was too important for her to want to risk the baby's life or well-being.

She shivered slightly at the sight of the priest up at the edge of the vill. He was leaning against a tree, wiping at his face as though to clear away sweat. Rather than go and speak to him, Jeanne turned away and walked towards the ford.

It was peaceful here. There was an old tree stump near the river itself, and she sat upon it, gazing into the water. Here at the boundary of the vill, she already felt a little happier, as though simply being on the road that would lead her homewards was itself enough to reassure her.

In the distance she heard hooves in the clear, still air and wondered who would be travelling along here today. Probably a tranter or carter of some sort, carrying fish or wine to the monks of Tavistock or even the nuns at Belstone. With the sun on her back warming her and gleaming in bright sparks on the water, it was hard to maintain her fear, and she began to feel a comfortable languor overtaking her. Gradually the water's sound and the light playing over its surface induced a pleasant drowsiness. The voice startled her when it spoke.

'My Lady, I am pleased to meet you again.'

Jolting to full wakefulness, her hand went to her breast as if to catch her heart before it could leap from her ribs. 'Master Bel!' she gasped.

'Oh, I am sorry. I worried you, didn't I?'

He was apparently attempting to soothe her, but his voice, now nasal and phlegmatic from the terribly broken nose that spread across his face like a flattened beetroot, failed to calm her.

'What on earth has happened to you?' Jeanne said faintly.

Ivo gave a dry laugh, then winced as another bruise complained. 'It's that wretched brother of mine – he will lose his temper. I was talking to him, and he suddenly flew off the handle, grabbed a staff and set about me. The man's completely mad! Not that he'll do it again for a while.'

'Why?'

'He's being held by the Reeve. He'll be lucky to get out before the Justices visit next, from what I hear. Reeve Alexander is to have him taken to Exeter to the gaol there. Then he'll regret his lunacy. With luck the bastard will swing. I doubt he'll have enough money to save himself – *and I won't fucking help him.*'

The last words were spat with virulent passion, and Jeanne shivered. Suddenly all her concerns returned to haunt her. If a man could attack his brother, surely it must be something to do with the place itself? It was aberrant behaviour, as was Ivo's apparent glee at Thomas's plight. A desire for revenge was common enough, but such a passionate hatred for his own brother was hardly normal. No, it was Sticklepath. Making her excuses, Jeanne left him contemplating the waters and walked back to the vill.

It was when she was halfway to the inn that she heard the hooves again.

Turning, she was in time to catch a glimpse of a small cavalcade as it moved between the trees, coming towards the vill. It consisted of one man of rank on horseback and five men on foot, acting as his guards.

They reappeared through the trees only moments later, and Jeanne got a better look at them. The man in the lead was a short, but powerfully built fellow with a round face and smiling eyes.

He wore a hot-looking velvet tunic, a hood over his head against the sun, and rode a magnificent rounsey. He was clearly a knight, from his spurs to his finely decorated riding sword in its scabbard – the quality was demonstrated by the engraving and enamelling on the pommel. In his hand he dangled a war hammer, a vicious weapon with a two-inch-long spike behind the hammer head.

Marching behind him, Jeanne recognised Drogo the Forester and his men, with Miles Houndestail bringing up the rear. He looked hot and tired.

'My Lady,' the knight said, taking in the quality of her dress, 'do you live here?'

'No, I come from Cadbury,' she said. 'I am wife to Sir Baldwin Furnshill.'

'Ah, I have heard of him. I am Sir Laurence de Bozon, from Iddesleigh – I fear we have not met?'

'I regret no,' she said, smiling when he bowed gracefully to her, never an easy feat for a man on horseback. She inclined her head. 'But I am sure that my husband will be pleased to meet you. We stay at the inn over there.'

'I shall look forward to seeing you both there,' Sir Laurence said courteously. 'First, alas, I have business to attend to with the Reeve of this place. Forester, which is his house?'

Drogo stepped forward, puffing a little. Jerking his chin, he said, 'It is that one, the one opposite the tavern.'

'I thank you. No hurry, then. My Lady, are you journeying far?'

'No farther,' Jeanne smiled. 'We are here to help the Coroner with an inquest. My husband is a Keeper of the King's Peace.'

'There is more trouble here?'

'There has been murder.'

'Well, my Heavens. It is terrible that there could be another death in a little place like this, isn't it, Forester? I trust there will be no more.' Sir Laurence laughed, but his amusement didn't strike Jeanne as genuine.

The reaction of the men about him also struck her as interesting. Drogo's features were bleak, Vincent Yunghe was sternly solemn, while Peter atte Moor was oddly excited, licking his lips and finding it difficult to keep still as though he was keen to get something done. Adam was the only one among them who looked unaffected by Sir Laurence's presence. All appeared to think that the knight's meeting with the Reeve would have dire consequences, although whether they were consequences only for the Reeve or for the whole vill she couldn't tell.

'I hope there will be no more violence too, my Lord,' she said. 'What are you here for, may I ask? It is rare to see so many guards about a lone knight.'

'Ah, these good Foresters are here to help me with my work and protect my body from attack, my Lady,' Sir Laurence chuckled. 'I am the King's Purveyor and I'm here to collect money or grain to help provision the King's host as he makes it ready to do battle in Scotland again. I sent for them from South Zeal.'

Jeanne smiled politely, but she was aware that this elegant man in his sweat-stained suit wearing that easy smile would be one of the most loathed men who could have arrived in any vill, let alone one which had already been so scarred by famine, murrain and murder.

'You think I could be in danger, my Lady?' Sir Laurence said, seeing her face. He continued, overruling her protestations, 'This is why I come with men. The last Purveyor for the King to come down this way disappeared, apparently.' He stared at Miles thoughtfully. 'At the time some thought he had robbed the King and run away with the money.'

'But not now?'

He smiled again. 'I find it more sensible to keep an open mind, shall we say? And in the meantime, I suppose, I should be about my business.'

'Collecting money for the King?'

'Yes. Although,' he glanced about him with his lip curled, 'it is hard to imagine a place like this could afford much. What a miserable collection of hovels!'

Jeanne didn't admit to sharing his scorn, and when she saw Drogo's hurt expression, she was glad. No man should insult another's home without reason.

Nicole Garde sat heavily on her stool and stared at her daughter, dazed. 'Are you sure?'

Joan burst into floods of tears and her mother gathered her up in her arms and cooed gently to her, rocking her.

It felt as though her life had collapsed around her. Naturally, she had always known that the people of the vill resented her, that they distrusted her husband and shunned her daughter, but that they should suddenly move against her family was terrifying. It was worse, somehow, than the treatment she had received at home before her husband brought her here to this rural English backwater. At least she could comprehend the strange detestation she aroused in the breasts of the local peasants in the town where she was born. Here it was incomprehensible.

So, for breaking the King's Peace, Thomas had been imprisoned in the Reeve's house and would be transported to Exeter as soon as a small guard could be mustered. There he would have to wait until he could be seen by the Justices, and all the time he was in gaol, he must pay for his own food and drink.

Nicole would have to find some way of sending money to him, perhaps even leaving their home here and taking on work in Exeter. Any sort of work – although she knew that she was only qualified for the one profession, and her belly lurched at the thought of being forced to earn money by selling her body. It was one thing to consider allowing Ivo to make use of her, another entirely to think of drunken men pawing at her, fondling her breasts and reaching up under her skirts in a darkened alley. And what would happen to Joan?

She gave a dry, hacking sob. While she was in Exeter, the farm and their house would fall apart. They wouldn't be able to trust anyone to look after them, not if the whole vill thought that Thomas was a child-murderer.

Joan looked up at her. 'If I ever find out who killed Emma, I'll kill him,' she said passionately.

'You mustn't say that,' Nicole said, but her heart was breaking. 'What about Father?'

Nicole stood and took a deep breath. In her wooden chest was her second tunic, and she fetched it now. Shaking it out, she noticed holes, but it was mostly undamaged. With hesitant fingers, she untied her apron, then doffed her tunic. Her shirt beneath was dirty and darned, but she couldn't help that. She pulled the fresh tunic over her head, tying a clean apron about her waist. Then, before her resolve could leave her, she slipped her tippet over her shoulders, raised the hood over her head and strode out, leaving Joan alone.

In some curious way she had always felt that Alexander de Belston's house matched him. He was a large, rugged man, and the appearance of the place fitted him so perfectly that he might have been constructed of the same materials. The walls were of good moorstone, rendered with cob to fill all the cracks, and then limewashed. It was redone each year, and the brilliant white gleamed in the sunlight, looking pure and awesome, especially in comparison with the other dwellings, whose limewash was older, and flaked or smothered in green streaks. His thatch was patched each year, too, all the holes filled, the peak checked and re-covered, the whole mass patted and combed into shape. It wouldn't do for a man as important as the Reeve to let his standards slip. After all, Alexander de Belston was the Lord's own representative. He was the law: both judge and gaoler.

As was usual, his door stood open. There was nothing for a man of his position to fear from thieves or draw-latches. Nicole entered the gloomy interior, feeling the atmosphere within settle over her like a chill, damp cloak.

Lighted by a large window high in the wall, the smoke from the fire in the middle of the floor rose up like a fine mist, with tiny gleaming motes dancing in it all the way up to the ceiling of dried thatch high overhead, which was blackened by the smoke of decades.

Beyond the shafts of light from the window, Nicole could see the hulking figure of Alexander de Belston, sitting alone at his table on the dais, slowly twirling a cup of wine in his hand, one foot on the table, the other jiggling up and down with nervous energy.

'I was expecting you,' he said gruffly. 'You're here for Thomas.'

It was a statement, given with no apparent emotion, and all the woman could do was nod mutely.

'You know why he's in gaol?'

'No.'

'Didn't he tell you himself what he intended?'

'*Non*. Reeve, he told me nothing. There can be nothing for him *to* tell – he is a good man. Honourable. He is no criminal. Someone has lied about him to make you arrest him.'

'In truth?' Alexander said, but now his eyes had moved from her towards the window. The sunlight was fading as a cloud passed by, and Nicole could see the smoke disappear, only to re-emerge from the gloom as the sun returned. 'But I cannot let him free.'

'We have little money, but I could pay a fine to—'

'He had none this morning.' His teeth showed in a humourless smile. 'You think I want paying?'

'Hold him in mercy.'

'In mercy,' he repeated. 'You want him released in exchange for a surety he will turn up at the next court.'

'There is so much work to be done, sir. We need him.'

'He's in prison because he has broken the King's Peace, woman, and his brother's nose.'

She shivered, closed her eyes, and stepped forward slowly, her feet feeling as though they were made of lead. 'I will submit to you.'

'You will let me have you?' He gave a dry chuckle. 'Ah, my dear, you are tempting a man who has been lonely so long . . . My God, it would be good to lie with you. But you will expect me to release your husband afterwards. Well, I can't, maid. He's in gaol because he's been accused of attempting to kill his brother Ivo. And while there's a Coroner and a Keeper here, much though I would like to take you, I think it wouldn't be safe.'

Nicole gasped, her face reddening. 'Is there nothing I can do?' she asked, stepping forward, her hand reaching up to her laces and pulling. Her tunic fell away. She could see him watching her with sad interest while she let her shirt fall open.

He stared at her breasts, then lower. His smile broadened, but there was no amusement in it, only sadness.

'Cover yourself, please. I can't take advantage of you. I am finished if I let him go, and I am ruined if I don't. I don't need your temptations to make my choices any more difficult.' He motioned as if swatting a hand at a fly, and she slowly donned her clothes. With great dignity, she turned away from him and went into the road.

Only there could she give herself over to her grief, leaning against a tree, her heart thundering with fear.

Her nightmare had returned.

Chapter Twenty

'This is it,' Serlo said.

Baldwin and Simon looked about them. There was no dwelling here so far as they could see. They had climbed a little way up the hill from the clearing towards the Cornwall road, higher into the woods, but there appeared to be no house nearby. As Baldwin stared about them, all he could see was trees and a low wall some distance farther up the slope. Aylmer went and sniffed at it.

'She wouldn't come to live with me, even though she knew I would have protected her,' Serlo said gruffly. 'I think her man gave her enough of a clue about what men would do. Not that it stopped her that once.'

'You mean her daughter?' Baldwin asked. He was still gazing about him, trying to see where Meg could be living.

'Yeah. Poor child. She was a nice little thing, too. Chubby and cuddly, if you know what I mean. Never had an ill word for anyone, even though they shunned her. And why? All because her mother was looked on as mad, and probably a whore to boot.'

'Her father was a Purveyor, I hear.'

'That's right. Ansel, he was named. Evil bastard, he was, too. Took Meg when she was young and hadn't a clue. But men will take advantage in those circumstances. There's nothing you can do to stop it.'

'Where is she?' Baldwin asked.

'Sorry, I was forgetting.' Serlo walked to the wall where Aylmer stood, his head on one side. Where the wall met a tree, there was a thick growth of ivy, and the Warrener pushed it to one side. 'I'll fetch her.'

Baldwin could see that the ivy concealed the entrance to what looked like a tunnel.

Simon saw his enquiring gaze. 'There's plenty of tin and copper all over the moors. I expect this is the result of some man's effort to find a new source.'

'You're right,' Serlo said, reappearing. 'This was a little attempt to see if there might be copper. It failed. So many of the mining attempts always do. This is Meg.'

Behind him, he had pulled a woman. He held her by the forearm, as though she was unwilling to come out into the light, but also as though she was frail and needed his support.

Baldwin smiled at her. 'Meg? Is that your name?'

She was wearing the same hood, the same grey shreds and tatters, remnants of an ancient robe, as when he had first seen her in the forest. And as her head lifted slightly so that she could glance at him from under her hood, as though it was a defence against him and all other adult men, he saw the wide-set eyes, the round face, the small tip-tilted nose, and realised how ridiculous had been his terror. He held out a hand to her, to the little half-witted mother of the dead Emma.

Nicole was so overcome with misery that she didn't notice Sir Laurence and the Foresters until they had stopped at Alexander's house. It was only when Sir Laurence began to roar for a groom to tend his mount that she paid them attention, and seeing them at the Reeve's door, she hurried away, towards her house.

The first thing was food, she told herself. Her man would need food tonight, and then he'd need more to be able to travel all that way. He was viewed as a felon, so he'd be set in chains and forced to walk the whole way. No one would waste a steed on a man like him, so he'd have to make the best he could of it.

He'd need money to buy things as soon as he arrived: bread, some cheese. A little dried meat. Even the water would cost him dearly in gaol, and he must be able to afford it, or he might starve to death! She couldn't face the thought of life without him.

'Oh God in Heaven, how could You do this?' she murmured so quietly that no one could hear. 'I suffered for my father's sake in France, and now I must suffer for my husband's. You do to my daughter what You once did to me! How much misery should one woman suffer in her life?'

She had picked up her skirts now, and was hurtling headlong towards her house. Mud splashed from her bare feet, and she didn't care about the dung she stepped in, nor the pools of urine puddled at the side of the road where the oxen had waited for a few moments before being led to their pasture. She was blind to the Coroner as he limped from the tavern's door. He stood propped with his staff, one hand on a sapling, gazing down the road, and then he happened to glance in her direction. Seeing her coming straight at him, her head bent, he had time only to gape in horror before she pelted straight into him.

'Oof!' she exclaimed, and fell back to sit on her rump.

'Christ's ballocks!' the Coroner roared, clutching at his upper belly, where her arm had caught him. Dropping his stick, he stumbled backwards, and his foot caught on a loose stone, wrenching his ankle for a second time. 'God's bones! You stupid bitch! Can't you look where you're going?'

She gazed at him in horror. In her mind's eye she saw herself chained alongside her husband as they were led from the vill and into captivity. In her terror she was mute.

'Well?' he bellowed roughly, gripping the wall to hoist himself upright. 'Are you dumb, woman?'

Jeanne had witnessed the scene, and she joined the Coroner, who was trying to reach his prop. She passed it to him, then crouched at Nicole's side. 'Are you all right? You fell with quite a thump.'

'I . . . I am well, I thank you,' Nicole stammered, rising and wiping her filthy hands on her apron, then remembering that it was her cleanest apron and her best tunic, she burst into loud, gulping tears.

'Oh, sweet Jesus!' Coroner Roger sighed. He licked his lips and glanced guiltily at Jeanne.

She saw his look, but she was already helping the other woman. Putting a compassionate arm about her shoulders, she led the weeping peasant into the tavern.

Coroner Roger rubbed at his belly, shaking his head. The damn woman had almost winded him, he thought ruefully. He'd been going to speak to the Parson to see whether he could learn anything useful, not that he held out much hope. Priests were always tricky. Getting information from them was like getting a free meal out of a Winchester innkeeper. Now, however, he'd lost interest. The distance looked too great.

He was standing before the inn rubbing at his ankle, when he heard a cheerful shout from the other side of the road.

'Coroner Roger, as I live and breathe!'

'Sir Laurence. It is good to meet with you once again,' the Coroner said, less heartily. He did not in all honesty like Sir Laurence, because the job of Purveyor offended him: it was simple extortion, to his way of thinking, but he was prepared to accept that the Purveyor's task was none the less necessary. After all, Roger didn't much like executioners, but someone had to do the job.

'I was told that I might find you here,' Sir Laurence said. He was idly tossing his war hammer in the air and catching it. 'A man called Houndestail said so. I have brought him back with me.'

Behind him, Coroner Roger could see the anxious features of Alexander in the doorway, peering over the knight's shoulder. As Sir Laurence spoke, Drogo and his three men pushed past Alexander and stood listening. The Coroner said, 'You are here to prepare for the coming war?'

'I think it will have already begun,' Sir Laurence said easily.

'No, I am simply collecting food and money to help support the effort.'

'I see.'

Sir Laurence smiled more broadly and he snuffed the air, taking a deep breath. 'Smell that? Shit and piss all over this place, isn't there?' he said conversationally. 'It's a revolting little midden, this. Still, we can't choose where we have to go, you and I, can we?'

'No,' Coroner Roger said. Behind Sir Laurence he could see that Alexander's face was mottled with rage to hear his precious vill so described. 'I suppose you have to come this way often enough? The road to Cornwall is paved with good manors, so I am told.'

'There are plenty of wealthy enough demesnes in among Lord Hugh's lands,' the Purveyor agreed. 'But this is my first trip so far south. Usually I deal with the northern pieces of the shire. There used to be another man down here – Ansel de Hocsenham. I don't know if you ever met him?'

Coroner Roger saw Drogo and Alexander exchange a glance. It was so fleeting that he could have mistaken it, but he was sure he was right. Ansel de Hocsenham, the man who had sired the girl whose body was found this morning; the man who Miles Houndestail thought had been murdered.

He turned his attention back to Sir Laurence. 'No, I never met him.'

'So if he died here, you didn't investigate his death?'

'Not so far as I remember, but while there are only two Coroners for the whole of Devon, it's not surprising. We have fifteen murders a year to cope with, and that doesn't count all the other sudden deaths I have to investigate or the wrecks I have to inspect.'

'Wrecks?'

'A Coroner's duty is to the King. If a ship is wrecked, the King owns any salvaged goods, so I am expected to rush to the coast at short notice to rescue any casks of wine or fine silks and have them sold for the King's benefit. It's not surprising that I didn't meet your predecessor. When did he die?'

'No one knows if he is truly dead, but he must be. He disappeared just about the time he was supposed to have arrived here in Sticklepath, oddly enough, but no one seems to know where he went or what happened to him.'

'Surely nobody would fail to report a dead body, would they?' Coroner Roger said, and shot a glance over Sir Laurence's shoulder again. Alexander met the Coroner's stare with an expression of despair, before turning his back and going into his hall.

If Roger hadn't seen him, he would never have believed that a man could suddenly appear so broken. Even Drogo looked sympathetic, and soon followed Alexander into the house, his men trailing after them.

The knight smiled lazily and pointed his war hammer at them. 'You could almost think he had a guilty conscience, couldn't you?'

'Surely not a Reeve like him,' Roger said drily.

Laurence de Bozon chuckled. 'Could you join me while I speak to him?'

'My leg, I . . .'

'Not right now. Leave us a little while. Let us say, when the sun is dipping below that hill. That should give me time to prepare myself – and leave the Reeve in a state of fright, wondering of which crime I intend to accuse him!'

Jeanne took the woman through the tavern to her own room. There, while Petronilla and Edgar hastily rearranged their clothing, she persuaded Nicole to sit on a bench and sent Edgar (when he had retied his hose) to the buttery for a jug of wine. Petronilla she sent out to walk with the baby, for Richalda was awake now and demanding her mother's attention.

'Tell me your name.'

'I am called Nicole Garde, *madame*.'

'You come from France?' Jeanne asked in that tongue.

Nicole started with delight on hearing her own language again. 'Yes, but how do you speak it so well?'

'I was raised in Bordeaux. Where were you from?'

'A village called Montaillou, near to Pamiers in Arrège.'

'And how did you come to be here, married to an Englishman?' Jeanne asked. Edgar returned as she posed the question, and the two women waited while he poured them a cup each, and then quietly left them.

'*Madame*, I was the daughter of the local headsman. The executioner. He was a good man to his family, but you know how people hate the headsman.'

'Yes,' Jeanne said. It was not only in France that the people loathed the man who represented the ultimate power of the Crown.

'When my husband Thomas saw me being mistreated, he rescued me and brought me here to live with him. I was nothing loath, for it is a healthful place.'

'Really?' Jeanne asked. It said little, she reflected, for Montaillou.

'But the people here have never accepted me. Nor, I think, do they wish my husband to remain.' Suddenly her eyes were brimming once more. 'Oh, *madame*, the Reeve, he has arrested my Thomas, and he says he will have him taken to Exeter to the gaol, to wait there for the next Justices to try. That could be a year . . . more. He will die there, and I shall be a widow, all for no reason.'

'What is he arrested for?'

'This morning they said he killed the child.' Nicole dried her eyes on her sleeve. 'This afternoon they said he tried to kill his brother. It is not true. He hates Ivo, but he is not violent. He is too calm and gentle to harm another, but they say that he will be taken away as soon as they can arrange a guard.'

Jeanne patted her arm comfortingly. 'Do not fear. My husband will look into it.'

'What can he do?'

'He is Keeper of the King's Peace. The Reeve will not dare to argue with *him*,' Jeanne said confidently.

'Keeper?' Nicole pouted doubtfully. 'You think so?'

'Why do you believe they should want to arrest your husband?'

'If they can have him arrested, the jury will convict him of murdering those children. You have seen how the people here are scared of strangers. They want to blame us for everything, and they will have Thomas killed, just so that the man who is really guilty isn't shown up. Why else would they arrest my husband?'

Jeanne shivered. Convicting a man because he was new to an area was a complete travesty of justice. 'Who is the real killer?'

'I do not know,' Nicole said miserably. 'If I did, I would appeal him before the whole vill and save my husband.'

'Are you wealthy? Perhaps someone covets your property.'

'We have very little.'

'Your only defence is to help show who did kill the girls.'

'I know nothing of them except Aline – she I knew. The others died before we came here. Ivo said that Denise died long ago, when he was buying provisions during the famine.'

'What was Aline like?'

Nicole thought a moment, her tears drying now that she was distracted. 'She was a quiet little thing, but it was the end of the famine, you know? All the children were subdued. They were so hungry all the time. Except, I know that Aline was . . .'

Her voice trailed off and she shot Jeanne a look from lowered lashes. 'Well?' Jeanne asked.

'*Madame*, the girl, she was with child.'

'Are you sure? But I thought she was only eleven years old?'

'I know. And she did not even have a boyfriend, you know? Her father would not let her walk about the vill on her own.'

'What of his wife?'

'She was dead many years ago. I never met her.'

'How well do you know Swetricus her father?'

'He is a neighbour, but I had thought that others here were

friends and neighbours. I will not call anyone here friend again.'

'I have not seen any other children. Does he have more?'

'Yes: Lucy is the eldest, then there was Aline, then Gilda and Katherine, but they rarely come to the vill to play with other girls. They are too shy, I think.'

'Perhaps,' Jeanne said, but even as she breathed the word, her mind was considering that the three young girls might wish to avoid others for another reason. So that their secret could not be spoken of.

She had never been touched by her own father, but Jeanne knew only too well that men were capable of molesting their daughters; especially their most beloved daughters.

'Swetricus,' she murmured. Could a man murder his own daughter to hide the fact that he had made her pregnant? And could he have killed the other girls as well?

Then she realised something else Nicole had said. 'Ivo told you about Denise, you say? Ivo was here when she died?'

'Oh, yes. He is often here, and knew Denise well, so he said.'

Chapter Twenty-One

Baldwin could see that the woman Meg was terrified to be confronted by Simon and him, and he tried to calm her nerves, smiling gently and speaking slowly and carefully.

Her voice was low, and although she had an impediment to her speech, she was easily understood. If she had been healthy, Baldwin considered that her voice could have been quite pleasing. By turns she was agitated and twitchy, picking at one hand with the other, and then calm, her round face vacant, as though uninterested in proceedings. Apart from that, as he spoke and as she gradually gained confidence in their company, he saw the signs of her affectionate nature. She held on to Serlo's hand, but with less and less of a firm grip. As she eased, she took to stroking his bare forearm, not a conscious thing, but merely a proof of affection.

They made an odd couple, Baldwin thought. The man so twisted and graceless after his terrible injuries, and she so dumpy and clumsy, but for all that the two had one thing that shone from them: love. She adored him, watching Serlo's face eagerly as he spoke, and for his part, when Serlo looked at her, his expression softened, like a man watching his own daughter.

Serlo was gentle as they explained about her daughter. 'You have to be brave, Meg. Try to be brave. Emma, she can't come back.'

'My Emma?'

Serlo glanced up at Baldwin, gave a short shrug which was a confession of his own inadequacy. 'She's dead, Meg. I'm sorry.'

He had his arms wrapped about her as he spoke, but Baldwin

saw her face crumble like a child's. She looked up at Serlo with desperate hope, as though thinking he might be joking, and her expression as that hope faded tore at Baldwin's heart. He hated to think how Serlo must feel. He regretted coming here like this, intruding on the grief of a poor, simple woman, but the alternative was to have some petty official come here from the vill, someone like Drogo, who would give her the news without Serlo to calm her afterwards. This was surely kinder. For a moment he tried to tell himself that so simple a woman could not appreciate her loss, but then he could have cursed himself for his callousness when he caught a glimpse of her face. This was no dim-witted girl he was watching, but a mother who had lost her only child. There could be no more hideous pain that that which Meg suffered now. Her very simpleness made her feel the pain all the more keenly. She could not imagine any alleviation of her grief.

'NO! Not my Emma as well! No!'

Suddenly shrieking, she struck feebly with her fists at Serlo's breast. He had to grab them and hold her, mumbling sympathetic noises, calling to her by name, and after some minutes she collapsed against him, weeping and shaking her head, her wrists still gripped in his hands.

It took a long time to calm her and prepare her to be questioned, and even then her face would occasionally become blank as her eyes appeared to turn in upon some inner thought or memory. 'She was my baby,' she said several times.

'I am sorry to have to tell you this,' Baldwin said, feeling stiff and formal in the presence of her overwhelming grief. 'I want to find out who killed her.'

Meg nodded, but there was little comprehension in her features. She responded dully to his initial questions.

'Tell us about Emma, Meg.'

'She was my girl.'

'When was she born?'

Meg turned to Serlo with a bewildered look on her face.

He answered for her. 'She was about ten years old. Not above eleven.'

'Who was her father?'

She smiled happily. 'It was my husband. He married me, in the field by the river, my lovely Ansel. He worked so hard, and he had to travel much, but he always came home to me.'

Baldwin stared at Serlo in confusion.

The Warrener sighed. 'Look, he made his promises to Meg about six years after the crowning of the King—'

'That would be about 1313 or so,' Simon muttered.

Serlo shrugged. 'I don't have much use for numbers. Only seasons. He made his promises, and he came back when he could. Emma was born, and Ansel came back for a couple of years—'

'Until about 1315?' Simon pressed him.

'Yeah, well, then he left, and didn't say farewell, and about a year later, Athelhard returned. He had heard that Meg had had a daughter, and he came to protect them and help as best he could. He wasn't happy with the situation, but which older brother would be? At least Athelhard had helped with money.'

'It was our home,' Meg burst out suddenly. 'Our house in the woods. Ansel built it for us. He liked it there.' A dullness came down over her face like a shadow from a veil. 'But he said he wasn't going yet. He promised he'd be about for another week. He would have said farewell.'

'Miserable bastard son of a whore and a dog fox,' Simon muttered viciously under his breath. He hated to hear of women who were taken for a ride, and all too often men could get their own way by pretending to marry someone. Litigation was expensive, thus many escaped censure or punishment. If the Purveyor *had* been murdered, perhaps he deserved his end.

Baldwin shot him a look to silence him, then, 'He said nothing? Gave no hint that he was leaving?'

'No, he just upped and went.' Serlo shrugged.

'Will Taverner said he'd left, but he wouldn't have, not without seeing me first,' Meg said tearfully.

'I see,' Baldwin said. 'What of the rest of your family?'

Her reaction startled him. She stiffened, and then her eyes grew wild. Suddenly she spun around, as though fearing an attack from behind her. Serlo had to catch at her wrists again and talk to her quietly. All the while she moaned with a keening noise as though mourning.

Serlo grunted, 'Her family died many years ago, all but her brother, Athelhard. He was older than Meg, and when their father died, he was all she had left, but he was away with the old King hammering the Welsh. When he died, Athelhard stayed in the retinue of a Marcher Lord. He did well and brought back plenty of booty, so that was fine, but he wasn't here for Meg. Like she said, when she was alone, she married but then her man disappeared and it was a good year later that Athelhard returned here to look after her and take over the assart.'

'Which assart was that?' Baldwin asked.

'The one where I met you today. It was theirs. Ansel had built the cottage for Meg, but it was Athelhard who started to clear the woods about it to create some pasture.'

'I saw you there, Meg,' Baldwin said softly. The recollection of the sight made a shiver of ice trickle down his spine, but he could sense the relief now that there was an explanation. 'You were standing at a tree with your arms behind you. Why was that?'

She sniffed, but couldn't answer. It was left to Serlo to respond for her.

Gruffly he said, 'They tied her to that tree when they set fire to Athelhard's house. To burn him out. He wouldn't come out even when they set fire to his thatch, and they wanted to make sure of him. They found Meg and used her, binding her to the tree so that she could see everything, and when she screamed, her brother came running. As they knew he would.'

'Who are they?' Baldwin asked.

'The vill. The Reeve, the Foresters – all of them. They thought Athelhard was a vampire.'

'Why should they have thought of vampires?' Baldwin asked quietly, his eyes going to Serlo. 'I can understand people being horrified by the thought that a child could have been murdered and her flesh eaten – but surely they knew that people can be driven to desperate measures from starvation. Why think of supernatural agents?'

'This is a small vill, Sir Knight. You are well-travelled and experienced, but many of the folk here have never been farther than Oakhampton. When they hear of cannibalism, it seems so inhuman that they assume a demon is responsible. And that means a vampire.'

'You mean they used Meg here to draw her brother outside?' Simon said with shock. 'Christ's cods!'

'They killed him,' Meg said brokenly.

Baldwin studied her. In some way the death of her brother was more immediate to her than the death of her own daughter, which at first he thought appalling, but then he found himself in sympathy with her. She had been forced to endure many years alone, and the loss of her sole remaining protector, especially since she was witness to his death, must have had a significant impact upon her, coming back and haunting her each night.

That was why she relived the terror of that day, he guessed. Perhaps she regularly returned to the assart, hoping that this time her brother would escape the flames and go to her.

Serlo shook his head. He could remember it so clearly: the stinking cottage reeking of burned meat, the blackened and twisted corpse in the doorway. 'They hunted him down, then slaughtered him like a rabid dog. That's why she can't sleep in the hut, even though I rebuilt it for her.'

Meg shuddered. 'I was there. I heard them walking, so I followed and saw them shoot at him after he had chopped wood. They chased him to the house and shot him again, and Drogo told

his men to light torches. I tried to scream, but a man caught me
and put his hand over my mouth. They tied me to the tree and
made me watch while they set torches on the thatch and waited,
and I screamed. The Reeve tried to make him come out, but it was
my screams that brought him out. He was hobbled, but they shot
him like a rat! Like a *rat!*'

She broke down again, wailing and snivelling inconsolably,
and it was some while before she could speak again. Baldwin
looked enquiringly at Serlo.

He shrugged. 'Far as I know, it's all true. She was there when I
found her. I'd seen the fire from my warren and went to look.
Thought it might be a house fire and someone needed help. Not
that they'd have asked me.'

'Why not?' Simon shot out.

Serlo gave him a scathing glance. 'Because I look like this.
Because people like you, people who are fit and well, hate to see
someone who's this twisted and wrecked. And they hate the way
that their own children prefer to come up and talk to me on the
moors than spend time with them here, that's why!'

'You were going to tell us about the assart,' Baldwin gently
reminded him.

Serlo's anger faded, although he ignored Simon and addressed
all his words to Baldwin. 'When I got there, I found Athelhard's
place burning. He was dead just inside. It was his funeral pyre,
poor bastard! They'd cut his heart out and burned him. The stink!
Christ Jesus, I shall never forget it!'

'No,' Baldwin said quietly. 'It is not an odour that ever leaves
you, once you have breathed it in.'

Serlo eyed him doubtfully. It had been a horror to him, but he
would have expected a knight to have smelled far worse in his
time. Yet when he stared into Baldwin's eyes, he could see that he
was serious. He looked like a man who could still sense that foul
stench in the air about them.

'I found Meg there and took her away. Later, I went back and buried her brother's remains. She stayed with me a while, just until she was better. Emma was with us as well, bless her. Then she took to staying in the vill.'

'Where?'

'With various people. Some took pity on her. They thought that a poor little creature like her needed all the help she could get. She was with the miller for some while, then with Swetricus, I think. I was sorry to see her go. I looked on her as my own,' he added quietly.

'Was there anything else?'

'Just one thing. When I found Meg, she was holding a piece of arrow. The arse-end with the nock and fletchings.'

'It was his, *his* – the Forester's,' Meg said. 'He must have killed my poor Athelhard. I saw them shoot him, and Peter cut out his heart, and then they picked him up and swung him onto the flames, but when they lifted up his body, I found the arrow on the ground.'

'Was there anything distinctive about it?' Baldwin asked.

She looked at him, then up at Serlo, who gave her an encouraging nod, and she darted off into the tunnel. A moment or two later she was back, gripping a six-inch length of arrow. She thrust it into Baldwin's hands.

'Ask Drogo about his arrows,' Serlo said grimly. 'And compare them with that. Then you'll have proof you have yourself a murderer.'

Baldwin nodded and carefully placed the splinter of wood into his purse to be studied later. The light was fading, and it was already too dark here in the woods to be able to distinguish much about it.

'I shall,' he promised. 'Except it would be a great deal easier if I knew why the murderer – or murderers if it was indeed the whole vill – decided to kill Meg's brother like that. It was not the random act of one man trying to rob another. Why should the people of Sticklepath decide to do such a thing?'

'You need to ask that? Because they thought he was a vampire
– a *sanguisuga*!'

'It was revenge, then?' Baldwin asked, whistling for Aylmer.

Serlo looked at him for a moment. 'I don't live in the vill. I am
a moorman, that is all. But I know this: the Purveyor disappeared,
then Denise died, and Drogo was keen to blame Athelhard. Very
keen.'

'Because Athelhard was foreign?' Simon asked.

'Perhaps. But there was another reason. Athelhard bought some
pork to feed Meg. It cost him a fortune, but he did it to keep her
alive.'

'So what?' Simon asked. 'Couldn't he have explained?'

'No one would have believed him if he had. They had already
jumped to the conclusion that he was eating human meat.'

'Why think that?'

'The priest had preached a sermon about the demons all about
us. He told the vill about vampires and how demons could turn a
man into one – so that although someone looked the same as they
had always done, underneath he could be a *sanguisuga*. That was
enough to seal poor Athelhard's fate.'

'I see. Now who would have had meat to sell during the
famine?' Simon asked.

'Ivo Bel,' Meg said clearly. 'He sold it to Athelhard to save
me.'

'Is that right?' Baldwin asked Serlo.

He shrugged. 'Probably. But I think it suited people to assume
the worst. What if Drogo had good reason to want Athelhard
convicted?'

Baldwin said, 'You suspect Drogo was the murderer?'

'No. I don't think Drogo could be so inventive. He's a God-
fearing man, for all his bluster, but I do think he could seek to
protect a friend or someone.'

'What are you hinting?'

'Ask Drogo. Ask the Forester.'

'I shall,' Baldwin promised. 'But before we leave you, where were you last night? Emma died and we must learn all we can about everyone's movements.'

'I was up at my warren until dark, and then I came here to see Meg.'

'Did you notice anyone about the vill?'

'I didn't pass near the vill. I came down the road from Belstone and straight up here. Hang on – I did see one man. Vin. He was going to the mill.'

'I see,' Baldwin said. 'One thing we haven't learned is, where would Emma have been sleeping last night?'

Serlo scratched his head. 'It varied. Sometimes with Swetricus, sometimes at the mill. Occasionally she'd stay with Thomas Garde.'

'Just one last question,' Baldwin said. 'Have *you* heard of Athelhard's curse?'

Serlo nodded slowly. 'Oh yes. He cursed all the men there, so they say – but I think he meant Drogo and the Reeve. He damned them both to Hell, and they will be there before long.'

Sir Laurence was enjoying himself. He always did when his job gave him the opportunity to exercise his humour at the expense of others.

'So, Reeve. I think I shall need to have most of your corn.'

His eyes twinkled with merriment as he spoke, the firelight giving him a cheerful aspect, but in Reeve Alexander's eyes, his smile was that of a demon grinning at the miserable fate of another.

'Sir Laurence, I am sure we would all like to do everything we can to assist the King's efforts in Scotland—'

'I am delighted to hear it. I assume that there is a "But"?'

'We have so little here. The famine, then the murrains, and no travellers to speak of. We don't have a market or fair like South Zeal. Couldn't you seek what you need from a more prosperous town?'

'I have already been to South Zeal. It is a pleasant place. All the burgage plots so well laid out, and the whole town prospering nicely. That, you see, is what happens when a place is run efficiently. But then you come here and what do you find? A midden! Look at it! The vill is falling apart, and it's all the fault of the man at the top. Laziness, that's what it is. I wouldn't allow it on my own manor, I assure you.'

Alexander gritted his teeth. He detested hearing his vill so denigrated, but he knew he must swallow his pride. 'These are difficult times for all the King's subjects, but for a little place like this with so few resources, it is even worse,' he said in a choked voice. 'Surely at South Zeal they would be able to afford a much larger stock of grain than we can?'

'Yes, I arranged for a little grain from South Zeal, but I feel sure that you will have enough stored away here to support the King.'

'We have nothing!'

'That is very sad.'

'My Lord, please! We have nothing to give, and we can't even pay the King money instead. We could never afford to compensate him.'

'Perhaps you could compensate someone who was of a lesser position?' Laurence asked, gazing at his fingernails with an air of mild enquiry.

'The last Purveyor used to find it served him to seek out the wealthier vills. They could afford to pay the King's Procurers enough to satisfy the King, but smaller ones like this, well, we could only hope to pay enough to satisfy one man,' Alexander said carefully.

'I see. And how much would one man be satisfied with? Say a man like Ansel de Hocsenham?'

'He would have been content with . . .' Alexander did a quick calculation. There was always the risk that Ansel – rot him! – had managed to let this new man know how much he had routinely milked from places like Sticklepath. Honesty was safest, although the thought of so much cash going again was sorely painful to him. It was all the money he had left. There was nothing after this. He swallowed. 'Three shillings and tenpence.'

'So little?' Sir Laurence yawned, but his eyes remained sharp. 'And that was the last time he came here?'

'There are so many felons and footpads on the roads,' Alexander said nervously.

'And some of them live in towns and vills like ordinary men. Like Reeves.' Sir Laurence was staring out through the window as though finding the conversation unbearably tedious.

Alexander said, 'He must have been set upon and robbed after he left here. Perhaps someone in Oakhampton will know of his passing through.'

'Curiously enough, the people there deny ever seeing him. It's most peculiar, but he never appeared there. But we know that he indeed left here, don't we? I was told that by Drogo Forester when I asked him.'

Drogo cleared his throat and shuffled his feet. Alexander didn't bother to look at him. Christ Jesus! It wasn't as though Ansel hadn't deserved his end. He was a leech in human form, demanding money from any Reeve who couldn't afford the King's Purvey, sucking their blood to within a few pennies of their conscience. Any more and most Reeves would have felt it worthwhile to tell the King that the Purveyor was corrupt, but Ansel knew how to gauge the amount to a nicety. He always left the people with just enough to live on: not enough to live comfortably, but enough for survival.

'He had an unsavoury reputation, you know,' Sir Laurence was saying, idly dipping a finger into his bowl of wine and licking it clean. He raised innocent eyes to study Alexander. 'It has been said that he was bent as hell, that he'd take money to release people from the King's demands.'

'I *am* surprised,' said Alexander with pointed sarcasm.

Sir Laurence didn't appear to notice his irony. 'Yes. And of course he'd force people to sell their grain at less than he was supposed to, and pocket the difference. Not a pleasant fellow, our Ansel, but still a King's Officer, when all is said and done.'

'Of course.'

Alexander wondered when all the play-acting would stop and they would arrest him. Peter atte Moor had left the place a while ago, gone off to get some sleep after the last two nights he had spent up on the moors walking about his bailiwick, but the others were still here. Drogo and two Foresters were behind him and it would take only a moment for them to bind him. One thing he was sure of – if he were to run, Drogo would have him dead in a moment; he would want Alexander to be silenced for good. However, the Reeve wouldn't give him that satisfaction, nor that relief.

Alexander's thoughts were interrupted when he heard the first dog begin to howl again. He hesitated, listening, but the dog continued, and he frowned. Forgetting Drogo for a moment, he rose to his feet.

'Where are you going?' Sir Laurence demanded harshly.

From the corner of his eye, Alexander saw Drogo make a sharp gesture with his hand and Vincent Yunghe appeared before him, an apologetic grimace on his face.

'I want to see what that dog is making such a noise over. The damned thing spent much of last night howling.'

'Wait here awhile instead,' Sir Laurence said silkily. 'We are having such a fine talk. It would be a shame to pause in the middle. Come, pray return to your seat, my good Reeve.'

Alexander slumped back into the chair, chewing at his lip. Outside he was sure that a second dog had begun to howl. They must be Samson's two in their kennels.

'That's right!' Sir Laurence said heartily. It was always pleasant to show that beneath his velvet glove there still remained a *main de fer*, a hand of iron. This man was cowed already, as he should be, but many a beaten man in the past had tried to escape by using a minor distraction like a howling dog or two.

It was an unsettling noise, true. There was a mournful quality about it that was rather eerie. There was also more than a little fear in those two voices, if he could hear them aright. It was odd, he'd never heard dogs howling like that before.

No matter, though. He eyed the pale and anxious features of the Reeve before him and told himself with satisfaction that there was more fun to be had in here, taunting this fellow, than in going out to investigate a pair of poxy, yapping curs.

Chapter Twenty-Two

Simon and Baldwin left Meg and Serlo soon afterwards. Serlo was comforting her as best he could, but Baldwin understood that the poor woman needed time to get over the first dreadful shock of hearing about her daughter's death, and of reliving her traumatic experiences in that wood. It was curious to Baldwin that she should wish to live in Sticklepath at all. The destruction of her brother by their neighbours must surely mean that she would hate all of them? But then again she was simple. Perhaps it was impossible for her to conceive of removing herself from the place where she had grown up and lived with her brother, especially since Serlo had shown her kindness. Where else could she hope to find that? Sticklepath was not only a place of horror for her, but somewhere with pleasing memories, too.

'Well?' asked Simon.

They had reached the roadway. Baldwin rummaged in his purse and took out the fragment of arrow, studying it in the faltering light. 'Peacock feathers. A bit grand for a poor little vill like this.'

'I dare say a Forester like Drogo knows where to catch such birds and make use of them.'

'True – but do they work any better than a goose quill?'

'No. This was used purely for ostentation. It's the sort of thing a young squire would do to impress his lady-love.'

'It was apparently good enough to kill this Athelhard,' Baldwin pointed out mildly. 'It shows that they were not scared of being discovered, doesn't it? There was no intention of concealing their crime from local people.'

'If Serlo was right, the whole vill was involved anyway.'

'True, and if the vill was convinced that he was responsible for killing and eating their children, it is no surprise that they would wish to take such a savage revenge.'

'Let us hope that Drogo can enlighten us.'

'It is horrible to think of dying like that,' Baldwin mused. 'All alone in your own home, while your neighbours fire arrows at you. No one to turn to. No protection.'

'And then they try to cover up their crime by throwing you back onto the flames of your own house. Sick!'

'Yes,' Baldwin said. He called to Aylmer, who was falling behind them, sniffing at every bush. 'And this happened a short time after the death of Denise, if the Parson is to be believed.'

'You think he isn't?'

'Well, he didn't tell us the whole truth about how Athelhard died, did he? Never a hint that the vill rose up as one and murdered him.'

'Maybe the folks went to him to confess. That would seal his lips.'

'Perhaps,' Baldwin agreed. 'It also explains why Gervase is such a nervous wreck and why the people here live under such a cloud. A country priest with little education could all too easily jump to the conclusion that a murderer who ate his victims was possessed—'

'Not only a country priest,' Simon said shortly.

'Simon, I apologise. I did not mean to pass comment on your own views. I was merely thinking aloud. But it would explain Gervase's attitude, wouldn't it? They killed the man whom they had blamed, and then they were forced to confront a terrible nightmare! They thought they had destroyed the beast who had slaughtered their children and eaten them – and then the killings continued! They must all be aware that they killed an innocent man.'

'That's what happens when the mob takes control and ignores the law,' Simon said ponderously.

'Do you really blame them, Simon? After all, you do share some of their feelings about ghosts and demons.'

The Bailiff grunted but didn't speak. There was a world of difference in his mind between someone who believed in the supernatural and was sensible enough to fear demons, and someone who was prepared to break the law for whatever the reason. Apart from anything else, he was certain that the best people to control demons of any type were priests. Everyone else should steer well clear of them.

'Perhaps,' Baldwin said thoughtfully, 'they didn't feel that they would receive any help from the law.'

They had reached the vill now, and were passing the cemetery. Simon cast a quick look at the cross with its drooping cross member. 'And your point? Other than to irritate me, of course.'

'That was not my intention,' Baldwin protested. 'All I meant to say was that there *are* precedents for cutting up a body and burning it on a pyre. Sometimes people feel that it's the only way to cleanse an evil soul.'

'They must have been terrified of Meg's brother,' Simon considered.

'Very.' Baldwin stopped to whistle again at Aylmer, who was staring out over the cemetery with his head tilted to one side.

'But although there were more murders, they didn't attempt to kill anyone else.'

'No,' Baldwin said.

'You sound unconvinced.'

'I am unconvinced by everything I learn here. I had assumed that the deaths of the children were committed by one person, but that the death of the Purveyor was a separate murder. Now I wonder . . . what if the Purveyor was killed by the same person?'

Simon looked at him curiously. 'Why should you think that? He only disappeared.'

'Yes. But I wonder whether his body had been mutilated, too? We'll never know unless we find it,' Baldwin said. 'And then we would have a case where one murderer over a period killed one man, perhaps got a flavour for human meat, and then killed other, easier victims over time. That would make sense to me.'

The Bailiff shivered, but then a thought occurred to him. 'If that's the case, why should the murderer hide the first victim, the purveyor, and Aline, but leave the others to be found?'

'A good question,' Baldwin said. 'Oh, what is the matter with the dog? Aylmer, get over here!'

It was at that moment that they heard the first dog begin to howl, and as Simon saw the sudden intensity of Baldwin's face, he felt the hairs on the back of his neck and arms begin to rise.

Gunilda shivered and licked her lips as she kneaded the dough for their supper. All about her the mill felt full of shadows, and whenever she looked up, she saw faces peering at her: in the darkened corners of the room, in among the timber baulks that made up the shafts, in between the great leather straps that connected one axle with another, even in the wattle of the walls. Everywhere faces were staring, watching and slavering in the dim candlelight.

'Go away!' she whispered as another one caught her attention. 'He's dead now, you can't touch me. You don't scare me.'

'Mother, can I—'

'Shut up, child!' Gunilda snapped. 'You can't know anything. Leave me in peace.'

Felicia sagged back. She felt the chill too, but she daren't comment again. It had been fearsome living here with her father, knowing that he would come to her bed at night and make use of her like a whore, but somehow now that he was gone, her mother's sudden collapse was still more terrifying.

It was impossible for her to trust the boys in the vill. Several of them had made advances as she grew up, usually at harvest-time when the cider and ale had been flowing faster than usual and their blood was hot, or at springtime, when the weather warmed and the young shoots began to break the surface of the soil, and the thoughts of all the lads and lasses in the vill turned to rolling in the fresh grass. Not many had appealed to her. Peter atte Moor had grabbed her once, trying his luck; so had Drogo, one night when he was drunk, but Samson had been near, and Drogo soon released her. Not that she was interested in any of them. Only Vin. Vin was the one who had really tempted her. That was why she had given herself to him at the river that day. And why she had gone with him again last night.

All through those years of abuse, her mother had been a source of sympathy; she had listened and comforted Felicia, often weeping with her as they rocked each other to sleep beside the snoring bulk of her father. Gunilda was desperate and lonely. She had lost her husband to her daughter, and witnessing Felicia's nightly rape was tearing at her heart as her own misery grew, Felicia could see that. But Gunilda had never dared try to stop Samson. Every night as he roughly pushed or pulled at Felicia and mounted her like a dog on a bitch, Gunilda turned away, but that was all. Except recently she had taken to holding Felicia's hand, just placing her fingers in Felicia's palm as if to reassure her.

Felicia had hoped that once Samson was dead, she and Gunilda might be able to live normally, free from the fear he inspired in both of them. It had felt like a miracle when she heard Gunilda scream, then her father's hoarse cry, and had run to them to see her mother standing, her fists clenched at either side of her mouth while she shrieked. Felicia had felt concern that her father was hurt, but not because she thought that he might die: she hoped he would. He had been an unholy menace to her. She hated him.

And when she realised he was dead, she felt no sadness, only a cold glee that had frozen her belly. There could be no more beatings, no more drunken fumblings. Now she need only submit to a man when she wanted to.

Like Vin, she thought, smiling as she recalled the last night. He was beautiful, with his large eyes shining, his lank fair hair fine and silken in her hands, his skin gleaming in the bright moonlight. She had always liked him, and now she knew he loved her. It was only ever her father that separated them, he said. His fear of Samson.

Gunilda moaned again as she stared at a dark corner of the room stacked with empty sacks. Her face was working, Felicia saw, and her eyes glittered with hatred. 'Leave us alone!'

Felicia was about to ask who she was talking to, but then Gunilda's attention turned to her. Somehow her eyes looked through her. It was as though Felicia wasn't there at all. On the woman's face was an expression of utter terror.

Whatever it was that Gunilda saw, or imagined that she saw, it was not human, Felicia knew. She threw a scared look over her shoulder, but there was nothing there. And then suddenly, Felicia could hear it: a voice that sounded oddly familiar – a voice filled with rage and fear.

And the dogs began to howl.

Simon entered the inn with a sense of genuine relief. It felt like a tiny sanctuary, away from the terrible noise outside. Seeing Meg had unsettled him, but the howling of the hounds had given him the willies, especially when he saw Aylmer bristle. Only when he was inside and could breathe the smoky atmosphere, see the light flickering on the walls from the candles and fire, did he feel safe.

Baldwin was behind him, his teeth shining as he grinned. 'You aren't imagining that William of Newburgh's stories could be true, are you?'

'It's all very well you talking smugly about superstitions and foolishness, but I tell you, ghosts exist, and many live on the moors,' Simon said hotly. Christ, he needed a drink.

The knight smiled and did not argue with his friend, but instead called to the taverner and demanded wine. 'And where is the good Coroner?'

'He has been asked to visit the Purveyor, sir. At the Reeve's house,' William said.

'Husband, I am glad to find you here again,' Jeanne said, entering behind him.

'My love.' Baldwin was about to greet her more warmly when he saw the other woman with her.

'This is Nicole, Baldwin, wife to the man Thomas Garde.'

'I have met your husband,' Baldwin nodded.

'You helped save him from being arrested, my Lord, and I am grateful,' Nicole said, bowing nervously. She had never spoken to a King's Officer before, and it was daunting. 'He paid his fine.'

'I am glad to hear it.'

'But Baldwin, the Reeve has had him arrested again,' Jeanne said impatiently. 'This time for participating in a fight with his brother.'

'Is this true?'

'Yes, sir. Alexander had him thrown in gaol as soon as he could. He says Thomas tried to kill Ivo, but my husband would not attack anyone without being provoked.'

'Good Heavens! Where is this fool Ivo?' Baldwin demanded.

Taverner muttered something about the stables, and was sent to find him.

'There is something else,' Jeanne said. 'This woman says that Aline was pregnant when she disappeared.'

'A girl so young? She was only eleven or so!' Simon burst out with all the anger of fatherhood.

Jeanne kept her gaze fixed upon her husband. 'Nicole thinks that Aline had no boyfriends.'

'What are you trying to say?' Baldwin asked, holding up a hand to stem Simon's outrage.

'That this peasant Swetricus has regularly slept with his daughters, and when he got Aline pregnant, he shut her up in the only way he knew.'

Baldwin frowned. 'If that were so, Jeanne, why should he kill the other girls? It is surely no coincidence that Denise and Mary and Emma were killed as well.'

'There is one last thing. Ivo Bel was here when all the deaths occurred.'

'How do you know? The first two girls died before the Gardes came here, so Thomas said,' Simon interrupted.

'It was Ivo who told us about their deaths,' Nicole replied. 'That was before he insulted me and tried to steal me from my husband.'

It was then that Ivo entered with Taverner, and he overheard her last words. 'I did nothing of the kind!' he spluttered angrily, his voice still thick and nasal. 'I have only ever behaved in an honourable manner to you, woman!'

Simon felt his mood lighten to see what a hammering Ivo had received. 'One man did that to you?'

'I warned you, didn't I? Tom's rages are ferocious. You should be careful when he is angry, Bailiff.'

'Enough!' Baldwin said sharply. 'We are not here to bicker, Bel. We are here to learn what you did to make your brother react so.'

'He has wanted me ever since he first met me,' Nicole said.

'Rubbish. I am happily married,' he scoffed.

Simon peered at him. 'Really? Have you forgotten that it was only this morning that you told me you regretted marrying your pig of a wife, and praising the "lovely thing", your brother's wife Nicole?'

'I said that?'

'By the river this morning.'

'No, Bailiff, you are mistaken. I could never desire a poor creature like this.'

Ivo threw out a hand to indicate Nicole, but he had misjudged the distance. His hand caught her about the eye, and with a startled cry, she snapped her head away. Then it was Ivo's turn to squeak as he became aware of Simon's sword blade at his throat.

'If you so much as look at her again, Bel, I'll shave your throat closer than ever before, you miserable dog's turd! You slithering little worm! If nothing else, that action convinces me that you were lying. Weren't you?'

Ivo felt the wall at his back, but his eyes were fixed with appalled fear on the solid steel blade that pricked at his Adam's apple. He was convinced that he could feel the sharpness of the point puncturing his neck, and dared not swallow lest he stab himself in the process. 'Um hmm.'

Simon withdrew the sword slightly. 'Did you desire your sister-in-law here?'

'I admit that I find her attractive.'

'You told me this morning that your brother was a berserker when roused. Did you set him up to have him arrested?'

'I may have taunted him a little.'

Nicole spat out, 'He said I had slept with him three times! My daughter heard him.'

Baldwin joined Simon. His face was calm, but there was a look in his eyes that Bel didn't like. 'Is this true, Bel? Did you tell the husband that you had cuckolded him?'

'I may have said something like that in the heat of the moment.'

'In that case, you are lucky to have got away so lightly. Bel, you are an unnatural fellow. I will demand that you be amerced to appear in the next court to answer for your dishonesty. I shall also offer to appear in that court to see you convicted. Do you understand me?'

'Yes, Sir Baldwin.'

'Is it also true that you sold pork to Athelhard the brother of Meg just before he died?'

'I did that in good faith. I never expected that someone else would think he had killed a child. Why should I? I sold it to him before anyone knew Denise was hurt and—'

'Where did you get it from?'

Ivo grew pensive. 'Ah well, it was a long time ago.' As Simon pushed the blade forward, he jerked his head back. 'It was some meat given as a gift to the Prioress at Canonsleigh,' he said rapidly. 'I stole it, all right?'

'Leave my sight, wretch. You make me want to puke!' Baldwin said contemptuously. 'I shall be writing to Canonsleigh. I recommend you don't bother returning there!'

While Bel scampered from the room, his terrified gaze on Simon's sword, Baldwin smacked his balled fist into his palm. 'The useless bastard!'

Nicole shivered. She was wearing a light cloak which Jeanne had lent her, but tonight she could not get warm, not with her man in gaol. 'My Lord, what about my husband? Please, Sir Knight! I cannot sleep knowing that my man is locked away in a cell fearing what the morning might bring to him. He could die in there, and if I didn't do all I could to have him released, I should be a poor wife indeed.'

She had thrown herself at Baldwin's feet, and he nodded, fully in sympathy.

'Yes, I quite agree,' he said, his anger not yet gone. 'We shall go and speak to the Reeve immediately.'

The noise of the dogs was getting on Coroner Roger's nerves. He had stood outside the Reeve's house for some while before entering, gazing towards the cemetery, trying to work out what had made them start this confounded howling, but he couldn't see anything.

He had heard of such things before, baying at the moon for no reason, but he hadn't experienced it and there was an odd edge to the dogs' voices, an edge he didn't like. There must be a full moon, he thought, but when he glanced upwards, the moon was hidden behind a single cloud. It looked as though it was illuminated from within by a pure white light, and was so beautiful that he had to stop and stare at it, delighting in the shadings within the cloud. At one moment he was almost sure that he saw a face in it, but then the face was gone, and instead he was confronted by the moon, whose clear brilliance put the stars to shame.

Reluctantly he trailed into the hall, where the Reeve sat at his table, the Purveyor a short distance from him.

'This man just tried to bribe me,' Sir Laurence said cheerfully. 'I appeal him before you, Coroner, so that you can witness my evidence.'

'It's not true,' Alexander said wearily. 'But you want your scapegoat, so go on and arrest me. I'm past caring.'

He was sitting with his arms on the table, his eyes downcast. Roger thought he looked the picture of a man who had lost everything.

'Bring me a seat,' the Coroner snarled at Vin, who was leaning against the wall. Roger sat, grunting with the pain, and then cast a look at Alexander.

There was a spark of defiance remaining in the man, Roger noted. Laurence hadn't quite broken his spirit.

He was right. Alexander could feel the anger simmering within him, but was determined to keep it concealed. He could achieve nothing by losing his temper. Not that it was very difficult to appear tired. For the first time in his life he was experiencing the bone-deep, numbing fear that came from the knowledge that he was lost. He could not persuade anyone of his innocence.

'You deny trying to bribe me?' Sir Laurence asked in his deceptively hearty way.

'I did not offer. You demanded. You made it plain you wanted money to leave us alone.'

'Is that what you heard?' Sir Laurence asked Drogo, who stood scowling at the wall behind Alexander.

'This is ridiculous,' Reeve Alexander said. 'I'm not stupid. I wouldn't say such a thing. You think that I have never dealt with a King's official before? How many stewards or Reeves would address a stranger and immediately offer a bribe in front of witnesses without first finding out more about the man? If you want to arrest me, do so, but don't insult my intelligence or try my patience with this foolishness.'

The Coroner studied him. It was always worse when men denied their guilt. If the Reeve was to fight the matter, it would be a lengthy case, and ultimately he would probably submit or confess. Men always did eventually.

Reeve Alexander saw his expression in the dim light of the room, and sighed. There was no defence against the killing of the Purveyor. Drogo certainly wouldn't protect him. No one would. The truth didn't matter to anyone. Everybody demanded *justice*, he sneered to himself, but most people wouldn't recognise it if it came up and smacked them on the jaw. Justice was always flawed. The only thing that mattered was that justice could be witnessed – and that meant that he could go hang. It was ironic, really. He had been willing to sacrifice Thomas for the same reason. The man would have been a good suspect. He fitted the vill's prejudice perfectly: arresting him for the murders would be so much easier than trying to arrest someone who was from the vill itself.

Damn those hounds! They were making enough noise to raise the dead, he thought inconsequentially.

'Alexander, I would speak with you for a moment.'

Baldwin's firm and displeased voice broke into his thoughts and when he looked up he found himself being studied not only by Baldwin and his dog, but also by Simon and Nicole in the doorway.

Sir Laurence clearly thought that the interruption was intended to release his prisoner, and he moved to the wall, his war hammer in his hand. Immediately Aylmer growled deep in his throat.

Baldwin called to the dog, but his eyes went to Alexander, then to the Coroner. 'It would appear that we are breaking into a meeting. I apologise for that. Roger, would you mind if I spoke to the Reeve for a moment?'

Coroner Roger grinned and pointed his staff at Sir Laurence, introducing him.

On hearing that Baldwin was a Keeper, the other knight relaxed visibly. 'I am glad to meet you, Sir Baldwin. How may I serve you?'

'I came here to demand the release of this woman's husband,' Baldwin said, snapping his fingers to his dog.

'I can't just release him. He attacked his brother with a staff and tried to kill him,' Alexander objected.

'Ivo confesses to taunting Thomas in an attempt to have him gaoled. He wanted Nicole here for his own.'

Alexander waited for the knight to expose the bribe Ivo had given him, and was relieved that Ivo had apparently not mentioned it. 'He has no money to free himself.'

'How much would it cost?'

'At least six pennies to keep the Peace and swear to present himself in court.'

'I shall pay it for him. Now order his release.'

'I can't until the money . . .'

'Do you suggest that I would offer money and then renege?' Baldwin asked silkily.

Alexander shrugged and shouted for a servant. When a thin, fearful-looking man appeared, the Reeve snapped at him to set Thomas free and bring him to the hall.

They were all silent as they waited. Nicole stood with her head averted from all the men in the room, nervously clasping her hands before her breast like a woman who was herself condemned and awaiting the arrival of the rope, but when her man appeared, drawn and anxious, she gave a short sob and flung herself at him.

'You have Sir Baldwin to thank for your freedom, Thomas. Now piss off and leave us in peace. I'll want you to appear before the next court, but until then, keep out of my sight,' Alexander rasped.

'No! Wait,' Baldwin commanded. 'I want an end to this. Thomas, you fought with your brother today?'

'I didn't want to, but he made me, insulting me and my wife

until I saw red. I couldn't help it. You know me, Reeve. I've never got into fights before, have I? I'm not the sort to resort to my fists after a drink. Drogo and his Foresters are often quarrelling with other men in the tavern, and Samson always used to brawl, but nobody has ever suggested that I was violent, have they?'

'Why should your brother want to provoke you into fighting?' Roger asked.

'He wants my wife. If he could have me hanged, he could take her,' Thomas explained.

'Your own brother would do that?'

'He's wanted Nicole since the day he met her.'

Baldwin said, 'Thomas, I think your brother will leave you alone now. You have broken his head and he has confessed to us. Perhaps you have knocked some sense into him. Anyway, he has gone.'

'I never want to see him again.'

The couple made as if to leave, but Baldwin's soft voice stopped them.

'One last thing. Thomas, you have been accused of murder, and you have been gaoled because of a fight which was not your fault. Why? What have you done to deserve this?'

'Ask *him*,' Thomas said disdainfully, jerking his head at the Reeve. 'He's been hunting me down for no reason.'

'Rubbish!'

'You tried to have me arrested – twice now. And why? Just because I wasn't born here in Sticklepath. The men of my own vill have had me thrown into gaol, they would have had me accused of murder and hanged, just to protect their friends here. They hate me not because I am a danger, but merely to serve their own interests. Why, Reeve, eh? What have I ever done to you?' There were tears in his eyes now, tears of frustration and incomprehension.

It was Simon who answered, speaking with the weary air of a

man who has witnessed injustice before. 'That's just the point, Thomas. You are an outsider. You didn't merit protection, not in his eyes, because you weren't a friend he'd grown up with.'

'Is this true?' Baldwin demanded, facing Alexander. 'You sought this man's imprisonment to protect your vill?'

'And what better motivation could there be? It would have proved that we don't tolerate murderers here, it would have explained things neatly! And without staining the character of the people and the vill itself. Thomas is a stranger here. A foreigner.'

'Oh yes, and I came from the north, didn't I?'

'What does that mean?' Baldwin asked.

Simon sighed. 'Everyone knows that only bad luck comes from the north.'

'Oh!' Baldwin sneered. 'More *superstition*.'

The Reeve said, 'Who else could I arrest? There was no one in Sticklepath who could do such a terrible thing as killing the girls and eating them.'

Vin heard his words and could not help but glance at Drogo. The Forester had been in the area with every fresh body discovered, and he never seemed to suffer from hunger, not even at the height of the famine. As the thought occurred Drogo's cold eyes met his, and Vincent looked away. Drogo made a bad enemy.

There had been silence after Alexander's words, but now Nicole ducked her head and spoke to Baldwin with her head lowered as though fearful, her eyes avoiding the knight's.

'Sir, there is one man I have heard who might have been guilty. The Reeve himself.'

'How dare you!' Alexander said, his voice growing in volume as the anger flared in his breast. He felt as though his chest must burst with rage. 'You accuse me?'

'Speak!' Baldwin said.

'It was Ivo who told me. He said that he had a hold over the Reeve because of something he had seen many years ago – that the Reeve had killed a man, and Ivo had seen him.'

'That's a lie! I didn't kill the Purveyor!'

'That's not what Ivo said,' Nicole said firmly. 'You passed the blame to my poor Thomas to protect yourself.'

'How did you hear of his guilt?' the Coroner asked her.

'Ivo told me that if I would leave my husband, he would see to it that the Reeve would not support Thomas but would declare our marriage annulled.'

'The Reeve doesn't have that power,' Simon grunted.

'That may not prevent an arrogant shit like Ivo from telling it to the woman he hankers after,' Coroner Roger pointed out. 'Many a man will promise the target of his affections that black is white if it gives him an opportunity to lie with her.'

Sir Laurence said, 'Wonderful! Reeve, you are a man of enterprise and determination! To throw all suspicion onto other men so swiftly, that is the act of a genius.'

'I didn't kill him. I have never killed any man,' Reeve Alexander said woodenly. The fight was gone. He knew now that he was dead. There was no one to protect him. 'And I didn't kill the girls.'

'I don't care about the girls, whoever they may be. No, I need only concern myself with the body of Ansel. Where did you bury him? Won't talk? Never mind. We shall find him.'

'Oh, all right!' Alexander sighed and allowed his head to fall into his hands a moment, collecting his thoughts, before speaking through his fingers. As he spoke, he lifted his head a little way, so that he could meet Baldwin's gaze. All the time he was aware of Drogo behind him, listening carefully.

Before he could rally his thoughts, he saw Baldwin eyeing him with a contemplative expression while he fiddled with the thong tying his purse.

'This can wait until the morning, can't it?' Drogo said gruffly.

Baldwin looked into his eyes as he pulled out the splinter of arrow and threw it onto the table in front of Alexander. There was a sudden silence in the room, and Baldwin watched Drogo's eyes go blank with shock.

The Forester knew that his own fate was sealed.

Chapter Twenty-Three

Peter atte Moor was uncomfortable in his bed. Although he was exhausted after the last two nights of patrolling his bailiwick, watching and listening for any sign of trouble, sleep evaded him.

Once he had been a cheerful, tolerant man, but all that had changed one afternoon. One moment's passion, and his life had been infected, his soul branded, and now all he could do was seek out evil and destroy it. He must fine felons and see them hanged. It was his vocation, it was his only road to salvation. It was his penance.

The others couldn't understand. Peter had been born and bred here, like Drogo and Adam, but they had lived most of their time down in the vill, not up on the moors like him. He knew how capricious the moors could be. They could tempt a man to go and investigate them, and then, once he was miles from safety, they would strike; a mist would come down, so swiftly that he had no time to take his bearings, and so thick that he couldn't see two paces in front of him – and then the wandering soul would be led to a mire from which there could be no escape.

Peter had been tempted once – they all were, every now and again – but his temptation had caused his destruction.

It was a girl. He saw her up at the extreme end of his bailiwick, where a stream had been dammed to create a large pool. Massive rocks behind were drizzled with water which cascaded gently down, making the rocks glow in the sunshine as though they were made of glass. It was a beautiful place. Peter had always adored it, and seeing the girl there made him feel as though it had been blighted. This was his own private hollow, and she had ruined it for him.

She clambered from the pool, stood on the edge, and jumped straight back in. Tall, with long, pale limbs, and thick brown hair that looked almost black now it was wet, she was utterly beautiful, breathtakingly so. Peter had felt his heart thunder in his chest like a caged lion.

He had gone down to her, his eyes feasting on her as she climbed once more from the pool, shaking her head free of water, self-absorbed and unaware of his presence. There was a rushing in his ears. This girl had appeared from nowhere, as though she was a gift from God, an angel dropped into his bailiwick. When he reached her, there was a strange feeling in his head, as though he was more than half drunk, and there was a weirdness about everything. He could hear nothing. Certainly she must have protested, must have asked him to leave her, for he knew she struck at him and opened her mouth as though to scream, but he couldn't remember anything about it. He didn't hear her. It was as though his hearing was cut off. All he was aware of was a high-pitched whistling noise in his ears, which overwhelmed all other sounds.

It didn't take long. Afterwards, he knew he was defiled and so was his hollow. She had been a virgin, that was obvious as he surveyed her immature, weeping form on the grass before him, and, realising what he had done, he was sick. The noise in his ears had gone, his lust had flown, and he was left appalled and terrified. A small, frightened man who had lost his life's direction in a moment of passion.

Later, he heard that her body had been found by a lay brother from the convent. The girl had been a novice nun, and it was thought that she had slipped on a rock and knocked her head, falling unconscious and drowning. For all he knew it was true: he hadn't killed her, and he felt sorrow that she had died. He prayed it hadn't been suicide. He wanted to confess his sin to the Parson, but somehow didn't feel he could. The rape of the novice was a crime which must wait to be confessed until he lay on his deathbed, begging Absolution before dying.

God's punishment was dreadful. For his sins, his family were to pay with their lives. Within a year his wife died, leaving him to bring up their daughter Denise alone. And then she too died, murdered in the cruellest way. Never again could he know contentment. Now his only comfort was walking about his bailiwick; guilt his constant companion. He couldn't even enjoy a whore! Not after Exeter.

Peter had ravished a Bride of Christ, and he must suffer the weight of God's displeasure. All he could do to win favour from God was seek out other felons and make them pay for their sins. But although he found pleasure in seeing them destroyed, it wasn't enough. It was never enough.

He turned restlessly. His body, his very soul, ached with exhaustion, but when he closed his eyes, his brain refused to shut off. And then he realised why – it was the noise from the blasted hounds of Samson.

He almost prayed that he might be finally punished and released from this hell. Death would be a reward he could embrace with thanks.

Baldwin stood staring at Drogo for a moment, then he looked down at Alexander. 'Remember that, Reeve?'

'I couldn't give a tinker's fart for all this,' Sir Laurence said. 'All that matters is that this man is accused of the murder of Ansel de Hocsenham. Is that correct?'

'Yes,' Nicole said. 'He told me that he had control over the Reeve because he saw the Reeve burying the Purveyor's body. The Reeve had killed him, and Ivo swore not to tell anyone, but the Reeve obeyed his whims, he said.'

'Well, Alexander?' Baldwin asked.

'Jesus Christ! All right,' Alexander sighed. 'Yes, Ivo Bel found me out on the Oakhampton road with a shovel. Next day the Purveyor was missing, and yes, I had hidden him. But I didn't kill him.'

'Was he stabbed?' Baldwin asked.

'No. Strangled.'

'Don't interrupt, good Sir Baldwin,' Sir Laurence said. 'Let's have the whole story, eh? From the beginning.'

Alexander ignored him and spoke to the Coroner. 'It was the beginning of the famine. Ansel had been the Purveyor for years. He'd got Meg with pup two years before, but when the famine was really hurting, he arrived just when the harvest had failed, looking like a drowned kitten, bedraggled and soaked. I recall it was a Wednesday when he rode into the vill, and the rain was pouring down. It did every day that summer, or so it seemed, and the summer after. The weather didn't settle down until this year.'

Baldwin grunted. 'You reckon this year is settled?' he said, as he remembered warm, balmy days in the Mediterranean.

Alexander wasn't listening. 'He demanded a vast amount of grain, although he knew full well that we couldn't supply it, for he could see how poor our store was. I didn't realise what he was up to at first, I thought he simply didn't understand. My Christ, I even took him to the ovens to show him how poor the grain was, how water-sodden it was, and he nodded and said he understood.'

The bastard! He'd just stood there with that supercilious smile, agreeing that the harvest had been shite, and then he'd put his boot in, saying that the King still needed to feed his army, and it was the duty of all *loyal* subjects to supply his wants. As if the King could give a fig for the people of Sticklepath! Edward was too interested in his boyfriends to care about a vill collapsing and the people dying.

'I explained, I reasoned, I pleaded and I begged. Christ! I all but crawled on my knees to him, but the Purveyor didn't want to understand. I can see him right now. As I spoke, the shutters came across his eyes.

'I told him: "Ansel, if you do this we'll starve."'

'He said, "That is a great shame."'

' "Look at the people here, you're sentencing them to death, man! Can't you see that?"

' "All I want is the grain, Reeve. And you must supply it."

'He was stiff and matter-of-fact, glancing casually at the people labouring out in the quagmire that had once been a field. He didn't give a damn.

' "Ansel, *please!*" I said. "This is me – Alex – you're talking to. Look at me! The folk here are already suffering from scurvy and starvation; you can see it in their faces, you can see the way the kids are becoming listless. We had two children die last month. Both of my sons are weak. Do you want to execute the whole vill?"

' "I've got nothing to do with it. If you're hungry, you should improve your husbandry."

' "Come on, Ansel! There's nothing to eat. You take our food and we'll die. And not just the folk here, either."

' "What do you mean?"

'I said, "It won't only be the people of the vill who will suffer, it's going to affect the folks in the assarts and all about here."

' "You threaten me?"

' "I'm not threatening anyone! I'm telling you the facts, man. If you starve the vill, Meg and Emma will starve with the rest of us."

'And that was when Ansel's face altered. His eyes lost their concentration and he looked quite blank for a moment. And then he roared with laughter.

' "So you *are* trying to threaten me? Oh Alex, I am sorry, but if you think you can save a mouth or two, go ahead and starve them. She was only ever a comfortable bed for me. Why do you think I never stayed at her assart when I came past here? No, you can starve her or kill her any way you wish, and you can drown her whelp at the same time. It will save me the embarrassment of having to explain them to my wife."

' "You are already married? You can't be! You told Meg you'd married her!"

' "Oh yes, I did, didn't I?" he said. "Never mind. She'll soon forget. She was never very bright, was she?"

'He left me then, still chuckling. It was clear enough what he was after. He wanted the full quantity at a set rate per bushel, which was the same cost as the previous year before the prices all rose. That meant he would pay us between one sixth or one seventh of the actual value of the grain. The vill would never be able to replace it.

'But he knew he could get more elsewhere. It was as plain as the nose on his face that what he really wanted was money. Purveyors always do. They prefer to line their pockets than do the King's work.

'In the end we settled on three shillings and tenpence. It was all I could promise to collect in a short time, and he gave me a few days to collect it. He said he would wait at the inn and rest until I found it. Afterwards I heard that he had spent much of his time with poor Meg. She can never have known how he spoke of her, prepared to see her starve, and her child, for his own profit, the bigamous son of a poxed ferret!

'It took me almost a week to cajole, wheedle and threaten the money out of everyone. There were many who had nothing, but some of the locals had a few pennies stashed away, and generally I knew who they were, but it was hard. Very hard. No one had that much. This one man was taking another's yearly income – more! – in a bribe. Extortion, that's what it was. Give me all your money, or I'll take all your food and leave you to starve. What a choice! But what choice do we have? We are serfs, villeins, peasants – call us what you will. Our lives are not our own. I once heard a smartly dressed Prior riding through the vill, and when he looked at us all, he overheard a man talking about the cattle we owned, this was before the murrain, of course, when we lost the herd, and this *churl*, this man of God! Do you know what he said?'

Alexander was all but spitting now at the memory of that fool on his great horse, fat and smug in his velvets and furs and silks, peering about him disdainfully.

'He said: "These fellows are slaves. All they own is their bellies."

' "Their bellies"! Well, all we owned then was our hunger, and fear of dying. I had seen my wife die, and my two boys, during the famine. They were all I ever loved, and I wasn't alone.'

'This is most interesting, but perhaps you could come to the point?' Sir Laurence yawned.

Alexander looked at him, his face carefully composed. Sir Laurence was no better than that Prior: a knight like him had no sympathy for the sufferings of the poor. If the whole of Sticklepath were to perish, Sir Laurence might utter a few words of polite commiseration to Lord Hugh de Courtenay for the loss of his serfs, but that would be all. Peasants mattered less to him than his hunting dogs.

The Reeve swallowed his frustration. 'The point is, I got him his money, and he took it and returned to the tavern for the night. Except he didn't stay there. I went there myself later that evening, only to be told that he had left. I saw Meg the day after, and she was asking where he had gone. She'd been expecting him to turn up at her place the evening before. Poor maid, she was tearful and distressed. He'd cleared off – that was obvious. I didn't worry myself about it. At least I'd saved the vill from his greed. But that night his body was found lying in the valley leading up to Belstone.'

Alexander didn't look over his shoulder. At this moment he knew he held Drogo's ballocks in his hand. He could almost hear the Forester's tension, like a bowstring ready to snap, but he was damned if he would accept all the responsibility. He wouldn't be the fall guy for Drogo.

'I knew it was Ansel. He'd been throttled with a thong, a simple strip of hide, and dumped.'

'And?' Baldwin asked keenly.

'Sir Baldwin, please don't interrupt his fascinating speech,' Sir Laurence pleaded.

Alexander sighed. 'Yes. As if that wasn't bad enough, he'd been eaten, too. Not by animals. I mean, dogs and the like had chewed at him and his eyes had been pecked out, but those wounds couldn't hide the fact that a man had butchered him.

'It was too much to bear. I knew that the result would be more than a straight fine: this could cost the vill very dearly, perhaps even cause us all to starve to death. I'm not joking, Keeper. You remember how bad that famine was?

'So . . . I had to choose, and as Reeve, I chose life for the vill. I deliberately hid the body. I found a shovel and buried him, and I came home and . . . God! Won't those damned hounds ever shut up?'

Baldwin eyed the silent man at the wall. 'Did anyone help you?'

'Drogo did. It was he and his Foresters who found the body,' Alexander said firmly.

'You fucking—' Drogo's forward leap was halted by Baldwin's bright blue sword, which was suddenly at the exposed gap between his jack and his hose. He could feel the razor-sharp point at his groin.

'Did this Purveyor have a purse on him?' Simon asked. 'Could the butchery have been to hide a robbery? I've known Foresters who've turned to robbery themselves.'

'Whoever killed him certainly took the purse.'

'This is most intriguing. I have all I need,' Sir Laurence said, rising.

'Wait, Sir Laurence.' Coroner Roger smiled politely. 'I am the Coroner, and this witness is helping me to conduct an inquest.'

'Without a jury?'

'That will be organised tomorrow, or perhaps the day after,' the Coroner said happily, knowing that the knight would not want to wait more than a single day.

'I see,' Sir Laurence said. He gave a faint smile and nodded to the Coroner, acknowledging that he had lost, and resettled himself in his seat with a good grace, waving a hand and murmuring, 'Please continue.'

Coroner Roger nodded. 'So you say Drogo was First Finder?'

'Yes. Him and his men. They fetched me.'

Drogo felt the colour rising to his cheeks. He hated this: he had expected the Reeve to mention him, but then it had appeared that Alexander wasn't going to. Now he knew his fear was plain. His face always reddened at the drop of a hat; it didn't matter a damn whether he was entirely innocent or not, it was the mixture of embarrassment and irritation that mingled to bring on his flush. Vin's eyes were on him, too, but he daren't look at the lad.

Baldwin asked, 'Where exactly was the body?'

'Under some furze near the river.'

To Baldwin, Drogo looked like a man who was losing his temper quickly. 'What do you say, Drogo?'

'It's true that I found him. I sent my man to fetch the Reeve and stood with the body until he returned, and when he did, I carried the corpse with the Reeve and buried it with him.'

'Who was sent?'

'Adam.'

'You confirm this, Adam?'

'Yes. On my oath.'

Drogo said, 'The Reeve was worried, of course. We both were. I sent Adam and Peter away and fetched a shovel myself. Then I started digging.'

'Where?'

Alexander smiled without amusement. 'You remember I told you that the wall kept falling where Aline was found? It is all too common. Probably because of the tree roots there. Anyway, the wall had just been rebuilt. All we had to do was dig down a short way in the soft soil and put the body in.'

'What? Aline was buried in the same grave? That was why you

saw different material where Aline had lain, Simon!' Baldwin realised.

'Yes. Dig a little deeper; you'll find him.'

Baldwin looked at him very closely. 'And then this girl was buried on top of him by someone who knew that Ansel was already there. It was the perfect hiding place for Aline, wasn't it? Somewhere the Reeve himself would have been careful to make sure was *never* searched. Is that right? You prevented people from searching that place for Aline's body?'

'Nobody suggested it,' Alexander said heavily.

'But the person who concealed her there must have known about Ansel,' cried Simon. 'It's too improbable that someone could have buried the girl on top of an existing grave without knowing it. The burial right there must have been conducted by someone who had been involved in hiding Ansel. And that means you, Reeve, or you, Forester.'

Reeve Alexander stared at Drogo for a moment. 'I swear I did not kill Aline.'

Drogo's face was suffused an angry-looking crimson. 'Are you saying I did? Do you accuse me in front of all these people, Reeve?'

'I don't know. I didn't kill her myself, that's all I know.'

'Well, neither did I! And there were no other people there so far as I recall.'

'Hold, Forester!' Simon called loudly. For a moment he had thought that the Reeve was going to launch himself at Drogo. Clearly Adam thought the same. He had set a hand on his knife hilt as though readying himself to pull it free. Vincent had drawn away. Simon could see that he hadn't learned the first rule of fighting: never retreat, always go in aggressively; when fists might begin to fly, don't step back, but go in close.

Drogo stood clenching and unclenching his fists. 'I didn't harm that girl.'

'We already know that Ivo saw the Reeve there. Perhaps

someone else did too,' Simon said. 'And seeing that, later realised that they had a perfect grave. First, who could have hated Ansel enough to kill him?'

'How would you feel about a bent official like him?' Drogo sneered. 'He was the dregs, the bastard. I've vomited more powerful stuff than him, the pus-filled bag of wind.'

Baldwin and Simon exchanged a look, and seeing it, Drogo suddenly realised his peril. 'Of course I didn't like him, but that's not the same as murdering him! I knew he was going. Why should I kill him?'

Simon cleared his throat. 'Perhaps because you wanted the money? You were alone with the Reeve to bury the man, yes?'

'Yes.'

'But you had men with you when you found him?'

'Peter and Adam, yes.'

Simon's eyes narrowed. 'What of the other man in your team? Vincent – where were you?'

Vincent blinked in genuine surprise. 'Me? I was off at my own bailiwick, I suppose. It's a long time ago.'

'So you weren't there with Drogo. The other members of the team were, but not you.'

'So what?' Adam rasped. He had stepped forward, and now he glowered from one to another. 'What are you suggesting?'

'This: that Vincent didn't know where the body was buried; because he wasn't there. Peter and you were sent away, but you could have been interested enough to return and watch what the Reeve and Drogo were doing, couldn't you? And then later, perhaps, you killed a girl and buried her in the same place.'

Adam's mouth moved, but then he shook his head slowly. 'It could as easily have been the Forester here or the Reeve who killed the girl and buried her there. Anyway, I didn't go and watch them. I went to the inn with Peter, and a short while later Vin turned up as well.'

'Did you ask where he'd been?' Baldwin pressed.

'I had other things on my mind,' Adam sneered. 'Christ! Me and Peter had just found a body.'

'Did you tell Vin? Did he leave you? Could he have gone to watch?' Simon asked with some excitement.

'No, Bailiff. Peter left not long after, though.'

'Perhaps Peter went up there to watch,' Simon said. 'He could have sneaked up there and seen the two men digging, and later he might have realised it would be a perfect hiding place for Aline.'

'But what of his own daughter? She was the first girl to be found,' Reeve Alexander said.

'It is not unknown for a child to be murdered by her father,' Baldwin said.

'Why should he kill Ansel?'

'For the same reason anyone else in the vill could have,' Simon pointed out. 'None of you would have been keen to have had a man like him demanding bribes. And Peter was hungry, just like the rest of you. Hatred and hunger are powerful motives.'

'Christ Jesus! Will those hounds never be silent?' Coroner Roger muttered under his breath.

Baldwin knew how he felt. The atmosphere was thick, as though there was a thunderstorm on the way, and the hall was charged with emotion and fear. Drogo looked anxious, but then so did all of the vill's men. Sticklepath was like a place under siege, rather like Acre just before the collapse. Yet there were no armies at the gates, only the ghosts of victims.

He decided to change tack. Picking up the fragment of arrow, he stood turning it in his hands. There was little which could be learned from so old a weapon. It had been used some six years ago, if the story told by Meg and Serlo was to be believed. Looking up, he saw Drogo's eyes were on it. 'Who uses peacock's feathers in his arrows?'

'I do,' Drogo admitted.

'Do you recognise this?'

'It could be one of mine. I can't be certain.'

'This was one of the arrows used to murder Athelhard, Meg's brother.'

Drogo bit at his lip.

'You and your Foresters helped to kill him, didn't you?'

There was silence. Drogo stared down at the arrow with a face that whitened visibly. 'This is the devil's own work,' he muttered, but there was a thick, husky note in his voice.

'What does that mean?' Simon demanded.

'Come on, man!' Coroner Roger rasped. 'We don't have all day to stand here like women washing clothes!'

'It was the vampire,' Reeve Alexander said quietly. 'Gervase told us that vampires killed people, ate them and drank their blood. The killings all started when Athelhard returned here.'

'Only because of a coincidence!' Baldwin exploded. 'You slaughtered him for *superstition*! The poor man murdered, his sister forced to watch, and all for your intolerable beliefs!'

'It wasn't just that,' Drogo said. 'His sister told the priest that her brother had given her a large portion of meat, of pork, Keeper, only the day before. What would you have thought? We only did what any God-fearing, sane men would do; we struck at him to destroy him.'

'Ansel died before Athelhard arrived, didn't he?'

'No. Athelhard was just returned when Ansel died,' the Reeve said. 'And a short time after Denise was found we heard of this meal given to Meg. It was obvious. Athelhard told her he had bought it from a traveller. Would you have believed him?'

'Yes. Until he was appealed in court, and had had a chance to prove his innocence,' Baldwin said scornfully.

'And had a chance to kill others. You know that these *sanguisugae* can fly through the air like birds?' Drogo said. 'And no lock will hold them out.'

'Nonsense! There are no such things as vampires,' Baldwin said.

'The Parson told us. If you want a debate with him on the merits of his case, fine. For us, we wanted to prevent any more deaths. Perhaps you'd feel different if your own child stood the risk of dying for your beliefs, Keeper.'

'You tied his sister to a tree to force him to come out.'

'The Parson told us he had demons within him. He was possessed. What else could we do? We had to protect ourselves, and that's what we did. There was no one to advise us. At least we killed him swiftly, which is more than he did with Denise.'

'It was murder!' Simon declared hotly.

'And what would you have done, Bailiff? Let him carry on? We thought it was just a desperate, starving villager who was responsible at first, when we found Ansel's corpse, but then, when Peter's girl turned up, and the priest told us about vampires, we realised it was something worse.'

'But why think it might be Athelhard?' Baldwin interrupted.

'It seemed so obvious!' Drogo burst out. 'We had the shock of Denise's murder, then we heard that Athelhard had been cooking meat. And Athelhard was a stranger. If anyone had brought evil into the vill, surely it was him!'

'But others have died since his death, so it wasn't him,' Simon pointed out.

Drogo was silent, but the Reeve put his head in his hands again. 'You are right. I know it, and I regret it. But what else could we have done?'

'And who was the real guilty man?' Simon asked, and then wondered for the first time whether it might not be a woman. Meg had plenty to avenge, after all.

Sir Laurence smiled. 'This is all beyond me. All I know is, I have two men here who appear to be suspects.'

Sir Roger returned his smile. 'Yes, you do. But I am the Coroner, and when I hold my inquest, I shall decide what to fine them for their misdemeanours as well as amercing them to be present at the next court.'

'I think you'll find you should have them thrown into gaol,' Sir Laurence said, his amusement becoming more brittle. He weighed his war hammer in his hand again.

'You think so? I disagree,' the Coroner said cheerfully. 'And right now, this meeting is concluded. Reeve, don't try to leave the vill. Forester, get out of here and make sure that you don't tempt me to regret my actions!'

In his room, Swetricus sat on his stool facing the door, a pole slotted into the handle of a sharpened billhook. It was his only weapon, but it was enough. Or so he prayed.

Thomas and Nicole had walked here to fetch their daughter, both so taken up with their own relief that Swetricus had not seen fit to remind them that their problems weren't gone. While Reeve Alexander and Forester Drogo wished to blame someone, Thomas remained the ideal target. He may have survived this accusation, but there would be more.

His dog was agitated now, walking from one side of the room to the other, sniffing first at one door, then the other, constantly moving, as though to remain still was to die, but Swetricus was sure that it wasn't only the row from Samson's hounds.

'What is it, Daddy?'

'Shut up!' he said gruffly. The girls had no idea about all this. They sat now, huddled on the family's bed near the fire, which still roared with the faggots Swetricus had thrown on. At this time of night he would usually be there with them, snoring gently, all of them huddled together against the cold, the fire doused for safety, but not tonight. Not with Samson's hounds howling like the souls in torment the Parson had told the vill about when Athelhard was thought to be the vampire.

He picked up his firkin and drank a long draught of ale, setting it down and wiping his mouth.

After Athelhard, they had believed that the deaths would cease, but they hadn't. Only two months later, the poor orphan Mary had died, her mutilated body found discarded like an apple core. Athelhard was dead. The vill knew that there was someone else, someone who had been living among them, and suspicion had fallen upon several, but the only obvious man was Samson. However, there was no proof. And no more deaths – until Aline disappeared two years later. Swet had his suspicions, but if he had appealed Samson, he would have been laughed out of the court. Where was the body? Aline could have fallen into a bog and drowned.

Now Emma was dead although Samson was already in his grave. Some might say that proved Samson's innocence – but Swet knew better. He remembered the sermon which the Parson had preached on the day they all went and killed Athelhard. He had said that vampires could become possessed, and the demons could make the body fly through the air. That was why, he said, Athelhard should be buried with a prayer written out on a piece of parchment, to explain to his soul how to find peace so that he wouldn't haunt the vill afterwards. It was Alexander who had said that they should burn his body instead. If there was no body, he reasoned, there would be nothing for the demons to use.

Samson had died, but he had been buried. His body was there still, and Swet was sure that last night he had escaped from the earth and murdered Emma. Swet was sure, because the hounds were baying incessantly. Scruffy and mangy, they were, to be sure, but they knew as well as Swetricus did that tonight was no time for sleep. They had been bred to keep felons away, but now they howled to keep their dead master from them.

Gripping his staff more firmly, he tried to control the savage beating of his heart.

Evil was abroad tonight, but Swet would not lose another daughter.

Chapter Twenty-Four

'In God's name, give me peace!' Gervase shouted, walking about his room, his arms wrapped about his body so that he looked like a great raven in his dark habit. No matter how he struggled to hold down the panic that assailed him, it didn't work. Nothing could keep away the horror.

He wanted to go to the chapel, but somehow he felt easier here, among his few possessions, and that knowledge gnawed at him: he should want to go to the altar and kneel penitently before Christ's symbol, but he daren't. That would take him nearer Samson's grave.

The Miller's soul was abroad tonight: Gervase could almost hear a cacophony of demons calling to each other in the darkness. Pouring more wine into his mazer, his hand trembled so violently that he spilled a large amount on the table. Cursing, he lifted the mazer and drank, heedless of the flood that coursed at either side of his mouth and dribbled onto his breast. He let the cup fall, closing his eyes, his breath sobbing in his throat.

'Please, God, just make it be silent! Bring peace to his poor soul and drive away his demons,' he prayed, head bent.

He knew what was happening. This was his nemesis, his destruction. It was his own fault, all because he had accused the other fellow. Poor Athelhard. It was Gervase's sin which had led to Athelhard's death. He had learned from Meg of the pork which her brother had bought for them, and at first the Parson had felt only jealousy. The famine was already biting, and the idea of rich, juicy meat made his saliva run. He had mentioned her good fortune to Reeve Alexander, in the hope that the latter might force

Athelhard to share his bounty. Perhaps he would have, too, Gervase realised. He had been a decent fellow.

Then they had discovered little Denise up in the fields and Gervase realised quickly what that meant. The meat served to Meg, and the cruelly butchered body, pointed to the one conclusion.

It was Gervase's drunken telling of the story to Samson which had sealed Athelhard's fate. Samson went to see Drogo, and on the way he spoke to Peter atte Moor, and Peter was by then desperate for revenge. Who could blame him? His daughter was dead, throttled and cut about like a side of pork. And it made sense. Athelhard was a foreigner; it was only natural to believe that he was responsible.

Yet he wasn't. That was the hideous truth. Gervase dropped to his knees again, his breath wheezing as he pulled at his robes and bared his breast, opening it like an offering to his all-seeing God. Spreading his arms wide, he wept as he stared up at the ceiling. 'What else could I have done, Lord? I wanted to stop the murders! I did it in good faith, Lord, thinking that the man was possessed. Why did You let me be misled, Lord? Why did You let me think it was Athelhard?'

But there was no answer.

'Jesus, You let me sentence an innocent man – why?' he cried out. 'He was destroyed like a lamb, like *You*! How could You let that be done to someone else? Was it to punish me? Well, punish me now – take my life. I can't live on knowing I caused a man's murder. Don't leave me here to poison others.'

He felt a sudden burst in his heart, like the onset of a marvellous dream, and for a moment he believed he was about to see a vision, perhaps even an angel, but then the lightheadedness passed away and he was left alone, a huddled, shrunken man kneeling fearfully on his floor. God wouldn't listen.

Perhaps if he had himself gone to the Reeve it would have been all right, but as soon as that fool Samson heard the tale, he fell into a drunken, roaring rage. He was the father of a girl too, and he'd be buggered with a red-hot poker if he'd let some foreign shit ballock about with his daughter. Fuck that! Some shite had eaten Denise? Samson would stop him; he'd cut the bastard's throat, then he'd slice off his prick. That'd serve him out!

Thinking about it, it was strange that Samson hadn't been so vociferous about the other girls who had died. It was as if Denise's death had shocked him and he had seriously wanted to avenge her, but when Mary was found, and then Aline disappeared, Samson withdrew into himself. He didn't help try to catch the killer, said little about the killings, and either changed the subject or stopped talking. It was almost as though he felt a guilt about the deaths, or a deep shame.

But on that other day, Samson was enraged as only a bone-headed fool could be. When Peter passed by, Samson bellowed at him that he was letting the foul murderer of his daughter go free. Wouldn't he see the foreign git hang? Samson was insistent until all the men in the tavern had sworn to avenge Denise.

They left the inn and went to Alexander's house; the Reeve demanding to know what their rioting was about. Gervase found himself being thrust to the front of the men, and made to tell the story again, but this time he found that his audience was still more receptive. Only later did he wonder whether Alexander had known of another murder.

There was a sour taste in his mouth when he had finished and he could stand and listen to the men discussing Athelhard and the dead girl no longer. Suddenly he felt a pricking of conscience: this was wrong. They shouldn't go and execute Athelhard like a felon. Even over the haze of alcohol and the demands of vengeance, a small, quiet voice seemed to warn him that this was an awful act. Athelhard would have no opportunity of defence. This crowd was a mob determined to destroy. They had decided that Athelhard was a vampire and that was sufficient for them. At that point, Gervase became aware of his own doubts.

Surely a man who was possessed would have hesitated to enter the church; he would have refused the Mass and Eucharist, wouldn't he? And wouldn't Gervase himself have felt something when in the presence of evil?

After the event, Gervase had done all he could to bring the men of the vill to a joint understanding of their shared guilt and he had prayed for Athelhard's soul, lost though it was, since it had not received the last services, Extreme Unction or Sacrament. Yet although Gervase hoped that Athelhard's innocent soul was safe, he had no such hopes for Samson's.

Samson it was who had listened to the story of Meg's meat; Samson it was who had roused Peter; Samson it was who had persuaded the mob to kill; Samson it was who had led the way to Athelhard's assart. Samson it was who had fired the first arrow, missing his mark as Athelhard bent to his bucket.

There was another long-drawn-out howl from across the way and Gervase felt it like a stab in his chest.

Now Gervase knew why Samson had been so keen to lead the attack against Athelhard. Since Gunilda's visit, he knew everything. Oh, yes! He knew that Samson had molested his own daughter, and others. It was Samson who got Aline with child, and just as surely he had killed her and the others too. Samson atte Mill was the vampire.

It all made sense now. With a resolute air, the Parson stood and picked up his mazer, then refilled it. Lifting it, he toasted God in an almost heretical manner, bitterly angry to have been forced to cause the death of a man like Athelhard for no reason. Then he opened his mouth and tipped in the wine. It was cheap and rough, but it was enough to strengthen his resolve. He was a failure as a priest, he had failed his congregation, he had failed Athelhard, and he had failed God. That was the cause of the noise at the cemetery: Samson's unresting soul. His dogs knew, which was why they howled. And Gervase knew, which was why his spine tingled with fear.

Samson's body was in thrall to demons. That was obvious, because he had killed Emma after his own death. Now Gervase must free Samson from the demons which possessed him. Throw them out and allow Samson to lie in peace . . . and protect the other folk of the vill.

The wine had given him courage and now he felt he could face Samson's ghost. He knew what he must do. On his table was his scrip, and he opened it, studying the small piece of paper and the phial. Satisfied with both, he carefully tied the scrip by its two leather thongs to his belt and took up his staff.

With a deep breath, he threw open the door. Outside, the wind was blowing steadily from the moors, and the air was thick with mizzle. Tiny droplets of rain landed softly on his bared breast, but he didn't care.

The hounds sounded more mournful out here in the open, their voices shuddering on the wind as though they were calling in desperation to their master, begging him to come back. Now that his decision had been made, Gervase felt calm. The indecision of the last couple of days had sapped his strength and now that he had chosen the route he must take, his soul was strengthened.

Squaring his shoulders, he set off to Swetricus's house. He hammered on the door with his clenched fist, waiting for it to be opened. When it wasn't, he struck the door with his staff and called out, 'Swet, you miserable cur, open up! It's me, Gervase, your Parson.'

There was no reply, and then he heard the slow scrape of the wooden latch being lifted. The door opened a little and a suspicious eye peered out at him.

'Swet, you've heard him too, haven't you? Fetch a shovel. We have work to do.'

Felicia shivered as her mother paced back and forth in the mill. The hounds were still calling, as if they could sense the approach of some foul creature from the moors. Perhaps it was true, what she had been told when she was a child, that devils lived out on the moors, and that they would torment the men and women who lived on the fringes.

'Mother, won't you come to bed?' she called again. She had already lost count of the number of times she had asked her mother to join her on their palliasse, but Gunilda didn't seem to hear her. Dark shadows under cheekbones and eyes made her look gaunt, almost as though she was herself dead.

'He's coming. I can hear him,' she said, and laughed.

It was a terrible sound, and Felicia gasped with horror. Her mother was going mad, and she felt that she must surely follow. This constant walking up and down, staring out through the open windows down at the cemetery, was petrifying.

'We did our best, we did, but he's coming back. I can hear him, just like the dogs can. Samson wants you again. We can't let him have you, though. No, never again.' Gunilda walked to the family's chest. It was a rickety old thing, ancient and wormeaten, but it was the only secure container. Reaching inside, she brought out a long-handled knife. Then she went back to the door, chuckling to herself.

'Yes, my lover. You hurt us, oh so often, and you want to hurt us again, but now you've gone I won't let you back. I only have Felicia, and I won't let you harm her again.'

Swetricus was breathing heavily as he pulled off his leather jerkin and hefted his great shovel. He was aware of a sick feeling in his belly, but it was no good. He had to go ahead. He had no choice, not if his girls were to be safe. Unless he helped the Parson, his other daughters might be killed like Aline.

He gazed at the white features of the Parson, then up towards the cemetery and the howling dogs, and as he did so, clouds passed over the moon. The mizzle stopped and a thin rain fell, and the cemetery was hidden. When the clear light shone out once more, the rain suddenly stopped, and he almost expected to see a ghostly figure standing there by Samson's grave, wrapped in a white shroud. It was with enormous relief that he saw the place was deserted.

'Come, my friend. We have to do this now,' said Gervase.

'When I've fetched Henry.'

'There's no time.'

'I'm not leaving my girls alone,' Swetricus said with blunt finality. Gervase could see the determination in his eyes, and nodded. Together they walked to Henry Batyn's house.

Henry lived with Peter atte Moor since his own house had collapsed, and it was Peter who opened the door. 'What do you want, Parson?'

'Look after Swet's girls. We're going to destroy him.'

Peter blinked. 'Who?'

Swetricus answered. 'It was Samson. He killed Aline, and your Denise and Mary and Emma. We're going to kill him.'

'He won't persecute us any longer,' the Parson said confidently.

Peter gaped. Then, 'Bring the girls here, Swet. Henry will guard them and I'll come with you.'

'Good,' said Swetricus, and returned to his own little place. Soon they could hear him calling his daughters over the whistling of the wind.

'First, I'm going to find Drogo,' Peter continued, tugging on his jack.

'No. We have to strike him while we can.'

Peter looked at the Parson. 'You'll need torches,' he said. 'I know where to get some.'

'Forget them. We don't need them.'

'If you're right and he killed my Denise, I want to see his face,' Peter hissed, leaning close, so that his own face was scant inches from Gervase's. 'This turd killed my daughter, Parson, and he *ate her*. I want to see him dance as we kill him.'

'Oh, get the torches, then, but hurry!' Gervase said reluctantly.

Peter nodded, then set off purposefully for the vill. He passed

Swetricus, who ushered his girls into Peter's house. Henry stood with his wife and sat the girls at the fireside. 'I'm coming too,' he declared.

'You should guard the girls,' Swetricus growled.

'If he can escape you, they'll not be safe with me looking after them,' Henry said simply. He reached behind the door and selected a shovel.

It was only a short walk, but even in the time that it took to get to the cemetery gate they could see other men gathering in the road by the inn. They gripped torches, the flickering yellow flames flattening and dancing in the gusting wind. Some stood nervous and uncertain, fearing to follow their Parson, but then the crowd began to move towards the cemetery.

Gervase felt better than he had for a long time. The howling ceased to trouble him now that he was fixed upon a course of action; the wine he had drunk had left him feeling clear-headed and warmed, as though God had breathed determination into his very bones. In truth, he felt as though he was at last performing God's will. After so many years of blaming himself for Athelhard's death, he knew what he must do. It was so refreshing, he almost felt he could sing and dance in praise of God.

'Give me strength, Lord, to do Your will,' he breathed, and began to sing the *Pater Noster*.

Behind him, Swetricus and Henry strode silently, not exchanging a glance, only keeping their eyes fixed firmly on the graveyard. They passed through the gate, and set off behind the Parson, heading for Samson's grave, and it was there that they saw her.

Dressed in tatters, the clothing ripped from her body, shreds flapping in the wind, she was recognisable as Gunilda only from her thickset body. She knelt at the grave of her husband, raking her hands through the sodden soil, then beating at it with her hands. As they approached, they could hear her.

'Shut up! Shut up! You killed them all – aren't you content? Can't you leave us alone? You would have done it to Felicia again, wouldn't you? But I won't let you. You couldn't keep away even when you were dead, could you? You had to come back and kill Emma. Why can't the devil take you? Shut up!'

Swetricus glanced at the priest, but Gervase was standing and swaying as though to music only he could hear, a beatific expression on his face. Grunting, the peasant stabbed his shovel into the soil and took Gunilda's arm. He lifted her to her feet, and she stood alarmed, cowering at the sight of the men converging on the grave.

'It wasn't my fault! He killed them, but I didn't know it. I didn't . . . I'm so sorry, so sorry! And now he's coming back to take her from me! He wants Felicia!'

Gervase smiled, then stopped her mouth with his hand. 'Child, it wasn't your fault, nor was it mine. This is the devil's work, and his minions are among us.' He jabbed a finger down at the ground even as the vill's men arrived, the torches casting a lurid light over them all. 'Friends, listen to me! The man we knew as Samson was the killer of our children. He killed Denise, he killed Aline, he killed Mary, and last night he killed Emma!'

There was a low hiss from the crowd, then an intake of breath.

'Yes! I say he killed Emma too. He has been taken over by demons, and we must exorcise them. Men! Dig, dig down into his grave, and bring out his body. I must lay this holy message on his breast, and then his soul will be free. He will never come back to trouble us. We can save him – we *must* save his soul. It is God's will!'

Leaving the house, Coroner Roger winced as he put weight on his ankle. 'This is not getting any better – and keep your damned dog away. Moth-eaten mutt nearly tripped me!'

'Put your hand on my shoulder,' Baldwin said. 'What are those hounds crying for?'

'God knows,' the Coroner said. He was glad to be leaving Alexander's depressing room. It aped a great lord's hall, but after today it would only have the feel of a gaol for him. Seeing Alexander sitting at his table, a broken man, had touched a nerve in Roger's heart. It was terrible to see a man at bay in his own home.

'The place needs a woman's hand,' Baldwin continued, seeing the Coroner's expression. 'It reminds me of my own hall before I married. Something is missing, some spark of life or joy.'

'You think a woman adds joy?'

'Some women do,' Baldwin smiled contentedly.

'Wait until you have been married as long as me before you make another comment like that,' the Coroner said. 'You'll realise your error. Isn't that right, Bailiff?'

'Hmm?'

'Wake up, Simon! Aren't you listening? We were talking about women and—'

'You were thinking the same? A woman could have done it?'

Baldwin caught his tone. 'What do you mean?'

'The deaths: Athelhard was killed wrongly because the vill took against him, and then the girls started to die. Couldn't Meg have decided to take revenge?'

Baldwin snorted. 'And what of Denise? She died before Athelhard; that was why the people decided to execute Athelhard in the first place.'

'True, and of course Ansel de Hocsenham was already dead as well,' Simon said. 'But Meg could have killed them too!'

'Perhaps,' Baldwin said without conviction. He asked Roger, 'What did you think of the Reeve's story?'

'I have to confess that I found it believable.'

Simon grunted. 'Up until now I was happy to believe that the Forester or the Reeve could have killed the Purveyor, but I think you're right. Their denials were convincing.'

'I had thought that the death of the Purveyor was separate, but as I said after we met Meg, what if his death was the first in a sequence?' Baldwin said, and now there was a growing excitement in his voice. 'Now we know that he too was murdered and eaten. Surely he must have been killed by the same person.'

'Why would the guilty person kill a man and then go on to slaughter children?' Simon asked. 'Ah! Perhaps because the first was an opportunistic murder, trying to stop the hated tax-gatherer from thieving the vill's money, and the killer didn't want to waste the flesh. He was starving, so he cut some portions to eat. Learning the meat was good, he killed again, and then even after the famine was done, he had a taste for human flesh.' He shivered at the thought.

'It is a possibility,' Baldwin said. 'But we also have the strange fact of Aline's concealment. Why should someone hide her when all the other victims were left in plain view?'

'If it was someone who knew her well, perhaps it was to give her the merest imitation of a church burial?' Simon suggested.

'Someone who cared that much surely would have found a different victim,' Baldwin said. 'No, I think it must have been for a different reason. Maybe the killer was anxious about being discovered. Or could it have been done to offend someone – the girl's father, for instance? To hurt his feelings, or to leave him in pain. Or maybe it was just punishment of the girl?'

'Did anyone have a motive for the murders?' Simon said. 'I've always tried to see who might have made money or got some other benefit from a crime, but in this case where is the motive?'

'There is always a motive, no matter how obscure,' Baldwin said with conviction.

Coroner Roger grimaced as his bruised foot caught on a tussock of grass. 'Are you sure?'

'Yes. I have known men to kill because they disliked another's eye colour; to show that they were men; to impress women . . . and so on. There is always a reason, if you could but see it.'

Simon held out his hands in a gesture of bafflement. 'But what could the motive be in this case?'

Baldwin was silent a moment. He was watching a crowd gather

outside the inn. 'Let us walk on. Those men look boisterous. Now,' he continued as they left Alexander's house behind them, 'The first death, that of Ansel de Hocsenham, may have been an accident.'

'The Purveyor was hated by all about here,' Simon reminded him. 'Perhaps he was killed because of that hatred, or maybe he saw something . . .'

Baldwin agreed. 'Let us suppose he was not only seen by someone who hated him, but that his killer was also starving. Perhaps the two motives came together.'

'What of the girls?' Simon said. 'Do you think he got a taste for the flesh of humans?'

'Perhaps. But I think it is more than that. Most of his victims were young girls. Children. All of about eleven years of age. That is curious. Surely it was a man trying to gain power over those weaker than himself. Any man could go and make use of a tavern's whores if he needed, so was this a man who had no money, or was it a man who felt threatened by women – so threatened that he sought to take them by force?'

'But he didn't take women,' Coroner Roger scoffed.

'No,' said Simon with dawning understanding. 'He took the only women he could, young girls who knew little better, who couldn't physically protect themselves against him.'

'So we have a weakly man,' Baldwin said, 'who was extremely poor during the famine and couldn't afford food, nor did he have any growing at his home.' He curled his lip. It was not convincing.

'At least that means we should be able to free some people from suspicion,' Coroner Roger said.

'Yes,' Simon said. 'And the more the better.'

'Listen to those blasted hounds!' Coroner Roger burst out. 'Why *are* they still making that infernal racket?'

Baldwin cast an eye up towards the mill. 'They miss their master.'

'A dog would usually have got over the death of a master by now.'

'Shall we see if there's something else wrong, then?' Baldwin enquired.

Simon looked from one to the other. 'I suppose you want to walk through the bloody graveyard to get to them? After all, what could be more pleasant on a chill and damp evening than a wander among rotting corpses. There's only your wife, Baldwin, and mugs of hot spiced wine waiting for us in the tavern; nothing to hurry back for.'

'You don't have to join us,' Baldwin said mildly.

'Ah, bugger it! If we're going to take a look, let's get on with it,' Simon said, and began to march towards the mill and the howling dogs – although Baldwin noted that he skirted the cemetery and didn't attempt to walk through it.

Aylmer sprang on ahead, but it was not easy for the men, especially for the hobbling Coroner. Although the day had been mostly dry, there had been enough drizzle during the evening to fill the puddles and make the mud even more thick and glutinous than before. Roger tried to hop between the ruts, but it was not easy because carts had created hard rails of rock-like dried mud which wouldn't soak up moisture so speedily, and he found himself slipping and swearing as he made his way to the source of the noise.

The mill was in darkness, and as the three approached, the wind seemed to grow in strength. Simon could hear a large piece of cloth flapping. It sounded like the wings of an enormous bird or bat, a bizarre, unwholesome sound, and he wished that he could silence it, but he couldn't see where it came from. Probably a length of sacking covering a window, he thought.

Just then, the moon was covered again and the yard became utterly dark. A few heavy drops of rain fell and Simon muttered another curse, hunching his head down between his shoulders, as though that could help, but then the moon was free again, and suddenly he felt his fears leaving him. There was no need to worry about spirits in a place like this. The mill was open to view, and there was not the slightest space for a man or ghost to hide.

In fact, Simon thought it was a pleasing view. The moonlight was almost as strong as the mid-day sun, or so it seemed, and all about, the land was bathed in a silvery light. Puddles sparkled and glittered, and even the river, which he could glimpse through the trees, shone like a ribbon of silk.

The dogs were held in a kennel between the mill and the cemetery, Aylmer standing before them wearing a puzzled expression. They did indeed remind Baldwin of his own great raches, but they were not guarding tonight; they had no interest in him or the others. Their concentration was devoted to the moon, Baldwin thought at first, but then he saw that they only howled upwards. Between each sobbing cry, they stared out over the cemetery.

'What in God's name is your trouble?' Coroner Roger demanded, bending to the nearer of the two. He spoke with exasperation and bemusement. 'Come on, you monsters, can't you see that some people want to get back to their inn and find a meal?'

'It's something over there,' Baldwin said.

'Where?'

Simon saw Aylmer trot away towards the wall. 'The cemetery?'

'There is no need for you to come as well, but I shall take a quick look.'

'You assume that I fear a cemetery at night?' Simon said. His voice sounded strained even to his own ears. 'I wouldn't have it said that a mere Keeper dared to rush in where a Bailiff did not!'

'Are you sure?'

'Yes.'

Baldwin gave a half grin, but there was a challenge in his eyes. 'You seem alarmed, though. Why?'

Simon sighed. 'The other night, I was walking along the road when I heard something.'

'What sort of something?'

'Like a voice from under the ground. Like a . . . ghost.'

Baldwin's grin froze. 'In the cemetery?'

'It came from where Samson was buried.'

'My Christ!' Baldwin said, appalled. 'Don't you see? The poor devil must have been buried alive!'

'Hoy, what are those men doing up there?' the Coroner interrupted them. 'Torches and all sorts.'

'Come quickly!' Baldwin said, leaping forward and springing over the low wall surrounding the cemetery. 'We have to protect him from their madness!'

Coroner Roger stared after him. 'This is all very well, but I don't mind confessing that I feel as scared as though the devil were at my arse! Do you really mean to enter that place at this time of night?'

'Not happily,' Simon admitted. 'But I daren't leave him in there alone. It looks as though the whole vill is there!'

The Coroner glanced down at his leg with a grimace. 'Come on, then. The sooner it's done, the better.' And he grasped his staff more firmly as he lifted his leg gingerly over the wall, and set off after Baldwin.

Chapter Twenty-Five

Vin didn't want to be here in the cemetery. The place was scary at this time of night. However, Drogo had insisted that he come. The Foresters' leader seemed a bit nervous himself. Vin knew about him burying the body of the Purveyor with the Reeve, but what else could there be to concern him? There was the small matter that every one of the murders had occurred when Drogo was away from Vin. The latter couldn't recall every one of those nights, but certainly Drogo had been out at his bailiwick when Emma was killed, or so he said. Perhaps he had come back to the vill and throttled her, then taken his pieces of flesh back up the hill to his camp fire?

But why should he do such a dreadful thing? And why eat them? Because he liked the flavour? Vin shuddered. He recalled meals with Drogo demanding bloody meat, remembered the man's chin dripping in gore, and suddenly Vin felt queasy.

Swetricus had already dug down several feet with Henry's help, and had just stepped down into the grave to dig out the rest when Baldwin pounded up. Behind him, the Coroner had caught sight of Swetricus's work, and immediately his face reddened and he roared, hopping over to join Baldwin.

'Just what is God's name is going on here? Get out of that grave, you bastard. Parson, what the Hell is this?'

Gervase stepped forward, motioning with a hand to Swetricus to continue. 'Coroner, this is Church land. Your jurisdiction ends there, at the wall.'

The Coroner was appalled. 'What are you doing here,

condoning this . . . this desecration! Why?'

'Because—'

Before he could answer, Swetricus dropped his shovel, ashen-faced, and sprang from the hole as a hideous shriek erupted from it.

Simon felt his stomach churn and took a pace back. That scream sounded like it came from the bowels of the earth itself – and then he corrected himself: it came from Hell. There was nothing earthly about it.

All about him, the men of the vill had moved away from the graveside, muttering and shaking their heads, one or two sidling towards the gate that gave out onto the road. Only two men stood firm: Baldwin and Gervase, with Aylmer at their side.

Gervase was smiling. This was the proof! He had known he was right! Now the vampire's cry showed it. Nobody could doubt the evidence of their own ears. Seeing Swetricus standing a yard or two away from the grave, the Parson indicated that he should continue. The peasant, his face showing his fear, wiped a forearm over his brow and stared down at the ground. Then he resolutely stepped forward, carefully lowered himself into the hole once more and picked up his shovel.

'What was that?' Coroner Roger exclaimed.

Baldwin spoke tightly. 'The poor man's not dead. He's still alive.'

'No, Sir Knight,' Parson Gervase said. 'He's dead, but demons have taken him over.'

'Don't be stupid, man,' Baldwin spat. 'He must have been buried alive by mistake. It's not surprising, seeing that he was knocked on the head. I've heard of men who have been buried alive before, when all they received was a bad knock. The poor devil—'

'He is no poor devil, Sir Baldwin. Ask his wife. She told us before you got here. Samson was always molesting young girls, including their own daughter. This man deserves no sympathy.

And if he was buried alive, as you say, how did he escape to kill Emma last night?'

'He didn't,' Baldwin said flatly. 'Surely you can see that this is only superstition? You cannot be thinking of killing the man just because *we* made a mistake and buried him alive!'

'You say I am thinking of killing him,' Gervase said reprovingly. 'I would do no such thing. I cannot: he is already dead. His soul has been taken over by demons because he died suddenly and couldn't receive the Extreme Unction which would have forgiven all his sins. So I must put this paper on his chest.' He opened his scrip and took out the sheet upon which he had so carefully scrawled. 'And anoint him with oil.'

Of all the men of the vill, Henry Batyn was nearest. He peered over the Parson's shoulder, his face falling. 'You're going to stick that on him and anoint him?'

'It will show him how to gain salvation,' the Parson smiled.

Peter atte Moor pushed his way through the crowd. Snatching at the paper, he stared. 'You've written things on it.'

'Yes, it tells him how to—'

'He couldn't read, Parson. What good'll this do?'

'His spirit can receive the message,' Gervase said, but a note of doubt had entered his voice. He hadn't heard that there was any need for a recipient to be able to read. Women in childbirth had prayers written down and laid against their inner thighs to help them cope with the pain whether they could read or not, didn't they? And Gervase had heard of demonic possession of corpses where this was the correct procedure.

'Ballocks!' Peter scoffed. 'This evil bastard couldn't read when he was alive, and he won't be able to if he's dead. Anyway, he killed my Denise when he was alive, and Emma when he was dead. I'll not see him reburied so he can murder any more.'

'He'll get out again,' came a voice from the crowd, 'and this time he may not kill a girl. It could be any one of us!'

'That is nonsense!' the Parson said. 'He won't be able to hurt anyone once I have put this on his chest and anointed him.'

'So *you* say, Parson, but how can we know?' Swetricus asked, clambering out again. 'I've lost one daughter. I won't risk another.'

'Get back in the grave, Swetricus,' Gervase commanded.

The peasant raised his arms. 'Who else here will let the ghost kill their children?'

'What else can we do?' Peter atte Moor asked.

'We know what to do!' It was Drogo, who now shouldered his way through the press with Vin and Adam in his wake. They stood at the graveside and stared down into it, and then Drogo looked at the men all about. 'Every household, bring faggots. We'll burn him, like we did Athelhard, and scatter his ashes so he can't come back and trouble us again.'

Baldwin felt his heart lurch. 'No, you must not! This man is alive still. He was interred by accident. Just think of it: he has been in there for a day, in a tiny space, praying for someone to rescue him. You must not raise him, only to throw him onto a pyre.'

'If you won't help us, leave us,' Drogo said curtly.

'Watch your tongue, Forester. I have only just given you your freedom,' Sir Roger growled.

'And I am grateful, Coroner, but I won't betray the trust these villagers have in me,' Drogo stated uncompromisingly. 'And I won't see another girl killed by this evil shit.'

Gervase stamped his foot and bellowed that the men should ignore Drogo, but even as he spoke, he could see that most of them were disappearing, streaming away to the vill to obey the Forester's command.

Baldwin saw them leave with growing anger and trepidation. There were so many. 'Simon, we must stop this.'

'How can we? Just look at them all!'

Men were running eagerly over to the mill's sheds, seeking sticks and tinder, collecting whatever bits and pieces they could find which might burn. Others hung around, but all had the same expression: fear mingled with excitement, just like the crowds at any hanging.

No, Baldwin corrected himself, he was being unfair. They were not happy to see a man being hanged, because they did not believe that this *was* a man; to them he was a demon, a child-killer. They would be destroying an agent of the devil, a *thing* which could attack and kill men, which ate children.

It made him shiver with horror. He couldn't face the idea that there should be a burning here, the burning of an innocent man whose only crime was that he had been buried alive by mistake. Baldwin had seen too many men die in the flames. The Knights Templar who refused to confess their guilt or, worse, who confessed under the tortures only to later recant, were bound to stakes and fired before massive crowds. From the Grand Master, Jacques de Molay, to the lowest Sergeant, all had died, and the odour of their roasting flesh had mingled with the sweet wood-smoke of apple and oak branches, to create a cloying smell that would linger in his sinus for ever.

As the men drew near with their faggots, Simon put a hand on Baldwin's shoulder. 'You mustn't interfere, Baldwin. They will kill you as well if you try to stop them.'

'This cannot be permitted.'

'You're right,' said the Coroner, but his eyes went to Simon. 'Only I cannot imagine how to prevent them. Simon is correct. These churls aren't going to let you get in their way. They don't see this as an illegal execution, it's just turning off a devil. And if you were to save him, what then? He'd be sought out, especially if another girl were to die. Would you be able to hold that on your conscience?'

'You believe that this poor fellow could break loose and climb up through the soil to kill Emma? No! So he didn't kill Emma, which means he didn't kill the others either. He's innocent!'

There was a sudden roar, and the Coroner spun around. Two men were hauling on ropes, while Swetricus climbed from the hole. He walked to the ropes and threw his own weight behind them, more men pulling and groaning, until suddenly there was a harsh rending and scraping, and the timbers which had been set atop of Samson came away bringing a shower of soil with them.

From the crowd there came a great collective sigh, and Roger instantly glanced at Baldwin.

The knight had a pained expression on his face. He could hear a low wailing moan, and he knew that it must be Samson. It would be a miracle if the miller hadn't lost his mind, left to suffocate and die under a ton of soil.

There was a general movement towards the grave, and Baldwin felt the men pushing him forward. At his side, he saw Simon being swept on, his eyes being drawn reluctantly downwards, although when he saw the winding sheet, he averted his face.

'He's fucking alive!' a man wailed. 'Oh, God! It's true, he's a demon!'

Even Simon couldn't help but glance into the grave.

No one could have looked less like a demon. The miller lay back whimpering, his face covered with both forearms as though petrified, as though he was already in the pit of Hell and feared that he would find himself confronted by demons tormenting him. When a man sprang down into the grave and pulled his arms away, Samson's eyes were wild, darting from side to side. As torches were brought nearer, Simon saw him wince and squeeze his eyes tight shut, then try to turn his face away into the dirt.

Until that moment, Simon would have been happy to see him burn, but that single childlike gesture of defence made all his fear melt away. Baldwin was right. This was a man who had been buried in a hole only slightly larger than his own body, without food or water, left to think that he would die slowly and horribly.

The men at the side of the grave were silent for several minutes, but then Gervase stepped forward, holding out his piece of paper and pot of oil. 'Let me down,' he instructed. 'I have to anoint him.'

Simon glanced at Baldwin and saw that his friend was preparing to halt this obscene event.

'Let me pass!' Gervase demanded again, pushing at the men nearest him, his shoulder jostling into Baldwin.

'No, Parson. Sorry, but no. He killed my daughter.'

That was Peter atte Moor, and Baldwin saw that he was backed up by Swetricus. Drogo was still nearby, but he looked as though he might be prey to the same doubts as Baldwin himself now that he had an opportunity to see Samson's grave. Baldwin, acting on an impulse, strode to Drogo's side and was about to speak, when suddenly Peter atte Moor shouted with a voice filled with horror.

'Christ Jesus, look! He's still covered in her blood!'

Baldwin turned, stared at Peter, and then down at Samson. Peter was holding out a torch, sending a lurid flickering light into the grave, and now he pointed, his finger shaking.

'You say he's no threat? Does any man here think he isn't a danger to us all? Look at him!'

Baldwin pushed his pointing hand aside. In the folds of his winding sheet, he could see the stains. Much of the staining came from the sodden earth, some was soiling from Samson's fear, but there were other marks on the cloth. 'Rubbish! You fool, it is not Emma's blood, it is his own.'

In his abject terror, Samson had tried to claw his way to freedom, and his fingernails had torn away as he scrabbled desperately at the timbers above his head. His head wound too was bleeding; not with a massive effusion, but enough to spatter his face with blood, making him look suspicious.

'This is the man who killed my daughter,' Peter said. His eyes were wild, and Baldwin could see the spittle flying from his mouth as he spoke. 'He killed Denise, and Aline, and Mary, and Emma too! How many more must die? He's possessed – we know that. We have to burn the demons from him.'

'I said NO!' Baldwin bellowed, but the crowd was already pressing forward. The pyre was almost complete, a large cone of faggots atop of sacking and straw, with a tree in the middle. People reached down to grab Samson, and he was lifted, screaming with an odd, shrill voice.

'Leave him!' Baldwin shouted again, but he was ignored. Filled with a rushing torrent of rage that washed over and through him, he put his hand to his sword's hilt and pulled the blade free. The sword was a bright peacock blue that flashed and shone like a lightning bolt in the darkness. 'STOP, I said!'

Simon heard his roar, saw the crowds begin to separate, saw the whirling of metal, and felt the blood course more swiftly through his veins. He couldn't allow Baldwin to be overwhelmed by the mob. It was unthinkable; Baldwin had saved his life. Crying, 'St George!' he pulled his own sword free and shoved men from his path, striving to reach his friend. He heard the sudden snarl and savage bark of Aylmer, a cry, and a man leaped back. ''Ware the hound!'

'Kill him as well!' a man shouted, and a torch was thrust almost into Baldwin's face. He felt the heat, heard the hairs of his beard fizzle, smelled the acrid burning, and snapped his sword up into a half-guard, cutting deep into the wood of the torch before the owner could remove it. The head of the torch fell away as Baldwin saw another figure at his side, and moved to avoid a blow as a fist holding a knife whistled past his shoulder. He thrust once and heard a scream.

Simon roared, kicked at the man before him, and was almost at Baldwin's side when he saw her.

She came through the crowd like an avenging spirit, her face set into a vicious mask, her hands clenched into claws, and for a moment Simon thought she wished to attack Baldwin, but then she darted under Baldwin's sword arm, ran past the Parson, and reached the edge of the grave as Samson was being raised. Simon saw her scratch at the face of Samson, her husband. He screamed

again, lifted his hands in a futile gesture of defence, but then his
voice altered. Suddenly it became a hideous bubbling sound, and
as Simon watched, he saw that Gunilda's hands were dark, and in
them was a knife. It rose, yellow and evil in the torchlight, as
though she was holding a flame in her fists, and then it flashed
downwards, only to rise and gleam with a fresh, crimson fire,
before plunging into Samson's breast once more.

'You were killed once. I can do it again, and again and again,'
she spat.

The Parson wailed; two men scurried away from her, and
Samson's cries became a hoarse coughing as he fell to his knees.
Simon saw him tumble to his side, the obscene flap of skin from
his head sliced away entirely as his wife flailed at him, striking
him in the head and chest.

Then the shock which had made his feet leaden, left Simon. As
others pulled away from her knife's reach, the Bailiff ran behind
her; the next time the knife rose, he caught her wrists and held
them. Gripping her tightly, he forced his fingers under her own
until she gave a sob and dropped the blade into the mud. Only
then did Simon glance at Baldwin.

The knight had dropped to his knees at Samson's side, and now
he looked up and shook his head wearily. 'He is truly dead this
time, I fear.'

Felicia was relieved. It was done now. Even the hounds appeared
to have realised and both had stopped their howling. When they
had stopped, she didn't know, for she had been watching the
events at the graveside, but now that she turned back, she noticed
that they were both silent in their kennel.

She left them and walked through the crowd, pushing her way
onwards until she came to her father's body. All about him were
the men of the vill, standing and staring down sombrely, while
Gunilda knelt weeping nearby. Felicia looked at her, feeling a
curious detachment.

There was an almost total absence of feeling for her mother. It was strange, but now, as she looked at Gunilda, she felt only a vague sympathy for her. Gunilda had tried to protect her from Samson, but she had failed.

Then the knight was in front of her, turning her slightly so that her attention couldn't focus on the dead body of her father.

'Are you all right?' Baldwin asked softly. 'This is a terrible place for you to be, child.'

'I'm fine. Why shouldn't I be?'

Baldwin studied her for a moment. She stood quietly, her eyes steady. If he had to bet, he would gamble that she was less affected by the dreadful scene than he was himself.

'I have come to fetch Mother,' Felicia said.

'Yes,' Baldwin said, standing aside. He saw the Coroner glowering, and walked to him. 'Don't worry, Roger. There's nothing to concern you here.'

'Nothing? I just witnessed a murder!'

'Maybe you saw a woman stab an already dead man. I don't know, we shall have to discuss the matter with the Church authorities. I may be able to talk to the Bishop. Essentially, it is an ecclesiastical affair. Nothing to do with us.'

'I can just see the King's Sheriff taking that view,' Coroner Roger scoffed, but then he nodded. 'Whatever happens, though, I'll be able to consider it more rationally tomorrow morning after a good night's sleep and a meal.'

'Yes,' Baldwin said, but he was troubled as he watched Felicia go to Gunilda's side. She bent, taking her mother's arm, and Gunilda gazed up at her with alarm, as though she could not remember her own daughter's face. A young lad walked over to them, and Baldwin recognised Vincent. He took Gunilda's other arm, and she allowed herself to be led away between the two youngsters.

Baldwin could not help but think that he would himself prefer death to life, rather than see such a lack of sorrow on his own daughter's face. Felicia had witnessed her father's murder, but she looked as triumphant as a woman who has seen her husband's murderer executed.

Felicia opened the door and thrust it wide with her hip. Carefully she pulled her mother inside, and Vin trailed in their wake, half-heartedly holding Gunilda's hand.

'I'll leave you, then,' he said.

'There's no hurry,' Felicia said, settling her mother on a stool and wiping Gunilda's brow.

Vin looked away with embarrassment. He thought there was every chance that Gunilda would be taken for the murder of her husband, although there was the claim of homicide while her mind was unbalanced. Anyone could believe that, having witnessed the scene. Perhaps she was fortunate that the Coroner and Keeper were there to see the whole terrible affair.

Felicia was silent. Passing him a jug, she drank deeply from a cup, then said, 'You remember that day by the river? You ran away then. Why?'

He couldn't meet her eyes. 'I was scared of your father.'

'You're safe from him now, Vin.'

'I know,' he said with a half grin. 'That was why I came back last night.' Her hand touched his, gripping it and lifting it to her heart, where she held it gently cupping the swelling of her breast. Leaving his hand there, she tugged at the laces of her dress. Both hands now, pulling the material apart so that he could glimpse the rounded flesh beneath, and then the cloth of her tunic came away and he could see her flat belly, the rising dark hairs at the base, her thighs.

'Do you want me again?' she murmured, shuffling out of her clothes and reaching up to kiss him.

He responded eagerly. 'I thought last night proved that well enough.'

'You seem to like my body,' she smiled, chuckling throatily, the hard points of her nipples almost brushing his chest. He had the fleeting impression that they could stab him to the heart.

'Your father . . . I was scared. He'd have killed me,' he said as she picked up her clothes unselfconsciously, bundling them into a ball and throwing them into a corner next to a little torn apron.

She took his hand and lifted it to her breast, feeling how he trembled. 'He'd never have known, Vin.'

'*Bitch!*'

They had both forgotten Gunilda, who had remained seated on her stool, and who now stood and hurled herself at her daughter, flailing with her fists.

'Get away from him! What are you, a she-devil? You would whore in my own house? Get out, you fool, leave this place!' she shrieked at Vin, and he retreated from her.

'You call *me* a bitch?' Felicia bawled. 'You dare call me that after lying back and letting *him* rape me every night? And you know what he did with those girls, don't you? When they batted their eyelashes at him, he went with them! And you let him, you old cow!'

'Get out, boy! Have nothing to do with her!' Gunilda shouted at Vin.

All he could do was flee, and he pelted from the place, out to the yard. He could remember every curve and swell of her body as though it was there before him, and the thought of lying with her tore at him, making him wonder whether he should go back, ask her to walk out with him, away from the house, back to their riverbank, but as he reached the main roadway, he paused and leaned against a pollarded tree, resting his brow on the bark. A thin mizzle was falling, kissing his face with a touch as light as a fairy's, gentle little kisses that began to soothe him.

Then, listening to the river, he realised that he now knew what had happened. And he couldn't tell anyone.

Chapter Twenty-Six

Baldwin rose with the first light, and was up at the table before the host had woken or stirred the fire.

He was more concerned than he could remember over the events of the previous evening. Never before in England had he witnessed that sort of crowd behaviour, with a whole vill joining together against the law, prepared to destroy a man from the worst motives, from bigotry and superstition. It was a hackneyed word, 'superstition', one which he had used too many times recently, but it was the only one which fitted the behaviour of the mob last night.

The memory of that terrible anger, and of his own frustration, and worse, the image of that dagger rising and plunging again and again into the breast of the hapless Samson, made Baldwin feel physically sick. He was not squeamish, he had killed men himself: he had killed one already this summer, but that was different. This was the slaughter of a man whose only crime at the time was that his own companions and neighbours had mistakenly thought him dead when in fact he was only wounded.

At least his murder was less cruel than leaving him buried alive. Not that the reflection was itself particularly comforting. The man had been rescued, only to be struck down. No matter how brutal he had been in life, he didn't deserve that end.

The people had wished to burn him alive, believing him to be guilty of the murder of the vill's children, and yet Samson was already buried when Emma died. The killer must be someone else.

Baldwin leaned on his elbows, resting his chin on his hands.

There had been six murders, if he was right. First Ansel de Hocsenham in 1315, the first year of the famine. That happened before Thomas and Nicky arrived, so they were innocent. From what the Reeve had said, Denise died in 1316, so she too died before Thomas got here, and Athelhard was killed that same year; the other girl, Mary, was strangled a little while after his death, as though the true killer was cocking a snook at the vill. Aline died in 1318, and Emma now in 1322. There was no logic to these deaths in terms of the gaps between each one, no apparent sequence that Baldwin could detect.

Surely all the deaths were committed by the same person. Peter was presumably innocent. One of the victims was his own child, and although parents did kill their offspring, Baldwin had never heard of any being tempted to cannibalism. Likewise, he was inclined to believe that Swetricus was not the murderer because of his daughter Aline's death. And the Reeve would always have had enough food. He wouldn't have needed to kill.

Baldwin was content with his earlier reasoning. He could imagine someone killing the Purveyor and then taking the opportunity to fill his empty belly. But why should that person then turn to killing children? Presumably because they were easier to kill, less able to defend themselves.

Baldwin frowned. He seemed to recall someone telling him that Ansel de Hocsenham had been a large, brawny fellow. That would mean that only a similarly large fellow would have been able to overwhelm him, surely, or a group. Perhaps the Foresters had had a part in his death, for all their protestations of innocence.

Or could it have been Drogo alone? The Forester appeared to be as concerned as the Reeve to conceal whatever had been going on in the vill. He had been surly and uncommunicative from the very beginning. And Vin too was an odd fellow.

Baldwin recalled thinking that there was a pattern, and then he realised that it was the girls' ages. There was something about their ages which appealed to their killer. He was considering this when Simon spoke.

'Couldn't sleep?'

'You are awake too? I had thought I was quiet enough to leave you sleeping,' Baldwin said, shuffling along the bench.

Simon donned his shirt and sat with him, scratching at his groin. 'Damned fleas get everywhere.'

Baldwin moved a little further away.

'So what do you think?' the Bailiff yawned.

'We must speak to Swetricus and see what he has to say,' Baldwin said with decision.

He was determined to leave early and get to Swetricus before the peasant left to go out to the fields. The Coroner asked them to go ahead without him. Roger's ankle had swollen considerably overnight, and now he was unable even to pull his boot on. Baldwin and Simon drank a little water, and walked out, Aylmer trotting from one scent to another.

The clear sky promised good weather, with a thin veil of clouds which looked very far away and insignificant, and Baldwin felt almost ridiculous as he walked up to Swetricus's door. To be talking in the broad daylight about ghosts and vampires felt ludicrous – and even to discuss a murderer seemed out of place. Nothing so appalling should exist in the glare of this perfect weather.

Another thing he noticed was that as they passed houses, there was chattering and even a couple of people laughing. The fear which had apparently lain over the whole vill had departed.

Swetricus opened the door and stood blinking at the two men.

'We want to talk to you about these murders,' Baldwin said, and Swetricus ungraciously stood aside for them to enter, Aylmer following.

About a low table were three children, all girls. As Baldwin walked in, all three rose and fled to their father, hiding behind him and peering around him at the two strangers. Baldwin smiled and tried to put them at their ease. He gave Simon a glance, and saw the quizzical expression on his face.

'It is obvious that you are a good father,' Simon said to Swetricus.

'Try to be.'

'I have a daughter myself,' Simon said, looking at the eldest of Swetricus's girls. 'She is about your age, I would think. Her name is Edith. What are you called?'

'She's Lucy,' Swetricus said, looking down. There was unmistakable pride on his face as he tousled her hair. 'Pretty as her mother.'

'She died?'

'Not long after this: Katherine. Bleeding.'

'I see. Sad,' Simon said, automatically copying him and falling into a monosyllabic frame of speaking.

Baldwin was less empathetic. He propped his backside on the table and peered about him. The house was a typical peasant's hovel. No rushes to cover the floor, so the bones and detritus stood out against the packed earth. There was a bed, which was a pile of fresh ferns with a rug thrown atop, three stools, and one tiny chest that looked as though Swetricus himself must have made it with ill-designed tools. Aylmer went to investigate the garbage about the table.

'We are here to ask about the deaths.'

'Denise, Mary, my Aline, and now Emma.'

'And the curse.'

'We all feared.'

'Because of the dead Purveyor?'

'And Samson. He was a devil.'

'Your daughter Aline – did he rape her?'

Swetricus looked away. 'I never guessed. No one told me. She disappeared; thought fallen in mire. Now I think different.'

Baldwin looked at the girls. 'Would they know?'

The three were undernourished and filthy, but from the way

that Swetricus put his hands on them, it was obvious to Baldwin that the man loved his girls and that his love was reciprocated. His protective stance didn't alter as he said, 'No, they don't know.'

'What of you? Do you think that Samson killed all those girls?'

'I don't know.'

'And the Purveyor? Would Samson have killed Ansel de Hocsenham?'

'Maybe. Samson hated taxes.'

'Did the miller suffer from hunger during the famine?' Simon asked.

'The miller, he had food. Not hungry like others, like his wife and daughter.'

'They did not eat so well as him?' Baldwin asked.

'He said he needed to eat to work, to feed them. Took most for himself.'

Baldwin nodded, considering the man. 'Swetricus, I am confused about much which has happened here in the vill. One thing that niggles at me is, why should your girl Aline have been buried? Denise and Mary were left where they had been killed. So was Emma. Why was Aline different?'

'Don't know. It hurt. Hurt lots. Not knowing . . . It was cruel to hide her like that.'

'Do you have any idea who could have done such a thing?'

Swetricus looked at him, and a cold, bitter anger glittered in his eyes. 'If I knowed, I'd kill him.'

'One last question, Swetricus. Where was Emma supposed to be sleeping on the night she died?'

'At the mill, I think. They let her stay in the barns.'

They left shortly afterwards. The Reeve had sent men to recover the Purveyor's body, and the group could be seen wielding their spades up on the hill. Baldwin stood a while watching, trying to ignore Aylmer, who was crunching at a bone of some sort just behind them.

It was Simon who broke into his reverie. 'Isn't that the Foresters up there? Shall we see if Vin is there?'

Vin didn't notice them at first. It was only when Adam stopped and muttered a curse under his breath that Vin glanced around and saw them. 'Shit! Are they here for you, boy?'

'Shut up, old fool,' Vin said boldly. If Adam called him 'boy' one more time . . . Somehow he knew that they were coming to question him again. Leaving his spade, he rubbed at his back and stretched. To Baldwin he looked as though he was tense, preparing himself for an interrogation.

The other Foresters were watching and no doubt listening with interest, but Drogo seemed furious as he greeted the two men with: 'What do you want now, eh? Not happy yet? You've seen off Samson, you've seen the ruin of Reeve Alexander and probably me, and now you're determined to attack my Foresters, is that it?'

'It's nothing for you to worry about. We just have some questions to ask this fellow,' Simon said.

'I have nothing to hide,' Vin said.

'Glad I am to hear it,' Baldwin smiled. 'Where can we talk in peace?'

'I have nothing to hide. We can stay here,' Vin repeated.

'Perhaps,' said Baldwin. 'But I would speak with you in private.'

Drogo walked to Vin's side, then led them away to a fallen tree farther down the hill, where all could sit. He took his seat next to Vin on a heavy bough, while Baldwin and Simon rested upon the trunk. Aylmer wandered away to sniff at a stone wall nearby. Soon he had disappeared in among the furze.

Baldwin eyed Drogo ruminatively. 'You appear very keen to look after this fellow.'

Vin curled his lip. The man had no idea how harsh Drogo made his life.

'Someone has to, now his father is dead,' Drogo replied stiffly.

Baldwin said, 'You were a friend of his father's?'

'He was a good man.'

'You did not answer my question, Forester,' Baldwin observed, studying him closely. 'And I think I begin to comprehend some words of Serlo's at last. I have been astonishingly foolish! Vincent: I am worried about your efforts in all this. You lived up on the moors when the Purveyor was killed, and you were still there when Denise died?'

'Yes. Until my father died, in the second year of the famine.'

'And then you were in your bailiwick when Mary and Aline died.'

'Yes.'

'Where were you when Emma died?'

'At the tavern with Drogo and Adam.'

Baldwin saw Drogo shoot him a quick look, then nod and say, 'That's right. At the inn.'

'Odd, isn't it,' Baldwin smiled, 'how you Foresters share so many things? You all confirm each other's stories, no matter what you think is going on.'

'We're often together, because of our work,' Vin protested.

Drogo was returning Baldwin's stare with a narrow, suspicious gaze. 'What are you driving at, Keeper?'

'Only this: if you had been prepared to tell the truth and trust to the judgement of the Coroner and me, you would have saved us time, and perhaps saved Emma's life. You are a fool, Drogo. You sought to protect Vincent here, and for why? Because you didn't trust him.'

Vincent felt his mouth fall open, and he gawped from Drogo to Baldwin and back again. 'What's he mean?'

Drogo broke away from Baldwin's gaze and stared upwards at the sky. It was bright, clear, and clean-looking, a good day to confess the crime he had committed so long ago. A good day to die, he thought. Glancing down at the vill, he could see a thin smoke rising from several houses as the fires were lit for cooking,

could just hear the rumble of the mill. Gunilda and Felicia must
have restarted the mechanism.

'Well?' Baldwin prompted.

'What would you do? If he was your son, wouldn't you have
protected him to the limit of your strength?'

'We had heard that Vincent was the son of your best friend,'
Baldwin said.

'He was,' Drogo groaned. 'She was the best, truest friend a
man could wish for. I loved her. I would have married her, but her
father wouldn't hear of it. He didn't trust me, preferred a miner.
But before the marriage, she gave herself to me, and she knew
two weeks later that Vin was my son.'

'She died young?'

'Too young. It was my sin, my crime, which did it. God took
her from me.'

'And you married as well.'

He sighed. 'Yes. A good woman, who bore me a daughter. I
tried to make her happy, and I think I succeeded, but then she died
and, during the famine, so did my daughter. My poor little Isabelle.
All I had left was Vin. I couldn't lose him.'

Vin gaped. 'How can I believe that? My mother wouldn't have
whored for you!'

'She was no whore, Vin, just a good woman who truly loved
me. As I loved her. She raised you as her own, and as her husband's
own, for she grew to hold an affection for him. She did not pin the
cuckold's horns on him. And she loved you.'

'I don't believe you! You're lying!' Vin declared, stepping away
and shaking his head.

'Vincent,' Baldwin said sternly. 'You were out on the nights
when the deaths occurred, weren't you? Were you with Drogo
each night?'

'No. Only when Aline and Mary were killed. And Emma.'

'You were with Drogo all night long?'

'Not all night, no. I went to see my woman,' he admitted.

'And you thought your son could have killed those girls, didn't you?' Baldwin pressed Drogo.

'I did.'

Vin shook his head in disbelief. 'Why would I have killed them?'

'Drogo, could your son have struck down Ansel de Hocsenham?' Baldwin demanded.

Drogo gave a wintry smile. 'Ansel? He was a tough bastard, he was, but Vin was a powerful enough fifteen year old; he could have killed him, but I never thought that was Vin's doing.'

'He was throttled with a thong like the girls?'

'Yes. And a slab of meat was carved from his thigh, almost from groin to knee.'

'What do you have to say, Vincent?' Baldwin asked. 'Where were you on the night the Purveyor disappeared?'

'I was with my girlfriend,' he said, feeling a certain pride in the words. 'We were out at the river, and then I heard Samson bellowing, and then he called for her, and I ran. If he had found me with her, he would have torn me limb from limb!'

'What did he call?' Simon asked.

'Oh, I don't know. It was just some shouting. And then he called for Felicia.'

'So you bolted.'

'Yes. To the ford, then up along the road, then I headed homewards.

'That was the night that Ansel disappeared, then. And it was the next night that you found the body, Drogo?'

'Yes.' Drogo didn't meet his eye. 'I found the body with Adam and Peter. We were all coming down from the moor, heading for the inn. It had been a long day. And there, under a bush, I saw a cloak and a boot. I sent Adam to fetch the Reeve, and he and I agreed that the crime should be concealed. We swore the others to secrecy, then brought the body up here because the wall had only recently been rebuilt. It was easier to dig there, and no one would notice that the soil had been moved.'

'Then who killed him?' Simon grated. 'It seems that every time we find something new, there's more damned confusion. Who in God's name did it?'

'If I had to guess, it was Samson,' said Drogo. He shrugged. 'The body was nearer to Samson's house than any other.'

'Why should Samson have harmed him?' Baldwin enquired pensively.

'Who knows? It's a secret he's taken with him, but Samson was always prone to swing with his fists at the slightest provocation. Maybe Ansel annoyed him?'

'We have heard that Samson raped girls in the vill.'

'He did, the devil. Aline was pregnant, and many thought it was Samson. But he had a hold over the girls, he made them fearful. They dared not tell anyone, not even their parents.'

'Is there any proof of this?' Simon asked.

'None. The girls he molested are dead. Unless his daughter or wife could confirm the truth.'

'Have you anything to add, Vincent?' Baldwin asked.

Before he could answer, Simon leaned forward eagerly. 'Wait! You said that Samson called – could he have shouted because he thought someone was attacking his house?'

'He could have, I suppose. So what?'

'If a man knew his daughter was outside, and he heard a stranger's footsteps, wouldn't he go to make sure his daughter was all right?'

Vincent said heavily, 'His daughter, yes. Any man would go out to protect her. But Felicia was more than that. She was his lover, too.'

'Did you hear Gunilda's words last night?' Baldwin asked Drogo after a moment.

'Yes. And I know what you think, that she might have attempted to kill her husband before he was mistakenly buried alive.'

'It would make sense. She must have hated him for his treatment of her daughter, and perhaps she too thought that he was the murderer. That he killed the Purveyor, then the children.'

'It is possible,' Drogo said. 'And she thought to protect herself and her daughter by destroying him.'

Simon frowned. 'I heard his yell, *then* her scream. So you reckon she killed him, then pretended to be horrified.' But he didn't believe it. There was something wrong.

Baldwin was struck by something different. 'You are being very open with us now. Why?'

'You know almost everything already. There is one last thing. When we slaughtered Athelhard in front of his house and butchered him, he had already taken his revenge. He had cursed us to Hell.'

'My God!' Simon breathed.

'His curse had no force,' Baldwin said irritably.

'You may think so, Sir Knight. I have a feeling that my time is not long, though. I have to make amends as I can and make sure my confession is heard. If Alexander has any sense, he'll do the same.'

Before they went to speak to the woman, Baldwin walked up to the edge of the grave and watched the Foresters expose the corpse of the Purveyor.

His clothes, albeit stained and rotted, were still recognisable, especially a leather jerkin which was undamaged. Simon, seeing the material, cursed himself for failing to realise what he had observed earlier, when he had stood staring at Aline's grave. He had seen the cloth sticking up through the soil, but hadn't realised what he was looking at, and now he felt foolish. If he had looked closer, he might have been able to speed the investigation, perhaps even save Emma's life. And then the man's face came to light, and Simon had to close his eyes and turn away. Empty sockets, grinning jaw, gaping nose, threads of hair, wisps of moustache and beard; but there was no flesh left upon Ansel's face.

Baldwin glanced at Drogo, who merely nodded. 'It's him.' Carefully the Foresters transferred the bones to a large rug at the side of the grave.

'We shall take him back to the chapel. It's most fitting that the Coroner should perform his inquest there,' Drogo said.

'Yes,' Baldwin said. Drogo's tone was gruff, and Baldwin thought he must be thinking of the additional fine to be imposed upon the vill. Concealing this death was a serious crime. 'Let me have a quick look to satisfy myself. When you found his body, did you remove the thong from his neck? There is nothing in the grave.'

'Of course I cut it away,' Drogo said. 'It looked obscene there. He was dead.'

'I see.' Another point in Drogo's favour, Baldwin noted. The other corpses were apparently found with the thong still in place, like Aline, but Drogo's first reaction was to give some respect to the corpse. He murmured, 'It is hard to feel sympathy for a Purveyor, especially one who was seeking to extort a bribe from a vill on pain of starvation, and yet seeing a decayed corpse like this is sad.'

Drogo looked as though he would be happy to spit on the skull. Vin was trying to avoid puking, and he coughed slightly as the last of the bones were added to the pile.

'Be glad, boy,' Adam said unsympathetically. 'If the body was fresher, you'd have the smell to cope with as well.' He was still in the hole with Peter, but now he leapt upwards, locking his arms on the edge of the pit, and swung his good knee up to gain purchase. Reaching down to help Peter out, he added, 'We saw enough bodies during the famine.'

'Of course,' Baldwin said absently.

He was frowning, and Simon noticed. 'What is it?'

'I was just thinking – you are quite sure that you heard him yell and then heard Gunilda scream?'

'Yes.'

'Yet when you arrived at the scene, Gunilda was outside.'

'Baldwin, you have that look on your face. The one that says you've just realised something we'd missed. What is it?'

'Simon, it wasn't her!'

Simon and Drogo exchanged a glance.

Ignoring them, Baldwin pointed into the hole. 'May I see his thigh bones?' he said urgently.

Drogo shrugged and pulled both from the pile. 'Here.'

'Ah. This one has scratches on it,' Baldwin said, studying it carefully. There were nicks which could have been made from a knife cutting through the meat of the leg.

Peter stood at the side of the body peering at it with loathing. 'He deserved it. Bastard!'

As Drogo and Adam picked up the corners of the rug to carry it to the vill, Baldwin suddenly cried, 'Wait!'

He reached down to the skull. As the two Foresters had picked up the rug, the skull had rolled over, exposing the back. Now Baldwin picked it up and wiped at it with his sleeve, studying the yellow stained bone with keen attention. 'Simon, look at this. Oh, come on, man, it won't bite! Now,' he continued as the Bailiff unwillingly joined him. 'See this star-shaped series of cracks here?'

Simon tried to forget that this had once been a man's head and imagined it as merely a sphere of bone or ivory. Where Baldwin had polished, there was a chip, with fine lines radiating irregularly from it. 'What of it?'

Baldwin's eyes were gleaming. 'I had thought that only a large man could subdue someone who everyone agrees was a strong, burly fellow like Ansel, but here we have, maybe, a sign that his head was stoved in!'

'So?' Simon asked. 'You think that when Vin spoke of a bellow from Samson, that was because he and Ansel were getting into a fight?'

'Vincent, on the night you were with Felicia, some six years ago, you said Samson shouted once, and then called for his daughter?' Baldwin said, turning to the lad again.

'Yes. He gave one loud roar, then a short while after, he shouted for Felicia.'

'Was it a roar of anger – or did it sound like a shout or cry of pain?'

Vincent stared at the ground doubtfully. 'It could have been pain.'

'Could it have been Ansel crying out in pain as he was knocked down?' Baldwin asked eagerly.

'I . . . suppose so.'

Simon understood now. 'You think that the first cry was Ansel because Samson had attacked him?'

'And then Samson called to his daughter – perhaps because he didn't want her to stumble over the body, or maybe because he wanted her to serve him his meal,' Baldwin said, staring down towards the mill.

'And then Samson carved up the body?' Vincent said.

Baldwin shook his head. 'If the miller had meant to do that, why tie a cord about his victim's neck?'

'To kill him.'

'He struck, surely with anger, in the heat of the moment, but didn't kill the fellow. No, someone else did that. Someone who was starving, who came along afterwards and found an unconscious man, and who hated that man enough to want to destroy him.'

'I didn't find him, sir!' Vincent said quickly, anxiously.

'No. If you had, you'd have used that,' Baldwin said, pointing to his knife. 'But a woman? Some women find the thought of stabbing too messy and unpleasant, while slipping a thong about a throat and stopping the breath – why, that is clean and tidy, isn't it?'

'A woman?' Simon breathed.

'Yes,' Baldwin said flatly. 'You were right yesterday when you suggested a woman could be responsible, Simon. One who was jealous of others, one who could easily win the confidence of her young victims. One who was hungry and found a source of meat, then learned that she liked the flavour.'

He tossed the skull into the air and caught it so that the empty eyes faced him. 'Ansel,' he told it, 'I think you have just explained your death to us. You shall be avenged.'

Chapter Twenty-Seven

Gunilda stood beside her fire, kneading dough. It was settling to her spirit, to be engaged on a task which she had performed nearly every day of her life. She knew she must prepare the bread before Samson came home. He would be cross if she hadn't got his food ready. He would beat her.

With a start she realised that the pottage wasn't in the pot over the fire. It made her squeak with alarm, especially when she looked out at the sunlight. He must be home soon, and his food wasn't waiting. Gunilda knew what he was like when she was late, and she dreaded the feel of his lash over her back. 'Soon, soon,' she muttered as she pushed her whole body's weight against the dough.

Felicia was watching her anxiously, picking at her faded green tunic. Gunilda was driving her up the wall; she was mad, quite mad. Her brain hadn't been able to cope with the horror of the night before. When the men appeared at the open doorway, she was glad for the interruption. 'Lordings, how can I serve you?'

Baldwin entered and smiled at her, studying her with interest. 'We are just come from discovering the body of the murdered Purveyor.'

'Yes?'

'Would you mind answering some more questions? Only a few, Felicia.'

'Yes, but get the dog outside. Dogs upset my mother, and she's in a bad enough way as it is.'

'Of course.' Baldwin took Aylmer out, and the dog sat and waited, but even as Baldwin closed the door, he caught a glimpse of a large cat, all striped brown and orange fur, with arched back and hissing mouth. Aylmer stood and Baldwin saw him slowly stalk the cat.

'Tell me, Felicia. When Ansel de Hocsenham died, you would have been about fourteen, wouldn't you?'

'I suppose. It's hard to keep track.'

'Of course. And you were hungry then, too, weren't you?'

'Everyone was.'

'Except your father. He had enough to eat.'

Felicia pulled a face. 'My father always made sure he was all right.'

'He loved you, didn't he?'

'Most of the time, if you could call it that.'

'Did he?'

Felicia sighed. 'He never said anything to me.'

'He merely raped you,' Baldwin said understandingly.

'Baldwin, shouldn't we be including Gunilda in this?' Simon said quietly, indicating the woman at the fireside. He was vaguely uneasy about questioning this young woman about the incest in her family.

'I think we shall hear little sense from your mother. What do you think?' Baldwin asked Felicia.

'You're just worried I'll be upset,' she said. 'I don't care. You know he took me almost nightly. What of it? Mother was unhappy, though. He didn't want her any more.'

'And not just you. He raped other girls, didn't he?' Baldwin said.

Felicia's face froze. 'I don't know what you mean.'

'Of course you do. He was a strong man, full of blood and lust.'

Gunilda had stopped her restless kneading, and now she stared at them with a frown on her face. Baldwin tried to give her a reassuring smile, but his lips wouldn't work. Instead he turned his attention back to Felicia. 'Tell me,' he said: 'which window was your father using to grease the machine when he fell under the wheel?'

Felicia jerked her head towards the machinery. 'The one behind there.'

Baldwin walked to the wall behind the turning shafts. There was an unglazed window there, a good-sized hole in the wall which was designed to light the great cogs. He stood on a wooden step beneath the window and looked up. Just within reach was the timber axle, but if he tried to touch it, he would be slightly overbalanced. An easy target for someone who wanted to push him out.

'Your father couldn't swim, could he?' he asked mildly as he returned.

'No. He had other things to do than waste his time on frivolous pursuits like that.'

'Of course. Now – your mother. You say she was jealous of you?'

'He preferred me.'

'Naturally,' Baldwin said. 'You were younger and more attractive. I suppose he was always affectionate to you?'

Felicia laughed shortly. 'When he wanted my body, he was. Otherwise, he would beat me, and even then he wanted me afterwards.'

'Were you upset when he wanted these other girls?'

'Me? No. I was glad. It meant he left me alone!'

'But accidents happened. Like when Aline became pregnant.'

'She was a strumpet. She had no shame,' Felicia said scathingly.

'And Mary, the orphan girl. She was no better.'

'She threw herself at Father.'

'Of course it was terrible to kill them. But understandable.'

Felicia almost nodded, but stilled her head.

'Poor little Emma, though. It was sad to kill her.'

'She was as bad as the others, showing off in front of my father,' Felicia said. Then: 'Why are you saying all this?'

'It was odd that she should be found in Thomas Garde's yard.'

'She deserved her end. She thought people wouldn't notice, but she was always after men in the vill. Not only Father. I saw her with—'

Baldwin watched her with a faint smile as she snapped her mouth shut. 'She was a plump little thing. Do you know what? If a man had killed her, I would wonder whether she had been killed somewhere else and then planted in Thomas's yard; if she was killed by a woman, though, why – I would think she had been lured into Thomas's yard and killed there. Why should Emma mistrust a young woman?'

'She was very trusting,' Felicia agreed. 'In some ways, Emma was innocent, you see. But you mustn't blame her murderer. She couldn't help it.'

'Why should she be killed there, Felicia?'

'Because she thought that it would point the finger at Thomas. She heard Ivo Bel talking about how his brother had a terrible temper, and she thought that either Thomas would get blamed or Ivo would, for trying to make Thomas look guilty. But it was *her*.'

'Who?'

Felicia threw a fearful look at her mother. 'She couldn't help it!'

'Me!' Gunilda gasped.

Baldwin ignored her. 'Why do you think Aline was buried when the others weren't? Denise and Mary were left out in the open, weren't they?'

Felicia set her jaw. 'It was her own fault. Aline wanted his child and Mother couldn't bear that, so she dug a hole to stop her getting a Christian burial. I think that was cruel.'

'It's a lie!' Gunilda screamed hoarsely. 'I didn't! I wouldn't!'

'She hid poor Aline to punish her, the whore, for persuading my father to bed her.'

'Ansel the Purveyor was different,' Baldwin said steadily. 'He wasn't murdered because of the girls, was he?'

'How would I know?'

'No. The killer of the Purveyor saw his unconscious body lying in the road, and at a time when everyone was starving, this was just a joint, a whole piece of meat.'

'You think you know so much.'

'I do. I do. Your father had an argument with the Purveyor. What about, I do not know.'

'He demanded money from my father. Said he would arrange for all our grain to be taken away from the vill and ground at Taw Green or another mill. It would have ruined us.'

'He tried to attack your father?'

'Samson was a strong man. He didn't wait to be attacked, he jumped on Ansel and beat him down.'

'And what happened then?'

'My mother throttled him to take his leg for meat.'

'Your mother did?'

'I did not!' Gunilda groaned.

Felicia ignored her. 'Yes. Just as she killed the other girls. And then killed my father.'

'I see.'

'While he was leaning out of that window, she pushed him. He screamed as he fell, and then she screamed too, maybe because she realised what she'd done. Ah! You don't know how good it is to be able to get it off my chest at last. I think she went on killing those girls because she thought Father loved them. He didn't, though.'

'When he fell I was outside,' Gunilda said clearly. 'But I saw my own daughter strike him on the head with a stone and push him out. I understood. Poor Felicia had been violated by him every night. My Christ, forgive me! I heard him, but I could do nothing. If I fought him, he'd beat me.'

'She's lying. She pushed him,' Felicia said calmly.

'She did it, Samson, not me!' Gunilda said suddenly. She was staring at Baldwin with intense fear twisting her features. '*I* couldn't have done it. You were talking to me, weren't you, through the window? And then she pushed you out.'

'Shut up, you old fool,' Felicia said brutally. 'You're mad. Your brain's addled like sour milk.'

'There is no need to hide the fact, Felicia,' Baldwin said. 'You only did what you knew was necessary.' His voice was gentle, but even as he spoke he could feel the horror deep in his belly. Madness was always terrifying, and Felicia was quite insane.

'What did they matter?' she said. 'The girls were just *things*. They were only bodies for him to cover, like a stallion with a mare or a dog with a bitch.'

'So you killed them to stop your father sleeping with them?'

'He loved their young bodies,' Felicia said, and suddenly her eyes brimmed. 'He left me for them. He raped me in our bed, and when he had used me, he found others. He scared them into doing what he wanted.'

'And you were jealous of them?'

'*Jealous*?' Felicia gaped at him, and then laughed. 'Christ's ballocks! Is that what you think? I hated him, Keeper! I hated him with a loathing that was so pure and strong that I could have done anything to hurt him. I killed his little lovers, I slaughtered them and ate them to show my utter contempt for them *and* him. And when the most recent of his little bitches came into heat and tried to wrest my Vin from me, why, I slaughtered her too. Only you should have thought it was Thomas Garde who killed her.'

'Emma?'

'Yes. The slut! She was making moony eyes at Vin, so I tempted her into the yard with a promise of sweetmeats, and then strangled her.'

'Tell me, how did you know where Ansel was buried? How did you know to bury Aline there?' Baldwin asked.

'I was waiting for Vin, but he didn't come. When I heard voices I hid, and saw the Reeve and Forester at the body. I walked after them to see what they did. Later I thought I could use that same hole.'

'And you killed your father.'

'He had raped me that morning. I was bruised and sickened, and when he leaned through the window, I saw my chance. I hit him with a rock, and out he went. The paddle hit him, and that was that.' She giggled.

'You saw her?' Baldwin asked Gunilda, but she wasn't listening. Her attention was fixed upon her daughter, horror in her eyes.

'You killed your own father! And you admit it so boldly.' She shuddered. 'How could you do that – and how could you be so cruel as to slaughter the others – *and eat them*! My God, my God. They were only little girls, Felicia.' Gunilda was standing now, her dough forgotten. 'It wasn't *their* fault your fiend of a father raped them!'

'But he regretted their loss!' Felicia spat. 'Don't you see? It spoilt his fun!'

Baldwin nodded. 'That explains it all,' he said. 'And now I think we should go to speak to Sir Laurence de Bozon and Reeve Alexander.'

'Why? I've got nothing to say to them.'

'They shall want to meet you, to talk about these deaths,' Simon said.

Felicia shrugged, but said nothing. She crossed the floor towards the door, passing near Gunilda as she went, and took up a cloak.

'Felicia, tell them it's not true,' the woman pleaded.

'I find it hard to believe such a feeble-minded, ugly old crone could actually be my mother,' Felicia said, curling her lip. 'Leave me in peace.'

Gunilda's mouth dropped wide open, but then she flew at her daughter, scratching, kicking and screaming. Felicia drew back, her hands up to protect her face, shrieking in fear and rage, and while Baldwin attempted to separate them and Simon tried to get behind Gunilda to hold her back, Felicia turned and ran towards the machinery. Gunilda chased after her, but Felicia was waiting for her. She had reached up to the rafter, and now she held her father's rope. It whistled through the air and Gunilda howled as it streaked down her cheek and breast. To Baldwin's horror he saw the blood welling on her face. Felicia brought it down again, and it was Gunilda's turn to retreat, crying pitifully.

The two returned towards Simon and Baldwin, but as the women approached, Gunilda tripped and fell on her back. Instantly Felicia was on her, raining blows on her head, and it took both men to grab her hands and lift her away.

Panting with the effort, Felicia screeched, 'You dare try to hurt me? Do that again, and I'll kill you!'

'Come with us,' Baldwin said strongly.

Felicia shook her arm free from him and walked to the door, waiting demurely while Simon and Baldwin stood back to let her leave first, and then suddenly exploded into action again.

In an instant she drew a knife from beneath her apron, and stabbed Simon in the hand, whirling to strike Baldwin in the forearm. Just for a moment, the men were stunned, could see only her blade, wavering between them both, and then she pulled the door to with a slam and was gone.

Recovering from his shock, Simon snatched at the door and yanked it open. He rushed out, through the yard and up to the roadway, but when he peered back towards the vill, he could see no sign of the girl. Surely there hadn't been enough time for her to disappear?

'Simon!' Baldwin shouted, and the Bailiff turned to see Felicia's figure flying away along the track towards Belstone.

Baldwin was already speeding after her, but when Simon saw Drogo and his men almost at the Parson's gate, carrying the rug rolled between them, he dashed over to them and blurted out what had happened. Immediately, Peter was off after Baldwin. Drogo swore, his eyes attracted to the blood trickling from Simon's fingers, then he grabbed for his horn and blew loudly on it three times. 'Murder! Murder! Murder!' he roared as loudly as he could, and then launched himself after Baldwin, overtaking Simon in a matter of a few yards.

The road passed along the valley at the side of the river heading southwards, wandering with the water. Baldwin splashed through thick puddles, black with peat, and almost copied the Coroner, turning his ankle on a large, slippery pebble, but recovered himself in time and pounded on. Soon he was jumping from one rock to another as the ground became wetter, but all the time he could see the bare footprints of the girl in the soil, or gleaming wetly from stones.

She crossed it where there was a slight broadening of the river. Too deep to be termed a ford, it nonetheless provided easier passage, and Baldwin didn't hesitate. He was into the water and through it to the other side in a moment. Here there appeared to be a rough track, little better than a sheep's path, climbing the hillside at the edge of a stream. A print or two further up showed that Felicia had taken this route, and Baldwin forced himself upwards as quickly as his legs would allow, his feet slipping on loose scree, once almost falling and catching himself by throwing his hand out into a furze bush and feeling the thorns puncture the flesh of his palm, fingers and wrist. Cursing, he carried on.

There was a lip and then the ground eased, giving onto a shallower plateau, and at last he could see her. She was running hard still, rushing up the hillside, then was out of view over another hillock. Baldwin took a deep gulp of air and was off again. His thighs aching, his lungs feeling as though they might burst, his head thundering with the rushing of blood in his temples; the bruises at his flank and torso throbbed as though they were licked with fire.

He had no idea where he was exactly, nor did he care; all he knew was that Felicia was attempting to escape by running over the moors, perhaps to hide somewhere down by the coast. She must not be allowed to escape. The girl was prepared to murder and eat her victims; she was a monster. She had to be stopped and executed before she could murder again.

The furze thinned, and soon he was running up over grass and heather. Birds exploded from the ground beneath his feet, darting away to chitter at him angrily, or swept upwards to sing melodic, liquid tunes, but he ignored them. His whole concentration was on the figure so many yards ahead of him. And then, just as he felt that he could not run any further, he saw her stagger a little, and realised that she was flagging.

He redoubled his effort, and as he did so, she turned. Instead of running straight away from him, she was turning right, across him. It was possible that he might be able to head her off. She was running on the flat, following the contour of the hill while he was still climbing, but the angle of his climb made it less brutal on his legs, and he thrust himself onward with what felt like the last vestiges of energy he possessed.

She was above him, rushing along a sheep's track, while he was climbing slowly to meet her, his calves feeling as though they were shrinking from sheer exhaustion. He was closer, much closer, when she turned and noticed him, and he saw the expression in her eyes.

The look stabbed his heart. It was like being stared at by the devil himself, and Baldwin quailed. Not from fear, but from shock. No young woman should be able to express so much malevolence.

With that thought, he lost his concentration. His foot caught on a root and he felt himself flying through the air: black earth came up to meet him, and he closed his eyes a moment before his arms and then his chin slammed on the ground with a force that knocked the air from him.

His wounds and bruises from the tournament at Oakhampton were raw agony now, as though he had been flayed, and even breathing was hideously painful; he sobbed with the effort as he looked up towards the horizon. She had disappeared now, running on around the curve of the hillside. There was no sign of Simon or Drogo, and Baldwin knew that he must somehow continue, or she would be lost to them.

Simon was about to set off after Baldwin when Drogo called him away. 'This way, Bailiff. Follow me!'

With that he was off, setting a cracking pace on the western side of the river. Soon the ground was boggy and heavy going, but Drogo bounded from one boulder to another, from a fallen tree-trunk to a low branch, ever onwards, ducking beneath low boughs, swinging over lower ones, until they began to climb.

Simon was to remember that chase for many years afterwards. He had never run so far on such uncertain ground, with the earth seeming to suck at his feet, as though trying to swallow him up like one of the mires on the high moor; every time he put his feet on a rock or a block of wood it seemed to move and threaten to break his ankle.

'There she is!'

It was Peter, who had passed Simon and now stood a few yards in front. Up on the hillside east of them, Simon could make out the line of the path from South Zeal to Belstone, and on it, near Serlo's warren, was the fleeing figure. Peter said no more, but hared off again, Drogo close behind him. Simon had to grit his teeth and push on.

Baldwin scrabbled with his feet for purchase and then he was up and running again. Ahead was a broad, slick expanse of water, and he rushed through it, the mud bursting upwards on all sides. As he came out the other side, he could see her again, and noted that Serlo was nearby.

'Warrener! Serlo! Catch her! She's the murderer!'

His voice was powerful enough, just, to reach the grim-faced man. Serlo hurried up to the path as fast as his legs would carry him, but he was not swift enough. The girl saw him coming and quickly darted around him without breaking her stride. But then Baldwin saw the Warrener frown and roar a warning, and to his horror, Baldwin spotted the figure of Joan, a short distance from Felicia, running downhill.

Felicia was at the top of the path which led to Belstone when she saw them: three men, all heading towards her, coming up from the river. She screamed, stamping her foot in a futile gesture of impotent rage. There was no escape that way; she could not return past Baldwin, and Serlo blocked her path down the hill. Clenching her fists, she shrieked her anger, and then set her face to the hill once more. Thank God Joan had disappeared, thought Baldwin. She must have concealed herself in among the clitter or behind some furze, and he was relieved that he need not worry about her safety.

The men were exhausted. They had run more than a mile, all uphill, and their bodies were beyond pain. Those who were barefooted had felt their flesh being slashed on stones, while the dead, dry furze thorns stabbed into sensitive arches; those with boots felt their muscles tearing with the effort of hurling themselves up the hill.

Bent double to catch his breath, Baldwin glanced up in time to see Felicia turn and look at them all. Her face was a mask of contempt, as before, but now she held no fear for him. He simply knew that she must not be allowed to escape. And then he saw the little figure bob up at her side.

'JOAN! NO!'

Simon heard his agonised cry and looked up to see Joan at Felicia's side. The miller's daughter reached for her with a reassuring smile on her face, and Joan smiled back, a happy child. But then there was a burst of movement as Felicia reached in behind her apron again, and Simon knew she was going for her knife. He opened his mouth to roar his own warning, but knew it was too late.

Felicia would have struck, or captured a hostage, before his voice could carry.

And then something odd happened. While Felicia's hand was in her apron, Joan ducked, shifted her weight, pushed at the older girl, and kicked out with her small foot. Felicia gave a loud curse, and then wheeled around, trying to keep her balance, reaching out with her knife towards Joan even as she began to topple, and then she gave a wailing oath as she fell from view.

Joan stood peering down, and Simon ran up to her side. At her feet was a wide gully, a fall of some ten feet, and at the bottom lay Felicia, an arm broken beside her, staring back up at him with a twisted grin. She coughed, and bright red blood erupted from her mouth. It wasn't from her knife: Simon could see that, lying on the ground a short distance from her. No, it wasn't from her knife, but as he stared down at her, dumbfounded, and as Baldwin and Drogo appeared at his side, he saw the crimson pool spreading on the rocks beneath her, and the spurting wound in her breast. At the same moment he noticed the blade in Joan's hand.

She saw his look. 'She killed my friend Emma.'

Chapter Twenty-Eight

The inn was full when the body of Felicia was brought in. Men thronged the main room as Drogo, Peter and Simon carried the dead weight between them, setting her down on top of a table, and causing the five drinkers to move. Behind them, Baldwin entered with Joan's hand in his, and he stood there for a while, surveying the room. The sight repelled him.

Here in the tavern the people of the vill had arrived in a party mood. They had been keen to destroy Samson, to burn him on a pyre, not because of his very real rapes, but because of superstition. His only crime had been to be buried alive; earlier, they had conspired with equal gusto to execute Athelhard and burn his corpse; now they jostled hungrily to view the body of the genuine culprit.

'*Silence!*' he roared, and the room fell quiet. He crossed the floor to the Coroner.

'Coroner, this is the body of Felicia atte Mill, daughter of Samson. She confessed to me, Sir Baldwin Furnshill, Keeper of the King's Peace, and before Bailiff Puttock of Lydford, that she was the murderer of Ansel de Hocsenham, the King's Purveyor; that she murdered Denise atte Moor, daughter of Peter; that she murdered Mary, orphan of this parish; that she murdered Aline, daughter of Swetricus; that she murdered Emma, daughter of the same Ansel de Hocsenham.'

'Is this all true, Simon?'

'Yes.'

Baldwin continued, 'She attacked the Bailiff and me with a dagger and fled. We raised the Hue and Cry and gave chase, following her all the way up to the warren of Serlo. There she attacked and would have killed this girl, Joan Garde, daughter of Thomas, but Joan Garde was able to defend herself. Felicia fell and died.'

Coroner looked at Joan. 'You confirm this?'

'Yes, Coroner.'

'Who else witnessed this death?'

Drogo stepped forward. 'I did, Drogo Forester, and so did my man Peter atte Moor.'

'I see. Then I declare her death to be justified in self-defence.' These words Baldwin heard as he walked from the room. He had no need to hear more. The whole matter was offensive to him, the attitude of the people repugnant. He left the inn and stood in the yard behind. Edgar was at the door to Jeanne's room, Aylmer lying apparently asleep at his side, and Baldwin nodded. 'They are inside?'

'Yes, sir,' Edgar said, standing. He could see the pain on Baldwin's face. 'Should I fetch you wine, sir?'

'No. I only want peace,' Baldwin said. He crossed the little yard to the pasture, and there he walked out to a natural hillock, sitting and putting his arms about his knees. Aylmer joined him, sitting at his side, alert, staring out at the moors before them, but not leaning or resting against Baldwin, independent and almost aloof. But when Baldwin drew a deep breath, Aylmer's head dropped and his nose touched Baldwin's hand, just once, as if in sympathy.

'May I join you?'

Baldwin did not need to turn around. 'Why didn't you tell anyone, Vin?'

'I didn't know until last night.' Vin sat beside him and shrugged. 'She was the only woman I'd ever lain with. In my way I loved her. I thought I could save her from her father, but I was petrified of him. Samson was an evil man. Evil and dangerous. I thought he had murdered the Purveyor, and that meant he had eaten the Purveyor as well. I couldn't tell people that. He would have killed me.'

'Was it mere prejudice led you to think he might be the killer?'

'A bit. He was a brutal git, always happy to fight anyone. God, the night the vill killed Athelhard, Samson was roaring mad. He was prepared to pull the vampire limb from limb. As it was he wanted to cut the man's heart out with Peter. That was one thing that has suddenly occurred to me.'

'What was?'

'I was young when Denise was killed, but I can remember the shouts and anger in the vill. Samson was beside himself with rage – yet when Mary died and Aline went missing, he was quiet, almost as though he knew who the real killer was and didn't dare react in case people guessed that it was Felicia.'

'But at the time . . .'

'At the time I wondered whether it was proof of his guilt. He avoided talking about the deaths, and that's not normal in a vill like this.'

'But you grew to suppose that it wasn't him, didn't you?'

'Samson was so often terribly drunk. He was violent, but I didn't think he was capable of killing a young girl. So I started wondering about others, and the only man who made sense was Drogo. I knew he was often away from his post when the girls died, and he was always so jealous of men whose daughters were alive. His own daughter – my little half-sister, I suppose – died at about the same age as the ones who were killed.'

'And that was all?'

'No. Regularly Drogo would leave me at my post. I thought it could be because he was off looking for a girl to murder.'

'Whereas in fact . . . ?'

Vincent sighed. 'In fact he was patrolling several of the tracks nearby making sure that there *wasn't* a murder only a few hundred yards from us. Never going far, you understand.' He looked up and met Baldwin's eyes with a wry grin. 'He didn't trust me that much, either. He wondered if I might be the murderer myself.'

'When did you realise it wasn't him?'

'Only last night. You see, I heard Felicia talking to her mother. She was saying that her father always went for girls who batted their eyes at him. Well, they didn't. No young girl would have. It was just her hatred talking. She said that they all went for him as soon as they were ten or eleven, and that made me think. They were all killed when they were about that age.'

'And that was enough to tell you?'

'That, and a little torn apron. I saw it on the floor near Felicia's bed last night, and I recognised it as Emma's.'

'What of Ansel?'

Vin hugged his knees. 'I think Samson had a row with him, Ansel turned to go, and Samson knocked him down. Then he called to Felicia because he feared he'd killed the man.'

Baldwin finished for him. 'You think she throttled him while he lay unconscious, then took a piece of his leg for her supper.'

'Yes. Remember, we were all starving then – and she was half-wild with hunger. And the next night Drogo and the others came along and found his body and decided to hide it before the vill could be harmed. It was just a lucky chance that the wall had fallen only a short while before.'

'But from then on, every time her father desired a new girl, he was signing her death warrant,' Baldwin mused. 'As soon as Felicia realised he had a fresh girl, she killed her, and as a supreme insult, ate her flesh.'

'But why should she have killed Emma?' Vin asked, puzzled. 'Samson was dead by then.'

'You were kind to Emma, weren't you?' Baldwin said.

'I hardly remember her.'

'One day I saw you outside the Reeve's hall. You picked her up and tickled her. Felicia saw you.'

'Holy Jesus! You mean that act of friendship cost that kid her life?'

'Let us hope that we shall never comprehend what went on inside Felicia's mind, Vincent,' Baldwin said slowly. 'That way madness lies.'

It was many weeks before Baldwin could bring himself to tell his wife the full story of the murders, not because of any squeamishness or fear for her own resilience, but because he did not know how to rationalise his own thoughts.

. He had been brought up in a chivalrous household, and the guiding principle belief lay in the generosity and love of women. To have found a girl like Felicia, who could murder children and eat them, was appalling. If the world could create such a one, Baldwin was not sure it was the sort of world he wished his daughter to inhabit.

Luckily there were many more people who were humanitarian; Baldwin had enough good friends like Simon to hope that whatever happened his daughter would be protected, but all the time at the back of his mind he knew that famine, war and pestilence could destroy not only families, but even the morals of people. Felicia had been tempted to eat other humans because of her starvation. In good years the miller would take one tenth of all the grain he milled as his payment, but when there was famine and no one had enough, they would grind their corn at home. And that meant that the miller and his family would starve. That was why Felicia had thankfully throttled Ansel when she found him, and taken a haunch from him. She was ravenous.

The children were different. They had committed no crime, she was punishing her father when she executed them.

It was one lazy, burning hot summer's afternoon when Baldwin told Jeanne the whole story. She had heard some parts of it when the matter was written up by the Coroner after the inquests into Felicia's and Ansel's deaths, but she had not appreciated the depth of Baldwin's own revulsion.

'What I don't understand is how the miller managed to keep his sexual wrongdoings secret from all the other folk.'

'He didn't entirely,' Baldwin said. 'Some knew, and others told friends, but when a man like Swetricus, who loves and trusts his daughters, is told that nothing has happened, he naturally believes them.'

'Why should his girl have concealed the rape?'

'Why should any? From shame, or perhaps from terror. Who can tell what threats or promises Samson used?'

'He must have been a truly wicked person!'

'Yes. His daughter, too.' Baldwin sighed. 'I blame myself, you know, Jeanne. If I had searched the grave more carefully, if I had noticed what Simon did, I might have made the right connection, found Ansel's body – perhaps saved Emma's life.'

'Do you regret the death of Felicia?'

'Her? My Heaven, no! She was deep into madness and had to be killed. I only regret that her death was brought about by a young girl . . . but then again, maybe not. Joan wanted her own revenge for the crime committed against her friend, and the fact that she could execute the killer may have given her some peace of mind, rather than merely hearing Felicia was dead, or even witnessing the hanging. How can I tell?'

Jeanne sat at his side and put her arm about his shoulder. After a moment he put his own about her waist, and they sat staring at the view, listening to the laughter of his peasants in the fields.

'There is something else, isn't there?' she asked after a short while.

'You know me too well, Wife. Yes. I have received a message from Simon.'

'Oh?'

'In it he says he agrees with you that the moors are too dangerous to treat without care. He says that superstition is a useful precaution.'

Jeanne smiled. 'I am glad you have a nagging friend as well as a wife.'

Richalda gave a great cry from the solar and Jeanne hurried indoors to see to her daughter. When she was gone, Baldwin took out the sheet of paper once more.

According to Coroner Roger, the curse appears to have been laid at last, he read. *Drogo and Alexander have escaped the court. They were both riding on the moors last month, illegally, after a fox which had attacked some piglets, when a mist came down and they fell into a bog. Serlo was at his warren and heard their screams. He tried to get to them, but the mist was too thick. He shouted, and they responded, but he could not reach them and had to listen while they drowned. He was very upset – but perhaps this means that Athelhard's curse has now been fulfilled. Certainly the people of the vill hope so.*

'Superstition!' Baldwin muttered, gazing at the dark, grim line on the horizon that showed where Dartmoor began. The only evil in Sticklepath came from one family. A father who was perverted, with his lusts for young flesh, a wife who was simple, and a daughter who was insane.

He read on: *Gunilda has adopted Meg, and both appear content in each other's company. Not that many of the vill were happy to learn that Meg had moved into the mill. Some still look upon her with dread, but she and Gunilda seem to have found comfort and Serlo looks in on them regularly, chopping their wood and helping tend to their animals.*

The letter ran on, but Baldwin put it away, musing on the violence and cruelty that lay at the heart of the murders: the brutality of Samson not only to Felicia's victims, but to his daughter as well.

Hearing another cry from the house, he murmured, 'Keep happy, Richalda. I shall never do anything to cause you such grief. That I swear.'

And then Sir Baldwin Furnshill stood and stretched. The

accursed bruises along his flank were healed now, and as he inhaled a deep breath of the shimmering summer air, he decided to take his horse out.

The evil was gone. Life was for the living.